Ruby, the White King, and Marilyn Monroe

Ruby, the White King, and Marilyn Monroe

by

F. L. Bicknell

Turquoise Morning Press
Turquoise Morning, LLC
www.turquoisemorningpress.com

Turquoise Morning, LLC
P.O. Box 43958
Louisville, KY 40253-0958

Ruby, the White King, and Marilyn Monroe
Copyright © 2011, F. L. Bicknell
Trade Paperback ISBN: 9781937389420
Digital ISBN: 9781937389437

Cover Art Design by Kim Jacobs

Digital release, October 2011
Print release, October, 2011

This edition is published by agreement with Turquoise Morning Press, a division of Turquoise Morning, LLC.

*For my husband, Matthew,
who has believed in me since once upon a time.*

*And for my agent, Dr. Uwe Stender.
Thank you for your wisdom, support and friendship.*

Praise for *Ruby, The White King, and Marilyn Monroe*

Packed with action, each scene moving forward at a clip-clop pace—don't blink your eyes once or miss a single paragraph *of Ruby, the White King, and Marilyn Monroe*. For if you do, you are sure to miss a piece of this literary puzzle!

One serendipitous meeting after another takes Ruby, her white king, and her quirky, hitchhiker friend Maureen on a frightening quest to get to Key West. With paranormal elements throughout, the sexual tension high, and the edge-of-the-seat factor not to be ignored, I could not stop reading until I reached the very end.

—Maddie James, Romance Author
www.maddiejames.net

Ruby, the White King & Marilyn Monroe is a well-written, intriguing book. It keeps you on the edge of your seat wondering what will happen next. With strong, well-rounded characters and tantalizing foreshadowing, this makes for a pleasurable read. Ms. F.L. Bicknell pulls the reader in, combining the paranormal with reality to give you a tale you won't want to put down.

—Jade Twilight, Author
http://jadetwilight.webs.com

A road trip fueled by blue lightning and irreverent humor, *Ruby, the White King, and Marilyn Monroe* jumpstarts a reader's heart!

—Tess MacKall, editor and author.

Over the past ten years, I've read hundreds of books, my favorite authors being some of the big names, but I must say I've just added a new author to my NY author list: F.L. Bicknell. *Ruby, the White King, and Marilyn Monroe* will have you laughing, crying, and yelling. I read this story in one sitting because I couldn't put it down! I can't wait to see if there will be a book two!

—Selene Noreen, Author
www.selenenoreen.com

Ruby, the White King and Marylyn Monroe is an edgy, fast-paced thrill ride with twists and turns that will keep you on the edge of your seat. This is one road trip I highly recommend!

—Shiela Stewart, Author
www.shielasbooks.ca

Ruby, the White King, and Marilyn Monroe has a fun voice that sucks you in and takes you on a fast-paced ride until its conclusion, rooting for Ruby all the way until you get there.

—Natalie Dae, Ellora's Cave Author
www.nataliedae.wordpress.com

Reincarnated over the centuries. Stuck with a ditzy Marilyn Monroe lookalike. Falling for a rich albino guy. It's just Ruby's luck for Hell's "real" angels to ride into this life and screw it all up.

Chapter One

Setting my boss's bra on fire and losing my job was not the best way to end a workday. My life sucked. I hadn't been laid in months, my uncontrollable powers scared the hell out of people, my father hated me, and it was so damn hot I could barely breathe.

Humidity hung over the quiet neighborhood. Ascending the stairs to my apartment, I pined for rain to cool the summer evening and a long shower to soothe my body and my foul mood. A twelve-hour shift at the sewing factory had me tired and irritable, but at least my sudden unemployment happened at the end of the day. I smirked. And my boss's face as she slapped at the flames eating her padded bra was almost worth it. Well, at least everyone wouldn't wonder anymore if her boobs were real or not.

Melting Latex foam stinks too.

However, most of my irritability stemmed from a feeling of unease and frightening visions, both of which had steadily grown worse over the past couple of weeks.

About to put my key in the lock, I cried out as a picture flashed across my mind. Demonic motorcycles rolled toward me, their headlights aglow. A huge, imposing man rode a Harley with a demonic horse head where the handle bars and gas tank should've been. The bike snarled, and I whimpered in terror.

The vision faded. I slumped against the door, banging my head against the glass. My legs trembled beneath me. For a moment I just stood there willing the fear and nausea to leave. Sometime during the afternoon, steady pangs of anxiety had begun to assault me, some so severe I felt ill, but this premonition left not only dread in its wake but also a sense of impending danger.

As I unlocked the door, entered, and shut it behind
me, I tossed my purse and keys at the kitchen table,
lunged for the sink, and turned on the spigot to splash
cold water on my face. Braced against the counter, I
willed the tremors in my knees to go away and my
breathing to slow. I knew from past experience to never
dismiss such feelings as stress or exhaustion, but just like
my other visions of late, this one made no sense either.

I groaned. If my boss hadn't grabbed my shoulder
while I was having such a vision, the end result wouldn't
have been Fahrenheit 451 tits.

The A/C in the kitchen window kicked on. I managed to stand without sprawling out on the floor, while
wobbling, I moved in front of it with my arms in the air.
Water trickled down my cheeks and onto my shirt. The
cold air on my wet face and sweaty body helped bring
me back to reality and settled my nerves. Slowly, the
sense of danger evaporated with the dampness.

Just inside the living room doorway, the phone rang. I
glanced at the caller ID: Nutter, Jackson. I grimaced and
answered the call.

"Where's my supper?" my father's voice barked
across the line.

"I worked a twelve-hour shift today, Dad."

Inwardly, I cringed. If I called to ask him what he
wanted for supper, he'd bitch that he was quite happy
with his junk food and six-pack. If I didn't call him, he'd
telephone and yell about his meal being late. I couldn't
win with my father.

"Don't bother cooking, then," he snapped. "Bring me
a couple of Big Macs, and make it snappy."

The line clicked.

"If you weren't my father..." I whispered. I rested my
head against the doorframe and suppressed the urge to
scream. Letting my anger get the upper hand would
awaken my curse, so I forced it down into the darkness.
That was the sucky part about my frightening 'abilities.' I
couldn't control them.

I placed the phone back in its base. "Well, Dad, you've waited this long. I'm taking a shower before I rush out to do your bidding."

My ire chased away the remnants of the vision and the sense of danger, but anxiety struck me again. The apprehension proved so intense it forced a gasp from me. I swayed, gripping the doorframe. Churning erupted in my stomach, and I bit back the need to throw up. I sensed things before they occurred and dreamed about places and people I'd never seen before, but I could seldom make any sense of it. However, something horrible was about to happen, something that was going to land right in the middle of my life again. The last time I'd felt such a strong sense of wrongness was the day before I accidentally killed my mother.

As always, guilt pierced me at the memory.

Its one thing to dream about strange places and people or to sense something before it happens, but I didn't know anyone else who could blast things with an invisible force. I could also start fires and move items or people around with it. And, if I was really upset, I incinerated stuff, blew them up. Mom's death and my abilities were the reasons my father hated me.

But the one thing I couldn't hide, the one thing that terrified everyone when it happened, was the warning sign before I annihilated something. I glowed. Hell, I was the one who did it and it scared me silly.

The shower beckoned me. My discarded clothes landed on the bedroom floor as I strode through it to the bathroom.

As I shampooed my hair, kaleidoscopic images I couldn't decipher assailed me. I fell against the wall, bracing my feet on the tub's side.

White.

White skin, platinum hair. His eyes, the color of ice and azure, tantalized me. The man's face remained obscured, but his eyes inspired fear. Something drew me to him, but that frightened me too.

A narrow gold crown encrusted with jewels encircled his head, and a mass of long, snowy hair fell over his shoulders as he reached for me.

The vision ended abruptly, and an overwhelming sense of loss consumed me. Although I hadn't seen his face, the man was familiar. It didn't make any sense. With my eyes closed, I sank to the bottom of the tub where I sat under the spray. The images had intensified my unease, but remorse, love, and a powerful sense of loss tumbled through my soul.

Shaking, I gathered my wits and finished my shower, all the while trying not to dwell on the vision. Afterward, I combed out my long, dark hair and slipped on a simple white sundress and a pair of Sketchers Shape Ups.

In the kitchen, I gathered my purse and keys, and yanked open the door to find my landlady standing on the landing, her hand in midair about to knock. Her mouth dropped open, and her coal-black eyes widened in fear.

"Oh!" I stumbled back. "Mrs. Enoch, you startled me!"

Heat flashed through my body until I thought I'd melt, and the air around me brightened as if someone had suddenly taken a shade off a one-hundred-watt bulb. The color drained from the woman's lined face as she watched me change from a normal woman to one whose body glowed bright white with neon coppery colors infusing my hair and fingertips.

"For God's sake, Ruby," the landlady squeaked, one hand shielding her eyes, "don't blow me up!"

"You should've called first." I struggled with the tingling that surged down my arms. Finally, the light emanating from me dimmed, and the heat flooding my body disappeared. It left me feeling slightly drained.

Last month, Mrs. Enoch arrived to collect the rent as usual, but witnessed my ability at its height. Some neighborhood riffraff had tried to mug me as I'd taken the trash to the curb. The thugs simultaneously frightened and pissed me off, and I'd lashed out before I could stop myself.

The old woman gulped. "I'm here for the rent."

"I have it with me." I pulled an envelope from my purse with the check in it and held it out to her. "Here"

She motioned to the counter.

Sighing, I placed the envelope on the worktop. She picked it up and slipped it in her dress pocket.

"Mrs. Enoch, I won't hurt you," I said.

"You're not natural, so why take chances." She turned to leave.

"What I did to those thugs was an accident."

"You could do that to me, too, you know," she insisted, a hard edge in her voice, one I recognized from my father and others who feared me. "Look, Ruby, I saw what happened." She shuffled out the door. "It's one thing to see you glow and your hair turn that weird color—and believe me that alone scares the shit out of this old body—but you blasted those kids with something not of this world."

Frustration ate at me. "I didn't hurt them."

"No, but you could have." Mrs. Enoch reached for the stair railing.

I hated to admit it, but she was probably right. After all, the melted-bra incident could've been a disaster. Luckily, one of my co-workers had a big Styrofoam cup of ice tea nearby that she dumped over the front of my boss' shirt.

"You shot one boy up into the branches of the maple on the corner where he hung screaming for someone to get him down, and the other boy landed upside down in Mrs. Cabbershot's chimney, his feet kicking as though he was running the Boston Marathon."

"I know, Mrs. Enoch. You don't have to remind me."

Slight prickling began in my gut. I had to change the subject. Otherwise, she'd continue to upset me and maybe find herself stuffed in a chimney too.

"If you're so afraid of me," I said, following her out the door and locking it, "then why don't you evict me?"

"Because you're the only tenant I have who pays on time and sometimes a month ahead. This damn economy has everyone by the balls." She hustled down the staircase to the side lawn as if she'd been goosed with a cattle prod.

Too bad I'm now unemployed. I sighed and headed to my parking spot.

Minutes later, I maneuvered my Jeep through a drive-through and bought Dad two Big Macs. He lived three blocks from my apartment, but the only time I ever saw him was when I stopped by.

When I turned twelve and my powers surfaced, my close relationship with my father dissolved. Dad changed, telling me I was an embarrassment to the Nutter family. I had no idea where my special abilities stemmed from or why I possessed them, but after Mom's death, things between Dad and me grew worse, and my every waking day was consumed with grief and blame.

I liked to think that if Dad had been a real father, if he'd been there for me, and if we could've come to terms with Mom's death together, then maybe things would have been different between us.

At Dad's place, I parked the car on the street. As I hurried along the walk to the front door, words whispered through my mind.

Come to us, Ruby. Your help is needed.

Frightened, I halted, dropping the take-out bag on the walk. Although I'd heard the voice in my head, I still glanced around for the source of the words. The visions I'd had at my front door and in the shower popped into my mind, and I sensed they were somehow tied to the voice. Shaken, I picked up the bag and sprinted the last few feet to the door.

"Dad," I hollered as I entered the house with my knees knocking together.

"It's about damn time you got here," he barked from his usual spot in the recliner.

I handed him his artery-clogging meal.

"What took you so long?" He opened a burger box.

Still shaken, I retorted, "What difference does it make?"

He snorted in disgust and bit into his food.

"Have you...noticed anything odd lately?" I asked. The question would urge him to be snider with me, but I had to ask.

"Besides you?" he replied around a mouthful of Big Mac. "Nope." He took another bite. "Why? Or should I ask?"

I knew better than to get my father going, but I always believed Dad had answers he stubbornly kept from me. I had to make some sense of things.

Determined, I braced myself for a verbal sparring match. "I have this feeling that something horrible is going to happen."

He guzzled the last few swallows of his beer and tossed the can in a small, overflowing garbage pail. "Something horrible has already happened."

"Like what?"

"You," he retorted, chuckling. "You see spirits, ghosts and things that go bump in the night, and you blow things up. That's about as horrible as it can get—unless you count killing your mother."

As always, guilt ate me from the inside out like a parasite hollows out a corpse.

"Dad," anguish squeezed my heart, "we've had this discussion a thousand times."

The misery in my voice pissed me off. Letting my father know he'd gotten to me was always a mistake, but bringing up Mom's death was his method of hurting me quickly. However, Dad couldn't talk about Mom without revealing his true feelings either.

I shut my eyes to avoid seeing my father's miserable expression and steeled myself for more of his barbs. Finally, I opened them again and said, "You *know* her death was an accident."

"It doesn't matter." He placed the burger in the carton and swallowed hard.

The torment in his voice always pricked my heart. My father might have lost his love for me, but he'd adored my mother, worshipped her. However, he wasn't blameless. Witnessing him talking to that "thing" in the garage that day had shocked me, and, unable to control my power, I'd set the building on fire.

"Dad, I'm sorry, but you were—"

"You saw nothing! Your mother's death was your fault, plain and simple," he ground out, his voice tight. "You shouldn't have been in the garage." He picked up his Big Mac again and bit into it with vengeance, but his other hand grasped the arm of the recliner so hard his knuckles turned white. "It was your infernal power that caught the rags on fire. You're lucky the police believed my story about the grease rags and a hot ash from my cigar."

Although Dad knew what had upset me so badly that day, I'd never told anyone what I'd seen in the garage. Besides, no one would've believed me anyway.

Leaning over, I reached out to Dad to apologize, but he jerked his arm away.

"Don't touch me!"

I grasped the recliner instead. Desperation, frustration, and anger formed a ball in my throat. The stinging sensation coursed down my arms, and I tried to will it away.

"Dad, I didn't—"

Smoke billowed up from under my hands, and I leapt back from his chair.

"Son of a bitch!" Dad thumped the arm of his recliner several times to beat out my smoldering handprints.

The aroma of melted plastic enveloped us.

Satisfied the danger was gone, he glared up at me. "Keep it up, Ruby, and I'll call the men in white coats to come get you." Dad returned to his meal and stuffed the first empty burger box into the bag and withdrew the second one. "You'll spend more time with a shrink like you did the summer you killed your mother."

"I went into therapy because I started seeing weird things like the dog-man that chased the mail carrier back to his truck!"

"Those things exist only in your mind." Dad took another bite of his meal. "I don't care what you think you saw in the garage that day. It was your imagination."

As I studied his craggy face and bushy brows, his mouth full of burger, and sauce clinging to the corners of his mustache, the urge to sob struck me. Why couldn't I have a normal father and have friends, a regular life—a loving relationship with a wonderful man? Instead, I was an outcast with a tyrannical jackass for a father and forced to endure a life of loneliness and isolation.

"Never mind," I said, defeated. "Let's drop it." Sighing heavily, I picked up the trashcan and debris surrounding it. "Do you need anything while I'm here? Clothes washed? Dishes done? Do you have plenty of Twinkies and Blatz?"

"No," he mumbled. "No again, and yes to the last two."

"Good. I'm going home."

He said nothing. Reaching for the remote, he flipped on the Speed Channel, burped, and yanked a can of Blatz from the full six-pack on the TV stand at his side.

In the kitchen, I gathered all the trash and carried it outside to the dumpster. When I walked back to the living room, Dad hadn't moved except to push remote buttons or lift his beer to his mouth.

"Night, Dad," I said as I opened the door. "I'm sorry about your recliner."

"Whatever." He belched again.

Loneliness slapped me, and I fought tears as I walked back to my Jeep. Exhaustion settled in my bones as I drove home. All I wanted was a good night's sleep so I could escape this shitty life I'd been dealt—and avoid more terrifying visions.

Once home, I locked the apartment, made my lunch for work the next day, then realized I had a sack meal for a job I no longer possessed. With a resigned sigh, I sat down and ate the sandwich and applesauce for my supper.

Finished, I changed into a thin nightgown, crawled into bed, and let the tears dampen my pillow.

****

A horn sounded in the distance, and I froze where I stood.

A few villagers filed out of their homes or pushed open shutters, their frightened faces pale in the gloaming.

The horn moaned again, the sound hollow and ghostly across the hillocks and through the shallow valleys.

No! It can't be. Not them!

The approaching thud of hoof beats followed, and the horn blared one more time, finalizing our pending demise.

"Run!" a man screamed. "Hide the women and children!"

Fear prevented my feet from moving.

Armored men rode into the village on monstrous horses with huge, furry feet. The warriors brandished broadswords or maces, and a few wielded whips.

A snarl reached me. Slowly, I faced the sound. A monstrosity crept across the ground in a swirling veil of indigo, black and gray mist. Long yellow claws glinted, and sharp snapping teeth filled a nightmare's face.

A lump of horror wedged in my throat. Unable to swallow, and with my heart hammering so hard spots floated in my vision, I feared the breaths I managed to suck in would be my last.

Villagers ran from their houses and into the darkness, their frightened screams impaling the night. The town harlot cried out, cowering against the community well. A few feet from her, another beast crouched, poised to attack. The woman had been kind to me, and secretly, I often left food and wine for her whenever I could sneak it out of our cottage.

I ran across the village to the whore, anger toward the intruders fueling my movements. I leapt at the fiend, but it dispersed only to appear again a few paces away. It formed a half-solid body as its bright yellow eyes assessed me through its camouflage.

"No! Leave her alone!"

"Tis a lowly whore," it hissed. "The masters can use her."

"You shall not have her." My innards quivered, and my legs shook so hard I feared I'd fall face down in the dirt.

More creatures drifted toward me and my paphian friend, their talons glittering in the light of the rising moon.

"Run," the harlot whispered. "Save yourself."

"No, I cannot leave you."

A fiery sensation bubbled up from my innards and flowed into my breasts, my shoulders, and down my arms. An invisible force shot from my hands and hit the beasts. With piercing shrieks, the fiends transformed into metal contraptions with wheels and demonic animal heads. Each one rolled away into the darkness, their abominable sound filling me with terror.

I frowned at the retreating things, wondering what sort of magic had created them, but approaching hoof beats resounded in the air. A glance over my shoulder spurred me into action. Framed by the red sky, a warrior, his black armor shining darkly in light of the rising moon, sat astride an ebony horse. The steed snorted, its feet sending a tremor through the ground. Terrified, and with my mouth suddenly dry, I grimaced at the panic slicing through my core. I sprinted for the narrow path between two cottages, the stones and pebbles bruising my feet through the thin soles of my slippers.

The animal's hot breath brushed the back of my gown. An instant later, the warrior caught me by the upper arm and hoisted me up and over his saddle.

I screamed...and screamed...

I sat straight up in bed, my scream shattering the quiet.

Chapter Two

Panting, my body aquiver and coated in sweat, I flung back the covers and leapt from the bed. The little toe on my right foot connected with a chair leg, and pain spiraled upward to my brain. Trying not to cry, I jumped up and down, my toe banging out an agonizing beat.

"Judas Priest and cherry Popsicles!"

I reached for the bedside table and steadied myself. A sickening, telltale sensation hurtled through my body. The air around me glowed, and warmth hurtled down my arms and into my fingertips which brightened to a brilliant copper-orange.

"No!" I jerked my hand back, righted myself. Invisible electricity crackled out of my right hand, zapping the lamp. The bulb flashed, followed by an abrupt pop and the aroma of ozone.

I breathed deeply. *In out...tamp down the fire and the need to blast the hell out of everything.*

Gulping, I glanced around the room as the sensation faded. The dream had been so real, including the absurd part where the smoke creatures had turned into motorcycles. I rubbed the fiery sensation from my hand.

The vision I'd had in the shower taunted me, which didn't help my state of mind. It was unfair to experience a phenomenal sense of lost love from a damn mind flash. I hadn't had a date for months. A relationship was out of the question, but it would be nice to get laid every hundred years or so. Well, it certainly felt like it a century since I'd had a good screw.

Hopelessness overwhelmed me. My job sucked, my neighbors hated and feared me, and my father wanted little to do with me, plus I sensed my life was about to change drastically.

I tensed as the aura of danger kissed my neck.

Ruby Nutter, we have need of you.

Still shaking and afraid to move, I stood staring at a tall chest of drawers.

Ruby Nutter, we have need of you. It's time to fulfill your destiny.

My gaze slid around the room, the sense of danger mounted.

Time to go, to get away. Go...go now—hurry!

Yes, come to us. Bring your son. He's in danger too.

Anthony! I had to see him, warn him.

But was I ready to see my son again? I'd only been fifteen when I'd given birth to him. After all, he was twenty years old, and he might not be too keen on seeing his biological mother.

Once Anthony turned eighteen, Catherine, his adoptive mother, sent me their address and phone number. It had been part of the adoption agreement. Anthony lived in Florida which seemed to be the direction I felt drawn to anyway. All that mattered was that he was safe.

If you want answers, then come to us, Ruby.

Against my better judgment, I made up my mind to go south and shrugged out of my nightclothes. Showering quickly, I rushed, dripping wet, back into the bedroom and jerked on the white sundress again, fresh undies, stuffed my feet into my Sketchers, and yanked a large suitcase out from under my bed. Within minutes, clothes and toiletries filled them. A small makeup case finished the ensemble.

After a brief breakfast of toast and jelly, I telephoned my landlady, explaining I'd be on vacation for several days, loaded my Jeep Wrangler, and locked up the apartment.

I should tell Dad I'm leaving.

Unlocking the door, I hurried back inside and straight to the phone. I glanced at the clock over the sofa. It was too early to call. Dad would still be in bed, and if I did call, he'd probably cuss me out. He wouldn't care anyway. The only reason he wanted me around was to wait on his needs, clean the house, and blame me for his mistakes.

Dad wouldn't even notice I was gone until I didn't show up for a couple of days or his phone calls went unanswered. I turned away from the phone and strode to the door.

Outside again, I paused to study the pale gray dawn streaking the sky over Columbus. Dots of light glowed in some of the neighboring windows as the homes' occupants readied themselves for work. Pigeons cooed in the eaves of Mrs. Tittle's rickety two-car garage across the street, and the distant roar of a garbage truck drifted up the street. The distinct odor of refuse from a cluster of cans on the corner floated on the air, and the flowery aroma of fabric softener spewed from someone's dryer vent.

Another rumble snared my attention, and a chill swept over my skin. I stopped with my hand on the driver's door and listened. Motorcycles headed this way. No one I knew of in this neighborhood even owned a moped let alone a suicide machine.

An overwhelming sense of urgency flooded my body again. The visions! I had to leave *now*. A whimper escaped me.

"Shit!"

Terror galvanized me into action. Keys in hand, I opened the driver's door and prepared to slide into the seat, but the sound of the bikes grew suddenly louder. First one, two, then several motorcycles rounded the corner down the street, their headlights pouring across the asphalt in silver beams. Recognizing the unfolding scene, I fought to draw air into my lungs. Fear slithered into my innards, poked its cold fingers into my brain, and jabbed my spine. For a moment I thought I'd hurl my breakfast on the asphalt.

Hide! But where?

I jerked the door shut, flattened myself across the bucket seats with my cheek pressed against the vinyl, and prayed I wasn't seen. The choppers passed, their reverberations penetrating my body. The thunderous sound vibrated my SUV, my heart thrumming in time to the engines.

Panting, I wiggled myself into the backseat so I could watch through the hatch. A dozen steel horses turned right, taking the street that led out to I-70, some with one rider, others with two.

The low, heavy growl of another one penetrated the quiet morning. I craned my head around the driver's seat. This straggler slowed to a crawl. Finally, he stopped in front of Mrs. Cabbershot's home just two doors up from my apartment.

If he noticed me, I was done for. I'm not sure how I knew this, but I sat so still I stopped breathing. Specks flitted in front of my eyes, and I wondered if my booming heartbeat would give away my location. Sweat covered my hands, and I tightened my grip on the sides of the driver's seat.

The man glanced toward the Jeep. I couldn't discern his facial features, but his eyes, bright yellow and glowing, surveyed my vehicle. My heart stuttered against my ribs. Fear nearly strangled me.

Please, God, don't let him see me.

He revved the bike and approached my vehicle. Ducking, I kept my gaze level with the window's rim, determined to see if the biker followed the others. As the steel horse passed, I saw enough of the man to know he wore all the buckles and metal trim of motorcycle garb and that his frame had to be well over seven feet, but the Harley he rode—or whatever the hell it was—was a different matter. The living head of a horse resided where the handlebars, gas tank, and the front wheel fender should've been. Above red, flaring nostrils, the horse's eyes shone flaming yellow. Serrated teeth filled its muzzle, and bands of silver ran from the corners of its mouth to the rider's hands. The thing snarled and gnashed its teeth against the bit as it rolled by.

The rider paused again, the bike's back tire almost even with the SUV's rear bumper. The man looked from one side of the street to the other. Something radiated from him, something primal, sexual.

The stranger parked the bike at the curb behind my Jeep. He sat the kickstand down, dismounted, and stood gazing up at my apartment. In awe of his size and stature, I could only stare with my mouth agape, my breaths tiny and quick. With purpose in his strides, he crossed the sidewalk and side lawn to the stairs that led to my dwelling and ascended them; his heavy footfalls were like drumbeats of doom as he climbed to the door.

He tried the knob, but when the door didn't open, he placed his hands flat on the glass which began glowing crimson. Stunned, I clapped my hand over my mouth to stifle the need to cry out as I watched the molten panes collapse. They dripped down the door and dribbled onto the landing until it had melted away enough that he could reach through and unlock the knob and deadbolt. He stooped over and stepped inside.

I turned my attention to the demonic Harley. The horse part snarled and shook its head, sending fright stomping across my nervous system. The silver reins jingled, and one fell, its tip brushing the pavement.

A squeaking noise finally penetrated the cloud of terror over my mind. I craned my head, scanning the backseat. I realized I shook so hard my sneakers were vibrating against the hard plastic of the opposite passenger door. I moved my foot and tried to steady my nerves, praying that the demonic bike couldn't sense or hear me.

While the man was in my apartment, I could've slipped into the driver's seat and sped away, but I was certain he'd hear the Jeep start up and come after me. Even if I managed to reach the next street, he'd easily catch up with me on the motorcycle. Maybe my proximity was the best camouflage.

Movement caught my attention, and the horse-demon thing growled again. The biker exited my apartment and mounted the motorcycle. He pushed the kickstand up, studied my home and the neighborhood for a long moment, and then pulled away. He turned at the corner, but this time, the bike looked like any other Harley, and, I realized, it was the thirteenth suicide machine.

Buzzing filled my ears, and I struggled to draw in air. Everything I'd seen had to be my imagination. Granted, I'd seen some freaky things in this world, including myself, but a motorcycle that was part demonic horse?

Tingles needled my forearms and bled into my hands. Light radiated off my body, heat singed my scalp, and my fingernails glowed red like embers.

Calm. Think calm thoughts. Chocolate peanut butter ice cream, cool, sunny days, a hot bath...

The sensations began to diminish, and, jackknifing out of the back, I struggled into the driver's seat and started the Jeep. My thunderous heartbeat crashed in my ears, and feeling inebriated with adrenaline, I took the long way around to I-70, first stopping at a mini mart for a big cup of coffee. I took the Interstate, heading due south. Somehow the dreams, visions, the voice, and the motorcycles were all tied together. I felt it in my bones.

However, not only was I in jeopardy, but so was my son. It bothered me that the first time I approached Anthony would be to warn him about a danger I didn't understand. He'd probably think I was crazy, but I had to try to protect him. He was, after all, my son, and regardless of the terrible circumstances in which he'd been conceived, I still loved him.

I had to make sure he was all right.

****

As I maneuvered traffic outside of Columbus, I pondered the motorcycles. They didn't make sense to me, but then nothing about my life ever had.

I could've gone to the Columbus Airport and flown to Florida, especially since I felt my son was in danger, too, but for some reason it was essential that I drive. A week earlier, I'd taken the Jeep to have it tuned up and replaced the worn tires with four new Firestones.

Before Mom's death, my father had taken us on many road trips, so I enjoyed them. Although frightened and uncertain of my future, I could still take pleasure in my sudden, unexpected "vacation."

Driving also allowed me to think. I needed time to sort through my emotions about my son and consider the whys and wherefores of this trip, the mounting visions and mind flashes.

Is Anthony cursed too?

The interchange for I-77 appeared, and I merged the Jeep with the traffic, heading toward the Ohio River and the West Virginia state line. Thirty minutes later brought me to a bridge where I crossed the dark, slate-blue river. The state sign loomed over the Jeep: Welcome to West Virginia, Wild and Wonderful.

I might be wild, but I'm not wonderful.

The thought annoyed me, and I punched the radio's ON button. The last few seconds of a pop song ended, but the beginning of "Copperhead Road", one of my favorites, filled the SUV and lightened my mood. Tapping the fingers of one hand on the steering wheel, I tried to avoid the heart of what bothered me, but it just wouldn't go away.

I'm weird. I don't belong. I have no purpose in this world.

Was I destined to always be alone? Never to love?

I'd believed Cole Vandercourt loved me, but he'd quickly proven otherwise. Handsome, blond, blue-eyed Cole, a senior and the most coveted boy in the high school had shown interest in me, a lowly freshman, the odd girl who no one liked. But once he'd gotten what he wanted and proven his fearlessness by doing so, he dumped me.

A week later, Cindy Sansburg and Jody Kefferstine befriended me, even sitting with me in the cafeteria of Whetstone High School. They'd insisted what Cole had done to me was wrong. They convinced me they wanted to be my friends, and as a trio, we could protect one another and watch each other's backs. Together, we went to the Christmas Snow Dance as a dateless trio.

That night Cindy told me I'd been named as the dance's Snow Queen.

I couldn't believe it, had been blown away by the news. It was too good to be true, and I should have realized that. The need for friends and acceptance had nearly gotten me killed.

Jody had led me to the girls' restroom to put on a tiara and cape before the announcement was made to the school.

Stunned, I'd followed them, but six other girls waited there for me. The tallest one pushed me so hard I sprawled out on the tile in my pretty red-and-white satin gown. The first kick landed in my ribs. The air had rushed out of my lungs, and pain radiated up into my chest and down into my groin. A series of kicks, slaps, and punches rained down on me. Blood and tears blurred my vision as shrieks burst from my lips like the cries of a snared rabbit. Even curling into a fetal position had done nothing to save me from their onslaught.

The power surged up out of my guts. It traveled along my arms, and I glowed so brightly the girls gasped and cowered together against the wall. With my hair whipping and flowing as if afire, and my fingertips as red as coals, the curse found its way out of me again. The water in the toilet bowls boiled and bubbled, cracking each one. The hems of the girls' dresses burst into flames, and they ran shrieking like banshees from the restroom. One tripped over me and hit the tile with a sickening "thwap."

She stared eye to eye with me, but finally realized she was still on fire and sat up long enough to smack out the flames eating at her gown.

"Why?" I asked.

"You're a freak," she said without looking at me. "You do weird things, know stuff before it happens, and you see visions, monsters, and talk about spirits. Freaks don't belong in this world." She jumped to her feet and ran sobbing from the restroom.

Later, during lonely, sleepless nights, their shouts of "freak," "weirdo," and "witch" echoed in my mind. Two months later, I discovered I was pregnant by Cole. The only thing Dad ever said about me putting his grandson up for adoption was that it was probably for the better because dealing with me was difficult enough.

I stared at the Interstate passing under the Jeep's tires. After a few brief relationships that ended in disaster once my freaky abilities were revealed, I resigned myself to a life of loneliness, but I still pined for a few good friends. Hell, I'd settle for just *one* good friend, someone to talk to and laugh with, someone who didn't care that I blasted things into oblivion whenever I was scared or upset, and one who wouldn't judge me because I saw things straight out of Grimm's Fairy Tales.

Irritated, I slammed my right hand against the steering wheel. The tingle began in my palm and seeped into my fingertips. My nails flared like large, flat sparks.

I tried to stop the surge of power, but failed this time. It wasn't the first instance of a window, mirror, or other shiny surface reflecting my power. Overall, the worst that had ever happened was a few scorched hairs or temporary flash burn to my eyes. However, I inadvertently jerked the steering wheel, veering into the emergency lane. Before I could right the vehicle, the Jeep ran over something on the berm. My SUV jolted, and a "whump" issued against the undercarriage. I righted the vehicle and manhandled it back into the correct lane of traffic, but the Jeep veered again, and the steering wheel turned sharply to the right.

With effort, I stayed in my lane, but let off the accelerator. Ahead, a young woman sat on the guardrail, early morning fog twirling around her. Hitchhiking on an Interstate is illegal, but she perched there all the same with her back to the traffic. She faced the opposite side as if admiring the swampy hollow below the road. I caught a glimpse of pale hair and a huge backpack as the Jeep whizzed by.

Gradually, I brought the vehicle back onto the emergency lane and slowed it to a stop, my hands clenching the steering wheel so tightly my palms cramped and my knuckles protested. I knew how to change a tire, but it had been several years since the last one and that had been on a Chevette.

I shut off the engine and groaned. Was this a sign of how the rest of the trip would pan out?

Screw it.

I'd change the tire, resume my journey, and buy a replacement as soon as possible.

A tractor-trailer roared by, its tailwind jiggling the SUV. At least the Jeep's color, a bright canary yellow, would be easily seen by motorists. Thoughts of all the caught-on-camera accidents along Interstate roadsides filtered through my head.

I waited for a lull in traffic. Frustrated, I clambered over to the passenger seat and got out on that side. Although still early, the humidity had become palpable. The aroma of heating asphalt and hot rubber pelted my senses. Every now and then, I'd catch the odor of swamp water wafting up from the shallow pond below the road. With a sigh, I removed the tire cover and bolts on the hatch's door, then retrieved the jack, rolling the spare around to the front. After positioning the jack, I reached for the four-way and squatted by the flat tire.

"Need some help?"

I paused with the four-way an inch from the first lug nut. There, at the back bumper, stood the blonde from the guardrail. She shrugged out of the backpack and dropped it on the pavement. I blinked. There was no way I was seeing a Marilyn Monroe lookalike with big boobs, wearing Daisy Duke cut-offs and wedge sandals.

"I've never changed a tire," she said in a soft, child-like voice. She stooped slightly, and her massive boobs surged to the edge of her scooped neckline. "But I can work the jack."

Yeah, I bet she's good at that too. I eyed her skeptically, my inner voice screaming this chick was pure trouble.

"So, do you want help?" she pressed. She placed her hands on her hips and shifted her weight to one foot so a healthy dose of ass cheek hung out of her shorts.

I wondered if Tits R Us could be of any real help.

"Sure," I said.

I focused on the lug nuts, turned to look for a pavement divot to set them in so I wouldn't lose them, and froze in horror. The woman's ass cheeks hovered inches from my face as she bent over to retrieve the jack. Appalled, I shifted my attention to the next lug nut.

"I'm Maureen Galbraith," she said in her baby-doll voice.

"Uh...Ruby Nutter."

"Nutter? You mean like a crazy person?"

"No, like the name."

"Oh."

I managed to loosen the other lug nuts. "Jack up the Jeep, please."

She stooped and started pumping the lever. I blinked again. Her breasts rushed forward in a wave of cleavage that was impressive to say the least. I fought the urge to duck.

A vehicle pulled in behind mine. The driver waited for a pause in the traffic, stepped out of the flatbed diesel and made his way over to us.

"Can I be of service, ladies?" he drawled and tipped his crumpled cowboy hat.

Instantly I sensed trouble. "No thanks," I said.

Maureen leaned over and resumed working the jack.

"Hoowee! Baby, bend over a little more!" The truck driver sauntered closer, ogling Maureen's backside.

"Do you mind?" I snapped. The look I threw over my shoulder should've fried him into a pile of ash.

"Yeah, pretty mama, show me that stuff between your legs!" the driver continued. His tone reeked of too many cigarettes and one too many hookers. "Bet I could poke you until you begged for mercy!"

That did it. I stood up, hands on hips, and glared at him. "Just the thought of that ten-gallon gut hanging over your one-ounce dick is enough to make me beg for mercy."

"GAWD, you're crude, Ruby!" Maureen straightened, her expression aghast.

I gaped at her. "ME?"

"Bitch!" the trucker snapped. "I stopped to help two pretty women and—"

"You stopped, thinking you might score a piece of ass, you jerk-off!" I retorted above the roar of passing semis. My palms itched. If I started glowing as I thrashed this guy's ass all over the roadside, I could only imagine the shocked motorists and resulting fender benders.

"Why you—!" He took two steps toward me.

The hitchhiker gasped and grabbed my arm. I leaned toward her, but whether for my comfort or hers, I wasn't sure.

A horn sliced the air, and a black, expensive-looking Ford Excursion slowed as it passed my Jeep to pull over in front of it. A door slammed.

Please don't be another jerk.

Footsteps crunched on the gravel littering the asphalt.

"Is there a problem here?"

Something in the stranger's voice shot an arrow of recognition through me.

"Not at all," the truck driver said. He backed away. "Thought I'd offer my help to these ladies, but they obviously have everything under control." He spun on his heel and bolted for his flatbed. As he pulled out into traffic, forcing a car over into the passing lane, a horn blared.

"That guy was giving you trouble, wasn't he?" the man asked.

I turned, and my mouth dropped open. Not one word would emerge from it.

The stranger smiled. I'd never seen an albino in person before. His pale skin almost blended with the dwindling fog and mid-summer haze. I caught a glimpse of a bad scar that dipped along his neck into his deep green Polo shirt that stood out starkly against his coloring. Hair like gossamer curled around his ears and collar. Mirrored sunglasses covered his eyes, which I could only guess were as white as his skin. Faded jeans clung to trim hips and slim, muscular legs. My gaze traveled down to a pair of expensive alligator-skin cowboy boots poking out from the hems of his jeans.

The only albinos I'd ever seen had been in movies. The character Whitey from the movie "Foul Play" and the twins from "The Matrix Reloaded" popped into my head. This man, however, wasn't what I'd deem unattractive, but he certainly looked unholy, eerie. Although some aspects of him were shocking and bizarre, I was simultaneously repulsed and drawn to him.

And he seemed so familiar. Somehow his pleasantly deep voice stirred memories, memories just out of my reach like a forgotten word dangling on the tip of my tongue.

"That guy was being nasty, but Ruby here," Maureen jerked her thumb over one shoulder, "can hold her own. She's got one hell of a mouth on her."

Frowning, I cast the hitcher a warning look. "He ticked me off."

"Would you like me to finish changing the tire for you?" he asked.

"Sure!" Maureen chirped.

I said nothing, just stepped back and watched him work the jack, wrangle the flat tire off and shove the spare on in its place, followed by the lug nuts and tightening each one securely. The muscles worked in his arms and shoulders, and my body responded. The guy wasn't my type. I liked tall, dark-haired men with dreamy green or brown eyes. This guy was just too—unnatural.

That's the pot calling the kettle black.

Shame warmed my skin, but I blamed it on the humidity and the sun.

He affixed the tools and flat in their proper places and shut the hatch. The man turned his attention to me, his full-lipped mouth spreading into a wide grin, revealing teeth whiter than his skin.

"All done," he said as he shoved his shades atop his head.

I withdrew a twenty from my dress pocket and held it out to him, but his gaze stunned me into silence yet again, a gaze of ice and azure that seemed to slice through my soul.

"Thank you for your help," I finally stammered.

I thought he was going to take the money, but instead, he squeezed my hand, and a warm smile lit up his face. His powder-blue eyes bored into mine, and the interest I saw in them rendered me stupid. It was almost as if I was meeting a long-lost friend or lover. Stranger still was that I had the overwhelming urge to step into his arms and snuggle my head against his shoulder.

"No charge," he replied. "Just helping someone in need."

"Thank you," I croaked. At the tremble in my voice, heat rushed to my cheeks.

The man continued to gaze into my eyes, and, with obvious reluctance, released my hand. "Maybe we'll bump into one another again sometime." He nodded to me and Maureen. "I need to get out of this sun and get going. You two take it easy and stay safe."

"We *will* see you again," Maureen called out.

He paused, glancing over his shoulder. Finally, he nodded again, but I sensed his bemused expression as he turned away. The man climbed into his Excursion and left. An odd sense of abandonment swept over me.

I eyed Maureen in bewilderment. What was this "we" talk?

"It was uh...nice meeting you," I said and climbed in on the passenger side to crawl into the driver's seat. Maureen opened the passenger door, flung her backpack on the back floorboard, hopped in shotgun, and fastened her seatbelt.

Flabbergasted, I asked, "What the hell do you think you're doing?"

"Riding with you," She blinked innocent, pale green eyes.

"Who says?"

She looked hurt. "I thought...I thought we were friends."

Eeriness washed over me. The voices of Cindy and Jody echoed in my ears. Hadn't I just been thinking of how nice it would be to have at least one real friend?

My eyebrows rose so high I momentarily wondered if they'd crawled up into my hairline. "We're not friends. I don't even know you."

"Please let me ride with you, Ruby."

The whine in her voice made me want to take my own life, but regardless, something about the woman both warned me away and urged me to give her a ride. Maybe it was the fact I needed female companionship, a friend, but despite the mental whispers, a louder, more insistent voice screamed over the rest. It said I "needed" to help her.

"I'm going to Florida."

"Really? So am I!"

I sighed. *How convenient.*

"All right, but if you try anything funny, I'll kick your ass out doing sixty-five."

She frowned as if confused. "What would I do?"

"Never mind," I started the Jeep and shot out into traffic before another car or semi appeared in my side mirror.

I didn't understand why I'd given in to her plea, but whatever the reason, the one voice out-shouting the others in my head had finally won. I hated that voice.

Chapter Three

"Where's your family?" I asked Maureen to pass the time and occupy my mind.

"I have my Aunt Lula in Indiana, but that's all," she said.

Her evasive tone snagged my attention. "So why are you hitchhiking?"

"I like to be on the move. Aunt Lula home-schooled me, and once I got my diploma, I decided I wanted to travel the United States. Everything I own is in my backpack."

"How do you survive without money?" I questioned, glancing at her French-tipped fingernails, which weren't cheap. "Where do you sleep?"

"If I want something, I do an odd job here and there. Aunt Lula wires me money when I need it, but I don't always rent rooms. If the weather is nice, I'll save my money. I've slept in doorways, barns, in cars, or wherever it's safe."

Safe? Was that possible in today's world, especially when there were things that went "bump" in the night?

I began the drive through the mountains of West Virginia. Ten miles later, I kicked off my sneakers. Wriggling my toes, I glanced down at Maureen's feet. How could she stand walking around in high heels? My unusual hitcher had to be a few bricks short of a full load.

I glanced over at her. "Why do you wear heels to hitchhike?"

"I only wear them when I'm not hitching," Maureen explained. "High heels make my legs look great, but these don't really count. They're wedges."

With my gaze on the road, I worried that I'd picked up Coconuts, the Fruit of the Loom guys' lost sister.

I tried turning up the radio, but Maureen talked over it until I gave up and lowered the volume. After an hour of listening to her constant chatter and high-pitched laughter, I started praying for a quick death. Kicking her out of my Jeep wasn't in my nature so long as she didn't do anything to "really" piss me off.

My thoughts strayed to the albino man. Despite his unusual appearance, something about the man seemed so familiar too. I knew I'd never met him before. It would be impossible to forget a man like that, especially one who looked like he'd just stepped out of the special effects department.

"What did you mean back there about us meeting that guy again?"

Maureen stared out the passenger window. "Oh, just that life can be weird. People bump into one another all the time."

"You expect me to believe that?"

"What do you mean?"

"You said it like you were certain we'll meet him again."

She shrugged. "It's just a feeling."

The gal was too much. Of all the people in the nation I could run into, it had to be a fruity Marilyn Monroe copycat, who played the baby-doll routine to the hilt and hinted she was psychic.

And I'd thought I was weird.

The miles passed under the Jeep's tires. Maureen prattled on about places she'd been and people she'd met, but I only half listened.

Oblivious to the fact I was only making noncommittal noises to her chatter, Maureen kept babbling. "I worked at a restaurant for a couple of months, but only because I had a terrible crush on one of the busboys..."

With Virginia not far away, I pulled into a rest area to pee and change my clothes. The August humidity had defeated me, and since my Jeep Wrangler didn't have air conditioning, I craved fresh, dry clothing on my body and a cold drink. Besides, Maureen's constant talking had me dreaming of driving into oncoming traffic.

Vehicles crammed the parking area. I found a vacant spot, parked the vehicle and shut off the engine.

"What are you doing?" Maureen asked.

"I have to pee," I snapped in irritation. "And I want to change my clothes."

The look I gave her would've silenced any other person, but not Maureen. She hopped out of the Jeep and followed me around to the hatch where I'd stashed my suitcase. I rummaged in it until I found a change of clothes. I shut the hatch and collided with Maureen's built-in air bags.

"Oh, for God's sake, will you put those things away!"

"Has anyone ever told you that you're not only rude but crude too?" she said in a wounded tone.

"Yep. Many times." I stuffed my clothing and purse under one arm and sidestepped Maureen. She was the epitome of a tag-along little sister who wouldn't let you have a moment of peace, but I still felt rotten for going off on her like that.

One woman in her late thirties used a squeegee on the outside plate-glass windows of the visitor's center. Sweat trickled down the sides of her face, and large ovals of perspiration stained the back of her uniform and underarms. In the picnic area, under the shade of oaks and maples, families ate from coolers. When I reached the bathroom, I ducked inside and nearly sprinted to a stall.

Moments later, Maureen's voice cracked through the air. "Ruby?"

I bit my tongue.

Louder, she called out again, "Ruby?"

"What?" Silently, I thanked God the restroom seemed empty. I didn't know how much more I could take of the woman without losing my temper.

"Just checking to see if you were in here."

"Judas Priest and cherry Popsicles!" I whispered. Had I left my common sense in Columbus? I still didn't understand why I'd allowed the woman to ride with me.

I struggled out of my sundress and slipped on the fresh clothes. "I swear I've never met anyone who talks as much as you do."

"Talking is how you get to know people," Maureen replied.

Frustrated, I shoved the stall door. It flew open on loose hinges and struck a woman—or rather an Amazon—on her way to the sinks.

"You stupid bitch!" She glared down at me through heavily kohled eyes. Her lipstick matched the bright red hair escaping from under a skull-patterned bandana, and she wore motorcycle attire.

Although I've always been considered tall, the woman towered over me. A bright yellow pigment flashed in her eyes, and for an instant I thought I saw elongated pupils. Shocked, my heart kicking up to warp speed, I stumbled back into the toilet stall. Danger radiated off the Amazon, and the overpowering urge to claw an escape route through the block wall assailed me.

"I'm sorry."

Fear coiled in the center of my chest, the sensation tight, piercing. Heat boiled up out of my gut and surged into my torso, down my arms. No! I had to contain the power, keep it from frying the woman and scaring the hell out of Maureen and anyone else who might walk in. Swallowing hard, I struggled with the sensation and managed to snuff it out—barely.

In a shaky voice, I added a little louder, "I d-didn't realize the door was loose."

The woman turned away from me as another thought somersaulted through my mind. *Is she one of the bikers from this morning?*

She didn't even wash her hands. With another glare over her panther-tattooed shoulder, her eyes normal again despite her anger, she muttered, "Fucking bitch."

She stormed out of the restroom, her large black boots thumping along the floor. If I followed the chick outside, I'd probably see her straddle a motorcycle behind a huge, tattooed dude wearing a mini machine gun strapped to his crotch.

Once the door swung shut again, the overwhelming urge to cry hit me. Tremors seized me, and shaking uncontrollably, I picked up my discarded clothes and exited the stall. I sucked in a big breath and looked around for something to use as a punching bag.

Maureen exited the toilet stall. She blinked. "What?"

"Nothing," I mumbled. Something about her seemed different, and I realized she'd changed her high heels. "What was wrong with your sandals?"

"The others were hurting my feet."

"So put on some sneakers."

"I like high heels."

"They make you look stupid." Oh, shit. I hadn't meant for my words to come out so mean.

She pouted, which transformed my shame into fresh irritation, neither of which mixed well with residual fear.

"No, they don't," she insisted.

Turning on a spigot, I splashed cold water on my face, hoping I could wash away the memory of the encounter I'd just had. Maureen handed me a wad of paper towels.

"You're very attractive, but you do look rather frightened." Maureen studied me in the mirror. "I bet you turn a lot of heads."

A chill swept over me. "What makes you say that?"

"You're long-limbed, tall, and have dreamy eyes and pretty brown hair with red highlights. Men love women like you."

Her comment sounded sincere, but it embarrassed me. I slung my damp dress over my arm and motioned toward the door. "We better get going."

"Yeah," she shrugged into her backpack, "we need to eat." She glanced at a big clock high on one wall. "It's nearly eleven. We could have an early lunch."

Outside, I could've sworn we'd stepped into a sauna. Throwing uneasy looks every direction, I walked to the concession shack with Maureen and bought us Coca

Colas and some Lifesavers to suck on once the sodas were gone.

"There's a family restaurant down over that way." Maureen pointed. "Let's get something to eat."

I debated whether or not to flop down in the parking lot and enjoy a good temper tantrum. Why did I get the feeling this woman was going to sponge off of me too?

She offered me a pleading look.

Fine. If fed her, I could probably leave her at the restaurant. Maybe some other poor, unsuspecting soul would give her a ride instead.

Side by side, we strode to the Jeep. A motor roared to life, and I stopped dead still, heart knocking so hard it wouldn't have surprised me if it had snapped a rib.

"Ruby?" Maureen grabbed my arm. "What's wrong?"

Another engine rumbled then another and another. The thunder of motorcycles assaulted the moist air and reverberated over the mountainsides.

A full-sized van with sleeping quarters backed out of a nearby parking spot. Hidden by the big vehicle, several Harleys lined the sidewalk. Two to a space, some with one rider, some with two, they each roared to life. Every hair follicle tightened on my body, and the word DANGER screamed in my brain. It couldn't be the same biker gang.

I counted. One, two, three....eight, nine...twelve, thirteen.

Each rider, whether male or female, stood well over seven feet tall. I scanned the bikes for the thirteenth rider, but didn't see him.

The Harley chick from the restroom swung onto the back of one of the motorcycles and settled behind a big, burly man in full leather, a coal-black beard and mustache clothing his face.

"RUBY!" Maureen shook my arm.

Her abrupt voice shattered my paralysis. Blinking, I stared at the rest area. Harried mothers ushered sweaty children back to RVs and minivans. Attendants picked up litter, their shirts dotted with perspiration rings.

"What's wrong with you?" my hitchhiker pressed.
"Nothing."

****

For once, Maureen sat quietly in the passenger seat. Every couple of minutes she'd look over at me. I said nothing. All I wanted was for the adrenaline to stop zinging through my nervous system and my heart rate to return to normal.

I concentrated on the traffic coming and going through the rest area as I maneuvered the Jeep toward the road leading to the restaurant.

The August humidity hung in twirling clouds over the steep West Virginia mountainsides. I couldn't wait to reach Florida. I loved the ocean, loved the aroma of brine and the way the sea breeze tugged at my hair.

I hope I don't have to buy a plane or boat ticket and travel farther than Florida.

Most of my family vacation memories centered on Florida and The Keys. Those were great times. Well, they were until my powers surfaced.

I drove along the narrow, winding lane to the diner. A graveled parking lot encircled the rectangular-shaped building called The Million-Dollar Cafe. Across the road, opposite the restaurant, sat a gas station and a souvenir shop.

A two-lane road cut through the area and twisted up the mountainside to parts unknown. I parked my Jeep amongst several pickup trucks. A chain-link fence lined the back of the brick establishment to catch rocks that might tumble from the steep incline. On the right side of the property, in an area riddled with murky puddles filled by unexpected thunderstorms, a rusty garbage dumpster crouched like a large, misshapen troll.

Maureen and I rolled up the windows, got out and locked the Jeep. We passed between a Chevette on the left and a dark green Ford 4x4 on our right. Behind me, Maureen wobbled across the gravel in her heels.

A dog lunged upward from the Ford's truck bed. I spun on my heel, inadvertently facing its snapping, foul-smelling maw, the dog's paws planted on the pickup's side. He strained toward me. Maureen screamed and yanked me back. We collapsed against the Chevette, clutching each other's arms, our heels digging into the gravel.

I fought to control the heat burbling up out of my gut. It traced my ribs, skittered beneath my breasts, and oozed down my arms toward my fingertips. Brightness surrounded me, and Maureen gasped, closing her eyes and turning her face away. Terrified at what I might do, I whimpered and battled the power.

If I didn't stop it, someone would have a barbecued dog.

Chapter Four

"Ruby? What's happening?"

Maureen's grip tightened, her touch both oddly familiar and disconcerting. I wanted to push her away, but feared making any sudden movements lest the dog break its tether.

Prickles raced along my skin, nausea landed in my belly and my fingernails turned from natural pink to light orange. Squeezing my eyes shut, I concentrated on controlling the energy threatening to burst free.

The monster's barks rang out over the lot. They were deep, angry barks that could inspire fear in a Kodiak bear. My insides grew hot, as if I'd swallowed lava, and my legs shook so hard I knew if I took one step I'd fall face first.

"I'm afraid to move," Maureen whispered, her eyes still shut against the light radiating from my body.

I forced the power down, shoving it back into the darkness where it resided. Finally, it succumbed to my will. The molten sensation obeyed and quieted, the brilliance around me faded. Shaking, I leaned against the car, my legs feeling as though someone had replaced the bones with mush.

Maureen blinked rapidly, her eyes full of amazement and curiosity. I blinked back at her.

Why isn't she afraid of me?

"Why were you...? How did you...?" She stared at me in wonder. "What or who are you?"

Ignoring her question, I wheezed, "What kind of idiot leaves an animal like that tied in the back of a pickup?"

"Hang on, ladies!" someone called.

Thankful for the distraction, I turned toward the sound of footsteps on the gravel.

A big man pushed between us and the snarling canine. He grabbed the leash with a meaty fist and pulled the dog off the truck's side. "BUFORD, DOWN!" He cuffed the animal over the ears. "Get down, you dumb mutt!" He pointed at the bed of the truck. "Lay down!"

With a last low grumble, the dog obeyed his master's commands. The sound imbued me with unease, and the image of the demonic motorcycle came to mind.

The man turned. "Sorry about that. Buford's really protective of my pickup. I'm a trouble shooter for the mines, and he goes everywhere with me."

"What would you do if he attacked someone?" Maureen asked.

A dark shadow flitted across his face, but an apologetic grin quickly replaced it. A billed red-and-gold hat with Coal Miners Do It in the Dirt embroidered across the front shaded his piercing blue eyes. Jet-black hair and high cheekbones hinted that he might have Cherokee blood running through his veins. His gaze slid over Maureen first then he appraised my body before his attention came to rest on my face.

Something slithered through my soul. *This guy is bad news.*

"I reckon I'd have a lawsuit on my hands," the man finally answered.

"Thanks for coming to our aid." I sidestepped along the Chevette and tugged Maureen with me.

As we passed, the man grabbed Maureen's elbow. She let out a squeak.

"Why don't you gals let me buy your lunch? It'll be my way of apologizing."

"That's not necessary—"

"Oh, that would be so nice!" Maureen chimed in over me. "I'm starved."

A big grin spread across the man's face. "Good, it's settled."

"I don't think—"

"Aw, come on, Ruby." Maureen pulled on my arm. "He's trying to make amends."

Her green eyes looked so childlike, and I wondered at the lack of common sense behind them. My gaze met the man's. He seemed harmless enough, but something whispered not to trust him.

"Oh, all right," I conceded. Somehow, someway, I knew I'd regret accepting his offer.

With a flourish, the guy motioned toward the café and walked with us. "Name's Wayne Blacktree. Are you two just passing through?"

"Maureen Galbraith." She nodded at me. "She's Ruby Nutter."

"Where are you from?" he asked.

"Ohio," I answered. His interest bothered me. What difference did it make where I was from?

"How about you, Marilyn?" He looked at Maureen.

The way his gaze traversed her body reminded me of a guy about to jump into a sports car and take it for a spin. I felt like stepping between them and telling him to keep his lust-filled looks to himself. Worse, however, was that Maureen seemed to be doing the same thing to him. I could almost smell the pheromones wafting between them.

"It's Maureen, and I'm originally from Indiana."

Wayne laughed and opened the café's door. "A Hoosier, huh?"

"Sort of," she grinned up at Wayne, "but I wouldn't say it's an official tag since I haven't lived there for more than six months at a time."

He motioned us inside. "I'll make sure the waitress gives me your bill. I'll be back for supper before I leave town so I'll settle my tab then." He tipped his cap to us. "Enjoy your meal, ladies." He spoke to a waitress and quickly left the café.

As I glanced around the eatery, my gaze landed on a head of snowy hair and a set of wide shoulders in a green Polo shirt.

My albino.

****

The classy style of The Million-Dollar Cafe surprised me. A shellacked oak surface ran the length of the bar. Small antler chandeliers hung throughout the establishment, their golden illumination cheery and bright. Philodendrons twined across the ceiling and down the walls of the café. Oak tables gleamed in a high-sheen gloss.

The early lunch rush kept the waitresses hopping from one crowded table to another. A server managed to oust a young guy from his table where he joined my white stranger at the counter. The waitress ushered us to our seats. Every pair of eyes in the place, whether male or female, watched Maureen sashay across the room. The albino noticed the whispers and pointed looks and turned, his pale eyes widening in surprise as his gaze connected with mine.

Again, something unnamable passed between us.

I thought about hiding under one of the floor tiles, but instead, I gritted my teeth and waited for the server to clean up some dirty dishes and wipe the table. What must he think of us? Especially when Maureen looked like the town trollop.

Oh, that wasn't nice. More shame whizzed through me. Where did I get off being so mean? *It's easier to deliver the first stab than it is to be on the receiving end of one.* Many others besides Cindy Sansburg and Jody Kefferstine had taught me that lesson, and I was a quick study.

I sneaked a glance at the man. How many hurtful remarks had he endured? How many cruel jokes had been played on him?

Everyone wants to be different...unless they are.

Maureen and I sat at the table. I was grateful for a menu to hide behind while the heat faded from my cheeks, but I still sensed his curious stare. Who was he? Why did he affect me so profoundly?

Studying Maureen, I wondered if she'd cause a stir everywhere we went. If so, I'd have to figure out a way to ignore the unwanted attention or dump her off somewhere.

"Ruby? What happened out in the parking lot?" asked Maureen.

"You were there. You saw and heard the dog."

"No," she said. "The other thing that happened."

"I don't know what you're talking about."

"You know," she insisted.

"Maureen, are you all right?" I asked.

Playing dumb was the only thing I could think of to derail her. The last thing I wanted was a confrontation about how I'd glowed and nearly blew up a pickup and the dog in it. I was lucky no one else had seen what happened, so maybe if I feigned ignorance, she'd have second thoughts about what she'd seen.

Maureen regarded me for a moment, her gaze too perceptive for her baby doll appearance. I squirmed, praying she'd let the matter drop.

"I'm famished," she said.

Guilt hit me again, and I wished I hadn't been so grumpy with her earlier. "When's the last time you ate?"

She blinked, and a blank expression settled over her face. "Yesterday, I think. I helped some guy out, and he paid me back with a burger and some fries." She met my gaze, blushed pink and shifted her attention back to the menu.

The waitress appeared and jotted down our orders. She removed two laminated cards from her apron pocket, placed them on the tabletop, and then hurried to the kitchen with our tickets.

I picked up one of the cards. A list of desserts, ice cream drinks, and sundaes covered both sides of it. One in particular caught my attention, and I blinked, disbelieving my eyes.

"This has got to be a joke."

"You mean Loretta's Million-Dollar Fudge Cake?" Maureen asked.

"Yeah, who would give a million dollars to someone for guessing the secret ingredient?"

"I would," a steely feminine voice said behind me.

A tall, stately woman in her late fifties stared down at me. Her deep brown gaze met mine, and for an instant, an odd sensation wriggled through me. A gold clip secured a twist of thick gray hair to the back of her head. Matching earrings hung from her lobes. She held a water pitcher in one hand and gestured wildly with her other. Big gems sparkled on the fingers of her right hand.

"Ask any of my regulars if I'll honor my claim," she continued. "I'm Loretta Detzer, proprietress of this café."

She focused on me again. A shiver of unease flowed down my back.

"The cake recipe has been handed down through my family."

"If it's so important, why give a million dollars to someone for guessing the secret ingredient?" Maureen folded her arms on the table edge and regarded Loretta with a look of awe, mouth ajar, eyes round.

"Because I can." The woman smiled slyly and walked away. She wandered about the café refilling water glasses and exchanging bits of gossip with her customers. Dressed in simple white slacks and a red summer blouse, she exuded power and wealth.

"Why would such a wealthy woman reside in this tiny, backwoods area?" I mused.

Maureen shrugged. "What about you? Do you have family in Columbus?" she asked.

"Just my father."

"No mother?"

"She died when I was a teenager."

"I'm sorry." Something in her eyes conveyed she truly understood my loss. "You don't have anyone else in or around Columbus?"

I shook my head. "Not that I'm aware of. Dad doesn't like to talk about the Nutters. Whenever I've pressed him for details it upsets him."

"Have you ever asked him why it bothers him?"

I rubbed away a greasy smear on the dessert menu. "Yes. He gets pissed and says 'the past is in the past, Ruby' so I stopped asking."

Maureen leaned forward, her boobs pressing against the table edge. The cleavage deepened, and I wondered if I should dive for cover. She cocked her head to one side and studied me intently.

"Ruby, what happened back at the rest area?"

"Nothing."

"You're lying to me."

I feigned interest in the dessert menu. "Maybe."

"You can trust me."

"Just drop it, okay?"

"Why are you traveling to Florida?" she asked.

"It's none of your business."

She didn't even blink. "Come on, Ruby. You can tell me."

"Why are *you* traveling to Florida?" I countered.

At that, she sobered. Unease and insecurity flitted through her eyes. "I have something I have to take care of in Florida," she said, her tone subdued. She looked away.

A few tables to our left, a baby wailed in its mother's arms. Maureen watched with a strange, melancholic expression on her pretty face.

"Like what?" I pressed.

"I don't feel like talking about it right now." She focused on the jukebox where an old man jabbed buttons as he perused the selections.

Shrugging, I settled back in my seat and watched the jukebox's decorative bubble tubes as they pulsed from bright blue to neon pink. "The Devil Went down to Georgia" filtered out of the ceiling sound system.

Our waitress set a steaming plate of food in front of each of us just as Loretta appeared at our tableside. She placed two dessert plates, heavy with thick slices of fudge cake, on the tabletop and stood with hands on hips. I met the elderly woman's gaze and sensed power. What sort of power, I wasn't certain, but whatever it was forced the hair to tighten on my nape.

"The cake is on the house," Loretta announced. She seated herself in one of the empty chairs. "Now, I have a business proposition I'd like to discuss with you."

My appetite evaporated. Staring eyeball to eyeball with someone while I'm trying to eat tends to do that.

"Have a seat." The remark popped out of my mouth before I could stop it, my tone scathing.

Loretta looked hard at me. Her eyes weren't dark brown at all. They were hazel green like mine, but something about hers was enough to send me screaming out into the parking lot.

"What's on your mind?" Maureen asked around a mouthful of potatoes.

I shot her a warning glance, but she ignored it.

"I overheard your discussion about Florida." Loretta leaned closer, her perfume, a curious blend of incense and cinnamon, wafted over me. "Since you're going there, I'd like you to drive to Key West for me. I want you to bring something back."

"I'm not running drugs," I said quickly.

She burst out laughing. "It's not drugs. It's an important document."

"If it's so important, then have it sent here by a courier," I replied.

"I don't trust the postal system or private couriers with this particular document." Loretta leaned back in her chair and crossed her long legs.

I breathed a little easier and finished the last few bites of my meal.

"Oh, come on," Maureen said, slurping her Coke. "What's it going to hurt to pick up a document and bring it back for her?"

I made a mental tally that this was the second time my Marilyn Monroe wannabe had opened her big mouth and obligated us. Rankled, I shot her a shut-the-hell-up look.

"We're going to Florida anyway," she added. "Traveling through The Keys would be nice too."

The fork, which I squeezed too hard, bit into my fingers, and I let go of it. The utensil dropped to the plate with a loud clink. Maureen's gaze met mine across the table. D*éjà vu* struck me again.

"Would you "please" shut up," I said, voice low, the warning tone enough to cause my hitcher's hair to burst into flames.

"I think driving to Key West together would be fun."

"Who said you were going all the way to Key West with me?"

"Well, I…" A glassy sheen slipped over Maureen's eyes. "I just thought maybe…"

If she started crying, I'd walk out and lay down in traffic. My gaze moved to Loretta's, who stared back with amusement.

I asked, "Why would you trust us with something so important?"

"Let's just say I have a knack for knowing a person's character." Loretta smiled.

Maureen finished the last bite of her dinner and shoved the plate aside. "She means she senses she can trust you."

"Are you incapable of keeping your mouth shut?" I snapped.

She shot me a wounded look, but upon seeing the slice of cake by her elbow, she brightened. Briefly, I regretted yelling at Maureen, but the woman could get under my skin in a nanosecond.

"I'll make it worth your while." Loretta continued with her soul-stabbing look and tapped her nails lightly on the tabletop.

As if I were one of those bobble-head dogs motorists place in their rear windows, my head swiveled back to her. I studied her for a few seconds, and, with suspicion thick in my voice, asked, "How?"

The woman's grin widened. "I'll pay you five thousand now and you'll receive another ninety-five grand at the address where you pick up the document." She held out a long-fingered, bejeweled hand. "All you have to do is bring the envelope back here to my café."

"Ruby," Maureen said around a mouthful of fudge cake. "That's one hundred thousand dollars!"

"No shit," I said without looking at her.

"Well?" the proprietress urged, still holding out her hand.

I couldn't resist. No matter how hard I fought it, no matter how loud that voice in my head shouted not to do it, I still placed my hand in Loretta's. Her fingers snapped around mine, her grip steely, almost painful.

A horrible feeling thundered over me as though I'd just shaken hands with the Devil.

Chapter Five

After Loretta and I worked out the details of our business proposition, I ate my slice of cake. It tasted of pure, sinful chocolate so moist it was almost pudding. Afterward, I felt odd, and a huge ball of unease settled in my gut.

Gulping down some water, I scribbled a note of thanks and asked our waitress give it to Wayne Blacktree when he returned.

Maureen and I spotted a ladies room sign over a hallway entrance. As I crossed the café with Maureen in tow, my gaze slid to where I'd seen the pale stranger.

He was gone.

Disappointment crashed through me.

Stymied by the sensation, I entered the restroom and made use of the facilities. Disgruntled that Mr. Enigma had left, I reached for the door, needing some time alone to think, which was exceedingly difficult with Maureen's constant prattling.

"I'll wait for you in the parking lot," I told her.

"You're not going to leave me here, are you?" She rinsed suds from her hands.

Actually the thought *had* crossed my mind. I paused with my hand on the doorknob, guilt tiptoeing through my heart. "What?"

"You're going to dump me here, aren't you?"

A stormy sigh burst from me. "No, I won't dump you...yet."

She seemed satisfied with my answer and smiled.

With needles of aggravation stabbing my skin, I stepped into the hall.

Standing in the dimly lit corridor, I secured my purse strap over my shoulder. A wad of one hundred-dollar bills resided in an inconspicuous section of my purse.

Later, I'd stash the five grand somewhere safer. Loretta wanted us to telephone her a couple times before we drove through The Keys. Although Maureen and I wouldn't receive the pending ninety-five grand until we reached the pickup point, Loretta still wanted the peace of mind that we were following through with our end of the bargain.

But, if I were in Loretta's shoes, I would've offered another five grand at the Key West pickup point, and then paid the pending sum when we returned to West Virginia.

Pausing, I considered this notion. Did the woman trust us that much? Or was it something else?

I put the phone number in the same place as the money.

The fact that I was now bound to the ditzy woman humming to herself in the bathroom bothered me almost as much as the deal with Loretta did. I liked Maureen well enough, but she grated on my nerves so much I wanted to lash out at her over the least little thing. It wasn't a good sign, especially for a long trip to Key West and back. Even worse, I felt badly for being so catty. It was part of my curse. Hurt before getting hurt, and then regret it when the person turned out to be harmless.

I'm the one who wanted a friend.

Heck, with a hundred grand I could go wherever I wanted, and if I invested a chunk of it wisely, the interest might allow me to live comfortably. However, I regretted being single. It would be nice to have a relationship with a man who didn't wig out every time I blew something up or set the sofa on fire. I'd always told myself a woman didn't need a man to survive. A good dildo with a steady supply of batteries can be a girl's best friend, but a battery-operated boyfriend can't share hopes and dreams.

The door to the men's restroom opened, and my fair stranger stepped out into the hall as my composure stepped out of the building. Blood rushed through my ears so loudly that when he said something to me, all I heard was boom-boom-boom.

Finally, words sifted into my brain. "Are you all right?"

I blinked. "Uh...yeah."

He walked closer, and the hall closed in on me. The corridor disappeared, and instead of floral wallpaper and soft overhead lights, I saw flat gray stones of a castle passage and a floor covered in rushes. A man stood with his back to me. A heavy black robe trimmed in gold flowed over his shoulders to the floor where it dragged along behind him. Pale hair hung down the robe, and I caught a glimmer of gold encircling his head.

"Hey."

A gentle hand patted my cheek.

My eyelids fluttered open, and I found myself leaning back in Mr. Enigma's arms, his face inches from mine, concern in his white-blue eyes.

Those eyes...I "knew" those eyes. His were the ones I'd seen in my lucid flashes and dreams. The world tilted slightly, and my breath caught.

"Sorry," I whispered. "I have these spells."

"You sort of blanked out, then started to fall," he said. "Are you okay?"

I nodded. "Yes, I'm fine."

Heat radiated from his body, warming me to the bone, and sending more warmth to pool in my lower abdomen. It was then I noticed fine scars crisscrossing his face. On the Interstate, I'd caught only a glimpse of the nasty one that traced a jagged line from his left ear and down the side of his neck.

His ice-chip eyes conveyed something powerful buried deep within him. Chemistry zipped back and forth between us. The feelings bombarding me raced past pleasant attraction and leapt straight into the need for let's-find-the-nearest-broom-closet sex.

"Ruby?"

The sudden urge to stab Maureen replaced everything.

He raised his head and straightened with me still in his arms. Leaning me against the wall, he smiled down into my face. "Are you sure you're okay?"

"Yes." At five-feet-eleven-inches tall, I still had to stare up at him. "I'm fine. It's going away now."

"My name's Solomon Xavier," he said.

"Ruby Nutter."

"And I'm Maureen," my hitchhiker chirped behind us.

"I guess your friend was right," he said.

"About?" I sensed he was going to leave me. At the thought, tears pricked the backs of my eyes. *Tears? What the hell's that all about?*

"She said we'd meet again."

The interest in his eyes nearly bowled me over. Unable to dredge up a response, I stared back at him hoping I didn't look as stupid as I felt.

"Well, it was nice seeing you again." His gaze bored into mine. He brushed a curly tendril back from my face.

The action was so sweet, so poignant. I almost sobbed with the emotion it stirred within me. Again, I marveled at the feelings the guy churned inside me and pondered why he had such a profound effect on me.

With a last soft smile, he turned and strode down the corridor.

"Nice ass," Maureen whispered. "I bet he's good in bed too."

I gaped at her.

"Shoot, Ruby. This is the first time I've ever seen you at a loss for words."

Laughter spilled out of her, and the sounds of the diner with its chattering customers seeped into my world again.

He was gone, and my life was back to normal.

Well, that was if I could call living with my curse and Titzilla normal.

****

Forty-five minutes later, we drove across the Virginia state line.

"Look, Ruby!" Maureen nearly poked me in the ear pointing at a sign. "An oddities museum. Let's stop."

"No."

"Why not?"

"Better yet, why should we?"

"Because they're neat!" she said with the enthusiasm of a ten year old.

"I don't want to visit a ramshackle building full of various animal parts glued together." I hugged the white line as a tractor-trailer whizzed by. "It's probably managed by Billy Bob and Bobby Sue too."

"Please?"

At her pleading tone I ground my teeth together.

"We're supposed to reach Key West as soon as possible. We've barely driven into Virginia." I sneaked a look at her, knowing I'd see her horrible pout. "Plus, I'm going to be in Florida at least a couple days before we can move on through The Keys."

Instead of her pout, tears streamed down her cheeks.

"What the hell are you bawling about?" Gawping at her, I nearly ran off the road.

"You're mean!"

"For God's sake, Maureen! You're not a baby!"

"See?" She sobbed harder.

"All I see is a childish woman with boobs that can smother the—"

My head started throbbing. Tingles invaded my palms. No, I couldn't risk a display of my power. But then again, maybe it would scare her badly enough I could dump her off.

Ready to pull over and throttle her, I shouted, "Aw, screw this!"

Maybe it wasn't such a bad idea to visit the museum on the premise of appeasing Maureen. I could hand her half the five grand and drive away. However, what would stop her from finding a ride to Key West and making the pickup on her own? The reality of what I'd done by letting her continue to tag along slammed into me.

Tears streaked Maureen's makeup, and snot dribbled from her nose. A wave of guilt rolled over me so intensely my breath hitched. Although there was something about her that caused temporary insanity, I knew too well how it felt to have someone treat me like shit, and the fact that I was the one now doing it made me feel as if I were an inch tall. Guilt turned into a steamroller and it flattened me.

In the passenger seat, Maureen sniffed in a very unlady like manner that made me wonder if she had any brain cells left.

"Son of a bitch," I muttered and opened the console between the seats. "There's a travel pack of tissues in there somewhere."

For the next three miles, I fumed at myself for my nastiness and Maureen's repetitious sniffles. I gritted my teeth until my jaw ached. The exit appeared ahead, and I flipped on the turn signal. A big, bright road sign declared: Gasoline, Souvenirs and The Museum of Nature's Oddities.

"Thanks, Ruby!" Maureen hiccupped. She rummaged in her backpack and yanked out a makeup kit. "You'll enjoy the museum. I promise."

"Don't mention it—and I doubt it."

"Besides," she blew her nose, "We're meant to go there."

"What?"

"You'll see."

"Whatever." I sighed and concentrated on the twisty road.

For several miles, we traveled a bi-way that twined up a mountainside. Another ten minutes of tall trees and breathtaking views brought us to a blacktopped lot and a large structure. I'd expected to find Cousin Bubba on a ramshackle porch spitting tobaccy into a Maxwell House can with several hound dogs sprawled around his rocking chair. Instead, several cars and a few motorcycles sat in the parking area of a building that looked like a new-age church.

The motion of the Jeep had kept the heat at bay, but once I parked the vehicle and stepped out of it, the humidity grew unbearable. I grimaced, imagining a frosty, salt-rimmed margarita and a hotel room with the A/C turned up so high icicles would hang from the curtain rods.

In her spiked heels, Maureen tiptoed across the smoldering blacktop.

"After we're done here, we're going to drive for several hours," I said firmly. "No more stops except to pee or grab something to eat, got it?"

"Sure."

As we crossed the lot, we passed a few motorcycles. Surely they weren't the same ones?

I counted them.

Seven.

"What is it with you and motorcycles?" asked Maureen, a note of wonder in her voice.

"Nothing."

I paid the five bucks admission for each of us, and we entered the building.

"When do I get some money?" Maureen asked, her voice shattering the stillness of the entrance hall.

"Later," I said. "When we have some privacy to divide it."

A corridor carpeted in slate blue stretched ahead of us. The faint aroma of new rug fibers, fresh plaster and paint upset my stomach.

Quiet permeated the building. Faintly, the distant strains of Enya's "Amarantine" wafted through the halls and rooms. The soft murmurs of the curious drifted to us. We wandered down another hall looking at framed pictures of huge vegetables. In a big display chamber, suspended from a hefty rigging system, a monster pumpkin sat upon a platform as if it were the Great Pumpkin from the Peanuts Halloween episode. A sign announcing its weight as nine hundred and ninety-eight pounds hung under it.

We followed a small group of people into a room full of authentic fruits and vegetables that could've graced any giant's dinner table. The hugest zucchini I'd ever seen stretched across a stand on our left.

"Too bad science can't do the same thing for men," Maureen said.

I burst out laughing, the sound echoing rudely throughout the building. People turned to stare.

She grinned back at me, a dimple appearing high on her right cheek. Our gazes locked. A strange and silent communication passed between us. Feelings I'd never felt before—camaraderie, hope, and even acceptance—awakened in me. The faint, vaporous stirrings of friendship surfaced, but I knew better than to trust such feelings and shoved them aside.

The subsequent room displayed everything from a preserved two-headed garter snake to a Holstein with three legs protruding from its back.

And I'd always thought I was the only genetic mishap alive.

A small cluster of visitors took the doorway to the right. I caught a glimpse of motorcycle chaps, biker boots, and the backside of a Harley tank top, revealing a bare shoulder tattooed with a black panther.

Fear knotted my gut.

Maureen and I stepped into a room full of albino animals. Snow-white cows, deer, goats, rabbits, and even a reversed skunk and a few preserved albino snakes stared sightlessly out of pink or pale brown eyes. The attraction which startled me the most stood at the front of the room.

Maureen reached up with two fingers and closed my mouth. "I told you we had to come here."

I threw her an irritated look, my gaze zipping back to the man waiting for the crowd to quiet.

Dark blue jeans hugged Solomon Xavier's trim hips and muscular legs. A tie-dyed shirt of blue and purple almost glowed against his skin. His pleasant, deep voice suited the lines and planes of his clean-cut look. How could anyone look so bizarre and yet so appealing. He certainly wasn't my type, but the draw was there all the same.

Slowly, Maureen and I edged closer. Solomon launched into an explanation about albinism.

Maureen nudged my arm. "Isn't he cool?"

He caught my gaze. A delighted smile spread across his face. The action reached his eyes, and something familiar tingled inside me, leaving me confused.

Maureen whispered, "He digs you, Ruby."

"No, he doesn't."

"Oh yes, he does." She leaned closer, and I caught a whiff of antiperspirant, mild sweat and citrusy perfume. "I can tell."

"Well, well," a female voice said behind us, "If it isn't the bitch from the rest area."

There was no reason to turn around. I knew the biker woman was part of the pack, but where was the rest of the gang?

Maureen tossed me a worried expression, and I barely shook my head, offering a stern look of warning.

"In conclusion," Solomon said, "there is one severe form of albinism called Hermansky-Pudlak Syndrome. Although rare, this condition involves—"

"Freak."

Silence fell upon the room. Museum patrons rubbernecked the crowd for the owner of the voice. The stuffed animals sat upon their perches, their sightless eyes accusing.

"What's wrong?" the male voice continued. "Is everyone else afraid to say it?"

I turned slowly. For a moment I wasn't so sure if it were me or Solomon who had been called a freak. The biker woman and her boyfriend moved through the group, head and shoulders above the rest, and stopped next to me. My insides quaked, and a new kind of fear permeated my thin façade. Maureen drew in a sharp breath and pressed against me so closely I smelled her hairspray. My gaze flickered over the biker dude's body tattooed in a menagerie of Harley emblems to snakes to weapons of mass destruction. A bushy black beard covered the lower half of his homely mug, and his nose looked as if it had been smashed and rearranged in the center of his face.

Something cold and dangerous radiated off the bikers. The image of the demonic horse head blazed across my mind's eye as well as the enormous man who had melted the glass in my apartment door. The beginnings of a tremor began in the soles of my feet and gradually ascended to my legs. If I lost my composure here...if the power awakened...

"You should be stuffed and put on display with the rest of these freaks of nature," the riffraff said.

His woman tucked herself against his side. She kissed his shoulder, leaving a bright red oval upon his skin.

The biker dude looked directly at Solomon. "You're a worthless freak."

Something inside me snapped. As usual, and despite my fear, my mouth popped open, and the words sprang from it like a jack-in-the-box. "Get lost, asshole!"

Maureen drew in another sharp breath.

Murmurs of approval rippled through the onlookers.

"You bitch!" The biker mama glared at me.

"I see you suffer a limited vocabulary too." Inwardly, I groaned at my lack of verbal control.

The woman let out a scream and lunged at me. The crowd parted, many people uttering gasps and startled cries. Frantic, I jumped to the side, dodging the chick. She landed in a heap on the carpet, got up, and let rip with another banshee screech. She sprang toward me again. Instinctively, I threw my hand up to block her, but I should've known better in front of a crowd of onlookers. My body began glowing, fiery colors infused my hair, and my fingertips lit up with bright orange color. The electrical sensation I detested so much zinged down my arms. The biker chick met with an invisible force, flew backward through the air and crashed against a wall. The impact of her body crumpled the drywall, and she sat up, shaking her head, her bandana falling from her kinky hair.

Total silence settled upon the room. As the glow surrounding me dissipated, I looked around at all the shocked faces. The momentary silence shattered as all hell broke loose. People shrieked and ran in every direction like ants in a knocked over hill. Many bumped into displays as they jostled one another to get out, the sound of collective footfalls overwhelming the room.

The Harley dude pointed at me. "It's her!"

"Back off," Solomon snapped. He stepped between us. "Leave quietly, or I'll call the police."

The power I'd sensed in him before at the diner emanated from him so strongly it felt like I was standing in an electrically charged box.

An expression of recognition slid over the man's face. He charged Solomon, who failed to get out of the way in time. He grabbed Solomon by the throat and tossed him aside. He landed at the base of one wall, narrowly missing a large deer mounted on a pedestal.

"It's him too," the biker said.

"Are you sure?" The woman focused on Solomon. Her eyes flashed yellow.

Terror erupted in my heart. I'd seen her eyes do the same thing at the rest area after all.

Solomon shook his head and staggered to his feet. "You two better run," he said to me and Maureen.

We didn't have to be told twice. I grabbed Maureen's hand, and we bolted from the room, her heels snagging on the carpet.

Within seconds, a shout sliced the air behind us. "Come back here, bitch!"

I glanced over my shoulder at the biker pounding down the hall behind us.

"Kick off those damn heels!" I yelled at Maureen.

She stopped long enough to step out of them and turned, throwing the shoes at the biker. One bounced off the top of his head.

We raced into the chamber housing the enormous pumpkin. Several people hurried out to avoid involvement.

The woman who had taken our entry fee shouted, "I'm calling the police."

"Then do it," I barked back.

She disappeared down a corridor.

"Where did he go?" Maureen asked, gasping for breath.

"I don't know, but let's get out of here while we still can."

We started toward one of the adjoining halls. The psycho jumped out of it with an animalistic howl. I cried out, but Maureen squealed like a little girl, stumbled backward and fell into a curtain. The drape ripped loose, revealing a lever that she caught with her elbow as she slid down the wall. A whirring noise drew my attention to the ceiling panels above us. The suspended pumpkin crashed to the floor. A deafening boom pervaded the chamber, and the squash burst apart like a piñata, spilling seeds and goo instead of toys and candy.

The biker grabbed Maureen by her upper arms and yanked her out of the curtain. He held her off the floor, feet dangling. "I know who you are too," he snarled.

Heat hurtled up out of my gut and out along my limbs. "Let go of her!" I swung at him, but since he was so tall, my fist only connected with his sternum. A whimper of pain burst from my lips, and I clutched my hand against my breasts. The pain pissed me off, and more of the lava sensation sped through my body. The glowing began, radiating off me so brightly the biker looked as if he stood in a spotlight.

However instead of being frightened, the jerk merely looked at me as if I were a pesky mosquito.

Still clutching my thumping hand, I stared up at him. *Why isn't he afraid?*

The guy's girlfriend jogged into the chamber. Upon seeing us cornered, she grinned.

"You're ours now." The biker dude chuckled.

"The lady said to let go of her friend."

The guy turned, his eyes widening. A few feet away, Solomon pointed a handgun at him.

Chapter Six

Slowly, the illumination emanating from me faded.

Solomon glanced at me curiously then turned his attention back to the biker. "Take your bimbo and get out of here."

The Harley mama issued a weird, sinister hiss that sent a shiver up my spine.

"And what if I don't?" the Harley guy asked, a sneer on his face.

"You'll deal with the police." Solomon waved the gun. "Until then, I can detain you in a storage room—after I shoot both your knees."

There was no doubt in my mind he meant it.

"You don't know who we are, do you?" the guy asked.

"Don't know," said Solomon, "and don't care, but I'm sure you don't want me to shoot you."

The woman looked at me and said, "You'll pay for what you did to us. We'll be back."

What I did to them?

But the little voice in my head insisted the Harley chick meant something else.

The biker couple left the museum. The receptionist re-appeared and announced she'd called the police for the second time.

Solomon held out a large, long-fingered hand with a big silver-and-turquoise ring on it. "Are you two all right?"

"I think so," I answered and clasped his hand. Familiarity washed over me. I did, however, recognize his eyes as surely as I knew my name.

"You know those characters?" he asked.

"We bumped into them at a rest area in West Virginia," Maureen supplied. She batted her eyes like a Southern belle trying to win over a beau. "Ruby accidentally hit the woman with a door."

Solomon seemed amused. His gaze locked with mine. "It seems you're special too," he stated.

I averted my gaze and pulled my hand out of his.

The receptionist announced the police had finally arrived, sparing me from any unanswerable questions Solomon might have asked me. The cops spent half an hour taking our statements. By the time they left, it was nearly the supper hour.

"I'm hungry," Maureen said, cradling a foam cup of coffee between her hands.

"Yeah." My stomach gurgled loudly. "Me too."

"Why don't you let me put you up for the night?" Solomon offered. He walked into the entrance hall. "The cops are gone, and the night crew can work on the mess in the display chamber, so I might as well close the museum early."

"This is "your" museum?" I asked.

"Yes, I built it a couple years ago."

"Cool," Maureen crowed. "It's your tribute to the misunderstood souls of the world."

Her cutesy tone of voice made me want to smack her into next week. Solomon favored her with a soft look, and I wondered if he was attracted to her. The idea irked me, and warmth flowed over my skin as I began to glow.

Shit! Go away, go away, tamp it down...!

Solomon cocked his head to one side, his attention on me again. The illumination halted almost as quickly as it had begun.

Acting as if nothing had happened, I asked, "What were you doing in Ohio when you stopped to help us change the Jeep's tire?"

"I was driving back from Pataskala where I'd purchased another piece for my museum," he replied. "The last two times I've had something shipped here the items arrived battered or broken. It wasn't a long drive, so I drove up to Ohio to pick up the piece."

His answer seemed plausible, but it bothered me this was the third time we'd bumped into him.

"So, what do you say? I'll feed you a grand meal and put you up for the night." He didn't wait for an answer, but indicated to his receptionist that she should secure the front doors. Turning, he disappeared down a hall.

"I didn't even get a chance to answer him," I said.

The woman laughed and locked the doors. "Solomon is a man who takes matters into his own hands. You'll be his guests tonight whether you want to or not. But don't worry. He's a perfect gentleman and a wonderful host." She returned to her desk.

"I take it you stay overnight often?"

Maureen spewed coffee down the front of her inner tubes.

Scowling at me, the receptionist pulled her purse from a desk drawer. "My-my, aren't you a witty one."

"Nah, just to the point," I smiled, hoping my bitch fangs showed.

"Let's just say you couldn't handle him, sweetie." She exited through a side door that locked behind her.

More like he couldn't handle me. And what the hell is wrong with me? I could care less who the guy has slept with.

A guilty twinge hit me for being so catty again. I don't know why the thought of her sleeping with Solomon bothered me, but I had the urge to rip her desk in half with my bare hands. The feeling didn't make a bit of sense, but it was there all the same.

We followed Solomon through the side exit. Outside, he slipped on a pair of dark sunglasses and used his cell phone to contact the clean-up crew. A black Ford Excursion sat a few spaces away from my Jeep.

The heat radiating from the asphalt permeated the soles of my sneakers. Earlier, one of the officers had found Maureen's shoes and returned them to her. She balanced on the balls of her feet so the spikes wouldn't sink into the blacktop.

Sunset wouldn't occur for a few hours, but the heavy humidity shrouded the sun's rays, so it seemed later than it actually was. Relieved the motorcycles were gone, I pulled my keys from my purse and stopped short. Both the front tire Solomon had changed for me and the back one on the same side looked like they'd melted into the pavement.

"I don't believe it." Fury ripped through me. "This has got to be the shittiest day I've had for a while."

Maureen halted and looked over her shoulder at me. "What's wrong?"

"Check out the Jeep's tires."

Solomon met us at my vehicle. "It seems like your biker buddies got one last dig in at you."

"Really? I thought maybe the tires came that way, and if I drove really fast they'd fill up with air." I didn't mean to be a smartass, but I had the overwhelming urge to smash something—something like a red-painted mouth that screeched like a cat in heat.

Surprisingly, he chuckled. "Take it easy, Ruby. I can tell you've had a rough day." He stooped and examined the back tire. Next, he moved to the front one. Nodding, he stood up. "Yep, both are knife slashes."

I crossed my arms over my chest and sighed. Once again I fought tears, and it pissed me off even more.

****

The A/C in Solomon's Excursion cooled my body and my temper. Soft Native American rock music played from an expensive sound system. Maureen sat shotgun, chatting non-stop to Solomon about the unusual places she'd visited while wandering the eastern U.S.

The steep landscape whizzed by my window. I'd had enough of Virginia. It was time to go further south, but that desire was postponed until we bought new tires for my Jeep. Yet another obstacle had landed directly in my path to Key West. I looked over at Maureen.

Correction. Our path to Key West.

The difficulties so far came as no surprise. For once, it would be nice to have something good happen. Was that too much to ask?

Solomon appeared to be looking at me in the rearview mirror, but with his dark shades, I couldn't tell for
certain.

"You're awfully quiet back there," he said.

"I'm still stewing over my slashed tires." Actually, I
entertained thoughts of using the biker dude's Harley to
peel out on his pecker. I guarantee it would be the first
time a woman had ever laid real rubber on his dick.

But the things the guy had said, the yellow eye blaz-
es... I shivered.

"I'll call a buddy of mine and have new tires put on
your Jeep first thing in the morning. For now, just kick
back and enjoy the evening."

"Yeah, Ruby." Maureen twisted around in her seat to
look at me. "We'll make up for our lost time. Don't
worry."

I added her enthusiasm and optimism to my list of
irritations.

"How is it that you can glow? And how did you
throw that woman across the room without touching
her? She's much taller than you and outweighs you by
about fifty pounds."

"I don't know what you're talking about," I lied, staring pointedly at Maureen in hopes she would take the
hint.

She didn't.

"You didn't touch her," she insisted, "and your hair
turned a different color, plus your fingernails were
glowing bright orange. I knew something happened in
the café parking lot, but you denied it."

"You imagined it," I said. The comment sounded
lame.

"I saw it too," Solomon stated. "It was amazing."

They were delving too deeply. Panic hit me. "You can
take me back to my Jeep now. I'll figure something out
on my own." Heart slamming painfully, I waited for the
SUV to slow, pull over, and turn around, but it didn't.

"Take me back to my Jeep!" Tears pricked my eyes,
and heat flowed through my body.

"Just calm down," said Solomon. "We're not—"

"I want to go back to my Jeep now!"

"I'm not taking you back. Where the hell would you go? How would you get there?" He slowed the Ford. "No one is around the museum for miles, and you'd have to walk—"

"Please, just turn around and drive me back." Light radiated off me, infusing the Excursion with brighter illumination than what was outside.

"Ruby, calm down," Maureen said. Her eyes grew wide. "Take it easy."

"Then just let me out!" Panic skewered my innards. "Pull over and let me out of this damn truck!"

Solomon pulled the Ford over and stopped. I fumbled for the door handle and lunged out of the vehicle. I started walking. *Calm, think calm thoughts. Tamp it down. Put it back. Stow it in a dark, safe place.*

"Ruby! Wait!" Solomon called and jogged after me, his feet crunching on the pebbles strewn along the roadside. "Let me talk to you."

"NO!" Sobs burst from me. "Just leave me alone. It's safer that way."

He caught up with me, grabbed my arm and turned me around. Instead of horror, he wore a mask of concern.

I blinked. That wasn't right. *He's supposed to freak out, cuss and tell me to get the hell away from him.*

"Look at me, Ruby. You heard what the biker called me. I'm the last one to judge you," he said with sincerity. "I've never seen anyone do what you did, but it didn't scare me. I think it's amazing."

"It should scare you." Angrily, I wiped tears away. I couldn't let a complete stranger see me suffer a nervous breakdown. *Oh, but he's not a stranger*, something whispered in the back of my mind.

Let him help you, Ruby. Give him a chance.

Terrific, now the voice was back. Trembling, I sighed and stifled another sob.

Before I could react, Solomon pulled me into his arms and snuggled me tightly against his body. With his hard length pressed to mine, his strong, sinewy arms around my shoulders and crossed over my back, and the intoxicating aroma of his own personal scent mixed with a spicy, fresh cologne, I found myself giving in to his embrace.

"Come on, Ruby. Let me take you to my place where you can chill out and have a fabulous meal. I have a roommate who can cook up a storm."

With another sigh, I nodded against his shoulder.

"Please tell me she's coming with us," Maureen called from the Excursion. "She has to stay with us."

Stunned, all I could do was allow Solomon to walk me back to the SUV and help me back into the back passenger where I sat quietly. With my mind in a whirl of disbelief, I stared out the window.

"What did those bikers mean by those weird comments they made?" Maureen asked.

I almost didn't hear her. My thunderous pulse nearly drowned out everything. No one took my weird abilities in stride, not even my father. No one ever hugged or held me either.

"Comments?" I finally managed.

"Somehow they recognized all three of us," she stated

"Whoever they are," Solomon interjected, "they certainly have axes to grind."

Yeah, I'd caught their words, too, but feigned ignorance. For the moment, I could only handle one thing at a time, and the main one was the fact that neither Solomon nor Maureen seemed to fear me.

I shrugged and finally looked at Maureen. "Maybe they have us confused with someone else."

She favored me with a skeptical expression.

****

The Excursion bounced down a gravel lane that ended at a beautiful log home. Surrounded by tall trees on three sides, the front of the home overlooked a shallow valley to the west. A small red barn stood behind the cabin. Solomon parked the SUV in the drive, got out, and walked around to the back to retrieve our bags.

I stepped out of the truck. Stiffness had settled in my muscles. Some of it stemmed from tension, but most of it was a side effect of my weird ability. I studied my surroundings and worked my neck and shoulder muscles. Crickets chirred in the surrounding undergrowth. Off to the side of the split-rail fence stood wooden statues of Papa Bear, Mama Bear, and Baby Bear. A hammock hung between two maples and rocked gently in a breeze soughing up from the valley.

I could get used to living in such a place.

The front door opened. A bundle of black-and-white fur bounded through it and rocketed off the porch. The canine monstrosity launched itself at me like a heat-seeking missile. The animal hit me square in the chest. I landed flat on my back in a bed of purple asters. A wet tongue and nose violated my face and insulted my nostrils with the vulgar scent of canned dog food.

"*Shunka Wakan!*" Solomon yelled. "Get off of her!"

The dog used my boobs as a springboard and leapt off of me with an excited bark. Dazed, I stared up at the hazy sky. Solomon's face appeared over me, worry lines creasing the corners of his mouth.

"I'm so sorry. Are you okay?"

Blinking, I wiped dog goobers from my face as Solomon helped me to my feet.

"Wow, Ruby. You went down like a ton of bricks." Maureen giggled from where she posed on a flagstone walk.

"I've never seen my dog react like that to anyone. He's usually reserved until he gets to know someone." Solomon brushed dirt and dog hair from my clothes. "Did he hurt you?"

"No, just slobbered me to death."

I imagined his ice-chip eyes smiling at me behind the sunglasses.

"Are you sure you're okay?"

"I'm fine, but I need a bath now."

His inviting lips spread into a hypnotic smile. "That can be arranged."

"I'm sorry, Solomon," a masculine voice said from the porch. "I had to open the door and let him out. I was afraid he would break the glass. One way or another, he was going out to meet you."

An elderly man hobbled down the front steps. He grasped the handrail until he reached the ground and stuffed both hands into his pockets. Simple leather moccasins shod his feet. Two long white braids hung on each side of his head, and a pocket t-shirt covered his lean torso. The old man could have been any age from seventy to a hundred.

"It's all right, Sam," Solomon said and picked up our bags from where he'd dropped them in the gravel. "You'll have to tend to your asters, though."

Sam shrugged, turned and started back up the steps. "They'll survive. They served their purpose by breaking that Nutter's fall."

At first, it didn't dawn on me the old Indian had called me by my last name. Astonished, I glanced up at Solomon, who shrugged. "Sam is the friend I was telling you about," he stated.

We followed Maureen into the cabin. I frowned at the amount of ass cheeks hanging out of her shorts as she climbed the front steps.

As Solomon showed us to our room, the Alaskan Malamute remained at my side.

"Make yourselves comfortable," Solomon said. He ushered us into a lovely bedroom with twin beds. "There's a bathroom off to the right." He motioned toward a closed door next to a cherry vanity. "Everything you might possibly need should be in there." He shoved his sunglasses atop his head and patted his thigh. "Let's go, Shunka. Give the ladies some privacy."

The canine padded to my side and sat on his haunches, his ears perked as if to say he had no intentions of moving.

"Come on, boy."

The dog promptly lay down and yawned.

"Looks like you made another new friend, Ruby." Maureen laughed and flopped down on one of the beds.

Solomon crossed his arms. "I've never seen him act like this before."

"What does *Shunka Wakan* mean?" asked Maureen.

"Sam named him. When Native Americans saw horses for the first time they thought they were very large dogs, so they dubbed them mysterious dog—*Shunka Wakan*."

"Well, he's certainly big enough to be a pony," she said.

Solomon leaned against the doorframe, his gaze drifting down my body and back up it again. The heat in his eyes ignited an ember of longing within me. Flustered, I turned and set my suitcase on the end of the other bed.

"The morning after I got out of the hospital," he gestured toward his face covered in fine scars, "that dog showed up on the porch and has been with me ever since. Sam says he's a spirit guide, but it appears his duty to me is finished. It looks like he's your spirit guide now, Ruby."

"Mine?" I looked down at the canine and wondered if drooling on the carpet was a spirit guide sort of thing to do.

"It's just a theory." Solomon laughed. He began pulling the door shut. "Supper will be ready in about an hour."

For a moment, I just stood gaping at the closed door. Could this day get any more bizarre? No, I didn't want an answer to that.

Chapter Seven

I had a soothing bath and changed into clean shorts and a halter top. Maureen showered and put on a mint green sundress. The garment's plunging neckline revealed cleavage that probably had Homeland Security scrambling to determine where the hell the unauthorized missiles had come from. Studying her from across the supper table, I knew her chances of survival in a head-on collision were significantly better than mine.

Sam served a delicious meal of greens, stir-fried chicken, cantaloupe and a spicy noodle salad. I admired the spacious kitchen done in red and black, complemented by stainless steel appliances. I would've never considered such a color scheme, but it exuded classiness that appealed to me.

We ate quietly, keeping conversation to pleasantries. Maureen babbled about her travels and her peculiar aunt, Lula. Once everyone finished, Sam began clearing the dishes. Without another word, Maureen stood and began handing him plates and glasses. The old Indian never acknowledged the help other than to accept the items as she passed them to him. He placed each dish into a dishwasher.

"Is there something I can do?" I asked.

"Go keep Solomon company on the porch," Sam replied brusquely. "I will bring dessert out when we are finished here."

"Go on, Ruby," Maureen said. She reached for the empty salad bowl. "You need to kick back for a while. You've been strung tighter than a banjo string today."

Her Appalachian expression brought a smile to the old man's face.

Turning, I found Solomon standing at my side. He offered his arm, and I threaded mine through his. This time I was ready for the familiar feelings that washed through me. At his touch, a tremor started in my feet. Together, we strode through the tastefully decorated home with its antler chandelier, plush beige carpeting, and southwestern flair. By the time we reached the front door, my legs quivered so badly I was afraid of falling on my face.

He's not my type, he's not my type, he's not...

"Hopefully the humidity isn't as bad as it was earlier today," said Solomon.

"Don't you need your sunglasses?" The tremble in my voice embarrassed me and I hoped he hadn't detected it.

"The evening light doesn't bother me."

The Malamute trailed behind us and slipped through the door before it shut on him. Solomon gestured for me to take a seat on the glider. With gratitude, I sank on the cushion, and he sat next to me. We relaxed quietly for several minutes, my thoughts centering on the mysterious man beside me.

Sprawled along the top step, the dog panted. Solomon and I began a slow back-and-forth rhythm that had me thinking erotic thoughts. Feeling a blush creep into my cheeks, I tried to concentrate on the western horizon and what the sunset might look like if the humidity hadn't camouflaged it.

"So...you and Maureen are heading to Key West?" Solomon said.

"How do you know that?"

"She mentioned it while we were waiting for you to come downstairs."

"What else did she say?"

He raised a fair brow and tipped his head to one side. He studied me long and hard. "Only that you picked her up in West Virginia and you decided to travel together since she's going to Florida too."

"Well, we didn't exactly *decide* to travel together." I broke eye contact. Something about the way he looked at me, or rather looked inside me, made me nervous and vulnerable. "It just sort of worked out that way. She's a likeable woman, but she…"

"She what?"

"She has the uncanny knack of making me want to take my own life."

Laughter rumbled out of Solomon. I hated to admit it, but the sound sent a pleasant thrill soaring through my body.

He grew silent and stared out across the valley. The spattering of fine scars across his face drew my attention. The muscles in his jaw worked, and he turned, staring deeply into my eyes. My breath caught, a butterfly of panic careening through my stomach.

"I got them in North Carolina one evening. I'd been out for an evening walk with my sister."

"Got what?" I stammered.

"The scars." He offered me a patient smile. "Gabriella, my sister, and me were visiting our uncle. We took a walk about dusk. It was in December during deer season, but since hunters must leave the woods at dusk, we figured we were safe. As we strolled back to my uncle's house, a truckload of hunters spotlighting deer roared across the field toward us. They were so drunk we smelled the whiskey from their pickup. When they saw me, they hollered something about a king. The ones in the back got out and held us at gunpoint."

Spellbound, I couldn't break away from his steady gaze, and although I sensed the sad outcome of his story, I still desired to hear every word.

"The driver and his two buddies got out. I didn't know whether to tell Gabriella to run, or what to do. With their shotguns aimed at us, she probably wouldn't have made it far before they killed her anyhow, but now I wonder if maybe she would've had a chance."

"They shot her anyway?" I asked.

"No." He closed his eyes, gulped and opened them again to stare out over the valley. "They grabbed my sister and raped her in the frozen pasture. I tried to reach her, but one of them cracked me over the head with a whiskey bottle, and another hit me across the back of the head with the butt of a gun. I went down, followed by another bottle repeatedly smashed into my face until I couldn't see for the glass, blood and liquor in my eyes. They kept shouting 'white king' as they bashed me with it."

"I'm so sorry," I whispered.

"When the hunters were finished with Gabriella, they stabbed her in the heart with a hunting knife and then gutted her."

Horrified, I gasped.

"I think I survived because they were so drunk they thought I was dead." He fell silent, and I thought his sad tale had ended, but he started talking again. "Sam found us a couple hours later. He managed to prop me up behind him on his snowmobile and take me to my uncle's house. The authorities investigated the scene and took my sister's body to the morgue."

"Where the hunters sent to prison?" I asked.

He continued as if he hadn't heard me. "The hunters disappeared. No one had seen them, and no one recognized their descriptions. After two long, grueling years of searching for them, I realized I wasn't going to find them."

"What do you mean? Surely the authorities would've had some leads."

He stared at the ridgeline as if searching it for answers. "Today at the museum, I saw the bikers' eyes flash yellow just like the hunters' eyes had that night they attacked me and Gabriella."

A chill enveloped me, and I began to shake so hard the glider vibrated under us. "Why did they call you a white king?"

He shook his head. "I have no idea."

"So why are you telling me this?"

We stopped swinging and sat very still. Tension hung in the air with the humidity. I sensed something deeper, something profound, but it dangled just out of my reach.

"Sam told me you were coming." He turned slightly so he faced me. "Sam dreams things that always come to pass in one form or another. He says many of his dreams are symbolic, but this one, the one about you, came to him in stunning clarity."

"I don't understand."

"Samuel Dream Wolf has a rare gift. He stayed by me for most of my recovery in the hospital. When I asked him to live with me here, he agreed, stating that his wolf guide told him he should. All of this," he waved his hand to indicate the cabin and grounds, "came shortly after I returned from the hospital. Shunka appeared on my porch the following morning, but at the time, I lived in a trailer on this site. That same day, on a whim, I bought a lottery ticket and hit it for ten million. A month later, the plans were underway for this cabin, I bought my Excursion," he pointed toward the driveway, "donated a sum to the Cherokee reservation, and began plans for the museum, dedicated to all the *ghosts* in this world like me."

His story seemed preposterous, but for some reason I believed him.

"Those bikers are after you, Ruby," he continued with conviction.

At that, I gulped and stared at the porch planks beneath my sneakers. Fear bloomed in my gut, sending tendrils of terror throughout my brain.

"They recognized me too. Despite one of the bikers being a woman, somehow I know they're two of the same hunters. They were stunned I'm not dead. And Maureen knows something's going on too."

"I'm not saying I believe your theory—"

"Yes, you do."

I ignored him. "But what does Sam, the dog, and winning the lottery have to do with all of this?"

"I don't know, but Sam says prosperity follows me, whatever that means. Anyway, I'm certain it's all connected somehow."

"What reason would they have for raping and killing your sister, then leaving you for dead?" I asked. This conversation was not what I'd expected.

"Why are those bikers after you?" he asked.

I thought of the bikers as they rolled along my street on demonic motorcycles. A chill fell over me, my skin feeling as though it had turned to ice, and the coldness seeped into my muscles, burrowing inside me. The big man who had stopped to investigate my apartment had to be the bikers' leader. Why was he looking for me, and how did them know Solomon?

"I never said they were." My ears detected the worry and denial in my voice as surely as he did.

"You know they are, Ruby."

I refused to answer or even look at him.

He sighed and sat silently for several long minutes. Finally, he said, "Okay, then tell me about yourself."

"Why?"

"I'm curious, especially after what I saw you do at the museum and in the backseat of my Ford."

"There's nothing to tell." I met his gaze again. "Talk about the weather, the museum, Maureen—anything else."

He blinked, his brow furrowing, which deepened the fine scars crisscrossing it. "I'm not being nosey, really."

Hurt before being hurt. Shut him up now before he turns on me later.

"You're not?" I countered.

Solomon's frown intensified. "I'm just intrigued, Ruby."

"Oh, really?" The bitchiness in my tone made me cringe on the inside.

His gaze hardened. "Yes!"

"I see."

An irritated sigh escaped him. "Are you always this frustrating?"

"Yes."

We sat eyeing one another like two rearing snakes about to strike. Finally, Solomon resumed the back-and-forth motion of the glider. The dog had raised its head, paying rapt attention during our verbal sparring match, but lowered it again.

He stared directly into my eyes and said, "I'd really like to know you better, Ruby. What I saw you do today was amazing."

He'd stated the same on the roadside earlier, but it was still the last thing I'd expected to hear. No one ever thought my abilities were amazing. Weird, frightening, and unnatural were some words that came to mind.

Sincerity resided in Solomon's eyes. I looked deeper but saw only curiosity and benevolence.

Tears pricked the backs of my eyes which pushed my annoyance into anger. "Trust me, the less you know about me the better for both of us."

"I've seen Sam do some really wild stuff."

This guy just doesn't give up.

I sighed. "I doubt it's anything like what I'm capable of."

"You'd be surprised," he said.

"Aren't you afraid of me?" Blinking, I willed the tears to go away and finally succeeded.

The stymied tone of my voice seemed to confuse him. "Not at all."

"Sooner or later you will be." I gazed back at Solomon, wavering back and forth between taking a chance and sharing some things about myself or choosing the safe route.

He seemed to sense my indecision. "I'll let it rest for now," he said. "Tell me about Maureen."

His interest in Maureen irritated me. "There's nothing to tell. She's seldom quiet and can piss me off quicker than anyone I've ever known other than my father."

"You don't let anyone in, do you?" he said quietly.

Words failed me. This man had zeroed in on my insecurities and fears and that was dangerous territory. "People always disappoint me." Feeling exposed and a bit frightened by the sensation, I shifted on the glider, preparing to stand. "Maybe I should just find a motel room—"

Solomon grabbed me and pulled me into his arms. A startled cry burst from me as his mouth claimed mine, and every thought or protest I might have had or said evaporated.

Worse, I responded to him like a brazen hussy. He deepened the kiss, and I wrapped my arms around his neck and half climbed onto his lap. A surprised sound escaped him, which turned into a murmur of approval. He slid his hands down my sides to my hips where he cupped my ass. I moaned into his mouth, pressing closer. Heat pooled in my lower abdomen. It nestled in my loins, but spread out along my body, too, climbing my internal thermometer. Recognizing the sensation, I stiffened. Appalled at my reaction to Solomon's embrace and fearful he'd push me aside, I broke the kiss. More heat blazed up my neck and into my face, the air around me infused with bright light, my hair flaring from its dark hue to brilliant red, orange and yellow.

Solomon blinked, his breath uneven. It took me a few seconds, but as we stared at one another with almost palpable sparks leaping back and force between us, I managed to subdue and conquer the power surging through me. The glow disappeared and my hair looked normal again.

His kiss awakened my abilities, but how?

The door swung open, and Sam stepped outside bearing a tray with four large dessert goblets brimming with whipped strawberries and ice.

Mortified, I quickly sat back, my sudden movement jostling the glider.

The old man paused. Surprise registered on his face, but delight settled in his dark eyes. Behind him, Maureen walked out onto the porch holding long spoons and napkins.

Sam distributed the desserts. As we ate, I took great pains not to look at the old Indian. Embarrassment still needled my skin and my conscience. Solomon said nothing as he concentrated on his icy confection, but his hands trembled.

Lightning flashed in the inky clouds. The clap of displaced air echoed throughout the valley and ricocheted off the ridges. Thunder always instilled a sense of doom within me.

Pushing the thought away, I spooned down to the bottom of my glass as the scent of rain blew across the porch. The taste of sugary strawberries blended with the sweet, refreshing aroma of rain. The combination triggered another vision. I stood on a grassy area at the edge of a dark expanse of water, peering up at a stone monolith, the sound of crashing waves reverberating in the air. A cloaked woman stood nearby, her head bowed. Thunder boomed over the water, and wind rushed across the waves, stirring them into white caps.

Hundreds of creatures, their bodies built of indigo and gray smoke, bore large, mysterious riders. I strained to see their faces as they rode full-bore toward me along the shoreline. I raised my hands to the sky...

Glass shattered, and something cold and wet splattered across my feet.

****

A soft light illuminated part of Solomon's living room. My head hurt and stiffness had invaded my body again. I blinked a few times to allow my eyes to adjust to the soft lighting. I rose onto one elbow and looked around the room. A lamp glowed nearby, and across from me, a cluster of burning candles sat on an end table, their wicks fluttering in the air conditioning. The aroma of sage and cinnamon greeted my nostrils.

"How do you feel?"

To my right, in a suede wing-backed chair, sat Sam. He looked at me with black, mysterious eyes, his face so deeply lined he could've passed for a wooden carving in the dim light, but his snow-white braids almost glowed in the darkness. Between his chair and the sofa, the Malamute lay primly on his belly, ears perked in my direction, his pale blue eyes watching me. The dog's eyes reminded me of Solomon's.

"I'm...I'm not sure," I said. "Give me a minute." I swung my feet to the floor and sat up. The room spun for a moment, and I gripped the sofa cushion. "I think I'm okay, Sam. Thanks."

"Solomon and Maureen are making coffee."

I rotated my shoulders, easing the rigid muscles.

"Do you have visions often?"

The old man's abrupt question caught me off guard. Solomon's comment about Sam soughed through my mind.

"Why?" I asked.

"They must be very powerful."

"Sometimes."

"You're a Nutter." Sam sat with his hands folded at his waist, fingers entwined, his legs stretched out and ankles crossed. His voice, low and powerful, whispered across the space between us. "Shunka Wakan says the Nutter family is unique. You have much to learn."

"I have much to learn about everything," I replied without missing a beat.

Raspy laughter rattled from his thin chest. "Yes, you do, but if you know that you are well on your way to finding your place in life no matter how strange it might seem to you."

"I don't think there's room in this world for someone like me," I replied.

"This life doesn't seem to fit me." As it often did, the horrible feeling of being a misfit smashed into me. Tears burned my eyes, and I glanced away unable to bear Sam's penetrating gaze any longer. "It's like trying to wear a pair of shoes that are two sizes too big. No matter how much paper you stuff into the toes, you just can't wear them properly."

"Maybe you should try moccasins."

His dry response eased the ache in my sould. I laughed.

A wry grin tugged at the corners of his mouth. He rose from his chair and shuffled toward the kitchen. "I'll go see what's taking so long with the coffee and scrounge up some Tylenol for your headache. I have a feeling you're going to need your powers tonight."

His blunt comment shocked me into silence. I watched him shuffle across the big living room.

And I thought I was weird.

Chapter Eight

That evening, Solomon's friend, who owned a local garage, arrived with my SUV and stated he had to go out of town first thing in the morning. Two new tires gleamed on one side of the Jeep Wrangler. Behind it, another man driving a small car pulled in the drive.

Once the guy left with his employee in the second vehicle, I asked Solomon, "What do I owe you for the tires?"

"Nothing. I took care of it," he said, a pleased smile on his face.

I didn't want any strings attached to our strange and tentative friendship. "I can't let you do that. I barely know you. You're already putting us up for the night, so let me pay for the tires."

"Ruby, it's okay. I took care of it." He looked directly at me, his eyes boring into mine with such force that something shifted in my heart.

Solomon reached out and steadied me. A snap occurred between us, the sound almost tinny. He let go and shook his hand, laughing.

"Damn static electricity." His smile turned into one of concern. "Are you okay?"

"I'm fine." It was difficult to do, but I stepped away from him. Solomon might find me fascinating, but if he knew what that little electrical snap had really stemmed from, he wouldn't be able to rid himself of me fast enough. Besides, after the kiss between us on the glider, the last thing I wanted to do was encourage more of the same. Well...that's not entirely true, but I sure as hell didn't want to set the entire mountain on fire either.

He looked at me quizzically, and I sensed my action had wounded him.

"If you're sure," he stated.

"Look, I'm sorry, but I really need to turn in for the night. I'm wiped out."

"No worries." He reached for the door and stepped inside. "I'll find you some towels if you'd like to freshen up before going to bed."

I tried not to stare at his tight ass in his snug, faded jeans.

Solomon continued, "A fainting spell means your body needs rest. To be honest, we all need to retire. I think the heat is draining everything and everyone."

"Maybe it will rain tonight."

Our small talk sounded hollow.

"I'm hitting the hay, Solomon," Sam called out as he exited the kitchen and headed for a room down a short hall.

"Night, Sam," Solomon and I said simultaneously.

The old man's laughter faded as he shut his bedroom door.

Maureen walked inside from the back deck. She carried her wedge sandals in one hand. "I'm heading to bed," she announced and crossed the room to the staircase. "You coming, Ruby?"

"On my way," I replied.

"I'll lock up down here and bring up those extra towels," Solomon said.

Once I reached our room, I found Maureen already in bed, her dress and shoes discarded on the carpet, her soft snores muffled in a pillow. She must have really been exhausted to drop off that quickly. I stood pondering her sheet-covered form as Shunka flopped down on the carpet next to my bed.

Why had life seen fit to pair me up with this woman? Maybe I should just abandon her at the next rest stop? No, I couldn't do that...not yet. Maureen irritated me, frustrated me, and could piss me off instantly. Those were reasons enough to dump her off somewhere, but I still couldn't bring myself to do it.

I don't need to like this woman. Liking her will cause nothing but trouble and hurt feelings.

A soft knocked startled me. I hurried to open the door.

Solomon's gaze connected with mine, and once again, I felt that irresistible connection between us. He passed me the towels, and I set them on the end of the dresser.

"Can I talk to you a minute?" he whispered.

Nodding, I stepped out into the hall and shut the door.

He reached out to touch me, but I drew back. His hand fell to his side, and he stared at me for a moment. "Ruby, I apologize for kissing you earlier. It's just that I thought you were into me too."

I said nothing, just focused on the soft amber glow of a hurricane lamp lighting the hall.

"You don't let anyone get close to you, do you?"

"Not if I can help it." But oh how I wanted to let someone into my heart. How I longed to be held and caressed and have someone whisper the words 'I love you' in my ear. Something about Solomon urged me to give him a chance, but I knew what would happen. Solomon would see what I could really do, and he'd abandon me just like everyone else did.

"Look, I know we barely know one another, but I'm due for a vacation and would love to travel to Key West with you and Maureen—that is, if you wouldn't mind."

My gaze flew to his. The direction of the conversation sent a thread of discontent trailing through my gut. "You can't be serious."

Obviously uncomfortable, he shuffled his feet. "At the very least, I'd love it if you'd stop by on your return trip. What do you say, Ruby?"

"You want me to stop by?" The question sounded ridiculous the minute it left my mouth, but his desire to see me rendered me temporarily stupid.

"I just want to get to know you a little better," he said, a smile tugging at the corners of his mouth. "There's something about you. I can't put my finger on it, but you're so mysterious. You're a beautiful and intriguing woman."

Don't forget dangerous.

"I don't think you'd like me if you got to know me," I returned.

"Why?"

"I'm different."

"I've seen that part of you. It doesn't scare me," he said. "You're not like other women, and you don't seem to judge me either."

"With all my flaws, I have no right to judge anyone."

He stepped closer, the expression in his eyes daring me to step away.

It was hazardous to be this close to him, but I stood my ground. Something banged at a frenzied pace against my ribs, and I realized it was my heart. I'd always been attracted to dark-haired, dark-eyed men. Solomon was the total opposite, but regardless, every time the man even glanced at me my pulse thrummed and heat settled in my crotch.

"What flaws?" he asked. "Do you snore?"

I chuckled.

"Fart in your sleep?"

At that, I burst out laughing then tossed a guilty look toward the guestroom in hopes I hadn't awakened Maureen.

"Maybe you spend too much money on shoes or gossip with your co-workers about who has put on the most weight?"

Still giggling, I said, "No, nothing like that."

"Then what?"

Best not to answer that one. I shrugged.

He gently touched one of my bare shoulders. The feelings that simple caress prompted nearly caused my panties to burst into flames. What was it about this man that stripped me of all my resolve?

"Ruby," he whispered.

I found myself moving into his embrace. With his hands on my waist, they rested there only momentarily before sliding over my hips to palm my ass. A whimper escaped me, and his mouth descended upon mine.

Heaven help me!

The heat that erupted in my lower abdomen spread into my thighs and swept into my crotch. Solomon's tongue pressed the seam of my lips asking for permission to enter. I parted them, and our tongues dueled in a rhythm that imitated what I wanted to do with our bodies. My pulse jumped in my jugular so hard it almost hurt. Oh, how I wanted this man! I desired to investigate every inch of his pale body. I wanted to straddle him and stare into his ghostly eyes as we made love, riding him until he claimed exhaustion and could no longer move.

He kneaded my buttocks, urging me closer. I pushed against him, the evidence of his arousal hard and prominent through his slacks.

"Ruby." The word slipped from his lips like a vague breeze. "I want you. Let me," he nipped the skin on my throat, "have you tonight."

How could I refuse him? I wanted him so badly it's a miracle the heat we generated didn't ignite our clothes.

"You don't know what you're getting into," I breathed against his stubbly cheek, my tongue tracing the scars along his jaw line. A gasp burst from me as he cupped one of my breasts.

"I know enough," he said and claimed my mouth again.

He moved with me down the hall, our bodies bumping, his lips never leaving mine. We jostled the little table supporting the hurricane lamp, nearly upsetting it from its perch. Solomon jerked away from me and righted the light. He took my hand and led me toward the door at the end of the corridor. Once there, my doubts resurfaced.

"No," I said. "You'll end up hating me."

"How could I hate you?" he asked, wonder in his eyes.

"Trust me, you will."

"No way."

"Solomon, I—"

He pushed me to the wall and kissed me until I struggled for air. My determination to change his mind faded and dispersed on a wave of sensation that left me powerless.

Solomon fumbled with the doorknob, and the door opened to swing inward and bang against the wall. He caught it on the rebound and kicked it shut. I barely had time to register the masculinity of the room before his fingers untied the straps to my halter top; the garment fell around my waist, and his palms quickly discovered my breasts and their dark, sensitive peaks.

I had no defense against him. My only thoughts were to have him thrusting into my body. Even as I reveled in the mind-blowing sensations he evoked, his touch and kisses still seemed familiar.

But how was that possible?

Fire awakened in the center of my body. As he kissed and touched me, the heat streaked out along my arms and legs. The light began softly, but the more excited I became, the brighter the illumination grew.

"No!" I pushed back from Solomon. "No, I can't do this. We can't."

He still held me, his arms loose around my waist. "Ruby, the glow doesn't bother me and you don't scare me."

"You don't understand." Still wanting him and frightened at the same time, I broke free of his embrace and walked backward to the door. "I also set things on fire and blow stuff up. I'd never forgive myself if I hurt you. I'm cursed, okay? Cursed."

"Let me decide for myself." He held his hand out to me.

Oh, how I wanted to lace my fingers with his and allow him to lead me to his bed. I wanted that more than anything.

"I can't, Solomon. I'm sorry." Turning, I hurried out of his room and down the hall to mine.

Once inside and the door shut behind me, I leaned against it and bit my lip to keep from crying. My body screamed for sexual release, but I wanted more. I wanted to be loved and held. With a sigh, I gulped back tears and strode to the bed to undress.

Chapter Nine

Something woke me in the middle of the night. I lay listening intently. The A/C kicked on, and cool air filtered into the dark bedroom. Moonlight illuminated the sheers. Blinking sleep from my eyes, I stared at the red glow of the digital clock on the nightstand which read 3:17. A few feet away, Maureen snored softly and muttered.

Something wasn't right.

I wiggled out of the covers, gently tugged my braid out from under the pillow, and got out of bed. At one of the windows, I peered down at the back lawn silvered in moonshine.

We're waiting for you. Come to us, Ruby. He will follow.

The last thing I wanted to "hear" at nearly three-thirty in the morning was that infernal voice. Come to them? And who was this he?

Images of the suicide machines bombarded my mind, followed by the thirteenth biker and what his proximity had done to me as I lain in the back of my Jeep.

I gulped and willed the ball of fear wedged against my heart to go away. A dark feeling tickled the edges of my consciousness. I crossed the room, and, knowing I shouldn't, turned the doorknob and opened it to the murky hall beyond. The door whispered across the carpet, the sound shattering the heavy silence.

Naked, I hesitated. Why was I so frightened? Granted it was a strange house, but Solomon had secured the doors and windows downstairs.

Perhaps I'd heard Sam up moving around?

Something is here that shouldn't be.

My robe lay on the foot of the bed. I swept it up and slipped my arms into the sleeves. Quietly, I opened the door. Shunka greeted me, bushy tail swishing to and fro.

"Come on, pal," I whispered.

The dog followed me, his eyes glowing an eerie white in the dim moonshine spilling through a hall window.

As I tiptoed along the balcony spanning the upper edges of the big living room, I kept my gaze on the downstairs, the banister cool beneath my palm. At the top of the steps, I halted. The Malamute stopped too and pressed against my leg. If I had any sense, I'd go back to bed and pray for sleep, but something bothered me and it wasn't in my nature to ignore such feelings. I'd learned the hard way too many times.

The Malamute issued a long, low whine.

"What is it, boy?"

The animal pressed tighter against my thigh and let out another worried whine.

"They're here, aren't they?"

He licked my hand.

I descended the stairs. With each step, my heart slammed harder. I didn't want to find what was waiting, but I had no choice. Something told me I had a job to do, an important task, but it scared me shitless.

The carpet felt cool beneath my feet. The A/C whispered from the vents, but sweat broke out across my body. The dog echoed my sentiments with his anxious panting. Something drew me to the kitchen where a door led out to the cabin's back deck. Maureen and Sam had sat out there that evening. Sam had even built a fire in the fancy, encased fire pit so Maureen could roast marshmallows. The shadows cast by leaping flames gyrated on the kitchen windows and created bizarre, mutated shapes on the appliances and red-painted walls.

Shunka's claws clicked on the tile as he padded to the multi-paned back door. There, I peered through one of the glasses.

Sam sat by the fire pit encircled by a patterned steel ring of stag-and-tree cutouts. He clasped a dried gourd painted in red and blue with turkey and eagle feathers hanging from it. In his other hand he held a long-stemmed pipe that he'd toke on every so often and blow blue-white smoke into the air above him.

Shunka began whining again.

Sam rose and dropped the pipe into the patio chair. He held his free hand out in front of him, palm flat like a cop halting traffic. I peered harder into the darkness beyond the fire ring. Although I'd somehow sensed their presence, the glow of yellow eyes still forced a gasp of fear and dismay from my mouth.

How could it be possible the creatures from my dreams were real?

Do you see why you must come to us, Ruby? Hurry! We're waiting.

Against my better judgment, I turned the doorknob and stepped out on the wide deck with my legs trembling and my senses acute. The dog remained close to me. The ruff around his neck stood on end, and a deep growl reverberated in his chest.

"I've held them off as long as I can," Sam said over his shoulder.

Something awakened within me. It stirred in the center of my chest, the feeling both invigorating and unsettling. With adrenaline slicing through my veins, I descended from the deck to join Sam. Shunka sat in front of us, ears perked, snout to the air, hackles raised.

The inky forms from my dreams and visions lined the perimeters of the deck. There were seven of them, each one a large, swirling mass of indigo and gray smoke, their eyes like yellow halogen lanterns, talons long, gleaming and as bright yellow as their eyes.

Crickets and bullfrogs sang macabre backup music, their bass in time with the frantic beating of my heart. Somewhere in the night, I caught the sound of a big cat screeching. The stars dimmed behind the haze of humidity, and in the distance, heat lightning backlit the sky.

Growls issued from the shrubbery and flowers planted in the beds that sloped down the backyard.

"She is here," one hissed.

"More powerful than the last time," said another.

"More powerful each time," a third snarled.

In unison, the forms said, "Free them and us! We have suffered long enough!"

Terror transformed into a dreadful feeling of intense electricity zipping throughout my body. Every pore and hair follicle on my body tightened. The aroma of sulfur and ozone invaded my sinuses. A nauseating sensation settled in my stomach, and what felt like liquid fire surged along each vein and into my fingertips. Glowing from head to toe, I moved to the top of the steps. My fingernails blazed bright red, and a bright coppery color flowed down through my hair, infusing the braid over my shoulder with the brilliance. Sam squinted against the light I emitted and finally held up one hand to shield his eyes.

Fire and fractured light erupted from my palms, my nails. The power snapped and crackled in the air, shredding Sam's pipe smoke into tiny fragments. The energy caressed the deck railing, rained sparks onto the steps, and lit up the surrounding trees as if someone had strung them with blue and white sparks.

The smoky creatures howled in fury and backed away in the forms of vaporous wolves, panthers, bears and birds of prey. The air crackled, the pops and sizzles as loud as firecrackers. Each bolt of energy pierced the half-solid, half-vaporous bodies, and the monstrosities bloomed into dark gray clouds to disappear with howls and indignant screams.

"We are not thwarted so easily...!" The words died on the evening breeze.

Somewhere a bullfrog croaked its irritation at the disturbance.

Exhaustion hit me. Drained, I slumped, and the deck raced up to greet my face.

Sam finally roused me. I sat up, blinking, and looked from one point to another, fearful I'd see a set of glowing yellow eyes.

"You and Solomon have bonded again. I think that's part of what drew those things here," said Sam so low I almost didn't hear him.

"Bonded again?" I echoed, shock in my voice. Fearfully, I scanned the deck and backyard.

"They won't give up. I held them off as long as I could."

His words shot an arrow of horror into my heart.

"You *are* the Nutter I dreamed of, Ruby. Your powers are growing stronger and your destiny is near."

Remorse filled me. "I've always had this curse. I hate it and I can't control it. I've done some terrible things because of it"

The old man helped me to my feet. "There is more within you, more you have yet to discover, but you need to go "soon." Go to Key West and do what is required of you."

"There isn't anything in Key West for me to do except to pick up a document."

He shuffled toward the kitchen door with me. "Yes, there is." His firm tone left no room for argument. "You don't now it yet, but you will." His onyx eyes glinted with an all-knowing power.

The old Indian wasn't making any sense, and his persistence began to irritate me. "I'm just being paid to pick up a damn piece of paper."

He smiled.

I remained quiet and struggled to breathe. My heart slammed against my ribs so hard I could barely breathe.

"Let's go inside," Sam suggested. "Neither of us will sleep anyway. I'll turn on some lights and make coffee and a batch of muffins and waffles."

Nodding, I let him open the door and push me into the kitchen. Shunka slipped in behind Sam.

Whatever Sam sensed, I did too. Although I desired nothing more than to climb into bed, there was no way in hell I could sleep now.

Somehow the monsters from my visions were real. I had to leave—and soon.

****

"I don't see why we have to leave at six in the morning," Maureen said through a yawn.

"We just need to get going," I replied as I finished packing my things. I'd dressed, shared a breakfast of eggs and waffles with Sam, and then hurried upstairs to rouse Maureen.

She sat up, the sheet pooling around her waist, her huge bazookas encased in a white satin bra. "Something's wrong, isn't it?"

"No, we've just wasted enough time—"

"Haven't you realized yet that you can't lie to me?"

Hefting my suitcase, I halted halfway across the bedroom. "What?"

"You heard me." She yawned behind one hand, her French-tipped nails curving outward like claws.

"Whatever." I left her to get dressed. "Come on, mutt."

The dog padded after me.

Against my better judgment, I strode down the hall to Solomon's room and peeked in on him. Wrapped in the sheet, he slept soundly. The sight of him awakened a familiar longing. No matter how much I liked Solomon, and regardless of the sexual chemistry that sizzled between us, he was better off without me in his life. Sure, he'd said he found my fascinating, said I didn't scare him, but if he suddenly changed his mind about me, I couldn't bear it. And what if something untoward happened to scare him out of his mind or hurt him? Sam seemed to accept me and my curse, but the Indian had also displayed a unique ability of his own, a natural power Solomon might not know about. Solomon might think he understood what it was to be different, but his albinism didn't hold a candle to my curse—or the things snapping at my heels. That was enough to convince me to get some miles between us.

Yet, Solomon had told me about the attack and how his sister was killed. He knew something was unnatural.

He'd even mentioned the yellow eyes of the bikers, their comments about knowing him, us.

But as I stood there watching him sleep, my heart cried out in protest. How could I leave him? We'd connected. I knew that, and so did Sam. Somehow our souls recognized one another. How, I had no clue, but knew it for the truth. For Solomon's safety and his sanity, I had to leave him. As long as I stayed, both Solomon and Sam were in danger. Leaving was the only thing I could do and I needed to honor my agreement with Loretta.

"Let's go," Maureen called.

I glanced over my shoulder at her. She stood in the hall with her backpack. She'd donned a different pair of Daisy Dukes and a t-shirt so tight it looked like it had been spray-painted on her.

Terrific. Another day of being blinded by boobs and ass. I picked up my suitcase again. "Let's go."

"You'll see him again, Ruby," she said with conviction.

With a shrug, I passed her in the hall, the dog right on my heels. Letting her see the tears in my eyes or trying to talk around the lump in my throat was not an option.

Downstairs, Sam handed Maureen a bag of apple muffins and two Styrofoam cups with lids. The aroma of freshly brewed coffee helped to wake me up. Sunshine began peeking through the windowpanes, and billows of fog rolled by the kitchen windows.

Sam helped us outside with our bags. "Solomon will be upset that you left without saying goodbye," he said, "but I'll explain things to him."

Cool morning air kissed my body, and sadness touched my soul. Condensation covered the Jeep and the Excursion. Fat dewdrops littered the lawn and adorned the purple asters planted along the drive and walk. Crows cawed in the distance, and mourning doves cooed under the shrubs. The Malamute trotted alongside me as I walked to the Jeep. I reached for the driver's door. The dog waited as if he wanted to hop inside. I opened the door a crack, and he shoved his muzzle into it.

"What's wrong with your dog?" I asked Sam

The Indian patted his leg. "Here boy, let her get in the Jeep."

The canine ignored him. I tried opening the driver's door wider so I could squeeze in between the dog and the seat, but the mutt shoved harder and wedged his head inside. I pushed the door snugly against his neck. The dog retreated and stood wagging his tail.

"Would you please do something about your mutt?"

Sam grabbed the dog by his collar and tugged, but the animal wouldn't budge. Putting his arms around his shoulders, he tried to pick him up. Shunka growled, the sound coming from deep within his chest.

Sam let go and retreated.

"Oh, for God's sake!" I snapped and shut the door. I swung my right leg up into the open window, followed by my left, and settled into the driver's seat.

Wobbling across the gravel in her platform heels, Maureen managed to get in on the passenger side before the Malamute realized she'd opened it.

"Do you have everything?" I asked her.

"Yeah, I think so."

I looked back at Sam, who raised one gnarled hand in farewell and ascended the steps. He slipped into the cabin without a backward glance.

"He believes it's bad luck to tell someone goodbye," said Maureen.

"I'm not so sure he's wrong," I replied, wanting to sob.

Chapter Ten

We drove through the remaining mountains of Virginia and into North Carolina. Maureen must have sensed my mood. She said very little—thank God. I concentrated on driving, watching the names of towns and cities on the Interstate signs as the pavement rolled away under the new tires. However, no matter how hard I tried, I couldn't keep my thoughts from straying to Solomon and the way he made me feel as he'd kissed me on the porch.

Then, on the flip side, the memory of the creatures encroaching on the cabin's back deck shot rockets of ice through me, freezing my innards.

It didn't take long to reach Statesville. There, we pulled into a truck stop to gas up and grab some cold-cut sandwiches and Cokes. I pulled the Jeep up to a pump, shut off the engine, and reached for my purse, which always sat between the stick shift and the console.

No purse.

Frowning, I looked on the floor, in the backseat, and even got out to rummage through the hatch.

"What's wrong, Ruby?" Maureen asked.

"Did you put my purse somewhere?"

"No, the last place I saw it was on Sam's kitchen table this morning," she said serenely.

"You saw my purse sitting on the kitchen table and you didn't pick it up?"

She twisted in the seat to look at me, both eyebrows raised in identical arches. "I figured you'd get pissed like you do everything else, especially with all that cash in it."

"You could've reminded me where it was!"

"Well, since you were the one who put it on the table, I assumed you knew where it was." Maureen's eyebrows lowered, but a furrow appeared between them. "Don't try blaming me for this one, Ruby."

Her response wasn't what I'd expected. For the first time since picking her up, my Marilyn Monroe hitchhiker was standing up to me.

"Shit!" Letting the hatch fall shut, I leaned against it and watched the endless stream of tractor-trailers entering and exiting the truck stop. I'd parked on the gas station side, but a large black, red and neon green billboard by the exit ramp advertised a traveler's restaurant around the back. A trucker's parking lot took up the far left. Heat waves shimmered up from the blacktop in huge silvery curtains. Two hookers, a blonde in a micro mini skirt and a redhead that was an obvious dye job, climbed out of a nearby truck.

Maureen got out of the Jeep and stood at my side. "What do we do for money now?" she asked.

I nodded at the prostitutes sashaying toward the next semi.

Her mouth dropped open. "Uh...do we really—?"

I gaped at her. "Jeez, Maureen, I was just being a smartass."

"Oh."

With a sigh, I felt in the pockets of my shorts. Empty. I walked around to the driver's side, searching through the console, the various pockets, shelves, slots and nooks for loose change or carelessly tossed bills.

"I don't suppose you have any dough put back for emergencies, do you?"

The sound of heels clicking on asphalt reached the passenger door, and Maureen poked her head through the open window. "Are you kidding? I've been bumming off you."

That brought a smile to my lips. She irritated the hell out of me, but at least she was honest.

"Well, I found three dollars and ninety-five cents." Straightening, I rubbed the small of my back. A tension headache had begun in my forehead and slowly crossed my skull to my spine.

"Good! It's hot and I'm parched."

"I was thinking more along the lines of telephoning Solomon."

"Do you have his phone number?" Maureen asked.

I wilted. "No."

I laid my head on my arms across the doorframe. The developing headache teetered on the edge of a stroke. Several minutes slipped away as I tried to clear my head enough to think straight. I didn't have any friends or any relatives other than Dad, and he'd never part with enough money for gas back to Solomon's. I could hear him now, "If you need money, use your damn power."

And to top it all off, I felt like an ass for the way I'd spoken to Maureen.

"Uh, Ruby," Maureen said.

"Not now," I muttered.

There was enough gas in the Jeep to go another twenty miles, give or take, but what then? Solomon's cabin was a good sixty miles behind us.

"Ruby," she said again.

"What?"

"Ruby Nutter?" a man said.

My head whipped toward the voice so fast that pain shot from between my shoulder blades, over my head and settled between my eyes. A North Carolina State Highway Patrolman stood looking at me with cool blue eyes. His black uniform with its rectangular arm patch outlined in gold promoted a high factor of intimidation. A round trooper's hat with the three divots in the crown perched on his head, and a black nametag trimmed in silver and gold adorned his left pec. I looked at Officer Sherman Zwight and wondered what I could have possibly done wrong.

"Can this day get any worse?" I moaned and leaned against the driver's door for support. Several other names popped into my head. I considered using Jane Doe, Cleopatra, Mary Magdalene—anything. "I'm Ruby Nutter."

"Are you Maureen Galbraith?" he asked, looking at my hitchhiker.

"Yes." Her voice sounded so small and scared that I felt like slugging the cop in the mouth for frightening her.

"I need you two ladies to come to the station with me to clear up an issue that was reported a few hours ago." He pulled out a notepad and scribbled on it with a pen. Upon his left shoulder, a mic imitated the sounds of a deranged chimpanzee. "Would you two please get in the back of my car?" He nodded toward the sleek black-and-silver charger parked a few yards away.

"What's this about?" I asked, my stomach falling into my sneakers.

"I'm not at liberty to say, ma'am," he responded and indicated that we start walking toward his cruiser. "This can all be settled at the station if you simply cooperate."

"Ruby, we better go with him," Maureen said, a faint quiver in her voice.

He smiled coolly and nodded toward his cruiser again.

"Shit," I whispered and urged my feet across the parking lot.

After he settled us in his car, he moved my Jeep from the gas pumps to a safe parking spot, locked it, and slipped my keys into his pocket.

Unshed tears sparkled in Maureen's eyes, so I refrained from saying anything for fear of starting a deluge. Besides, if she started bawling, I would too.

****

Except for the occasional squeal of the police radio, we rode in silence to the trooper's station. A female voice babbled across the airwaves with strings of codes, addresses and Interstate ramps mixed with perp information and details of traffic accidents. Maureen mutely stared out the window.

The officer took an off ramp, made a right onto a two-lane highway, and about a quarter of a mile down the road, promptly pulled into a parking lot on the left. The square brick building sat upon a small knoll surrounded by trees and one lonely radio tower protruding from the backside like a steely pimple. He parked the cruiser and helped us out of the backseat.

"Are we under arrest?" I asked somewhat snappishly and grimaced at the stricken look Maureen shot me.

He favored me with a bland smile that didn't reach his icy blue eyes. "No, we just need to ask you a couple questions, then you can be on your way."

"Does this have anything to do with those bikers who trashed the museum in Virginia?" Maureen asked.

The officer paused and quirked an eyebrow. "Should it?"

"Never mind," she muttered. Her gaze dropped to the toes of her platform sandals.

The cop led the way to the station's front door.

"Way to go, ditz," I whispered.

She offered me a helpless shrug. Disgusted, I strode slightly ahead of her. The clickety-click of her heels followed me as she stumbled over the stray pebbles strewn about the pavement.

Inside, the patrolman led us to a window where he stopped to fill out a timesheet and address a short, gray-haired man with brown eyes and a salt-and-pepper mustache. "These are the two women who were reported, Marty," he said. "I'll put them in a detaining room until our other party shows up."

"That's fine, Sherman." Marty glanced at me and smiled.

Officer Zwight turned and indicated that Maureen and I walk down a pine-paneled hall. He unlocked a door on the left and pointed for us to enter.

He shut the door behind me with a firm thud.

Maureen poured a cup of coffee and parked herself at a round table in the center of the room. A cabinet sat behind her as well as a cheap coffee maker and several towers of foam cups. Riddled with cigarette burns, an ugly turquoise sofa from the late 1960s occupied the left wall beneath a large print of the North Carolina state seal. The coffee-stained, mustard-yellow carpet clashed with the couch so badly I could almost hear the two hues screaming insults at one another.

"Wonder what they want to question us about?" Maureen mused, nervously drumming the nails of her free hand on the table's laminate.

"Who knows?" I sighed and pulled out one of the hard plastic chairs. "It could be anything from the bikers at the museum to Loretta Detzer paying us to pick up her document in Key West."

"Who could've known about that?" Maureen's eyes grew as big as her boobs.

"That diner was packed the day we were there," I said, deciding I would try the black syrup in the coffee pot. I walked over to the cabinet and poured a cup. "Anyone might've eavesdropped on our conversation and made up a lie to detain us. Then he could go to Key West and pick up both the document and the money. The way our luck has gone so far, I wouldn't rule out anything just yet."

"Good point," Maureen muttered.

Thinking back over the events of the past two days made my head throb worse. For the millionth time, I wondered why I'd agreed to let Maureen tag along. Her obvious fear of our situation only served to make me feel guilty.

Stirring creamer into my coffee, I sat down again. Maureen stared off into space, her fingernails still tapping the tabletop. She leaned against the table edge. The action created a tsunami of pale flesh that bulged over the neckline of her low-cut shirt. The sight disturbed me and I fought an overwhelming urge to duck under the table.

With the way things were going, maybe it wasn't the best idea to stop in Florida to see my son. No, I had to see him, warn him, make sure he was safe. But for now, it was best to concentrate on why we were detained at the highway patrol station. The clock on the coffee maker blinked 11:45. Placing my cup in the center of the table, I crossed my arms on the tabletop, laid my head on them and closed my eyes.

Maureen shifted in her seat and exclaimed, "Oh, good, a "National Geographic" to read."

The thought of Maureen reading "National Geographic" was pretty damn amazing. No, that wasn't fair. *Hurt before I'm hurt first.*

As I dozed, thoughts of Cindy Sandsburg and Jody Kefferstine rose unbidden. Cole Vandercourt's handsome face transformed into a cruel mask as he used me, and then dumped me in front of the entire football team and cheerleading squad, their jibes and jeers echoing in my brain.

The A/C breathed down on me from a vent in the ceiling. I dropped off into a deep slumber and heard his voice again, *'I never fucked a witch before.'*

When Cole, a senior and the handsomest and most coveted guy in school, started chasing me, leaving beautiful notes and letters in my locker, carrying my books, and calling my house, the other girls hated me even more.

The truth was that I'd always been smitten with Cole. His Italian heritage had blessed him with dark, brooding looks. He'd flash that perfect white smile, his blue eyes stark against his olive complexion, and I'd turn into a ball of goo.

Finally, despite my reservations he could have any girl he wanted, I went out with him. We hung out at the mall and then saw a movie. I had a great time, and Cole even kissed me at my front door, promising to take me to the school's biggest football game of the season.

I was so stupid for letting him talk me into going to the after-game party. So stupid to trust him, to believe he only wanted alone time with me.

As I always did, I saw the door burst open, the kids filing in to watch as Cole taught the witch a lesson. I fought...fought so hard, but although my power rose again, it didn't stop Cole. He'd boned the witch while she'd glowed and screamed for him to stop. He'd reveled in my power cascading over him as I cried. He'd used it to prove to the others how fearless he was.

And poor Anthony was the one who had paid for it all.

"Ruby?" a familiar voice said next to my ear. Something nudged me gently. "Ruby, wake up."

The sensation began before I roused fully. At first, I thought I was still dreaming, but the prickles and stinging flowed into my arms as my consciousness floated to the surface of my brain.

'I never fucked a witch before.' Cole's words stabbed my heart again.

The fiery sensation permeated my hands, shot into my fingers—I jolted awake. My concentration centered on my hands now flat on the laminate. Bleary-eyed, I tamped the urge, the need to fry everything, down into the well of my soul.

"Ruby, it's okay. Wake up," Maureen soothed.

The orange of my nails faded to natural pink, but the aroma of burning plastic tainted my nostrils. Sleep fuzzed my mind. My gaze moved to the coffee maker's digital clock: 12:33. Someone squatted next to me, and I turned to look into Solomon's eyes. He wore a look of relief and pleasure.

"What are you doing here?" I asked as the illumination surrounding me vanished.

"He brought your purse, Ruby," Maureen chirped from the sofa, the magazine spread across her lap.

"How did you know we were here?" I frowned at Solomon, my brain finally functioning properly as it chased the dream away and my power slumbered again. "I never got a chance to call you."

"I have a buddy on the Virginia State Highway Patrol," Solomon explained. "After I told him about you and that you'd left your purse with all your cash in it, he took down the make, model and license plate number of your vehicle and called another buddy, a Sherman Zwight, who got lucky when he found you at the truck stop outside Statesville."

A bright blue dress shirt accentuated his eyes and hair. His lack of natural coloring no longer seemed strange and alien to me. Oh, no. Solomon looked great, so much so my breath hitched.

"Zwight had the patrol station hold you here until I could drive down with your purse. I apologize for rummaging in something so personal, but I thought maybe I'd find something to help me get in touch with you. When I found the wad of cash and all your credit cards, I realized you were in an unfamiliar area without money, I.D., or even a couple of quarters to make a collect call for help." He grinned. "And nowadays, what woman doesn't carry a cell phone with her?"

I shrugged and grinned sheepishly.

"Isn't he a sweetheart, Ruby?" Maureen said like a lovesick girl.

Heat singed my cheeks. "I don't know how to thank you."

"Well..." Solomon smiled.

Suspicion fluttered in my heart.

"Let me go with you to Key West," he said. "I'll even let you drive my Excursion, and I'll pitch in for gas and other expenses."

"Why?"

"I already told you."

"You have money, Solomon. Why not travel to Italy or maybe Japan? You can certainly afford it."

"I find you fascinating."

He'd told me that last night. What was fascinating about me? Well, besides blowing things up, my sunshine glow and rapier wit.

His smile grew wider. He reached out and smoothed back that one stubborn tendril of hair that always dangled in my eyes. "Yes, Ruby, you're fascinating, even more so than going to a foreign country. There's more to you and I want to find out what it is." He cupped my cheek, his thumb caressing my lips.

"Yeah, she's rude, mouthy, profane, and sometimes she's downright mean," Maureen quipped.

I threw her a look that spoke volumes about my temper.

"See?" she said, but amusement danced in her eyes.

"If you don't like hanging with me, you can go back to hitchhiking," I grumbled.

"No thanks." She sat on the sofa again and picked up the magazine.

"So what do you say?" Solomon asked. "Sam says I need to stay with you to fulfill some sort of destiny, and if you ask me, it sounds like a good excuse to get to know you better."

I searched his eyes for some clue to his true intentions. How was it possible that such a compelling man wanted to spend time with me? Leaving this morning was how it always ended with the men in my life, especially if they found out how weird I was. His hopeful expression tugged at my heart.

"Come on, let me go with you."

"You don't even know why we're traveling south."

Solomon chuckled. "If it's with you, I know it will be interesting. I've even closed the museum for a couple weeks."

"You're better off staying away from me, Solomon."

"Let me be the judge of that." He brushed his lips against mine, startling me into silence.

I couldn't comprehend his need to travel with us. However, he did manage to find us through his cop buddies and had driven from Virginia to North Carolina just to bring me my purse full of cash. He could have easily taken it, claiming he'd never found my purse, but he was already wealthy, so that theory fell flat.

I hate it when I feel like I owe someone something. On the other hand, I was elated he wanted to go with me. I certainly enjoyed his company, and since leaving him that morning, I'd felt lost.

"Oh, all right, but if you turn into a jerk, I'll go to the nearest car rental and high-tail it to Key West without you." I felt like a bitch, but my wariness overwhelmed everything else—not to mention revisiting Cole during my catnap hadn't helped my mood. "Take it or leave it."

His schoolboy smile softened my heart. He stuck out one pale, long-fingered hand to shake on it.

Chapter Eleven

On the way back to collect my Jeep, Solomon explained he'd met his police pals through a detective who had worked on his sister's murder case. Minutes later, we arrived back at the truck stop outside of Statesville. He'd thought ahead and had brought a neighbor to drive my Jeep back to the cabin.

The downside was that Solomon had his damn Malamute with him. Thank God we were taking the Excursion and not my Jeep. Otherwise, we would've had to tie the mutt on the roof. I didn't say anything, though. After all, the man had traveled over sixty miles to find me and give me my purse.

Maureen and I waited on the sidewalk as Solomon filled his SUV with gasoline. He motioned to us, indicating he'd park around front when finished. We walked to the entrance. Rounding the corner, I stopped cold. A row of Harley Davidsons sat parked in a line in front of the entrance. I didn't need to count them to know there were thirteen.

"Ruby? What's wrong?"

Maureen's voice sounded like it came from miles away.

"Uhm...nothing."

My heart jittered so hard I wanted to vomit. What if the bikers saw Solomon too? But what could they really do to us here in front of so many people? And if they did start something, the State Highway Patrol was only a few minutes down the Interstate.

"Let's go inside," I said. "I'm hungry."

Maureen stopped so suddenly I ran into her. She tossed me a skeptical look. "I still say you're hiding some..." Her head swiveled toward the steel horses. "Something's not right about those—"

"Oh, for God's sake, Maureen!" I shoved her toward the door, almost pressing her nose against the glass. "Will you quit dawdling and go inside. It's damn hot out here."

She sighed. "Okay, I'm going, I'm going!" She opened the door and tippy-tapped inside, her heels loud on the tile.

I hoped Solomon didn't run into the same thugs who had trashed his museum.

The gas station sold hot submarine sandwiches in a tiny corner deli. We opted for sandwiches instead of waiting for a table at the restaurant next door. As we ate, customers chattered while paying for their gasoline and snacks, and the beeps from the cash register punctuated the store as a young black cashier cussed a string of vivid Ebonics whenever he punched the wrong buttons.

Solomon spotted us and slid across the booth's hard plastic seat.

"I got you a sub sandwich and a Coke," I said and pushed some condiment packets toward him.

He smiled. "Thanks."

Maureen ate voraciously, and Solomon said very little as he cast curious glances my way. Every time my gaze met his, I blushed to the roots of my hair. I feigned interest in the racks of snacks, travel kits and a long display of tourist trinkets and toys, but the store's lighting and garish theme colors only turned up the volume of my headache.

I finished my sandwich, took a sip of pop, and wiped my mouth and hands. Casting nervous looks around the place, I announced, "I'm going to visit the restroom, then we should be on our way."

"I went before we sat down to eat," Maureen stated around a mouthful of bread and lettuce.

"Well, I didn't." Solomon scooted out of the booth beside me.

A sign over another glass door pointed to public restrooms. We passed through it where the dinner chatter of the restaurant next door grew louder.

"I'll wait here for you." Solomon pushed open the men's room door.

Inside the women's, I found the last of six stalls empty. I did my business, flushed and stepped out to come face to face with the redheaded biker chick. She stood at the counter lined with small ceramic sinks and soap dispensers.

I could only stare at her. Where to hide? Back in to the toilet stall? Dread and fear roared through me. I took one step backward, my hand on the edge of the door to draw it shut.

The woman noticed me. Her eyes flashed yellow, and the little flame of fear in me turned into a mushroom cloud of doom.

"You!" she hissed through lips painted fiery red.

My fear didn't matter because my mouth shot off anyway. "Damn, you're not only big, but you're homely too."

"Bitch!" The chick slung water off her hands and wiped them on her shirt. "I'm going to kick your ass before I take you to Azazel!"

The other stall doors opened one by one. A little girl with her mother and two elderly women hurried out of the restroom.

I asked, "What did I do to you?"

"It's what you did to us!"

"Well, with your bad breath and body odor, it's a miracle everyone around you doesn't drop dead." Again, I wondered how long I'd live if I kept allowing my mouth free rein.

She let out a shriek that should've tripped seismometers all over the country. She swung at me. Although her punch missed my face, I didn't move fast enough for her to miss all of me. Her fist connected with my collarbone, and a jolt of pain zipped through my shoulder and chest. Spinning around, I pressed my backside against the counter's edge and gasped at the agony gripping my chest and shoulder.

She lunged for me again. The sensation that I'd just grabbed a live wire shot down my arms, and I threw my hands up to shove her back. The power roared through my body. My skin grew brighter until it looked like someone had switched on a spotlight in the restroom. The energy that shot from my hands sent the biker flying backward. She crashed through the stall door and smacked into the rose-and-vine wallpaper. She fell with one boot in the toilet bowl, her other planted on the floor.

The biker chick let out another piercing scream.

I ran, my sneakers squealing on the tile. I barely got the door open before I smacked into Solomon.

He caught me by the arms. "What's going on in there?"

"Come on!" I pulled him along. "That biker woman is in there."

We sprinted down the hall just as the homicidal chick yanked the restroom door open. "After we use you, I'm going to kill you!" she shouted after us.

Throwing open the door to the gas station, we hurried to Maureen. Solomon grabbed her by her upper arm and hoisted her to her feet.

"We're out of here. Now!"

"I haven't finished my root beer," she said, clutching the big cup in one hand.

The hellion stormed into the gas station. "Your ass is mine!"

"Let's go!" Solomon dragged Maureen along behind him as I veered around the shelves full of tourist junk.

"But, you guys—" In her hurry to keep up with Solomon, Maureen wobbled on her heels. She teetered, then took another step around the shelves, losing her right shoe, but somehow managed to hang on to her root beer. "Wait, Solomon. My shoe! I lost my shoe!"

"Now, Maureen!" I held the door open, panic nearly suffocating me.

The cashier yelled, "Hey, no fighting in here or I'll call the cops!"

Customers stared wide-eyed at us. One woman pulled her two children against her as she stared at us aghast.

The crazy biker snarled like a rabid animal. She hustled around the racks of chips and snacks, her boots clunking on the floor. She rounded the corner of the tourist gifts, stepped on Maureen's high heel, slipped, and toppled over backward, her arms windmilling.

The woman crashed into the shelving unit. Snow globes smashed on the floor in a shower of water, glass and tiny bits of imitation snow. A box of novelty balls crashed down, and the colorful orbs bounced all over the tile, landing upon shelves and rolling under others.

The cashier shouted a litany of curses that would have sent a priest to confession just for hearing them. A potato chip stand fell on top of the woman as she thrashed around on the floor. Miniature bags of Lay's, Snyder's and Doritos littered the immediate area.

Outside, we pounded down the sidewalk to the Excursion.

"My shoe!" Maureen cried. "Solomon, I lost my shoe back there!"

A herd of Harleys sat parked next to the Excursion. I yanked open the driver's door where I found the Malamute sitting as if he were the get-away driver. "Maureen, shut up and get in the SUV!"

I slid into the driver's seat. Starting the engine, I put the SUV in gear as Solomon jumped into the backseat next to the dog and Maureen hopped in shotgun.

The biker and his girlfriend burst out of the gas station's entrance, their boots whacking against the concrete like sacks of wet sand. "Azazel! She's here!" they both shouted toward a delivery truck parked next to the choppers.

An enormous man in leather chaps and a black t-shirt stepped out from around the truck. Everything in me turned ice cold. He was the thirteenth biker who had stopped at my apartment the other morning, but seeing him in broad daylight, I recognized him from somewhere—but where?

He strode across the sidewalk, his shoulders wide, arms powerful. His tawny eyes stared directly at me, mesmerizing me. Hair as gold as a rising sun brushed his shirt collar.

I couldn't move. Desire crashed through me, and I gasped. He continued to advance, but I couldn't break eye contact.

"*Ruby!*" Maureen's voice came from a galaxy away.

The guy they called Azazel reached the Excursion, his hand passing through the open window.

The need to have him, to have our bodies straining against one another rendered me powerless.

Cold wetness and crushed ice splashed my face and my shoulder. Snapping out of my fugue, I screamed and stomped the gas. The SUV lurched, and then the engine stalled.

"Ruby! Go!" Maureen shouted. She pounded her palms on the top of the dash. "Go, go, go!"

The Malamute lunged from the backseat. He sank his teeth into the biker's wrist. The guy cried out and tried to yank his hand back.

"Shunka! Let go!" Solomon yelled.

More bikers spilled out of the sub shop.

Maureen smacked my shoulder, sending pain through the same collarbone again. "Get moving!"

The rational side of my brain kicked in, and I threw the shifter back into PARK and started the engine again. The blond biker stumbled backward with his hand cradled against his chest. Blood soaked his black shirt with a laughing skull on the front.

The Excursion's engine roared to life. I shoved the shifter into DRIVE and stomped the gas. The tires squealed on the hot pavement. Hookers looked up from where they stood conversing with a couple of truckers. A man pumping gas into a Tahoe cranked his head toward the noise.

"Hey!" Maureen yelled, leaning out the window. "That looks like Wayne Blacktree over by the gas pumps!"

I almost side-swiped a rusty Chevy Blazer towing a pop-up camper. The truck horn blared, and the driver waved his fist at us. Maureen sucked in air and grabbed the sissy bar as the SUV fishtailed across the asphalt, its tires chirping every few feet.

Solomon yelled something unintelligible from the backseat.

We shot in between two tractor-trailers lumbering toward the big side lot, and then out onto the two-lane highway. I took the turn for the on-ramp too fast and fought to keep the Excursion from rolling. It righted itself, and I slowed down to merge with the I-95 traffic.

"What happened to you back there?" Solomon asked over the wind rushing through the cab.

"I...I don't know. I just froze for some reason."

What *had* happened to me? How was it possible the biker could control my body by simply seeing him? If he had touched me, I would've been in grave danger. Somehow I had to avoid physical contact with him. If I didn't...

Dark liquid dripped from my arm, and my hand grew sticky where I held the steering wheel.

Frowning, I wiped my palm on my shirt. "Why am I covered in pop?"

"I dumped my root beer on you," answered Maureen. "It was the only thing I could think of to snap you out of your daze." She sighed. "What am I going to do about my other shoe?"

"For God's sake, Maureen, I'll buy you another pair of heels if you'll just shut up about it!" Finally, I managed to meld with the traffic and set the cruise control for seventy. "We could've gotten our asses kicked back there, and all you're worried about is a stupid shoe!"

"They're my favorite pair!"

"Maureen, Ruby's right," Solomon said.

Glancing at him in the rearview mirror, I saw him patting the Malamute. The dog acted as if nothing had happened, but a red stain decorated the white fur around the animal's mouth.

"What are we going to do about those bikers?" I asked. "They're not normal."

"Let's hope we don't run into them again after this," Solomon replied. "Especially now that Shunka took a hunk out of that guy's hand."

Chapter Twelve

The time passed as did the miles. We listened to various radio stations, changing to different channels once we drove out of each signal's range. Tension hung in the SUV. I knew Solomon and Maureen were thinking about the motorcycle gang too. The biker bitch had called the blond man Azazel, and some of them had yelled that name when they'd rushed out of the sandwich shop. Who was Azazel, and why did he have an interest in me? Why did my brain shut down and my libido explode when he was near? And what had the chopper chick meant by saying 'what you did to us' when I'd never seen any of them until the morning I left Columbus?

'The past is in the past, Ruby.'

My father's familiar phrase left me with a sour taste in my mouth. Did he have something to hide? Had he done something years ago and now these people sought revenge on him through me?

Columbia, South Carolina was behind us, and after a couple more rest stops and a quick top-off of the gas tank, I took I-95 until we reached Walterboro around midnight. There, we found a nice, clean motel with a large pool.

Solomon volunteered to pay for our rooms that night. Gathering our gear, we entered adjoining suites.

"I'm starved," Maureen said.

"Me too." Solomon threw me a meaningful look, and I flushed white-hot from head to toe.

To distract myself, I picked up a phonebook and paged to the P section. "How about pizza and a two-liter of pop?"

Solomon nodded as he opened the door to his room and walked in to investigate, his dog obviously torn whether to stay with me or to follow him.

"Pizza sounds yummy, but no anchovies or hot peppers," Maureen said and tossed her backpack on the bed closest to the bathroom.

"I want extra cheese!" Solomon called from the adjoining room. He poked his head through the doorway. "I'm shutting the door for now. I need a shower." Looking at the Malamute, he asked, "Coming or staying?"

The dog let out a disgruntled sigh, made four tight circles on the carpet and flopped down. Solomon shook his head and closed the door.

My thoughts detoured to Solomon undressing in the next room. Fantasies about his body straining against mine shot a lightning bolt of need to my loins. With a mental shake, I scattered the erotic images in my mind. I was still sticky from the root beer, so I needed a shower too—a cold one.

"I'm so sick of this heat!" Maureen fished in her pack, pulling out various pieces of clothing. She took the lonely, shiny green high heel and tossed it in a trashcan sitting by a long, low dresser.

As I waited for the pizzeria to answer, I studied the room. Tan walls, earthy carpet, two gold-framed pictures with ocean scenes, pressboard furniture, and two double beds with chocolate-brown bedspreads finished the room's décor. My entire body ached, so I wouldn't have cared if the room had been done in pea green with purple polka dots. Driving for long periods always made my joints and muscles hurt, and all I wanted was a couple gooey pieces of pizza, a bath and a soft bed afterward. An image of Solomon naked beneath the shower popped into my mind, but I shoved the thought aside.

No need to complicate matters by sleeping with him during our trip.

A clerk returned to the line. I placed our delivery order and hung up.

Maureen withdrew an oversized t-shirt, panties, a jar of makeup remover and toothpaste from her backpack.

Of my two companions, I realized I knew more about Solomon than I did Maureen. Curiosity found its way to my tongue.

"Can I ask you a question, Maureen?"

She picked up a brush and looked at me over one shoulder. "Sure."

"What is it you need to take care of in Florida?"

A peculiar look crossed her face. Unease fluttered through her eyes. "Why do you ask?"

Stretching, I pointed at a bottle of pain reliever that had fallen out of her makeup kit. She tossed it to me, and I shook out three, swallowing them dry.

"I was thinking that I know more about Solomon than I do you, which seems odd since we've been together longer."

Her brow furrowed as she picked up the items she intended to take into the bathroom with her. "I guess you have a point." She sighed, leaning against the bathroom's doorframe. "I'm meeting someone."

"Oh? Like a computer romance?"

"No."

"A relative?"

"Yeah...a relative. One whom I haven't seen for several years."

"So you have family in both Indiana and Florida," I confirmed, rolling onto my side.

Her demeanor switched from perkiness to guarded. "Well, not really. After my mother died, my Aunt Lula raised me, but she's not really my aunt."

I hadn't meant to touch a nerve. Lord knows I had enough of my own issues that I detested people poking at any of them, but I only wanted a little more information about a companion who I not only shared my transportation and rooms with, but the money in my purse as well.

"I guess you feel a little insecure about traveling with me, so you need some information."

A chill swept over my body, and I thought about her prediction of meeting Solomon again let alone all the other little odd things she'd mentioned that had come to pass.

"Yeah," I conceded.

"My mom died when I was very young, and since Lula raised me, I go back every few months to make sure she's well." She hugged the toiletries as if they were the most important things in the world to her. "I've always known I had family in Florida, but I finally grew curious, contacted him, and we decided to meet."

"Makes sense," I said. "Where are you meeting him?"

"Florida City."

"That works out well. It's the last city before The Keys."

She smiled, but I suddenly felt as though she were merely humoring me.

"You said you had to take care of something in Florida," she reminded me. "Where?"

"St. Augustine."

She brightened at that. "I've always wanted to visit St. Augustine, but never did for one reason or another." She disappeared into the bathroom, pulling the door shut behind her. "I'm taking a shower," she yelled through the door. "Holler when the food arrives."

I sprawled on the bed and thought about what my Marilyn Monroe lookalike had just told me. So, she was an orphan who had been raised by a friend. How had Maureen's mother died? Somehow, I sensed it would be a sore subject to pursue.

Remembering Loretta Detzer's number in my purse, I decided to check in with her. I dialed out and then punched in the phone digits. An answering machine picked up, so I left a message.

Again, why were we being paid the remaining ninety-five grand in Key West? Why not give us a portion for picking up the document to ensure we returned to West Virginia with it?

The answer hit me. *She's not worried about us returning to West Virginia.*

That brought another question to mind. Aside from the document, what was so important in Key West?

There were just too many questions spiraling in my brain. I clutched my head in both hands, bracing my elbows on my knees, and sighed.

My thoughts strayed to the biker woman at the truck stop. How the hell were the bikers able to change their eyes in such a creepy manner? I know I wasn't seeing things because Solomon and Maureen had witnessed the same phenomenon.

Besides, I couldn't deny what had happened behind Solomon's cabin in the wee hours of morning. I didn't want to think about those things, but I couldn't get the image of them encircling the lawn and Sam out of my head.

"Come to us, Ruby. You know what they are. Hurry!"

Yellow eyes.

Smoke monsters.

Very large, unusual bikers with weird attributes.

A gasp ripped from my lips. I snatched at the bed covers in an attempt to keep the room from spinning, but the carpet rushed up to meet me. Lying there with the A/C whispering across the floor and over my body, I wrestled to comprehend the implications of my theory.

A knock sounded on the door, and I roused, scrambling to my feet, looking around wildly as my heart crashed against my ribs. The canine let out a soft woof before lowering his head to his paws again. I recalled where I was and that it was probably the pizza delivery person. My legs shook beneath me, and as I rounded the corner of the bed, I tripped over my sneakers and sprawled out on the floor next to the overgrown fur rug, who calmly licked my cheek.

I jumped to my feet again and peeked through the spy hole. Relieved, I grabbed my purse and opened the door.

"Pizza delivery for Nutter?" a girl, barely twenty, asked in a thick Southern drawl.

"Yes." I rummaged for a twenty in the bottom of my purse.

The girl left, and I studied the parking lot draped in shadows where the security lights didn't reach. Was something lurking out there? Watching? Waiting for me to slip up?

I shut the door with a bang and locked it.

****

The noise was subtle, but it awakened me with a jolt.

I lay listening in the darkness. The bathroom light had been left on, and the door stood ajar so we could find our way around the room should one of us get up. Maureen snored softly. I even heard the dog's breathing at the bedside. The A/C had shut off during one of its power-saver cycles. The distant rumble of tractor-trailers on the Interstate reached me.

Relaxing, I started to slip back into sleep. The noise roused me again, so I sat up. Finally, I identified the sound.

Someone is trying to jimmy the lock on our door!

At almost the same instant, the dark, shaggy form of Shunka's head rose at the bedside. The dog issued a rumbled warning. Every hair on my body stood at attention.

"Maureen!" I whispered.

She continued to snore. It was no wonder she slept like the dead, considering the woman had consumed four slices of pizza and three plastic cups of cola.

The doorknob clicked again, followed by soft metallic jiggling. The dog issued another menacing snarl. This place didn't have the electronic keycards like most motels and hotels used, so, if given enough time, whoever was trying to pick the lock might succeed.

"Maureen!" I whispered louder.

She kept snoring.

In just my Cleveland Browns nightshirt and a pair of cotton panties, I crept from the bed, padded around the dog and over to the door of the adjoining suites. Opening the door a couple of inches, I listened. Solomon's deep breathing drifted from his bed. As I peeked inside, total darkness greeted me. Plucking some courage, I stepped into his room and picked my way across it until I found the footboard and felt around the mattress to his side. Behind me, the canine panted in agitation.

"Solomon!" I shook him. "Someone is trying to break into our room. Hey, wake up!"

"Hmm? What?" He rolled over.

The streetlights' glow slipped through the edges of the curtains providing just enough illumination that his eyes glowed eerily.

"What's wrong?" he asked, sleep heavy in his voice.

"Someone is messing with our door." My eyes had finally adjusted enough that I picked out the other furniture.

He shoved back the covers and stood wearing only a pair of dark boxers, his skin luminous in the shadows. He slipped on his loafers, walked quietly to the door and opened it without a noise. The dog waited at his side, nose pressed to the crack in the door, tail swishing from side to side.

The memory of the bikers and my new theory about them returned fresh in my mind. I prayed they hadn't found us again. How were the riders and their demonic bikes linked to my visions? For a moment, the room swayed and spun. I placed my hand on the dresser and waited for the discomfort to pass.

Solomon situated himself so the Malamute couldn't get out the door. He stuck his head through the opening then pulled back and closed the door.

"You're right, Ruby, someone's working on the lock."

"What do we do? Call the police?"

"No, by the time they get here the guy will probably be inside. I'm going to let Shunka out to deal with him."

"If Shunka hurts the guy, the authorities will take the dog and prosecute you."

"Don't worry. He'll incapacitate the guy until the law does get here." Solomon patted the dog. "Ready, buddy?"

The canine shivered with excitement. He let out a gentle woof as if to say "Hell, yeah!"

Holding the animal's collar, Solomon opened the door, then leaned over to speak in the dog's ear. The Malamute padded out slowly as if he were a wraith gliding upon a night zephyr. It crossed my mind he should've been born a panther instead.

In moments, snarling like a rabid, foaming-at-the-mouth animal and a man's low, frightened voice punctuated the night.

"Easy, boy, easy. Just let me stand up and I'll be on my way. Easy now."

Solomon stepped outside. The smell of cooling asphalt, chlorine and exhaust fumes from I-95 wafted in and over me. The glow of the digital clock to my right showed it was just a few minutes past four a.m. Now, wide-awake, I felt as if I had swallowed a bottle of pep pills.

I moved out behind Solomon, peering down the walk where a man slowly stood. The Malamute advanced on the perpetrator, hackles raised, lips peeled back to reveal pink gums and white razor teeth. Growls raged deep within Shunka's chest.

"Easy, fella. I won't hurt you," the guy said and backed up.

Why did that voice sound so familiar? Frowning, I moved abreast of Solomon, my mind searching for an answer. As the perp continued walking backward, he moved into a security lamp's light.

With a sharp intake of breath, I shouted, "Wayne Blacktree! What the hell do you think you're doing?"

Wayne had been so focused on the Malamute he hadn't even noticed us on the sidewalk.

"Shit!" He whirled, sprinting for his pickup parked on the opposite side of the parking lot.

The dog took off. He barked loud enough to awaken the dead, his claws scrabbling over the asphalt as he hurtled after Wayne. That first bark set off a series of frustrated barks from the bed of Wayne's truck.

"Do you know that guy?" Solomon asked.

"Sort of," I replied. "We bumped into him in West Virginia. His dog wanted to eat Maureen and me, and Wayne interceded then bought us lunch."

Wayne yanked open the driver's door, jumped in and hurriedly rolled up the window.

"Shunka Wakan!" Solomon called. "Come!"

Reluctantly, the Malamute obeyed. He dropped to all fours from where he'd been standing with his front paws on the driver's door, his muzzle pressed against the glass. He turned and trotted across the lot, but Wayne's dog broke the tether holding him in the back of the truck.

The furry, snapping-teeth machine leapt from the pickup bed, barreling toward the Malamute. Solomon's dog whirled and took the first blow from Wayne's mutt.

I screamed, "No!" and felt Solomon grab me. I hadn't even realized I'd started after the canine.

Wayne jumped out of his four-wheel-drive shouting, "Buford, no! Buford! Truck! Now!"

Buford was too high on doggy adrenaline to give a shit. His buzz-saw mouth snapped and bit at the Malamute, but Solomon's dog stood up on his hind legs and lunged for Buford's throat. They struggled that way for a few seconds, their snarls background noise for a bloody scene in a horror movie. Several motel room doors opened, and sleepy tenants stared out at the dogfight in the parking lot. A few grew interested, but others turned, slamming their doors. One yelled an ear-numbing string of profanities, followed by a threat to call the police if the dogs' owners didn't break them up.

Wayne's dog let out a yelp, and a distant crunch prompted the remaining pizza in my gut to look for a quick exit. Shunka let go of the mutt. He stood sniffing him for a moment then padded back to Solomon.

"Buford?" Wayne called. He strode over to his dead dog and knelt next to him. He stroked his head and gently patted Buford's side. "Come on, buddy. Get up." He raised Buford's head, pulling a penlight from his shirt pocket and shining it in the dog's eyes. "Buford?"

"Oh, Solomon." Tears flooded my eyes. The guy was a virtual stranger, but his affection for the dog dredged up sympathy that rocked me with its intensity.

Solomon let go of me and walked out to Wayne. I couldn't hear what they said, but soon Wayne's voice cut through the night.

"No, I don't need your help," he yelled. "Get the hell away from me!" As his voice cracked with emotion, more tears slid down my face.

A woman three rooms down stepped out with a blanket in her arms. She walked across the parking lot dressed in fuzzy white slippers and a long, pale nightgown. A little boy about ten years old trailed her.

She stooped, said something to Wayne, and handed him the blanket. Quickly, she returned to her room.

Solomon helped Wayne lay the dead Buford on the blanket. He stepped back as Wayne carefully wrapped up his dog. The man stooped, slipping his arms under the enormous bundle, lifted the body and staggered with it to his Dodge. Solomon dropped the tailgate, and Wayne hefted the corpse into the pickup bed.

Even from that distance, I heard Wayne's sobs, and, despite my anger at him for trying to break into our room, I cried with him.

Wayne started the truck and tore out of the motel lot, tires squealing.

Once Solomon reached me, he pulled me into his arms.

"It's okay," he said softly.

Startled, I croaked, "Let go of me."

"You're crying."

"Whatever gave you that idea?" I pushed against his bare chest. His body was so warm, and my pulse raced in response. The aroma of shampoo, cologne and his maleness rendered me powerless.

"People are complex creatures," Solomon's voice rumbled in my ear. "In a matter of minutes that man went from criminal intentions to fear to acute grief, and as a result, he inspired emotion in everyone who witnessed it."

His arms loosened around me enough that I could look up at him. I shoved against his chest again. He gazed down at me, his eyes reminding me of a vampire's seductive look. If vampires were truly full of sex appeal as well as magic, I suddenly understood why people succumbed to them.

"What grief do you harbor, Ruby?" he said so quietly I wasn't sure I'd even heard him.

"None of your—"

His lips met mine, igniting a fire inside me. Stunned, I started to melt against him. However, in that instant, the sensation that I knew Solomon from somewhere before proved so sharp I gasped against his mouth and rammed my hands into his shoulders. I broke loose and fell backward through the doorway. My night shirt flipped up over my hips, the hem nearly reaching my breasts. Solomon's gaze met mine, and surprise settled over his face. He held out a hand to help me up and disappeared.

A man who looked like a king stood in his place. We wore a dark robe that fell to the rush-covered floor and a thin, gold chaplet around his head with a bright stone in its center. A fresh, pink scar sliced his face in half diagonally, but instead of making him appear frightening, it gave him a rugged look. A set of piercing blue eyes met mine and he held his hand out to help me to my feet. I glanced down at a long tunic-style dress with heavy embroidery adorning the hem.

Blinking, the vision was gone. It was him! I didn't know how or why, but man in my visions and Solomon was one and the same. Fear of the unknown pierced me, and I scrambled through the doorway of our adjoining suites on my hands and knees, my cotton-pantied ass in the air.

Solomon caught me by the ankle and dragged me, belly down, through the threshold and back into his room.

Chapter Thirteen

Solomon released my ankle, pushed the door shut and then locked it. He hauled me to a standing position. The vision I'd had and the sensation that we'd done this before made no sense to me, but it pierced my mind and heart all the same.

Drawing me close, he pressed his length against me.

"No," I whispered, the heat emanating from him almost searing my skin.

He stared directly into my eyes. Desire roiled within his, their coloring deepening to a steel gray. "How can you say no? You feel it, too, don't you?"

Words failed me. As bad as the vision had frightened me, I wanted Solomon so much it rendered me powerless. I remembered the mental flash I'd had while showering at my apartment, the way I'd felt such sorrow after it had ended, how I'd missed the man in my vision.

Solomon's entire body trembled. "I don't know why," he gulped and shut his eyes for a second, "but it's like I've done this with you before."

His words skewered me with a needle of unease, and I marveled that I had such an affect on him. What if I let him make love to me and it set something untoward in motion? Half-heartedly, I pushed against his chest, but he pulled me against him again, nibbling at my earlobe, hands caressing and rubbing my ass. His body scent, something all male and utterly intoxicating, swept over and around me, heightening my over-stimulated body. Electricity sizzled along my nerve endings. I was so carried away by the feelings he created, I momentarily forgot to breathe. My legs began shaking, and shock-waves cascaded throughout my limbs.

Solomon cupped one of my breasts, and my traitorous body responded by pushing closer, needing the ultimate contact. He grabbed the hem of my nightshirt and tugged it up over my body to toss it aside. I tried to cover myself, but he captured my hands, followed by his head dipping to my chest where he seized a nipple in his mouth.

Fire spread through my limbs, leaving me vulnerable and craving more. My head fell back, and the sounds that escaped my lips both embarrassed and thrilled me.

He straightened and slowly walked me backward toward the bed. The backs of my knees met the mattress, and together, we fell onto it limbs akimbo. He kicked off his loafers and wriggled free of his boxers.

Solomon glanced over at the television and then back at me. "Don't go anywhere," he whispered and kissed me softly.

He rose and flipped on the television, muting the sound. The glow from the screen illuminated his body. The Bible says that the sons of God—whatever they might have been—went in unto the daughters of men. I often thought, as many people do, that the sons of God were angels. If so, then I understood how those women were seduced if such immortals had been fair, muscled and well endowed like Solomon.

He turned to face me, and I could only sit and stare at him standing before me totally nude and unashamed, an impressive erection straining against his lower abdomen. I couldn't decide what fascinated me more—his chiseled six-pack abs or the erect, glorious cock surrounded with closely cropped platinum hair that was enough to make any woman pause in awe.

No! I can't do this. He'll just use me and toss me aside. He can't be trusted.

He stepped toward the bed, his desire for me proud and eager. I clenched my thighs together in anticipation. Who was this man preparing to seduce me? Was he a vampire like I'd fancied earlier, or was he a simple, caring man who seemed familiar for some unknown, unexplainable reason?

Solomon lay on his side next to me and propped himself up on one arm. His eyes glowed in the dim light, each orb a translucent raindrop.

"Tell me no and I'll stop," he said.

"I did tell you no." I blushed as he noticed the way my heavy breathing made my chest more prominent, the steely color of his eyes darkening more. "I thought I was clear on the no issue."

With his index finger, he traced the outline of each breast, creating little tingles upon my skin. "If you were clear on the issue, would you be here next to me now?"

We locked gazes again, and for an instant, another picture flittered through my mind. I saw Solomon with long snowy hair flowing over his shoulders, a thick pink scar running from his right temple, across his brow, over his nose, and down his left cheek. Upon his brow, a thin gold chaplet with a blue stone inlaid in the center rested just above his scarred nose. He smiled, removed the crown and reached for me. When I blinked, the real Solomon leaned over me, his mouth descending to claim mine.

I shouldn't do this. If I do, there's no turning back.

Resolve returned to my body. Somehow I sensed making love to Solomon would set something unnamable and disastrous into action. I still wanted the man, desired his touch, his kisses and his body joined with mine, but I couldn't sleep with him.

Don't be afraid, Ruby. Follow your heart.

The words in my head startled me. I stiffened. What if we were being watched? How did the voice know what I was doing?

"No, we can't do this."

He raised his head and stared down at me quizzically. "Why not? Give me," he brushed his lips across mine, "one good reason."

"I did." I struggled into a sitting position and scrambled off the mattress, looking for me discarded nightshirt. "I'm saying no and meaning it."

He said nothing, just watched me with his ghostly eyes, the disappointment in them obvious.

"I'm sorry." Shrugging into the garment, I hurried to the door leading to my room

"It's okay, Ruby. Really."

I didn't look back. If I did, I feared I'd lose my resolve. Making love to Solomon would lead to jeopardy.

Besides the obvious chemistry between us, I really liked Solomon, and that was the most dangerous thing of all.

****

Later that morning, a waitress poured more coffee into our cups. Although I'd slept soundly until the noise at our door had awakened me, I'd tossed and turned the rest of the night. I just couldn't shake the feeling that sleeping with Solomon would change something or set something extremely important into motion.

One plus of the morning was that I hadn't heard the infernal voice in my head for a few hours.

I breathed in the rich aroma of black coffee, wishing I could wake up. The blue-and-tan decor of the IHOP we patronized did little to improve my mood. Sunshine streamed through the window, searing my eyes, and the kid in the booth behind us jumped and jarred in the seat so much I felt as though I was riding in a hay wagon.

A sunrise beach photo hung on the wall behind Solomon. I slurped from my cup, eyeing the picture, and said to Maureen, "I can't believe you slept through all the noise."

At my words, Solomon lifted an eyebrow.

Memories of his touch, the way his kisses had made me feel bombarded my mind. Intense heat rushed to my cheeks.

More coffee. Desperate for a diversion, I looked around for the waitress. *I need more coffee!*

I waved to our waitress. "Wayne Blacktree made enough noise he woke Shunka, too, but the dogfight that followed probably woke all of Waterboro except for you."

Solomon grinned at me over the rim of his coffee cup. Mischief and a silent invitation danced in his eyes, but I wasn't taking the bait. Despite the heat pooling in my lower belly, I frowned at him and turned my attention to Maureen.

"I was tired last night." Maureen used her knife to scoop margarine out of a tiny plastic cup. She spread it over her pancakes, exercising great care to make sure every inch of both cakes had a thin layer of the artery-clogging condiment.

"Still," I picked up my fork, "there was enough racket it should have woken you."

"I told you I saw Wayne at the truck stop." Maureen glanced over at me and reached for another margarine container.

I sipped from my cup. "What other reason could the guy—?"

One of Solomon's feet bumped mine. I jumped, spilling my coffee.

Maureen shot me a perplexed look.

Mentally cussing the man across from me, I focused on my plate. "What other reason could the guy have for following us?"

"Maybe he wants the money you're carrying." She put down the knife and reached for the butter-pecan syrup. "If you hadn't awakened, he might have broken into our room and found the money. We wouldn't have known it was gone until we paid for breakfast this morning."

I sneaked a look at Solomon. With a pleased grin tweaking his lips, he focused on the dining room as if interested in our fellow patrons.

"The dog wouldn't have let him beyond the door," I said. "Shunka would have woken us with his barking or worse."

"He's after something, Ruby," Maureen said. "What else could it be besides money?"

An ill feeling settled in my stomach. Quickly, I opened my purse and felt for the money. Relieved it was still there, I set my bag in my lap.

"Well, you're right about Shunka," Solomon pointed out. "He probably would have taken a hunk out of the guy."

"I feel bad that Wayne's dog was killed," Maureen said around a mouthful of pancake.

"Yes, but that dog was a danger to everyone around it." I looked at her, wondering if her brain had gone on vacation. "That animal nearly ate us for lunch the other day!"

"But he was Wayne's companion." She picked up her coffee cup.

She was right. The mutt's death and Wayne's anguish bothered me more than I cared to admit. I met Solomon's knowing gaze and looked away.

Was our money the sole reason Wayne had tried to break into our motel room? Somehow, I felt he wanted more than just the five grand we carried. Sure, five thousand dollars was a lot of money to the average Joe, but something about the night's excitement hinted there was more to the scenario than just the obvious.

"His dog aside," Solomon said, reaching for the creamer, "what would this Wayne Blacktree possibly want besides your money?"

I admired the grace and strength of his long-fingered hands as he poured cream from the stainless-steel pitcher and stirred the java from black into buff. The silver-and-turquoise ring he wore looked regal against his skin. I imagined his hands on my bare body, touching, caressing...

When I didn't respond immediately, the conversation died at our table. I looked up and caught his gaze. My face flamed again. Obviously guessing my thoughts, Solomon grinned wider.

Thankfully, Maureen came to my rescue. "Maybe he wants the directions in your purse, Ruby."

"Directions?" Solomon echoed.

"Uh, yeah." I shifted uncomfortably. "The directions to the place we're going to in Key West."

"Why would he want those?" he asked.

"Because," Maureen glanced at me, "he might think if he gets the directions to our destination, he can muscle in on our job and get the remaining money."

"Speaking of getting paid," I said. "Don't you find it odd that Loretta wasn't concerned about the balance of the money?"

Maureen blinked at me. "I don't understand."

"Five now and ninety-five on our arrival?"

She blinked again.

Trying to convey the meaning with my eyes, I gave up and added, "Why not five now, five or whatever on arrival, and then the balance of the money when we returned to her café in West Virginia?"

Realization lit up her eyes. "Oh! That is odd!"

Solomon shook his head and finished spreading jam on a slice of toast.

"Do you think Wayne will try it again?" she asked.

The waitress appeared with the coffee pot. I waited as she refilled our cups, and Solomon asked her for another order of toast. The woman tried not to stare at him as she updated our order ticket.

When the server left, I replied, "Do you two think he might?"

Both Maureen and Solomon shrugged.

"I don't know all the details about your trip," he said, "but from what I saw last night, the guy seems pretty determined."

Would Wayne want to get even for the death of his crazy dog? I suddenly heard the Wicked Witch of the West's movie line in my head, but with a twist: *I'll get your money and your murderous dog too!*

****

Later, we traveled along I-95 again. The Malamute panted in the backseat next to Solomon who studied a road atlas. With her bare feet up on the dashboard, Maureen sat shotgun, staring out the window, her blonde hair stirring gently around her face from the force of the A/C. About every other tractor-trailer blew its air horn as the driver's stared down from their cabs at her inflatable boobs with Grand Canyon cleavage.

Passing a long line of traffic, I merged Solomon's Excursion back into the slow lane. At first, I couldn't figure out what I smelled, but as it grew stronger, my eyes began to water, then my stomach protested.

"Eew!" Maureen slapped her hand over her nose. She glanced at me. "What is that smell?"

"It's not me!" I fought the gag reflex threatening to make me spew breakfast all over the windshield.

Maureen turned in her seat, shooting an accusing look at Solomon.

"Don't lay the blame at my door," Solomon protested, laughing. "I told you not to feed Shunka that last slice of pizza last night."

"Maureen!" I coughed, my eyes tearing.

"Well," she said shrilly and clapped her other hand over her nose too. "He kept staring at me with those soulful blue peepers of his."

The odor grew worse. I hit the button for the power windows and pulled out into the fast lane, passing a Cadillac Escalade that I really didn't need to go around, but hoped the increase of air flow into the SUV would flush the noxious fumes out the open windows.

My gaze's met Solomon's amused one in the mirror. "Hang that dog's ass out the window!" I yelled over the air rushing through the vehicle.

He laughed harder. "Try sitting back here with me! You better pull over at that rest area." He pointed at the big blue interstate sign as we whizzed by it. "I think Shunka needs a restroom break."

We only stayed long enough to use the facilities and allow the Malamute to relieve himself in the pet area. We scrambled back into the Excursion and hit the road again. The next couple of hours took us past exits for South Newport, Pine Harbor, Darien, St. Simon's Island and several miles of the putrid odor regurgitated by the paper mills.

Gross!" Maureen said and pulled the collar of her shirt over her nose. "I don't know which is worse, the dog's fart or that awful processed-paper odor."

"The dog's fart," I said firmly.

Solomon's deep laughter rumbled in the SUV.

"Why don't we stop in Brunswick?" she suggested.

I merged with the passing lane. "What for?"

"We have plenty of time to reach Key West, so I thought we could get a couple rooms in Brunswick then make a day of it at the Jekyll Island Water Park. It's too darn hot to travel today." She took her feet off the dashboard and slipped them into the sandals she'd opted for that morning. "What do you think, Solomon?" Maureen asked.

"What do we do with Shunka while we're gone?" he returned.

"As long as we find a motel that allows pets, he can stay in a room with central air," she answered.

"Oh, all right," I said. I didn't want to admit I really didn't want to travel in the humidity either. The heat index had to be well past one hundred. Besides, after the chaotic night before and the mind-blowing sex with Solomon, I could use a day of relaxation too. "A day of just doing nothing sounds nice."

Chapter Fourteen

In Brunswick, we tried three small motels before finding one owned by an Indian couple who allowed us to bring the Malamute into our rooms for an extra twenty-five bucks. Suites were not available, but we did get our rooms side by side. They were small, clean, and smelled fresh instead of like mildew or stale cigarette smoke, which seemed common for out-of-the-way motels.

My swimsuit lurked at the bottom of my oversized duffle bag. Pulling it out, I threw it over my arm and grabbed a couple guest towels. When I turned around, Maureen had discarded all her clothes and stood naked in the middle of the room, the door standing wide open. She teetered on one foot as she slipped on a bikini that reminded me of two tiny Band-Aids.

I gaped at her. "What are you doing?"

"Huh?" She straightened and drew the bottoms up over her hips.

"The door is open!"

She turned, blinking innocent green eyes, her bare breasts swaying like two large gelatin molds.

I strode to the door and slammed it shut. "You're a real piece of work, Maureen."

"What do you mean?"

She kept staring at me, her expression clueless. I realized she was truly oblivious to what she'd done. I also wondered how the woman had managed to survive as long as she had when her mentality seemed so childlike.

"You just don't change your clothes with the door standing open." I sounded like a scolding mother. "What if Solomon had walked in? What if someone had strolled by and saw you? Someone could've come in and thrown you down on the bed."

"I don't think the human body is anything to be ashamed of," Maureen answered, unconcerned.

The Malamute issued a big sigh and stretched out on his side between the two beds.

I shot the dog a sympathetic look. *Yeah, buddy, I know how you feel.*

"Maureen, you have to be more careful."

"You worry too much." She pulled the ties of her bikini top behind her neck and tied them.

"Judas Priest and cherry Popsicles!" I hissed under my breath, flopping down on the bed.

She giggled at that and searched for something in her backpack. "I'll have to buy some sunscreen."

"There's some in my bag," I answered, staring at a water stain on the ceiling.

"I'm going to put my hair up and take off my makeup," Maureen said as she strode to the bathroom. "We should get one of those cheap foam coolers and buy some luncheon meat. The food at the water park is probably expensive."

Yawning, I answered around the hand I'd placed over my mouth, "We could get fries or something to hold us then have supper together somewhere."

"That sounds nice."

Rolling onto my side, I studied a television, a dark enameled dresser, shiny blue-and-white-striped wallpaper and an enormous and chintzy lithograph of The Glynn Marshes. My dad had brought me and Mom to Brunswick during our last vacation, and I remembered the marshes just north of the Sydney Lanier Memorial Bridge. The melancholy, desolate scenery, the white marsh birds, and miles of tall grass and brackish water had impressed me as a young girl. It was one of the most beautiful and melancholic places I'd ever been.

I sighed and rolled over.

"Ruby Nutter come to us."

How long would I continue to hear that voice? Would reaching Key West silence it, or would I have to buy a ticket of some sort and go farther?

"No, Ruby. Come to us instead! Why flee? You know you want to be with me."

Loud, bold and very strong, the new voice frightened the hell out of me. I struggled to rise but couldn't. Cold seeped into my body, darkness enveloped me, and my feet and legs were wet as if I stood in water. The sound of crashing waves surrounded me, and the aroma of brine and fish assaulted my nose.

"You belong to us, Ruby. You're a part of us. We need you. I need you."

Footsteps sloshed toward me, and terror clenched my heart. Where was Solomon and Maureen? Were they okay?

Something hot brushed my shoulder, and desire slashed my body, the heat of it piercing my core. My loins throbbed, and lust pooled in my lower belly.

"Go away," I whispered, remembering the biker at the truck stop and how his proximity had caused me to want him so badly.

"You don't really want me to do that. You want me, need me."

Something cupped my breast, and fire raged through my body. I wanted to lie down, spread my legs and let whoever he was join with my body, cock hard and relentless as he pumped into me. I wanted sex and I wanted a lot of it.

"Give yourself to me. Let me have you, love you and thrust into you until you scream in ecstasy."

The touch grew more insistent, and what felt like the pad of a thumb caressed my nipple. I sucked air through my teeth, the need for sex so strong I could barely maintain my sanity.

"Look at me, Ruby. Come to me. Let me have you, love you. The white one can't make you feel like I can."

How did this person know about Solomon? Who did the voice belong to? The dark gave way to a pre-dawn light. I picked out a shape before me, and a set of yellow eyes with serpentine pupils gazed back at me.

"I will have you," the being said. His eyes flashed a brilliant flame-yellow.

"Go away! Leave me alone!"

"Ruby?" Solomon said next to my ear. "Wake up."

Stirring, I finally roused, my gaze meeting his. Lust still pounded through my body, but my thrashing heart pushed adrenaline through my system, cleansing me of the delirium.

It had been a dream...hadn't it? For a moment, I lost myself in Solomon's mystical eyes. I wanted to throw myself into his arms and let him rock away my fear.

"What's wrong?" he asked, concerned. "You were murmuring in your sleep."

The A/C whirred under the window. Since the room's temperature felt so nice, and I'd had little sleep the night before, I must've dozed off.

At the dresser, Maureen hiked her short-shorts up over her bikini bottoms.

I shivered but not from the cool air. "Bad dream."

He frowned, and his tone told me he didn't believe me. "Is that all?"

How could I lie to him? Shrugging, I added, "I'm not really sure."

He cupped my cheek and brushed his thumb across my lower lip. Worry flitted through his eyes and settled over his features, features that no longer struck me as alien but handsome. His concern for me lightened my trouble heart. He really did seem to care for me. Somehow I knew him whether it made sense or not.

God help me, can I be falling for him?

The thought both frightened and saddened me. The enticing gaze of a man and heartache always walked hand in hand.

"Do you still feel like going to the water park?" Maureen asked.

"Yeah," I said as I rubbed sleep from my eyes. The vestiges of the chilling dream faded. "I think the heat just drained me. I'll be fine in a few."

Solomon left bowls of food and water in the bathroom for the dog. We grabbed our towels and my suntan lotion, locked our rooms and piled into the Excursion, heading out of the parking lot in search of Egmont Street. Several minutes later, I located the route and turned left. A couple more turns put us on South Ocean Highway. It wasn't long before we passed the marshes. I drove slowly, remembering when I was a little girl and how awesome I'd found the area with the pristine white, spindly-legged birds that kept vigil for fish.

Sadness struck me. *Mom would have liked Maureen and Solomon. Dad would have, too, if he hadn't changed into the nasty, bitter person he is now.* Sighing, I focused on the two-lane road in front of me.

The Jekyll Island sign passed by on our left. Live oaks, clothed in gray-green Chantilly gowns of Spanish moss, flanked both sides of a short, narrow bridge.

Taking a wrong turn, I maneuvered the SUV around the accessible areas, going the long way around the island to the park. Stopping the vehicle, I waited as a horse-drawn carriage full of tourists clattered by. Informative signs about repaving roads in crushed oyster shells, the paving product of choice over one hundred years ago, dotted the old-world landscape.

"What an incredible place," Solomon mused.

"It is beautiful," Maureen breathed, her eyes wide with wonder.

The trees with their long, mossy hair, the cool, shady atmosphere, the briny aroma of the ocean, and the lovely resort carried the perfume of history. Men such as Vanderbilt, J.P. Morgan and Rockefeller were responsible for the island's club-like atmosphere of the 1800s.

We rounded the other end of the island, and within minutes, a sign announcing Summer Waves appeared. After finding a parking spot, we grabbed our things and locked the SUV.

Solomon paid our way in. Once inside, I quickly changed in the women's locker area, and then we laid our blankets out on an unclaimed section of ground.

Under a rented umbrella, Solomon pulled a bottle from the pocket of his jams-style trunks and began slathering lotion across his torso under his t-shirt, which he left on. I noted the sunscreen was the highest SPF available.

"How about trying the water slides?" Solomon asked.

"Can you handle the sun?" I asked.

He held the bottle up for me to see. "I won't be in the sun long. That's why I rented an umbrella." He smiled. "So, are you coming?"

"You two go on," I said quickly.

"Oh, come on, Ruby," Maureen pleaded. "The water slides will be fun."

"Shooting along on my ass at speeds which are better left to things powered by engines is not on my list of fun things to do." I shrugged. "Besides, I need a pair of sunglasses in the worst way. I'm getting a headache from the glare off the water."

"Okay," she said, disappointed. "We'll meet you here later."

Earlier, I'd placed money in my bikini top, and since the sun had turned the sidewalk into a hotplate, I made my way over the grass to one of the tourist shops along the walk.

It didn't take me long to find a nice pair of shades, another bottle of sunscreen with higher SPF than I already had, and a couple of huge beach towels with the words "Summer Waves" on them. As I started to put my purchases on the counter, a rack of foam platform sandals drew my attention. Several pairs composed of brightly swirled colors took up the top shelf. The second level held pairs with geometric shapes cut out of the heels, and slip-on rubber straps that wrapped around the wearer's ankles adorned other sets.

A pair of hot ones with turquoise swirls and little hearts cut out of the foam screamed Maureen's name. I checked the size, added them to my purchases and picked up a pair for me too.

As I wandered toward the back of the little store, a display of summer dresses caught my attention. I spent a good fifteen minutes browsing through them.

Finished with shopping, I found Solomon under the umbrella. When he saw me, a dazzling smile touched his lips. My heart kicked into high gear. No one had ever made me feel that way, not even Cole. People who passed Solomon openly stared at him. However, I no longer saw someone strange and unnatural. Instead, I saw a man who possessed a honed body, a brilliant smile, glimmering flaxen hair, and eyes that cut straight through to my soul every time our gazes met.

On my way to sit with him, I dodged a small group of Hispanic children carrying sodas and large orders of French fries. A baby cried, protesting the fact her mother had taken her out of the wading pool, and the sound of waves began again when the machine for the man-made ocean kicked on. At that moment, I realized how much I was enjoying our day of relaxation.

"Do a bit of shopping?" he asked, humor in his voice.

"Yes." I sat next to him, scanning the park for Maureen's whereabouts.

"Maureen is dozing on her towel over there," he said, pointing.

She lay on her belly, her round bottom pointed toward the sun.

"She had a bit of misfortune at the black water tubes." Solomon nodded toward a tall structure with water chutes propelling the adventurous butt skidder nearly straight down in total darkness. "When Maureen hit the pool at the bottom, the impact ripped her top off."

Rolling my eyes, I groaned.

"I'm surprised you didn't hear the fuss," he said, laughing. "There were squeals of shock and catcalls for several minutes."

"What did Maureen do?"

"Laughed."

"That woman has no shame."

Solomon peeked into the plastic sack on my lap. "Hmm...towels, lotion, sunglasses." He withdrew the shades. "Summer dresses and shoes too." He removed the tag from the eyewear and handed them to me.

He met my gaze. Something clenched within me, something sweet and powerful. Flustered, I looked away.

"I want to apologize for last night," he said. He took my hand and squeezed it.

"It's okay." I squeezed his hand back, but still couldn't look at him.

"Are you going to wear some of your new stuff to dinner tonight?"

I shrugged, thankful he'd let the matter drop. "Sure."

"Good, I'll pick the restaurant."

Chapter Fifteen

Solomon made reservations at the Cargo Portside Grill in Brunswick.

After showers and watching a bit of TV, we fed Shunka then dressed for dinner. I kept my purchases hidden from Maureen. Once she went into the bathroom to shower, I pulled the bag out from under my bed and placed the pink dress and platform sandals on her bed where she'd see them. Minutes later, she emerged. She stood in her towel, another wrapped around her hair, and stared at the items with her mouth ajar.

"What are those?" she asked quietly.

"Clothes," I answered. It occurred to me I may have offended her with my gift, and a pang of worry stabbed my gut.

"For me?" She fixed her large green eyes on me, an almost liquid expression in them. "You bought me an outfit?"

"Yeah." I shrugged, occupying myself by taking items out of the shopping bag.

"I never had a friend buy me something before," she said so seriously it raised the hair on my nape. With trembling fingers, she traced the faint outline of a pale pink heart on the dress's hemline. "The dress and shoes are beautiful, Ruby."

"I thought maybe...well...I thought that..." Uncomfortable with the situation, I focused on taking the tags off my dress.

She grew suddenly quiet, and I sneaked a look at her only to wish I hadn't. She wore a silly, almost love-struck grin on her face.

"Thank you!" Something galvanized her into motion, and she hurried straight for me. Her boobs bounced like basketballs, and all I could think about was getting the hell out of the way before they smothered me. Quicker than I gave her credit for, Maureen reached me before I could take more than two steps backward and hugged me so hard I couldn't breathe. "And yes," she added, "the dress and sandals make up for my favorite pair of shoes and then some."

"Whatever." I untangled myself from her arms. I just wanted out of the room and away from the goofy look on her face.

She picked the dress up and hugged it to her, even sniffing the garment. "Thank you *so much*."

****

Promptly at seven p.m., Solomon parked his Excursion and helped Maureen and me out of it.

The Cargo Portside Grill stood on New Castle Street. The building's tan stucco, large wooden double doors and small awning with the emblem of a ship's prow added class to the historical location. Solomon took us by our elbows and ushered us across the street. Inside, the grill's atmosphere put me at ease. Diners relaxed, wearing everything from nice evening attire to golf shirts. I glanced down at my periwinkle blue dress sprinkled with dark blue orchids and wriggled my toes in my light blue wedge sandals. For once I felt attractive.

A host seated us at our reserved table. Solomon helped us sit and then ordered a bottle of red wine. For the first time in days, I felt comfortable. I studied the wide expanse of bricked wall covered with tinted photographs of historic ships that once frequented the waterways and coastal areas of Brunswick. An enormous painting of a steamship upon stark blue water with a burnt-orange-sky hung on the adjoining white wall. The hues looked incredible against the neutral expanse. The warm glow of the polished heart-pine tables and the matching bar completed the friendly, yet chic atmosphere.

Our orders didn't take long. Each of us enjoyed a wonderful seafood dish, the wine, and afterward, coffee and marbled cheesecake for dessert. Maureen didn't say much during our meal. She seemed lost in her own little world. I'd even managed to forget the visions, the bikers and the monsters for the most part. However, I noticed as the evening wore on that her cheeks glowed pinker than usual, and her stupendous cleavage had begun to match her facial color, both areas blending with her dress.

"Are you all right?" Solomon asked her.

She sipped from a glass of ice water. "I don't feel well."

"I bet you got too much sun today." I touched her left cheek with the back of my hand. "You sunbathed too long. You're skin is really hot."

"Now you know why I stayed under the umbrella most of the time, even after slathering on my sunscreen," Solomon admonished her gently as he wiped his mouth with a napkin. "Would you like to go back to your room and lie down?"

Maureen nodded. "If you two don't mind." She glanced at each of us. "I'll just let the A/C hit me and watch TV. You two go on to that after-dinner club like we planned. I wouldn't be much fun right now anyway."

"Are you sure?" It bothered me that she didn't feel well, and it didn't seem right to leave her alone.

"Yes," she said with conviction. "My skin is really starting to hurt and I feel queasy."

Solomon paid our bill, and I grabbed the bag holding our doggie boxes. On the return trip to the motel, he stopped at a drugstore and bought a huge bottle of aloe gel. We got Maureen back to the room, and he waited outside as I helped her shrug out of her dress and sprawl out on the cool sheets. After I smoothed the gel on her shoulders, arms, back and the backsides of her thighs, I turned on the television and handed her the remote.

"Are you going to be okay?" I asked. Sympathy for her assailed me. She looked like someone had spray-painted her in fuchsia.

She smiled wanly. "I'll be fine. I just got too much sun. Next time, I'll use sunscreen with a higher SPF like

Solomon told me to. I forgot to put it on again after swimming and then sunbathed too long, so it's my fault."

Shutting the door quietly, I turned to find Solomon leaning against the grill of the Excursion, his shades perched upon his head.

The sun sat low in the hazy sky behind him. The evening was still early, but it didn't feel right going too far from the motel room in case Maureen became really ill. I worried about sun poisoning, which could be dangerous.

He seemed to sense my reservations. "Do you feel uncomfortable leaving Maureen alone?"

"Her sunburn is getting worse. I'd rather be nearby in case she needs something—or if we need to take her to the nearest emergency room."

"You're a good friend." He walked around to the driver's side and hit the power button to roll up the windows then locked the doors.

Me? A good friend? I paused and pondered that for a couple seconds. Could I call my ditzy hitchhiker a friend?

"Well," I quipped in an attempt to hide my discomfort, "don't spread it around."

He grinned, and my heart flip-flopped in response. "I have a bottle of wine in my room," he said. "We can talk, play cards or watch television. Unless you'd rather call it a night."

With our erotic encounter the night before still fresh in my mind, I started toward his room.

I'm playing with fire. I should just turn around and go to my room. At the thought of being in his arms again, tingles rushed to my crotch, and I struggled to breathe properly. *So much for not getting involved.* I reminded myself that if we made love we would unlock something we couldn't control.

He used his keycard at the door. Inside, the TV still lit up the otherwise dark room. Maps from The Weather Channel flashed across its screen. He turned on a wall lamp above a small, battered writing desk and hooked his sunglasses on a corner of the television. The décor of his quarters had the same colors as my shared room except the artwork on the walls displayed old galleon ships on rough seas. Instead of a dark brown bedspread, a cover of cream with tiny anchor emblems in brown and black covered his bed. A small pile of dirty laundry lay against the long dresser shouldering the flat-screen television. His suitcase sat open on an easy chair riddled with cigarette burns and coffee stains. Clothing and various items spilled out of it.

He picked up a paper bag sitting on the nightstand. The sack rustled loudly as he pulled out a bottle of red Joseph Phelps Insignia. He also withdrew a deck of cards, a box of Ritz Crackers and a can of spray cheese.

I couldn't help but laugh at the combination.

"What?" He looked up, his pale eyes glowing in the dim lighting.

"Excellent wine, but crackers and spray cheese?"

"Hey, I'm a bachelor. What else did you expect?"

I giggled softly and shook my head.

"Somehow I feel I should be insulted," he joked.

"No, not at all. I'm used to being around my dad. He's been a widower for a long time now."

"Does your dad eat a lot of this sort of food?" he questioned as he set it on a small table by the window.

"Yeah, but I try to cook him a good meal at least a couple times a week."

"See? Men need someone to make them eat right."

I shrugged. "Most of the time he refuses to eat what I cook."

"How odd. What man would pass up a great meal?"

"You'd just have to know my father."

"Sam's a great cook, but his diet is almost as bad as mine. Fast food and packaged dinners are easier than a home-cooked meal." His deep laughter poured over me, inspiring a need in my loins that left me breathless.

Nodding, I pulled out one of the padded chairs and accepted a flimsy plastic motel cup he'd filled with wine. I clamped my thighs together to quell the need throbbing between them and peeled the Cellophane off the deck of playing cards.

"What sort of card games do you like to play?" I asked.

"Strip poker."

My gaze flew up to meet his.

He burst out laughing.

Heat crept out of the collar of my dress and flamed into my cheeks. I concentrated on shuffling the slick cards, but my hands shook so hard I kept dropping them.

Solomon pulled the string on a small lamp hanging over the table. I looked away quickly, hoping he wouldn't comment on the color of my face.

"How about gin rummy?" he suggested, sitting across from me.

"I haven't played it for a long time," I warned.

"We'll play to five hundred to start."

I shuffled the cards one more time and dealt a hand of seven for each of us.

An hour later, he'd beaten me by thirty-five points, and only a third of the Joseph Phelps Insignia remained. Pouring our cups full again, he tossed the empty bottle in the trash, handed my cup to me, and then relaxed in his chair. His hair shimmered silver under the lamplight, and his eyelashes shone luminously. My insides tightened, and all I wanted to do was undress and straddle him.

"Make yourself comfortable and turn the TV channel if you like," Solomon said, getting up. He bumped his head against the overhead lamp, sending it swaying. "I'm going to peek in on Maureen and make sure she's all right." He reached up and stopped the light's motion.

"No, you better let me." I rose. "Maureen stripped off her clothes and is sprawled on the bed."

He picked up the remote. "Leave my door open so you can come back in without the keycard."

Outside, the humid night air hit me as if someone had thrown a hot, wet blanket over my face. Grimacing, I used my keycard to go inside as the ice machine between our rooms clattered and clanked out another load of cubes. The door swung open, and the Malamute waited eagerly just inside the threshold.

Maureen dozed fitfully on the bed. Careful not to brush against her skin, I pulled the sheet up over her breasts, turned the volume down on the television and left the room. As an afterthought, I let the dog follow me outside. He trotted to a small area at the end of the parking lot where half a dozen palm trees loomed in the darkness. He watered one and then hurried to my side. I let him back into our room.

About to shut the door, I paused as Maureen shifted and rolled on her side facing me.

"He's here," she mumbled.

I stepped just inside the door to see her face better, but her eyes remained shut, her breathing even.

"Don't let him find you, Ruby," she muttered, her brow wrinkling with worry.

"Are you awake?" I asked.

She murmured something silly and settled back into fitful slumber.

Coldness seeped into the soles of my feet and traveled upward, icing my body as if an invisible sheen of frost covered it. The remnants of my disturbing afternoon dream came to me. My breath hitched, and, with a final cautionary look around the room, I backed out, leaving the dog there to guard my sun-poisoned Marilyn Monroe.

Out on the sidewalk, I scanned the parking lot. Humidity shrouded the streetlamps, a silver halo around each one. The palm trees drooped as did the tropical flowers and plants. The motel sat back away from the major hubbub of Brunswick behind a 24-lane bowling alley. A Waffle House's sign glowed yellow and white through the cloying atmosphere, and farther down the street a porn shop's shingle blinked red, purple and yellow.

Big puffs of fog billowed across the asphalt. Heat lightning flickered across the night sky, thunder boomed, and the ice machine punctuated the night with the clunk and rattle of its refrigeration cycle. Tires screeched somewhere on one of the neighboring streets, and the rumble of motorcycles drifted to me.

Both my heart and breath stuttered. Were the bikers closing in on us? All the disturbing occurrences of the past few days corkscrewed through my mind. Solomon had ties to the bikers through the murderous hunters, but Maureen was an innocent bystander. It wasn't fair to put her in danger, but how could I abandon her now?

And when the hell had my outlook on Maureen changed? I didn't owe her a thing. It was my kindness that had allowed her to hitch a ride with me, so I could just give her a chunk of money and go my separate way before something terrible happened to her.

But what about Solomon?

Dumbass! I can't fall for the guy.

I had to draw back, had to put distance between us and make it clear there would be no sex between us, no more getting to know one another, no more. I gulped, my heart hurting so badly it stole my breath..

The sound of the suicide machines faded, and I relaxed.

Calm down. Not every motorcycle is demonic.

The sound of footsteps spanned the parking lot, the noise hollow in the mist. I glanced around for the source, but no motel patrons moved through the humid night, no one went in and out of the lot, and not a single vehicle drove along the narrow side street either. A figure emerged from the rolling fog. A very large figure. One that headed straight for me.

Off to the left, movement caught my attention. Another man, this one smaller, walked half stooped along the building's side, as if he feared being seen.

Unable to move, my heart slamming so hard I saw spots before my eyes, I stood watching the second man come closer...closer.

He stood over seven feet tall. The fog obscured his clothing, but his eyes flashed yellow in the silvery murk. Fear exploded in my chest, and a pathetic whimper tumbled from my mouth.

Desire pierced me.

"Come to me, Ruby. Let me love you. Let us be together forever."

Somehow I found myself wedged between the ice machine and the door to Solomon's room. A thin column of golden light sliced through the opening where he'd left it ajar for me, but I couldn't seem to make my feet go that direction.

Vaguely, I sensed the smaller guy almost upon me, but I wanted nothing more than to walk out into the parking lot, lie down on the asphalt, and let the big fellow take me body and soul. Lust raged through my core, settled in my loins. Moisture dampened my panties, and tingling assailed my crotch.

I wanted him. I wanted sex. I wanted...

"Yes! You do want me, don't you? Come to me, Ruby..."

"No!" The word burst from my lips, startling me.

"Got you!" a voice hissed, followed by hands fastening on my upper arms.

I looked up into Wayne Blacktree's triumphant face.

"Finally! I'll get my reward," he said. Anticipation and zeal glowed in his eyes.

Fear smothered me, and a fiery sensation swept into my arms, down into my hands, my palms so hot I hissed at the pain. The area around me lit up as my skin glowed. Wayne gasped but didn't let go. Long tendrils of my hair hung around my face, each one infused with radiant orange.

The door opened wider, and the artificial light bathed me in its comfort.

"Ruby?" Solomon's voice drifted out. "What the hell?" He rushed out, hitting Wayne with his body like a human battering ram. "Let go of her!"

Although surprised, Wayne didn't loosen his grip. "Stay out of this, freak," he snapped and tugged me toward the parking lot.

"You are mine!" the voice in my mind shouted. *"The White King is not to touch you!"*

I screamed, struggling against Wayne. "Let go of me!"

The power surged through my body and exited my ember-tipped fingers. This time white sparks flew from my hands, hitting Wayne across the throat and collar bones. He hissed and let go, stumbling back a couple of steps but he shook off my power and grabbed me again.

Solomon threw a punch. How he missed me and connected with Wayne's jaw, I don't know, but the resulting crack urged my belly to flip. Wayne cried out, released me and toppled ass over teacup on the sidewalk.

"Fool!" the approaching big man shouted. "You the White King get the best of you!"

Holding my hands out in front of me, I allowed the diamond-like fire to surge from my palms. It illuminated the night and dressed the fog with glittery periwinkle hues. The finger-fire hit the hulking man, but instead of a cry of pain, a scream of fury sliced the air instead. A security light blew up, and white sparks rained down on the pavement. Ozone permeated my nose, seared my sinuses.

Wayne scrambled to his feet, and, clutching his jaw, ran off the way he'd come, his footfalls echoing dully in the heavy mist.

Strong arms encompassed me, my surroundings brightened and a door slammed.

I blinked up at Solomon, my senses returning.

Chapter Sixteen

"Are you all right?"

Mouth ajar, shock and awe on his face, Solomon looked down at me. He let go, and, lunging for the door, engaged the lock and slipped the chain on.

"I'm fine, it was just—"

The thud against the door frightened me so badly I stumbled and fell to my knees. Solomon slipped his arms around my body and pulled me to my feet again.

"What the hell's going on, Ruby?" he said next to my ear.

"I'm not sure."

"Give her to me!" a deep, furious voice shouted through the door. "She is mine!"

"You won't touch her," Solomon shouted back. "I'll kill you first."

Silence.

I gaped at Solomon. Myriad of emotions twirled and danced through me. He'd kill the guy for me? Did he care about me that much?

Visible tremors passed through his body. Was it from fury or fear?

He jerked his thumb toward the door, his expression shifting into something I couldn't identify. "Do you know the big guy?"

"No, not really."

"I think we should call the police, especially since this is the second time we've had trouble with Wayne Blacktree."

"It won't do any good," I said. The shudders in my body turned into a full-fledge earthquake. "Remember the hunters?"

He tightened his arms around me but turned an ashen color at my reminder, his face stoic despite the uncertainty in his eyes.

"If you open this door," the voice on the other side growled, "I won't hurt the White King. I will leave him in peace, but only if you go with me, Ruby."

Sweat coated my body. My senses spun. I gulped and said as calmly as I could, "Your promises are worthless. You're full of deceit."

Did I just say that? Why did that sound like me and yet not, and why do I feel like I've said it before?

Solomon released me and placed both hands against the door. "What are you talking about?" he asked over his shoulder.

"I'm not sure."

"Ruby," the voice said in a verbal caress. "Come to me. You know you want to."

Lust ravaged my body. Oh, how I wanted to throw open that door and let the big man have me. But I couldn't. I knew the feelings weren't real and that I'd be lost forever if I succumbed to them. How I possessed such knowledge didn't matter, but I had to do something to protect us.

"Get out of the way, Solomon," I said.

"No, you're not going out there."

"I don't plan to. I'm going to do something else."

He backed away from the door, pausing to caress my cheek before moving to the window where he peeked through the part in the curtains.

"Damn, that guy's huge," he whispered, amazement in his voice. "I've never seen anyone that big before."

"Don't touch the window," I told him.

"Ruby!" the man shouted.

Thumping assaulted the door, and I jumped at the barrage. The outline of hands appeared in the metal as if it was putty.

I had to do something and fast. If he could melt glass he could probably do something similar to metal too.

"What the hell?" Solomon said, his tone incredulous, eyes huge as he stared at the clay-like surface. He moved toward me, intending to pull me away from the door, but I shook my head sternly and motioned for him to stay put.

"I *will* have you," the voice said. "This time you'll be mine."

"You asked for it," I muttered and allowed the electrical current I despised so much to overcome me. With my hands pointed at the door, the power raced through my body and exited my palms. I didn't know how I knew to blast the place where the man's prints appeared, but the following howl of pain from him soothed my fear. White sparkles skittered over the door.

The unexpected sense of how to use my power shocked me. Closing my eyes, I imagined the current exiting my body, and then covered Solomon's room in a protection bubble as well as the one I shared with Maureen. I blanketed the SUV for good measure. We'd be safe for now.

"I'll find you, Ruby Nutter. You can't avoid me for long."

Something hit the door, the sound deafening. Shunka Wakan's barks breached the wall separating our rooms. The door glowed red around the edges, and more ozone pervaded the air.

The dog barked one more time.

Silence.

"Is he gone?" I asked.

Solomon peeped through the curtains. "I don't see anyone. After all that noise, it probably won't be long before the motel manager tells us to leave too." He let the curtain fall and looked over at me. "You know more about this strange stuff than you've been letting on."

"I didn't want to scare anyone unnecessarily, and I didn't want you to think...to think..." I gritted my teeth and ordered the tears not to fall.

"To think you're a freak?" he supplied. "To treat you like shit because you're different, or that you're not what people consider normal?"

"No," I lied, "it's just that—" The sob ripped free of me before I could squelch it.

Solomon crossed the room and folded me in his arms, holding me so close I heard his heartbeat. Now was the time he was supposed to go crazy with fear, yell obscenities, call me names, and then leave so fast his shoes would catch on fire.

"Why?" he said.

Sobs still spilled from my mouth, but I managed to squeak, "Why what?"

He leaned back and peered deeply into my eyes. "Don't do that."

"Do what?"

"That."

I pushed against his chest, but he held me still.

"Why do you clam up or run away whenever someone asks you something personal?"

I sniffed and tried to avoid his penetrating gaze. "Maybe because it's none of your business?"

"Look, I'm not asking you to tell me all the deep dark secrets you might have." He let me go and crossed his arms over his chest. "The fact that something unnatural is going on aside, I'd like to know a little more about the women I'm traveling with, that's all."

He had me there. Hadn't I gone through the same thing with Maureen last night?

"For starters," he said, "I'd like to know more about the incredible things you do."

"I honestly don't know how I do them." I risked looking at him and wished I hadn't. The expression on that man's face said he was determined to find out more. "Can we discuss this another time?" I turned away, needing some space. Most of all I needed time to process the fact he wasn't already packing his bags. "I promise I'll answer a couple of your questions if we can do it some other time."

"Fair enough." He sighed. "So you really think that guy is tied to the hunters who murdered Gabriella?"

"Yes."

"Come to think of it, the men who attacked my sister and me were really big too. I can't remember many details about them now other than their yellow eyes and the smell of booze."

"Solomon, you're in danger if you travel with me. You should go home."

"No. I refuse to leave you, Ruby. You might be able to ignore the chemistry and feelings between us, but I can't."

That was the last thing I'd expected out of him. For a moment I said nothing. I couldn't let Solomon know how much I cared for him, how much I wanted him. If I did, there was no doubt it would all come crashing down. At least for now he was still with me.

Pressing onward, I changed the subject. "I should ditch Maureen, but I just can't bring myself to do it. She's...there's...ah, hell. I can't even explain it." Irritated, I sat at the table and stared at the wood veneer.

"She's your friend," he said.

Nothing like hitting the nail on the head.

"I better go check on her," I stood and looked out the window, "and make sure Shunka isn't chewing a hole through the door."

"You're not going out there alone," he said behind me. His hand settled on my shoulder. "I'm coming too." Solomon gently pushed me aside and unlocked the door. Slowly, he opened it, peered out and nodded. "It's okay."

"Stay close to the building. I don't know how far the protection bubble I created extends, but we should be safe for the night. Somehow I get the feeling they're less apt to try anything in broad daylight."

"How do you know this?"

"I honestly don't know," I replied, "but I know it's true."

We kept close to the building, skirted the ice machine and let ourselves in to check on Maureen.

The dog sniffed at the threshold but didn't go any farther, as if he sensed the invisible barrier there and was satisfied with its presence.

Maureen stepped out of the bathroom, pulling a light robe around her sunburned body.

"How do you feel?" I asked.

"Terrible, but it'll pass." She sat on the edge of the bed and winced. "Shunka woke me. Anything wrong?"

"No, just thought we'd check on you."

"You're lying again."

I blinked, and Solomon chuckled.

"I feel too bad to even care right now." She sighed wearily. "So I'm going to lie down and watch TV."

"We'll be next door if you need anything," Solomon said and pulled me out onto the walk. He shut the door, propelling me back to his room. After he engaged both locks, he asked, "Want more wine? I have another bottle of Joseph Philips."

"Sounds great. My nerves could do with a sedative."

He withdrew the wine from a paper bag and opened it.

"It must be nice to enjoy the finer things of life when you want to. What did you do before you struck it rich?"

A gentle smile turned up the corners of his mouth as he worked the bottle. "I was a welder. I repaired coalmine equipment and came home on the weekends." He refilled our cups. "Where are you from?"

"Columbus, Ohio."

"What do you do for a living?"

"I'm the dayshift supervisor at a sewing factory."

"Really?" He tipped his head to one side, studying me. "That sounds interesting."

"Actually, it's a boring job, but the pay is decent. My mom died when I was a teenager, so when I finally graduated, I went to work to help my dad with bills instead of going to college. I'm the only close family Dad has. He just gave up on life and stopped doing anything after she died."

I sat on the bed, feeling a bit more secure since Solomon had turned the discussion to general life matters. It helped to talk about something mundane instead of worrying about the paranormal that might start banging on the door at any moment.

Solomon pelted me with another question and sat next to me. "Ever been married?"

"No."

"No?"

I frowned. "Is that so hard to believe?"

"You're a very attractive woman, but you're really bitter about life, so I figured you must have come out of a nasty divorce."

The fact I might have portrayed myself as a bitter divorcee had never occurred to me. "I've just had a hard life."

"Lots of people have tough lives."

"True."

"So why are you so bitter?" he asked.

"Because I want to be!" I snapped. Not the questions were veering into dangerous territory. No one ever asked me questions about my life, especially after they'd witnessed my supernatural abilities.

"Come on, Ruby, that's not fair."

"Why not?" Anxious to be away from him and his questions, I stood up.

The irritation in his eyes surprised me, and I felt bad for being such a bitch.

"You learned more about me in an hour sitting on my porch than I've learned about you in the past three days. Don't you think we should get to know one another beyond just being acquaintances?" He jumped to his feet and invaded my personal space. "You hold everyone at arm's length. You constantly hurt Maureen's feelings, but regardless, I can tell she truly admires you."

"I don't want her admiration."

"Why? Because you don't feel you deserve someone's friendship or their loyalty?"

Oh, boy. He was hitting too close to home. I clenched my fists. The last thing I needed to do was let him upset me so that I zapped him.

"Loyalty is a myth. Admiration is for super stars." I whirled, stomping over to the door. "And your questions and observations are full of shit!"

I pulled the door open just as his hand hit it, slamming it shut. Solomon spun me around by my shoulders and glowered down at me. It wasn't exactly anger in his eyes but more of the determination I'd seen earlier. I felt for the door, backing up until my rear touched it.

"If anyone is full of shit, it's you," he said. "You spout off one flippant remark after another. No one here is against you, Ruby. Maureen surely isn't. She wants nothing more from you than your friendship. She's a free spirit, a woman who has no desires except to see what's over the next horizon."

"What about you?" I whispered so softly that at first I didn't think he'd heard me. My heart flailed against my ribs, and blood thundered in my ears. "You've seen what I can do and you're still here. What do you want from me?"

A series of emotions flickered through his eyes. Male emotions had always baffled me, and most of the time I believed men only possessed base feelings such as hunger, lust, jealousy, anger and competitiveness. The expression in Solomon's eyes didn't fit any of those. His face turned stoic, and his mouth flattened into a thin line.

"Well?" I prompted.

"I'm not sure."

"You're not sure?" Anger welled up inside me. "So, that must mean you're after *something*."

"No, it doesn't." He let out a big breath.

"Then what?" Deep inside, I'd begun to quiver as if I'd caught a chill. At that moment, I knew what I truly wanted from him and was ashamed of myself for being so weak. Solomon's body scent mixed with the aroma of wine and a musky aftershave wafted over me. My heightened senses even detected the breezy odor of fabric softener in his shirt. However, I had to be strong. If I succumbed to my desires, it would set something into motion that I wasn't sure I could handle.

Solomon strode away, leaving me feeling abandoned. "You would never understand what I want."

"Why?" I asked.

"You can't see beyond the end of your nose," he said gruffly. He stared at the floor like a forlorn little boy then turned, looking at me. "You're incapable of understanding."

"Now you sound like a woman," I quipped.

"No, I sound like you," he threw back.

"You son of a—"

He stormed toward me. I couldn't get my feet to shift into reverse fast enough. He jerked me into his arms, his mouth claiming mine with such passion my senses reeled.

Pushing him back, I gasped, "Don't!"

"Don't kiss you?" he breathed into my ear, sending gooseflesh over my shoulders and down my back. "I guess you're incapable of passion too?"

"Shut up!" I shoved against his chest again.

"How about I shut you up?" Solomon retorted, his lips against my neck, his hands sliding over my ass.

He kissed me again, his mouth firm but soft, questing, tasting, leaving me breathless and—God help me— wanting more. The sensation of his hands on my body turned everything inside me into steamy liquid, as if mercury had replaced my bones. Dimly, I heard the television playing and the shriek of a car horn outside, but the sound of Solomon's excited breathing captivated my ears. He wanted me. He desired long-limbed, smart-mouthed Ruby who could wield freaky powers.

"Let me make love to you," he murmured, his face buried in the scooped neck of my dress.

"We shouldn't," I gasped.

Solomon's tongue slid over the swell of one breast. "Please, Ruby...I can't stay away from you."

"Heaven help me," I replied, quivering from head to toe. "We'll regret this."

"No we won't," he said into my ear. "We're meant to be together. I don't know how I know it, but we are."

"That's what scares me," I whispered.

He tore at my clothes, and I yanked his shirt up over his head. Our garments flew helter-skelter, and within moments, he drew my naked body against his, and all rationale exited my head. With my breasts pressed against his firm, hot chest, my nipples hardened into painful peaks. He kissed my neck, his tongue swirling over the sensitive skin there, his hands roaming my waist, the small of my back, and over the curve of my ass.

An irresistible itch began in my loins, and the spring deep within my center started coiling tighter and tighter. What this man did to me! All I wanted was to join our bodies, strain against one another, and once we finished, start all over again.

He sucked my left earlobe into his mouth, flicked it with his tongue, his breath stirring the hair around my ear. He backed me toward the dresser, his manhood pushing eagerly against my lower belly. Once my rear connected with the furniture, Solomon hefted me onto its top. He bent his knees and slipped his cock along the folds of my crotch without penetrating me.

"Please," I said.

"Please what?" He nuzzled my neck again and trailed kisses down to my collarbone, his breath as hot as my fevered skin.

"You know what," I gasped.

"I want to hear it."

"Make love to me."

At my words, he pushed into my body. His member stretched my core as he continued to shove deeper into me. With my eyes shut, I reveled in the feeling of him inside my body. He stretched me so that it burned but it also felt invigorating. He filled a void and inspired more of the insane need to have him touch me, to fill me up more, tighter. Whimpering, I waited for my body to adjust to his size, and then wrapped my legs around his waist.

When I opened my eyes, Solomon was gone. Instead, I saw his older crowned version, his eyes rolling back as he rode me. Blinking my vision away, I concentrated on Solomon. He slipped his arms around me and held me close. My breasts made contact with his bare chest, and he groaned, beginning a rhythm that prompted an intense, insatiable heat deep within my body.

The head of his cock bumped my womb gently. At that point, he'd pause and push in harder, burying himself in me up to his root then move back to thrust again. The sensations he created within my core spiraled outward on corkscrew fireworks of desire. The fire within my pussy flashed through my body, and the need to jump off that precipice of pleasure silenced everything else within me. I couldn't get enough of this man. Even the aroma of his cologne, his own personal scent, and the musky pheromones in the room inebriated me with desire. Solomon could screw me until the end of time, and I'd die a happy and very sated woman.

"Harder," I whispered.

He started thrusting more forcefully. I tightened my legs, pulling his hips snugly against the apex of my thighs, his rod going deeper still. He bent and suckled one of my breasts, his tongue searing the nipple. A spear of need skewered me and propelled me over the edge. Insane with need, I bucked and arched vigorously. Solomon grunted and met every one of my hip actions. The mirror over the dresser banged on the wall as he bounced me across the furniture's glossy top and up against the television set.

Whimpers, groans, and squeals tumbled from my lips. I slipped my hands around his waist and palmed his ass cheeks, digging my fingers into the flexing muscles. I wanted more, needed more, needed him deeper, harder, more forceful. The coil within me continued to wind, I arched my back higher, and my heels dug at the backs of his thighs, urging him onward.

"Ruby!" he breathed an instant before seizing my mouth. He kissed me ruthlessly, stole my breath, bruising my lips, and I relished every moment.

The television fell off the dresser, and although it frightened me at first, I didn't let up. I wanted Solomon to release his seed within me. I wanted to hear his shout of triumph as he filled me up. Still, he pummeled me, his sounds that of a ravenous animal. Suddenly, Solomon paused, and before I could cry out in disappointment, he pulled me into a sitting position and slipped his hands under my hips. He lifted me and strode to the door where he placed me firmly against it.

With my back and ass pressed to the door, and Solomon bent slightly so he could fully penetrate me, I let out a scream of pleasure as his cock pushed into its limit. He thrust harder and faster, over and over. The coil shattered, and sensations crashed through me on one tidal wave after another. I could only hold on to him, his hips pistoning, his breath heavy and fast.

Finally, he stiffened, and an almost anguished groan fled his lips. His cock pulsed, and liquid heat bathed my insides.

"Yes!" he yelled and pumped faster.

Totally sated, I clasped him to me so tightly my arms ached.

Solomon coaxed the last few drops of his essence into my body then turned with me in his arms and carried me to the bed. He slid out of me and spooned my body.

With Solomon cradling me, I lay panting and enjoyed our afterglow.

What am I going to do when he decides to leave me?

He tightened his arms around me and kissed my nape.

I still couldn't shake the sensation that there was something bigger going on than both of us realized.

What have we set in motion by making love?

Chapter Seventeen

Bright light seared my eyelids. I floated to the top of consciousness.

"Hey, get up!" Maureen cooed in my ear. "It's a beautiful day. The humidity is down, the sky is blue, and I have breakfast."

Grudgingly, I opened my eyes. Reality washed over me, and I scrambled to pull the sheet up to my chin.

She laughed and stepped over to the table where about an inch of red liquid remained in the wine bottle. An open box of doughnuts sat next to it with the name of a grocery store splashed in green across its cardboard side. Three large coffees kept the doughnuts company.

My stomach grumbled. Sitting up, I clasped the sheet tightly and looked around for my dress.

"I packed your dress and laid out a pair of shorts and a halter top from out of your bag," Maureen said. She selected a long doughnut covered with white powder and oozing purple gel out one end. "Your clothes are in the bathroom along with your toiletries and your new sandals. I figured you'd want a shower before we check out this morning."

"You seem to feel better," I said, standing with the sheet wrapped around me.

"My skin is sore, but I don't feel sick anymore," she said. "As much sex as the two of you had last night, I'm surprised you can walk!" She laughed like a teenage girl who had just overheard a dirty secret. "You two woke me up at three this morning. Solomon must have the stamina of an elephant!"

"Maureen!"

"What?" she turned, looking at me with innocent green eyes. Jelly clung to the sides of her mouth.

Mortified, I moved toward the bathroom and tripped over the damn Malamute. Between the sheet twisted around my feet and the dog scrambling out of the way, I don't know how I kept from sprawling out on the floor. I stumbled through the bathroom door, slamming it behind me. Maureen's laughter taunted me from the other side.

"Solomon took the SUV over to the gas station to fill it up," she called through the door. "If you make it a quick shower, you can enjoy your breakfast without rushing."

"Okay," I mumbled and turned on the spigot.

As the water cascaded over me, I discovered my crotch and breasts were tender. Memories of Solomon's kisses and caresses filled my mind, and a hot blush covered me despite the tepid water.

The vision of the older, crowned Solomon surfaced. What did it mean? I knew the man wasn't Solomon, but he was too.

It didn't take long to wash my hair and shave my underarms and legs. I quickly toweled off and dressed, grimacing at the discomfort between my legs, but it was a good soreness. I stood looking in the mirror and contemplated my freshly washed face and combed hair. A look of fulfillment inhabited my eyes, one I'd never seen before.

A fast application of facial moisturizer and skin powder gave me a completed look, but I finished it with a light dusting of blusher on my cheeks and eyelids then applied mascara. Lastly, I put my hair up in an unfinished ponytail for a poofy bun look.

When I stepped out of the bathroom carrying all my toiletries, Maureen struggled with putting the television back where it belonged. Heat flooded my face as I remembered Solomon and me falling recklessly upon the dresser, his hips thrusting against mine. Luckily, a chain attached to the back of the TV set had kept it from hitting the floor.

Evidence of our later sessions of wild lovemaking littered the room. The bedspread and pillows lay on the floor. The lamp rested on its side on the nightstand, its shade askew. The chair holding Solomon's suitcase lay on its side, spilling the case's contents across the carpet. My gaze came to rest on the motel room door. A forensics unit would have a field day analyzing the imprint of my ass on its shiny paint and the vague outline of the biker's handprints melted into it.

Maureen glanced at me as she stooped to pick up the chair and suitcase. She grinned from ear to ear.

"I knew there was sexual tension between you two, but I had no idea how much!" She laughed.

"What are you talking about?" I asked, horrified she would say such a thing.

"And you think that "I'm" a bad girl!" She stuffed a shirt and a pair of trousers into the suitcase and zipped it shut. "I sure wish I could find someone who would make me holler like you did."

"All right!" I shouted louder than I intended. "That's enough! I get the point!"

Her lower lip popped out, and a childlike look entered her eyes. "Jeez, Ruby, you don't have to be so touchy about it."

"Well, it's not something I normally do, nor do I want to talk about it." Stomping over to my duffle bag on the floor, I dumped the toiletries into it and zipped it shut. "I'm just as surprised, if not more, than you are, okay?"

She straightened, placing her hands on her hips, her weight on her left leg, hip jutting. "I think you dig him more than you want to admit."

"No, because I made a promise to myself that I wouldn't allow another man to hurt me." The words popped out of my mouth so fast I couldn't believe I'd said them.

"Who hurt you?"

"Just a guy."

"Were you married?"

"No, I was very young, and I don't want to talk about it."

She sighed, and to my surprise, let the issue drop, but her next words startled me. "It's nice to finally find a man who makes you feel like a real woman, isn't it?"

Speechless, I could only stare at her. Maureen was right. For the first time, I felt like a woman both physically and emotionally.

I wondered, deep down, were we all simple animals? Was it possible a good roll in the sack—on the floor, the dresser, and against the door—could change a woman's perspective? Was I so deprived or perhaps even that shallow? Or had Solomon merely filled a primordial need that I hadn't realized was lacking?

Or, as strange as it might seem, had we reconnected after years of being apart? We were familiar to one another, so what other answer could there be?

"You like Solomon," Maureen stated.

"Sure, I do."

"No, I mean you like Solomon a lot." She watched me in a way that told me there was more to Maureen than she let on. "You're falling for him."

"Shut up."

"See?"

"Maureen, I just met the guy three days ago."

"So?"

"So, you have no idea what you're talking about, and you're getting on my nerves," I snapped.

"Have it your way," she said sweetly, which made me want to slap her silly.

****

Later, we sped along I-95 again, but this time, Solomon drove. Maureen opted to sit in the back with the slobbering canine while I rode shotgun. The earlier conversation with Maureen haunted me. Occasionally, Solomon would throw a curious glance my way, but he never reached for me as a new lover would, and I was grateful. I needed time and a little space.

No one said much of anything over the next few hours. Solomon found a radio station playing a nice mixture of music from oldies to contemporary tunes. The dog snored in the backseat, his head on Maureen's lap. Once in a while, Solomon would sing along with something.

We passed the Florida State line sign. The terrain still looked like Georgia's, but within a few miles, the landscape would grow steadily more tropical. As the road followed the eastern edge of the state, the air quality would change, too, becoming briny instead of the putrid stench of the paper mills.

Over the next few minutes, we passed the exits for Fernandina Beach and then the Timucuan Ecological and Historic Preserve, followed by the packed-and-jumbled atmosphere of Jacksonville. Traffic finally cleared enough we could again travel with speed, leaving the city behind us.

Solomon asked, "What's our next stop?"

"St. Augustine," I answered, realizing just how far away I'd been during the last few miles.

"Really?" He turned the music down. "I was there once years ago. My mother used to have a friend who lived close to St. Augustine's historical section."

The quiet of the backseat prompted me to twist around and look at Maureen. She sat with her head tipped back, forehead resting against the doorframe, eyes shut, mouth slightly ajar. The Malamute mimicked her.

"She's been out for the last hour," Solomon said.

"I'm getting hungry." I reached for an open bag of Doritos at my feet. Its gaping top had enticed me too long, and I withdrew a wad of ranch-seasoned chips. "How about supper as soon as we secure a room?"

"Fine with me," he answered. "Our exit is coming up right now."

His words inspired intense anxiety in the pit of my belly. The real reason I'd wanted to stop in St. Augustine hit me, and now I wasn't so sure I could deal with it. The anxiety dispelled my hunger. Nausea set up residence, and I realized if I didn't get a grip on myself fast, I'd be hanging my head out the window, painting someone's windshield with old coffee and confetti Doritos as we passed by.

"What's wrong?" Solomon questioned.

I glanced at him sharply. "Why do you ask?"

"I sense waves of tension coming off you." He slowed for the exit ramp, following a dump truck loaded with junk. "Didn't you say St. Augustine is where you need to take care of something?"

"Yes, and that's all I want to say about it."

"Okay." He braked, waiting for the truck to make a right turn. He checked traffic before turning left. "I'm not going to pry."

"Good."

"You didn't seem to have trouble sharing some things with me last night." He glanced at me with a devilish smile, his tone seductive, suggestive.

The hiss that passed my lips forced his smile to grow wider and prompted a giggle from the backseat.

"You're supposed to be asleep!" I snarled over my shoulder.

"I am," Maureen quipped, nudging my elbow with the toe of one foot. "See? My eyes are still shut."

Solomon's laughter drifted out the driver's window. The car next to us had its windows down, too, and the occupants stared at him as if laughter were a heinous crime.

At that moment, I had to agree with them.

****

The sun bore down on the Excursion as we cruised through the beautiful city of St. Augustine. On our left, a Ripley's Believe-It-Or-Not Museum sat back from the street like a miniature medieval castle. Live oaks dotted the landscape, their branches dripping Spanish moss dreadlocks. Regal palm trees surrounded the fortress-style building, their fronds waving in a stiff ocean breeze. Off to the side of the unusual attraction sat a sequoia log converted into a house trailer.

"Where should we stay?" Solomon asked. "We're here during tourist season. Everything will be booked solid."

When I'd dashed out of my apartment a few days ago, I'd never considered I'd be traveling during the peak of tourism. I groaned. "Let's stop for gasoline, and I'll check the phone book. Maybe someone can recommend an out-of-the-way place."

"Sounds like a plan," he answered, "but I can access the info we need from my cell."

He pulled into a gas station and looked up motels and inns on his iPhone. He placed a few calls, the last one to a bed-and-breakfast. The proprietors had just forced some people to leave for being disruptive and we could rent the rooms, providing we allowed them an hour to clean up the quarters. To pass the time, we drove around St. Augustine taking in the sights.

"Can you tell us who you're meeting here?" Maureen asked behind me.

"No," I answered. "If I recall, we've already had this discussion."

"You're so secretive, Ruby," she persisted. "This person must be someone important."

"Maybe."

"Why all the secrecy anyway?" Solomon questioned, breaking for a horse-drawn carriage full of tourists.

"It's no one's business except mine." I understood their curiosity because I was curious about whom Maureen was meeting in Florida City, but there was no way I was going to tell them anything about my son.

Solomon cast a jealous look my way. He thought I was meeting a romantic interest. Not able to contain myself, I shot him a sly smile and deliberately turned my attention to the entrance of the Ponce de Leon Park.

"You're not in any trouble, are you?" Maureen asked. "Because if you are, I think we have a right to know since we're traveling together."

"You already know about the bikers. I just need to warn someone important to me that he might be in danger," I replied irritably. "Are you going to tell us about your stop in Florida City?"

"No."

"Then we're even," I said.

A heavy sigh escaped Solomon, and he shot me disturbed look.

Guilt nudged me. He thought I was seeing another man. I was, just not the type of man he was thinking.

Solomon handed me his cell, and I punched the B and B address into the dashboard's GPS. He followed the system's directions, and within minutes, we pulled up in front of the establishment. The place didn't allow animals in the rooms, but they did have a kennel out back for pets. Solomon fed and watered Shunka then helped us unload our bags.

The Tropical Flower Bed-and-Breakfast possessed old-world charm. Every paint chip on the outside of the building and each stick of furniture and decoration on the inside looked as if it had been magically transported straight out of the mid 1800s. A woman in her early twenties signed us in and escorted us through the inn, but as we passed through the lavish sitting room, three women dressed in dark, flowing dresses and wearing gothic makeup, caught my attention.

The women reclined in the center of the room, their garments stark against the pale furniture. They watched me until I started up the stairs.

"Not to be rude," I said to the young woman ahead of us and lowered my voice more, "who are those women back there?"

She smiled over her shoulder and held up one finger. Once we reached the top and started down a long hall, she replied, "They're part of a coven in town for a convention on alternative healing and the powers of crystals. A convention is held here once a year for things mystical and magical."

"How cool," Maureen said, but as she followed us into our room, she let out a delighted squeal. "Oh, Ruby. Isn't this gorgeous?"

"Yeah," I raised an eyebrow, "gorgeous."

Maureen and I shared a room with two single beds, and Solomon had one across the hall. I grimaced, feeling as if I'd just walked into a honeymoon suite. Done in pink and red, the room was the epitome of a flower garden. The rose-printed bedspreads, a deep pink carpet, and twining rose wallpaper all made me feel like I stood in a garden designed by a flower zealot. Fresh white and pink roses stood proudly in a lead crystal vase upon a breakfast table in one corner. Pink sheers billowed in a breeze soughing in from a small balcony. Through the open French doors, a nice view of the river presented itself, and the salty aroma of the nearby ocean perfumed the room.

"Breakfast is from seven until nine, but if you'd rather have it in your room," the woman pointed at the little glass-top table, "then it's an extra ten dollars per day for the   room   service."
The young woman indicated the bathroom off to the left. "The bath is through that door." She turned toward the hall where Solomon waited. "There's a wonderful lounge just down the street that serves great meals. Enjoy your stay." She shut the door.

"Isn't this room lovely!" Maureen stepped out onto the balcony.

"Yeah, lovely," I muttered, wrinkling my nose at the room's frilliness. How any man could stay in this room was beyond me.

"I'm going to take a bath," my hitchhiker announced and ambled into the bathroom. "There's a claw-foot tub in here and all sorts of bubble baths and oils to choose from!"

"Go soak until you turn into a prune," I said, suddenly feeling drained. "I think I'm going to lie down for a while."

"You feeling okay?" Maureen stuck her head through the doorway, her face a mask of concern that I found rather endearing, much to my dismay.

"I'm fine." I hoped I'd kept the anxiety out of my voice.

I chose the bed closest to the balcony and sprawled out on top of the cover, watching as Maureen gathered toiletries and her robe. She disappeared into the bathroom and left the door ajar. The sound of splashing water drifted out, and the aroma of something rosy wafted across the room.

I closed my eyes and hoped there was more to choose from than just rose-scented oils. My thoughts wandered to the reason I'd stopped in St. Augustine.

Fear clenched my heart. Would I regret my decision to see Anthony?

Chapter Eighteen

Believing Cole loved me, I gave in to him. The quick, brief pain took me by surprise, but not as much as the door bursting open had. Juniors and seniors filed in, their bawdy laughter loud, their expressions vicious, arrogant, and even a few embarrassed ones. Cole held me down, his vivid blue eyes steely, smug. I pushed against him, but he wouldn't budge.

"Teach her not to mess with any of us," someone shouted.

"Yeah, Cole. Show the little bitch-witch who's boss," a girl said snidely.

Jibes and foul words of encouragement punctuated the bedroom like a hundred squawking and screeching birds.

I began to sob and quickly realized my upset gave them pleasure, but most of all it excited Cole. Even as the light burst from my skin and my hair and nails glowed brightly, the kids jeered louder and Cole thrust harder and faster. His aroma, one of sweat from the football game and too much liquor, invaded my nose and clung to my skin. No matter how much I sobbed and pleaded, Cole wouldn't listen.

Finally, something warm coated my insides, and I knew I was doomed...

My eyes fluttered open, and for a frightening moment, I didn't know where I was. The throes of the dream faded, and I swallowed hard, my throat dry.

A small table lamp glowed next to the opposite bed, and an electric candle burned behind the sheers in the large window. As I gazed at the gaudy rose wallpaper, everything came back to me. I glanced over at the balcony, wishing I could rid myself of Cole's memory, what he'd done to me, and its result that had tainted my entire life.

I pushed the disturbing memories and the residue of my dream away and used the facilities. Finished, I discovered a note from Maureen on the dresser. She and Solomon had gone to the lounge down the street. They'd be at the bar until eight.

I looked at the clock on the dresser. It was six-forty-five. I'd been asleep for three hours and had missed supper, but there was plenty of time for a soak before making my way to the lounge for a drink and a late meal.

Gathering my toiletries, I left my robe on the bed and padded into the bathroom. The remnants of roses still lingered in the small room. I rinsed out the tub, put in the plug, and turned on the hot water. Instead of rose oil, I chose lavender.

I shut off the spigot and slipped into the water, exhaling a sigh of contentment as the lavender-scented water enveloped my aching body. I'd always been an uptight person, but thus far the trip south had been more stress than I'd experienced for a long time. The water soothed my feminine areas, which were still tender from night before.

My mind wandered over the events of the past few days from picking Maureen up outside of Columbus to Loretta Detzer's business proposition, the bikers, Solomon, and the mysterious man who could... Well, I didn't want to think about "that."

Not to mention the memories the trip had dredged up like prehistoric fossils.

The pending phone call I would make had me thinking of skipping it altogether. Why not let sleeping dogs lie, or, as my father would say, 'leave the past in the past.'

Then there was Solomon who had become my lover against my better judgment. My insides flamed with the thought of him making love to me again. Falling for him was something I hadn't expected. The bathwater suddenly became too hot for comfort. How could I let my guard down? What had I been thinking?

My desperation for attention and comfort got the better of me. I've got to step back so neither of us gets hurt.

Thinking of Solomon created longing within me and simultaneously worried me. Frustrated, I turned my thoughts to the dilemma at hand—the phone call. I needed to make it or dismiss it.

Maybe I should let Anthony go on without me. Why show up and become a speed bump in his life?

No, I had to see my son. I'd never forgive myself if I didn't warn him and something terrible happened.

I must be out of my mind to entertain the thought of seeing him again.

Opening my eyes, I saw the silver-haired king standing over me with a crystal goblet full of amber liquid. His chaplet crown caught the overhead light, a band of brilliance dancing along it to the bright stone at its center.

I sloshed upright and uttered a strangled cry.

"Calm down, Ruby." Solomon backed away from the tub as I splashed water. "It's getting late, so I got worried and came back to see if you were joining us at the lounge. When I came in, I figured you were in the tub, so I brought you a glass of champagne to enjoy while you bathed."

"You scared the hell out of me!" I rasped, my chest heaving, adrenaline flying through my body in the form of an invisible lightning bolt.

"I'm so sorry. I thought you heard me come in and call your name."

Blood thundered in my ears. Shutting my eyes, I relaxed against the bathtub's sloped back. The vision of the other Solomon, the one who ruled over some unknown territory, had seared a vivid image into my brain.

"Where's Maureen?" I asked.

"She's still at the lounge. She met a couple from Indianapolis and has been talking to them for the past half hour." Tentatively, Solomon passed me the glass of champagne. "Here, you probably need this to mellow out now."

At the wry humor in his voice, I smiled. Taking a sip, I wrinkled my nose at the bubbles.

"Where'd the champagne come from?"

"Complimentary bottle," he answered. His eyes darkened to a smoky color. "Want me to wash your hair?"

"Is this a ploy to get me in bed again?"

"Maybe."

As enticing as his offer was, I'd already made the decision to pull back from Solomon. I couldn't risk getting hurt again and I didn't want to hurt him either. "I think I can handle it. Give me fifteen and I'll be out of the tub." I swallowed the last of the champagne, hoping the alcohol would enter my bloodstream quickly and slow my galloping heart rate. "Wait for me in the bedroom."

"What do you want to wear?" Disappointment and confusion landed on his face. "I'll lay it out on the bed for you."

"The yellow sundress and my new sandals." I couldn't look at him. If I did, I'd yank him into the bathtub and let him have his way with me.

He turned, hesitating in the door. Finally, he walked out.

I breathed a sigh of relief and simultaneously berated myself for not taking him up on his offer.

****

That night, we returned to the bed-and-breakfast as drinks were being served out on the garden patio. The clatter of a carriage reached us from the historic Bridge of Lions, and the water lapping at the riverbanks set the mood for a romantic evening for those so inclined. The aroma of sea brine, fish, spicy food from the lounge down the street, and the cotton candy fragrance of a Pygmy fringe tree in the garden produced a bizarre blend that assailed one's olfactory senses. A breeze blew softly, stirring the moss hanging in the surrounding live oaks. A lizard ran across the flagstone at my feet, and I shuddered.

"Hello," said the hostess, who had checked us in earlier that day. "Would you like to join everyone for a nightcap? We have a well-stocked bar on the patio."

"That would be nice," Maureen said, sashaying toward the bar.

We watched her as she relayed something to the older gentleman tending the drinks. He handed her a tumbler full of amber liquid, and then dropped a twist of lime into it. Movement drew my attention to the walk leading from the B and B to the garden. The three witches from the sitting room stood regarding the scene. Their gazes met mine, and one of them smiled. They ambled toward the bar too.

"What would you like to drink, Ruby?" Solomon asked. "Another Irish coffee, perhaps?"

"Yes, but I have to make a phone call, so I'll be back in a few minutes."

He studied me suspiciously. "A phone call? Are you all right?"

"I'm fine." As soon as the lie popped from my mouth trembles began in my knees. "I'll be back in a few minutes." I turned to walk inside, hoping I didn't bump into one of the gothic-dressed women when I returned. Something about them stood my hair on end.

"I'll wait a few minutes before I have the bartender make it for you," Solomon called after me.

I nodded and grimaced at the uncertainty in his voice. Maybe if Solomon thought I had a love interest in St. Augustine he'd back off. However, just the thought of not feeling his caresses or kisses again sent a pang of regret through me. No, I had to be strong. I couldn't allow him to be a casualty of something disastrous whether I inadvertently caused it with my crazy abilities or the bikers did something terrible.

I followed the flagstones placed in the shell-littered ground to the back entrance. With my heart performing a bizarre dance beneath my breasts, I made my way through the stylish manor. I glanced at the enormous oil paintings of men in full beards and dark suits as they posed next to women in tight bodices and voluminous skirts, their upswept hair arranged in a multitude of curls. The muted lighting throughout the bed-and-breakfast emphasized the surrealism of the establishment. For just an instant, it was as though I were in the 1800s.

The stairway harbored more oil paintings, some from the period, some from modern day artists who obviously preferred sea themes boasting old galleons and stormy skies. Heavy sconces supported battery-operated candles. As I ascended each carpeted step, I wondered how many women had climbed them before me. How many ladies of the past had carried guilt in their hearts? How many of them bore dark secrets they feared would find the light of day?

For now, the only woman who fit that description was me.

"Ruby Nutter, bring him to us."

The sudden voice shocked me into stillness. My shoulder bumped the wall, and I leaned there under a painting of a beautiful redheaded woman.

"Bring him to us. He's in danger too."

Solomon?

Sorrow flowed through me. Pain and regret rode in on its waves. I'd inevitably hurt him through association with me.

"Time is running out, Ruby. The others are getting too close. You must hurry!"

The voice galvanized me into action. Using my key, I entered the room and rummaged in my handbag for the hidden phone number.

The phone rested on the bedside table placed between the twin beds. With a deep breath, I snatched the portable out of the base and quickly unfolded the paper.

Each digit beeped on the touch pad. I waited. The line rang five times. About to hit the disconnect button, I nearly dropped the receiver when someone answered.

"Hello?"

My voice evaporated with the residual scents of lavender and roses floating from the bathroom and out through the open French doors.

"Hello?" a woman asked a bit more forcefully.

"Uh, hi." I hated the quiver in my voice. "Mrs. Gottrick, this is—"

"I know who you are."

Shocked into silence, I mentally riffled through my brain for something intelligent to say.

"I'm sorry," Mrs. Gottrick finally said after my long pause. "I don't mean to be rude. Are you in St. Augustine now?"

"Yes." Something flipped over in my stomach, and for a moment I thought I might hurl all over Maureen's bed.

"Do you still want to see Anthony?"

"Yes." If my heart beat any harder I worried it would explode.

"All right, Ruby." Papers rustled on the end of the line, and the woman sighed. In my mind's eye, I saw her studying some sort of gadget with an electronic calendar. "I'll take Anthony to the Castillo De San Marcos. Be at the entrance gate tomorrow afternoon and follow us through as we tour the site. That way he'll think you're just another tourist. Agreed?"

"Yes."

"Okay, Ruby. Two o'clock tomorrow. Until then," she said.

The line clicked.

My knees shook so badly I collapsed on the bed.

I am such a wuss and a dumbass. I gathered all the courage I could only to say yes three time? The woman must think I'm an idiot.

After several minutes, I remembered Solomon waited for me on the patio with my drink. Quickly, I slipped into a pair of shorts and a tank top, stepped into my flip-flops, and hurried downstairs, my gaze avoiding the accusing stares of those immortalized on canvas.

A string of Chinese lanterns and a few sets of red novelty chili peppers glowed from wires threaded through the night-blooming trees. Half the guests had retired to their rooms, including the three witches. Maureen sat at a wrought-iron table playing Parcheesi with an elderly black man. Next to the fountain of a lion, Solomon reclined on a glider. He waved at me and motioned toward a cup sitting on the little table placed in front of the glider.

"What took you so long?" he asked.

"The phone call took longer than I expected."

Skeptical, he studied me, his pale eyes glowing eerily. Somehow he sensed I'd lied to him.

"I'm going to walk Mr. Jebbstart to his room," Maureen announced. "I think I'm going to go to bed too. My skin is still tender, and I can't stand wearing this dress any longer."

"I'll be up later," I told her.

The black man ambled over to Maureen, offered her his arm and bid us all goodnight. They strolled up the flagstone path to the rear entrance.

"There just went the next Anna Nicole Smith," I muttered under my breath.

"Hey, cut Maureen some slack."

Solomon's comment shot a needle of regret into my gut. He was right. I was taking my frustrations and stress out on Maureen.

"Sorry."

"What's up with you?" He stretched his arm across the back of the glider, his fingers resting on the rounded portion of my shoulder. The delicate touch sent sparks zipping to my innermost region. "You've been uptight all evening, more so than usual."

I shrugged.

"Come on, you can tell me."

"I have trust issues, remember?"

He blinked. "I told you about me and Gabriella. That wasn't easy, and it's not something I've discussed with anyone other than my parents and Sam."

"Lucky me."

"Wow, you can be a royal witch when you want to."

The word "witch" sliced through me like a shard of ice. I substituted the W for a B. Sometimes I "had" to be a bitch. It was all I had to keep me strong, to prevent those in the world from destroying me like before and it served in helping me deal with my father. Sure, Solomon wanted to know more about me, but I didn't want to tell him the long, sordid history, and he should have respected that.

Besides, if I did tell him, he'd call someone and have me hauled away to a room with padded walls.

I picked up my cup of liquor-laced coffee, stood and walked to the door without a backward glance.

There was no way in hell I was going to allow him to see the tears streaming down my face.

Chapter Nineteen

When I awoke at seven-thirty the next morning, Maureen snored softly in her bed. Quietly, I dressed in the yellow sundress I'd worn the night before, slipped on my comfortable sandals and fixed my hair in a French braid. I thought about makeup, but the day's weather report had forecasted high humidity. The last thing I needed was to end up with raccoon eyes if I happened to come face to face with Anthony.

Finished, I scribbled a note to Maureen and hurried downstairs. The proprietors had laid a breakfast out on the patio tables. I enjoyed a glazed yeast roll with a cup of strong coffee, hoping Solomon didn't appear before I finished my breakfast.

An ocean breeze invaded the back lawn, and I breathed in the aroma of salt and fish mixed with the sweet perfume of the garden's flowers. My roll finished, I decided to chance another cup of coffee. After a bit of shopping and playing tourist, I would meet Mrs. Katherine Gottrick at the Castillo De San Marcos. Once I got a good look at Anthony and give Katherine my warning about possible danger, I'd return to the bed-and-breakfast, enjoy an evening meal with my traveling companions, and try not to think about the past anymore. The next morning, we'd be on the road again heading for Key West and ninety-five thousand dollars.

The clear cerulean sky soon faded to a silver haze as the morning progressed into an oven-like day. The hours passed with a walk through the Ripley's Believe-It-or-Not Museum, a tour through the chocolate factory, followed by enjoying a cup of cold lemonade as I sat under The Old Senator, a live oak approximately six hundred years old in front of the Howard Johnson Hotel. I walked down the only original street remaining of the settlement, its cobbled surface reminiscent of the late 1600s. Tiny shops full of handmade jewelry, trinkets, scarves and lovely clothing lined the narrow thorough-fare. I spent two hours examining the goods available, making jewelry purchases for myself and Maureen, and something special for Solomon as an apology for my behavior the night before.

I looked at my new silver wristwatch. Its abalone-shell face showed it was nearly two o'clock. My heart felt as though it somersaulted in my chest. Gathering my packages from where I rested on a bench, I hurried to the Excursion, stowing everything in the back, and drove to the fort across the river.

It was hard for me to comprehend that twenty years had passed since I first gazed upon Anthony. Time seemed to have no meaning where he was concerned. It just didn't seem possible that I had reached the point of truth, a truth that would haunt me for years to come if I didn't make this effort to protect him in my feeble manner.

Parking the SUV, I made my way along the sandy path to the enormous fort. With perspiration tickling my skin, I shouldered my purse and scanned the people entering and exiting the Castillos gate. My gaze settled upon a tall, angular woman with a sun hat hiding most of her thick, strawberry blonde hair.

Anthony's adoptive mother.

Next to Mrs. Gottrick stood a gangly young man. As I approached, I couldn't tear my gaze away from him. He studied Mrs. Gottrick with impatience, his dark hair gleaming in the hazy sunshine. His lean build hinted at the man he would become later down the road.

"Hurry up, Mom," he grumbled. "It's cooler inside the Castillos." He pronounced Castillos with a perfect Spanish accent.

"I found it," Katherine said, pulling a wallet from her purse. She handed a bill to the woman taking entrance fees, and as she waited for her change, she sensed my gaze and recognized me instantly. A sympathetic expression crossed her face, and, nodding to me, she accepted her change and took Anthony's proffered arm as he guided her inside the fort.

After I paid my fee, I followed them closely. A tour guide took us and other tourists through dark, dry storage rooms constructed of stone to soldiers' barracks, officers' quarters, and then out to the grassy courtyard littered with crushed shells. Along the top of the fort's wall canons faced the ocean where they once fired at potential enemies who encroached upon the settlement's shores. At one point, I could've sworn I'd spotted the three witches from the B and B with another tour group, probably whiling away the time between mystical lectures.

I couldn't recall much about the guide's historical monologue. My attention remained on Anthony. He caught me staring and looked long and seriously at me, his wide-eyed gaze piercing something in my heart I hadn't realized existed until that moment. The pain it inflicted nearly knocked me off my feet, but then Anthony favored me with a beautiful smile, and its balm healed the searing agony in my soul.

Our little group of sightseers filed into the souvenir shop. Anthony headed straight to a shelf full of history books, novelty items and Castillos replicas. I studied him as I pretended to be interested in a bag of cannonball chocolates displayed in a glass showcase.

"Are you satisfied?"

Turning, I looked at Katherine Gottrick, who stood waiting for the cashier to ring up a scenic puzzle of the fort and a pack of gum.

"Yes," I said with a quaver in my voice. "He has grown into a handsome young man. He looks healthy and happy."

"He is," she replied. "And he is "very" smart."

"Oh?"

"Straight A's throughout all of school. He's been accepted at the University of Tampa this fall. He's also a mathematics whiz and loves to read."

"That's great," I heard myself say, but I felt like I floated a million miles away. The tiny granules of information I'd gleaned about Anthony seemed to not only make me glad the boy was happy, but it made me feel cheated and I was the one who had cheated myself. "Does he know he's adopted?"

"No, we've never told him."

"Has he...has he ever...?" I swallowed hard. I couldn't even bring myself to say it.

A peculiar expression settled in Katherine's eyes. "Has he ever done anything strange?"

I nodded.

"No, he's not like you, Ruby."

"Oh. Well, that's good."

I suddenly felt ridiculous for being there. What was the point of all of this when I was actually no more than just another tourist?

"If you like," Mrs. Gottrick said hesitantly as she picked up her plastic bag of purchases, "I'll send you a picture each Christmas from now until—and if—you should decide you want to change things."

"That's very kind of you." The words nearly choked me.

"Do you still live at the same address?" She assessed me from head to toe, her dark brown eyes slicing through my tough façade.

"No, I don't." I quickly pulled a pen and a scrap of paper out of my purse and jotted down my address. "I moved out of my father's house several years ago. I live a few blocks over from him now." My hand shook as I handing her the piece of paper.

Katherine noticed the trembling and smiled sympathetically. "It must have taken a lot for you to summon the courage to see him, Ruby," she said. "Don't worry. You did the right thing, and I'm sure when it's time, Anthony will understand."

"I hope you're right." My throat constricted with emotion.

"I am." She put my address in her purse. As she stepped around me, she squeezed my shoulder. "I must be going."

"Wait." Fear attacked my heart, and I gulped hard.

She met my gaze, quirking an eyebrow. "Yes?"

"I also came to warn Anthony."

Although Katherine's expression remained stoic, terror flashed through her eyes. "Oh?"

"I don't know why, but I'm being followed by a biker gang." I lowered my voice and leaned closer to her. "They're not...uh...normal people."

She flattened her lips into a thin, gray line.

"I felt compelled to warn my son." Roaring filled my ears. I sounded like a complete idiot, but blundered onward. "I don't know that they'll go after him, but I still have this sensation that he's in danger."

Without any reaction to me, she turned and walked away. "Anthony, it's time to go."

"In a minute, Mom. I want to buy a couple of these books." He didn't look up from the reading the back of one of the paperbacks.

Once again, I felt torn, humiliated and alone. In a blur of tears, I returned to the Excursion. I suddenly felt very old, very stupid, and if I hadn't known better, I could've sworn someone had ripped out my heart.

****

It's funny how a person can go through life thinking things are a certain way then one day something happens, something small and insignificant to the casual observer, but upon closer inspection and thorough contemplation, the entire universe teeters in the balance of that one little thing.

I sat on a piece of driftwood on St. Augustine Beach and watched the sun lower toward the horizon as waves caressed the hard, gray-brown sand. Seeing Anthony had turned my world, as I knew it, upside down. It had caused a multitude of revelations to whirl through my brain, and in turn, it had also prompted a sense of hopelessness within me.

Regardless, I'd paid the price for my naivety and stupidity, paid it over and over every day I thought about Anthony. Had I done the right thing by giving him up for adoption? Hell, I was fifteen when I'd given birth to him. What does a fifteen-year-old girl know?

Seeing my son had been both wonderful and disturbing, but as a result, my heart was even more unsettled.

I had nothing to offer Anthony, and with my current circumstances, the bikers chasing me, the smoke creatures, the voices in my head coaxing me south, and the fact I possessed supernatural powers, he was better off without me anyway.

Besides, I'd never forgive myself if something happened to him. If one of those flame-eyed bikers hurt Anthony because of me... I shivered, picked up my purse and prepared to walk back to the Excursion. Although I didn't want to think about it anymore, I knew I'd done the right thing by warning Katherine that Anthony might be in danger. She'd thought me insane, which was a normal reaction, but she knew enough about me as a teen to heed my words.

I hurried on to the SUV. I'd been gone all day. Maureen and Solomon were probably wondering if I had abandoned them.

The Ford sat on a side street. I'd parked there and walked down to the beach through the small campgrounds separating the two. As I wandered along the sandy path and into the trees of a large, unoccupied section of the grounds, the sound of a Harley fractured the evening. The thrum-thrum-thrum of the bike froze me in mid-step. Terror claimed me, and my breath stuck in my throat.

Someone gunned the engine, bawdy laughter melded with its roar and what sounded like the squall of a cat—a very big cat—followed.

It can't be them again, can it?

There was no use denying it. I knew the answer. I stepped off the trail and quietly picked my way through the brush and trees until I reached a pine where I could hide.

Flames leapt and crackled in a fire ring surrounded by several tents. Eight men and five women, who were all extremely large, tall people, stood around talking or sat on the ground drinking hard liquor. The mouthy biker chick with the bright red hair and thick makeup reclined against her tattooed man. Her loud mouth would be difficult to miss even at a cockfight.

However, in the middle of a big area without any pitched tents, sat thirteen motorcycles—but only at first glance.

Not only was the big man's steel horse parked there, but the other motorcycles with it were part demonic animal too. The head of a black panther with fiery red eyes sprouted from one, and a set of silver reins ran from the corners of its mouth to lie across the seat. The forms of bear, stags, wolves, and even an eagle jutted from the fronts of the other "bikes." Each head sported glowing serpentine eyes of random colors and mouths full of sharp teeth. The same style of silver reins looped around muzzles or hung from their steely bits to lay draped across their seats. The panther shrieked again, and I jumped, pressing closer to the tree, its rough bark scraping my skin.

"Protect yourself, Ruby! Cast a protection ward around you—now!"

I didn't even question the voice in my head. The power bubbled up from within me, and the sensation of an invisible force flowed down my arms and out through my fingertips to surround my body.

My protection ward in place, I peeked around the tree. The biggest man stared directly at me. He walked in my direction. For the first time, I wasn't overwhelmed with lust, and I realized, too, that my ward prevented him from seeing me as well.

"Remain still! when he walks away, leave there immediately!"

The huge biker stared into the thicket for a few more seconds then turned and joined the others cavorting around the fire. One of them handed him a fifth of something. He put the bottle to his mouth and gulped from it.

As quickly and quietly as I could, I backed away from the tree and headed toward the trail with my knees knocking together and my heartbeat crashing in my ears. A startled ring-tailed raccoon chattered loudly at me and scampered off into the undergrowth, its long black-and-white tail puffed with fear. I kept walking and prayed its cry hadn't drawn attention, but with the noise coming from the campsite, I doubted the bikers had heard it.

What were those people and the things they rode upon? Why were they following me?

There was no doubt in my mind the bikers were the reason I was heading south.

But who or what was drawing me there?

Chapter Twenty

The sun hung low over the old settlement turned contemporary city. I booked our rooms for another night and headed upstairs to tell Maureen and Solomon.

As I passed the parlor, I spotted Maureen sitting at a checker table with Mr. Jebbstart. Behind them, at the big bay window, sat one of the witches dressed in a hooded, deep purple gown. She nodded politely and raised her coffee mug in greeting. I inclined my head and then focused on Maureen.

"Who taught you to play checkers so well?" the old man asked Maureen as I approached.

"My guardian, Lula, had a boyfriend who traveled a lot, but when he'd come to stay with her it would be for three or four weeks at a time," Maureen supplied. "He grew bored easily, so he taught me how to play several different skill games." She jumped three of his checkers.

"Damn!" The elderly fellow sat back in his chair. "I can't believe I didn't see that coming!"

"Hi, Maureen," I said.

"Hey!" She favored me with a bright smile, but it faded and a slight frown marred her brow. "Where have you been all day?"

"I did some sightseeing, bought a few things and visited the Castillos."

I met Mr. Jebbstart's gaze. Deep brown eyes, ones that bordered on black, stared back at me with a wealth of information.

"Hello," I said. "I'm Ruby."

"Yes," he replied. "Maureen has told me all about you."

I glanced at my hitchhiker, a sense of doom sliding over me. I could only imagine the horrible things she'd told him about me.

The old gent seemed to read my mind. He smiled broadly and added, "Don't worry, it was all good."

"What are your plans for tonight?" Maureen asked, king-ing one of the old man's checkers.

"I haven't thought about it, really. I just booked another night here. I really don't feel like being on the road for five or six hours only to rent another room."

"Me neither." She shrugged. "Besides, I've grown attached to Mr. Jebbstart and don't want to leave him just yet."

"Well, my beautiful sweetheart," the old man cooe,. "I'll be checking out tomorrow morn, so we must make the best of our last hours together."

I rolled my eyes.

"Well, maybe we can have dinner together?" Maureen queried, batting her lashes at him. She looked at me. "Or, if Ruby doesn't mind, the four of us can go out somewhere tonight."

"Let me get back to you on that," I replied, not wanting to put up with their goofy, flirtatious games. "I'm going to take a cool bath and relax for a while."

Maybe a bath would wash away the day's events—at least I hoped so.

"Solomon is upstairs," Maureen said as she watched Mr. Jebbstart move a checker.

"So?"

"He's been worrying about you all day."

"Again, so?"

"Jeez, Ruby." Maureen sighed and kinged another checker. "Give the guy a break, would you? He's crazy about you and you're so—"

"What?"

"Cold."

Not a single scathing retort entered my mind. Without a word, I turned toward the staircase.

"By the way," Maureen said over her shoulder. "How's Anthony?"

A chill swept across my body. With my foot poised over the first step, I stopped. Eeriness settled in the pit of my stomach.

"How do you know about Anthony?" I asked without turning around.

"I don't."

"But you—"

"It's a name that surfaced for me when you were standing here," Maureen replied. "I thought it might be important."

"Don't worry about it," I said icily.

"If you say so."

As each day passed, my hitchhiker grew stranger and more complex. Had she overheard my conversation the previous night? No, it wasn't possible. I was certain she'd been with Mr. Jebbstart the entire time I'd been upstairs making the phone call.

I turned, studying Maureen, but her back was to me as she concentrated on the game. "Are you sure Solomon didn't come upstairs last night and then later tell you what he'd overheard?"

Mr. Jebbstart, however, regarded me with what looked like skepticism and unease.

"No, he stayed in the garden, ordered your coffee and sat waiting for you." She twisted in her seat to look at me. "Why?"

At that moment, I saw deep into my odd friend's heart and knew Maureen couldn't lie. The woman had a conscience that made her incapable of falsehoods.

"Never mind," I said. "I'll see you later."

Once upstairs, I shut the door and tossed my purse on the bed, having left my packages in the SUV since there was no point in bringing them upstairs only to load them again tomorrow. In the bathroom, I turned on the spigots. A bottle of citrus bath oil smelled great, so I poured it into the bath. As the tub filled, I stepped out on the balcony. Palm trees waved in a strong ocean breeze. The neigh of one of the carriage horses reached me, followed by the peal of a church bell or maybe a buoy.

The sound of a diesel engine drew my attention to the traffic along the street. At first, I dismissed the dark green 4x4 that pulled up to the curb four buildings down from our B and B. A man got out of the truck dressed in jeans and a short-sleeved flannel shirt. From my vantage point, I stood too far away to see enough details to identify the man, but he certainly resembled Wayne Blacktree. Leaning over the rail, I squinted against the hazy streetlights, but still couldn't make out anything to help me identify him. The guy entered a large house renovated into a hotel.

Was Wayne Blacktree still following us?

"What are you looking at?"

Gasping, I whirled. "Damn you, Solomon!" I yelled. "Stop sneaking up on me!"

"Sorry," he said as he sauntered across the room looking positively delicious. "The door was ajar."

The site of him heated my libido. I glanced away pointed at the green pickup, voicing my concerns. "I think Wayne Blacktree followed us."

I risked looking at my lover. The corners of Solomon's mouth turned down as he stepped out onto the terrace and noted the truck parked down the street.

"Is he following us because you and Maureen have more cash on you than you're letting on?" he asked.

"No, we have about forty-five hundred. It's a nice lump sum, but not enough I'd follow someone around for days only to land in jail over it."

He leaned against the doorframe, crossing his arms over his chest. "Still, I think we should be more careful."

Against my will, I admired his body, realizing how much I'd missed him as I'd been strolling about the city. Dressed in casual white slacks, a black leather belt encircling his waist and a black muscle shirt, Solomon exuded the unnatural and ethereal air I found so fascinating.

"Did you have a nice day out alone?" he asked.

"Yes." I strode past him and into the bathroom where I turned off the spigots. My thoughts had begun to stray to an area that always proved to be dangerous territory. "I did some shopping then toured the Castillos," I said as I returned to the bedroom.

"Ruby?"

"Yes?" I didn't look at him. Instead, I browsed through a dresser drawer where I'd stowed my nice clothes.

"I want to apologize for calling you a witch last night." A sigh full of regret burst from him "It was mean and thoughtless of me and I'm sorry. It has eaten at me all day."

"After all the barbs that fly out of my mouth, I'd say we're even." Picking out a cotton skirt with a black and white zigzag print and a simple white summer blouse, I laid the clothes on the bed. "Don't worry about it."

The instant he stepped from the balcony and into the room, the temperature seemed to spike. I put the bed between us, trying to gauge his intentions.

"I've never talked like that to anyone," he said. "But you..."

I couldn't look at him. If I did, I'd be in trouble. "But what?"

"You bring out feelings and sensations in me I'm ill equipped to deal with, and it's unsettling."

"Huh, try living my life."

"I think that's why you are the way you are. Your sharp tongue is your defense mechanism."

"Maybe." I hurried past him on my way to the bathroom. "I'm going to take a bath, so if you want to have supper later, let me know—"

His arm snaked out and encircled my waist. A little squeak escaped me. The tempo of my heart reached dizzying proportions, and heat flashed into my loins.

"Want to know the truth about why I lashed out at you?" he whispered.

Desire stampeded through my body, and a lump formed in my throat, so I could only nod.

"I was jealous."

I offered him an incredulous look. I couldn't help it. Jealous? A man was actually jealous over me?

I couldn't allow Solomon to know how he affected me. We'd already made love twice, but I couldn't allow it to happen again. The more involved we'd become, the more disastrous the end result would be. It never failed. I was never permitted to enjoy a relationship. Heartache was something I couldn't handle anymore.

"Why were you jealous?" The tremor in my voice betrayed me. Need thundered through my limbs.

"You're meeting someone here, right? And you didn't want anyone around when you made that phone call last night." He tightened his grip on me, and a shudder flowed through his body. "You've been gone all day."

"But—"

"You're driving me crazy, Ruby," he murmured, drawing me against his hard, warm body.

"I have that affect on a lot of people."

The retort fell flat. It's difficult to be a smart ass with raging hormones and panties that are ready to melt.

"You know what I mean," he said, nuzzling my neck.

The sensation that swept over me rendered my legs useless, and my arms became leaden weights. The chemistry between us affected my equilibrium, as if I was inebriated.

"Solomon, no," I said, trying to push him away but at the same time desiring him closer.

"No what?" He licked my earlobe.

"We shouldn't do this. Maureen might walk in."

"She's busy downstairs."

"This isn't right." I tried to dodge his lips as they traversed from my earlobe to my mouth. He kissed me gently several times, his mouth working magic that torpedoed throughout the rest of my body.

He stepped back, still holding onto my waist, and stared directly into my eyes. "How isn't it right, Ruby? Do you love this guy?"

"Yes."

He blinked as if I'd actually slapped him. His devastated expression clawed at my soul.

"It's not what you think," I rushed on. "I don't love him "that" way. He's not a romantic interest."

"Then who is he?"

His question was like a bucket of ice water in my face. "I don't want to talk about it."

Solomon frowned as he considered my response. "Then why can't we be together?" He nipped my neck, and the aroma of spicy cologne tantalized my senses. "What do you have to lose?"

"Someone will get hurt."

"What's wrong with enjoying one another?" he asked. "We're two consenting adults with a hell of a lot of chemistry raging between us, so let's see where it goes."

"It always ends in misery." I took a deep, steadying breath. The traitorous hormones coursing through me made it harder and harder to stand my ground.

He tugged me closer, and I placed my palms flat against his chest.

"Let me take my bath." My voice sounded calm, but on the inside an earthquake shook my foundations. "I'm hot, sticky and tired. Later, I want a good meal." Stepping out of his embrace, I turned, grabbed my clothes and walked into the bathroom. "Shut the door behind you, please," I called out. "I'll let you know when I'm ready to go." I shut the door, leaving Solomon standing in the middle of the room with a bewildered expression on his face.

I turned off the water, tossed my fresh clothing on a vanity stool pushed against a wall and shed my clothes. Tears caressed my cheeks, washing Solomon's essence from my skin. The scent of the citrus oil permeated the air. I hoped it could also penetrate my soul, easing the agony there.

I want to be with you, too, but I can't risk it.

The door burst open, forcing a sharp cry from me.

"I'm not giving up so easily, Ruby," Solomon stated gruffly. Determination flamed in his eyes. "I think we have something special if you'd just give it a chance."

Naked, I stood there grasping for something intelligent to say. I backed up until my rear hugged the tub's rim.

He pulled me against him, and I knew struggling or denying Solomon was useless. I wanted him, wanted him between my legs, his bare flesh against mine.

"I'm crazy for you," he murmured against my neck, his tongue hot and wet on the sensitive skin there. "I'm insane for your touch, your rare smiles, the way you gasp when I hit that one," he nipped my throat, "special spot."

A cry leapt from my lips. The intensity of need within that small sound might as well have screamed my desire. I wanted him so badly my legs shook.

"Damn you," I said as he trailed kisses across my collarbone and down over the swell of my breasts. "This isn't fair."

"Nothing in life is fair." He claimed the sensitive peak of one breast.

I arched against him and tore at his shirt, yanking it from his slacks.

"Tell me you want me," he said. He moved to my other breast and flicked the nipple with his tongue.

Clinging to him, I reveled in the flames licking my skin.

"Tell me, Ruby."

"No!"

It was a lie, but I would be damned if I told the truth. There was no way I was going to suffer through more heartache. I'd learned the hard way too many times.

Solomon slid his hand over my hip, around to my lower abdomen and down to palm my mound. I whimpered, clinging to him and mentally cussing myself. The aroma of citrus, his spicy cologne, and his distinct male scent assailed my senses like a hard-core narcotic. Solomon stroked my folds, the touch feather soft. A tingling sensation swept through me and into my thighs, my lower belly.

He knelt, his mouth claiming my sex, tongue searing. He delivered several licks that sent lightning bolts of need through me. Before I could utter a word, Solomon stood and slipped his hand between my legs again. He stared straight into my eyes, pushing two fingers into my pussy.

Whimpering louder, I tried to pull him against me, but he placed his free hand over one of my breasts and stroked his thumb over the nipple. Heat streaked downward to my loins as it simultaneously shot from my crotch and upward into my core.

"I'm not going to hurt you," he said, "so why can't you take a chance?"

With desire pounding through me, I whispered, "I know how it will end."

"The next time I make love to you," he whispered back, "you'll come to me first."

I glared at him. He'd played me, damn him.

He stepped away, tucking his shirttails into his pants, and paused in the doorway. "I'll wait for you in the lounge."

With that, he left the room, shutting the door softly behind him.

Shaking, I climbed into the tub and sank into the scented water, thankful for its coolness.

****

I hurried downstairs on my way to dinner, but as I passed through the sitting room, the three witches called out a hearty goodnight to me. I didn't want to appear rude, so I nodded and smiled as I opened the door and walked outside.

Dinner consisted of sautéed shrimp and fettuccini noodles mixed with strained conversation. The lounge, known to the locals as The Alley Grill, possessed a soothing, laid-back atmosphere. The night before, I'd admired the rustic air of all the lacquered cherry wood-work, including the bar and most of the tables. Brass accentuated everything from the stained-glass shades hanging over each table to the electric light sconces on the walls, but the odd glances from Maureen and the assessing looks from Solomon proved distracting.

Pouring each of us more house wine, Maureen set the bottle on the table and sat back, focusing on first Solomon and then me. "Jeez, what's with you two?" she asked.

Solomon didn't miss a beat. "Ask Ruby."

She turned her attention to me.

"Don't look at me," I said.

Sighing, she returned to her shrimp and steamed vegetables.

As the meal progressed, my hitchhiker prattled on about Mr. Jebbstart. After several minutes of listening to Maureen, I tuned her out. The meal tasted wonderful, but too much wine had dulled my senses, and a weepy state of mind settled over me. The last thing I wanted was for Solomon to see me cry. Three times in one day was too much.

The waiter arrived with three slices of key lime pie, one of my favorite treats. Although Maureen and Solomon raved about how good it was, I might as well have been chewing a piece of light-green sponge.

"Would you like some after-dinner coffee?" the waiter asked. He stood with his order pad and pencil ready, his acne-riddled face wearing a hopeful expression for a healthy tip. "Or maybe you'd prefer a nightcap?"

I glanced at my wristwatch. Ten until midnight. Standing, I pulled five twenties out of my purse and tossed them on the tabletop.

"I'll pay for dinner. You two go ahead and enjoy some coffee. I'm going back to the room," I said.

Surprise registered on both Maureen's and Solomon's faces.

To the waiter, I stated, "Keep the change. You worked hard tonight."

"Thank you very much!" he exclaimed.

It wasn't in my nature to be rude and walk out on someone during dinner. My impoliteness stemmed primarily from my mouth. However, I just couldn't handle Maureen's bubbly demeanor or Solomon's brooding glances.

Outside, a gentle rain had fallen, wetting everything just enough to stir odors. The air reeked of old fish, and the pavement and shell-strewn patches of earth smelled oily. The rumble and whir of vehicles crossing The Bridge of Lions sounded distorted and muffled in the misty atmosphere. Somewhere a parrot shrieked, followed by the scaly rustle of palms in the wind. Fog swirled through the tropical foliage, caressing the cars parked along the streets and in household parking spaces. An orange tabby cat lay curled on the bottom porch step of a large manor along the way. Upon hearing my footsteps, the feline stretched and wandered out on the sidewalk to mew a greeting.

"Hello, kitty." Stooping, I scratched behind his ears, and he rewarded me with a raspy purr. "What are you doing outside so late?"

The cat meowed. Giving him a final pat on his side, I bid the cat farewell and continued down the walk.

My mind bounced back and forth with thoughts of Anthony and Solomon. My son was a subject I could reflect upon later, but Solomon was a different matter. If only I'd refused to allow him to join us on our venture to Key West. Just like my hitchhiker, I was clueless as to why I'd allowed him to accompany us. Sure, I was attracted to him, cared for him, but it was also reckless of me.

But he doesn't seem to judge me because I'm different. Maybe it's because he's different too? Can it be that simple?

It had been a long time since I'd felt such attraction to a man, but the chemistry with Solomon went beyond anything I'd experienced before. Being close to him kindled a fire in me that I found both frightening and thrilling. What I didn't understand was why he seemed so familiar, and why I was certain he was the king in my visions. Besides, even if we both wanted more, there was no hope for us, no future. I would go back to Ohio, and Solomon would return to his cabin in Virginia.

The scrape of a foot across asphalt jarred me out of my musings. Gooseflesh rippled up and down my arms. All along my body the hair stood at attention. Again, the crunch of pebbles between sole and pavement sliced through the mist. Expecting to find Solomon dogging my heels, I spun around with a scathing retort on the tip of my tongue, but swallowed my words as Wayne Blacktree stepped through a wall of fog.

Chapter Twenty-One

It was stupid to walk back alone.

I turned to run, but one of my sandals slipped off, and with the strap still hooked around my ankle, I staggered against an old Pontiac parked at the curb. Hands grabbed me by the shoulders and shook me like a bed sheet.

"Don't make a sound!" Wayne growled.

"Let go of me!" I snarled back at him, hoping my head didn't snap off my neck and land in the top of a palm tree somewhere. If someone did, they'd probably think it was just another coconut. It's funny how one thinks such strange things in moments of panic.

"Don't cause any trouble!" he said forcefully.

I shoved him back, taking him by surprise. "Don't touch me!"

"I don't know why he'd want someone like you." He grabbed my arm again. "You're a mouthy bitch."

Several things about the situation just didn't make any sense, but the fact that he'd called me a bitch hit my hot button. Anger rippled through me, boiling up out of my gut.

"Why don't you go to the beach and start walking toward Cuba!" I pushed him off me again. If the jackass touched me one more time, he was going to tangle with a right hook full of fire—that was if someone didn't hear us and call the cops first.

"Come on, dude." Wayne caught me again as he scanned the street. "What's taking so long?" he shouted. "I've got her!"

You asked for it, buddy.

The stinging sensation I was so acquainted with burbled up from the center of my body and out along my limbs. My skin brightened and light radiated off of me, illuminating the sidewalk. It reflected off the car and the raindrops coating the palms and flowers. The hair around my face transformed from deep brown to molten orange, and tendrils escaping my braid twirled around my face and head like miniature serpents.

With my fingernails glowing neon yellow, I made a fist and swung, allowing the power building within me to exit. The knuckles of my right hand protested as they connected with his face. Upon contact, light exploded between us. The gasp of pain that tore free of me echoed oddly in the swirling mist.

Wayne staggered back and fell ass first into a low-lying hedge. He scrambled to his feet, his eyes wide with shock, one hand covering his cheekbone. A furious expression crossed his face, and he lunged for me.

I threw my hand up to knock him back, but electricity whizzed down my arm, building to an almost painful pressure in my glowing fingertips. I tried to yank my hand back or point it to the sidewalk, but wasn't fast enough. White fire erupted from my fingers, each one feeling as though the nails would explode. The halogen-bright flames blasted Wayne in the center of his chest. He let out a howl of pain, flew backward into the air, and landed upside down in a cluster of saw grass and elephant palms.

The tabby cat hissed from the porch. Like a fireworks display, the bright pinpoints of light danced in the wet sheens of the parked cars, and the surrounding rain puddles reflected the brilliance.

I started to turn, but lust roared through my body with such intensity I cried out and staggered against the Pontiac again.

No! Not him, not now!

"Yes, Ruby. It is me. I have come for you, and now you'll be mine."

Sensation burned my breasts, their nipples taut against my bra. Heat assaulted my crotch, and a thrumming began deep within my core, pulsing into my inner thighs. Whimpering, I pushed away from the car. If I didn't get escape or figure out a way to defeat him, I sensed I'd be lost forever.

"Come to me, Ruby. Give yourself to me."

A moan burst from me, and I managed to take one step backward.

"Don't fight it. We will become a force to be reckoned with. No one will thwart us, and we'll rule side by side forever."

He stepped out of the shadows. Fear slapped the hell out of me. Riveted where I stood, I could only stare at him as he approached. Dressed in motorcycle leather, he approached me in a leisurely manner, his golden hair almost luminescent beneath the streetlamps. He wore a smug expression, positive he finally had me in his grasp.

"You are mine. I will not allow the White King to interfere again."

He continued toward me. The cat hissed, spat and scrambled under the hedges lining the sidewalk.

Groaning, Wayne struggled to his feet and shook his head. "I caught her as promised, Azazel," he said.

"Idiot," the huge man said. "You detained her and nothing more."

"But you promised to reward me! I want my dog brought back!" Wayne took two steps toward the man, but halted as Azazel whirled on him, his face a maniacal mask of fury.

"I don't have her yet! Only when I possess her will you get your reward." He returned his attention to me and entered my mind again. *"Come to me, Ruby. Show me that you want me, and then we'll be together for eternity."*

"No!" I ground out.

"You can't deny me much longer. You know I will have you."

The need for sex overpowered me. It was nothing like I felt when I was with Solomon. With Solomon the emotion and physical attraction ruled me, but this man made me feel primeval, animalistic—demonic and twisted. What was worse was that I wanted it.

"Yes...yes, you do, don't you, Ruby?" Azazel moved closer until only three or four yards separated us. *"Concentrate on that. Let it flow over and through you. I will make love to you in*

such a manner you will beg me for more, beg me to never stop fucking you."

The word "fucking" hit me with the force of a lead pipe. It wasn't making love to him, it was fucking. It was a method of control, a tool.

Just another Cole Vandercourt.

That knowledge offered me a thin slice of resolve. However, as I tried to call upon my power, I realized being in Azazel's presence prevented me from accessing it. Somehow he was blocking it.

And that meant I was royally screwed.

Someone touched me, and I drew back instinctively, an odd feeling skittering down through my muscles and bones. I looked behind me to find one of the witches from the B and B. She nodded, her expression placid, eyes stern as she shifted her attention to Azazel.

Two other forms stepped through the swirling fog.

Azazel closed the distance between us. With only three feet separating us, the pheromones and power radiating from him finished me. An orgasm rolled through me. The strength fled my body, the orgasm intensified, and I cried in delight as I collapsed on the sidewalk. Wave after wave of pleasure pierced my loins, moistening my panties.

The beautiful man reached for me at the same instant the woman behind me spoke.

"Be gone, Azazel."

A bone-chilling growl rumbled out of him.

The gothic women from the inn surrounded me, their dark velvet cloaks swishing around their feet.

"Leave her!" one cried.

"Do not return," said the second.

The third, who appeared to be older than the other two, glanced down at me. Worry lurked in her gaze. As she focused on the beautiful blond man again, her expression changed to loathing. "You know there are rules you must follow, Azazel. It is up to Ruby if she chooses you, but she never has before, and I don't believe she ever will. You must wait for The Banishment."

"Be gone wielder of trickery," Azazel snarled. "I *will* possess her."

"Only if she chooses it to be so," the first witch retorted.

He glanced at me, and another orgasm roared through my body. I gasped, fighting it, but it was pointless. I lay panting on the walk and stared up through the twirling mist.

Someone slipped their hands under my shoulders and hefted me into a sitting position. Surprised, I screamed. Fear stabbed me again, and as I began to glow, white sparks shot from my hands.

"Whoa! Wait Ruby! It's me!" Solomon said. He protected his face with upraised hands.

I scrambled over to the Pontiac and leaned against it. "Couldn't you have said something to let me know you were there?"

"I did, but you didn't seem to hear me."

He held out one hand, and I put mine into it.

"Are you okay?" he asked.

"Yeah, I'm fine."

"Where's Wayne?"

I glanced over at the jumble of tropical plants where he'd landed. He was gone.

Shaking my head, I answered, "He must've run away. I blasted him, then the leader of those bikers showed up, followed by—"

"Yeah, Maureen and I saw what happened, but a fog bank passed between us and everyone was gone. We couldn't see or hear anything for several minutes. It was really weird."

"It was "him" again—Azazel." Shamed by what had happened to me, I dropped my gaze to the sidewalk. "He wants me," I whispered. "They took Gabriella from you, but now the leader of these bikers wants me for some reason."

With two fingers under my chin, Solomon tipped my head up. Fury raged in his eyes, but so did sincerity. "We'll figure something out. I meant what I said earlier in your room. We have something special, and I'm not going to let some overgrown jackass separate us."

As I stared up at him, I couldn't help but wonder how we could fight Azazel when he was already so powerful.

"Did you see the witches? The ones who have been staying at the inn?" I asked.

"Yes."

"Where did they go? What happened to Azazel and Wayne?"

He shook his head. "I don't know, Ruby. That's what I meant when I mentioned the fog bank. They were all there, and then when the fog cleared, they were gone and you were lying on the sidewalk."

The click-click-click of high heels drew my attention. Maureen paused by the car's bumper, her mouth a big O, eyes wide with awe.

"We decided to follow you back to the bed-and-breakfast," said Solomon. "You seemed so upset."

"Don't worry about me." I smiled, but the remnants of the orgasms and the freakiness of the situation wouldn't leave me.

He squeezed my hand, leaned close and brushed his lips across mine. Something in me shifted, and although it was after midnight, in my mind the sun suddenly shone upon me. If Solomon was with me, then everything would be fine.

"Are you okay?" asked Maureen. "What did Wayne Blacktree want?"

"He's the biker's servant." I wiggled my toes into the front of my loose shoe.

"What?" she asked.

"He was supposed to capture me for Azazel, the big, blond biker who wants me for some reason." Sighing, I closed my eyes, trying to steady my nerves. Finally, I opened them again to find Solomon and Maureen waiting patiently for me to finish. "Wayne said something about wanting his dog back as his reward for finding me. I know it sounds stupid, but he seems desperate for it."

"Where did Wayne go earlier today when you saw him get out of his truck?" Solomon asked.

"I'm not sure now." I looked up and down the street. "I don't see his truck parked anywhere."

"Let's go back to our rooms." Maureen cast uneasy glances at the fog-cloaked gardens and manors. "Those two might come back."

Solomon slipped his arm around my waist. I enjoyed the contact and his protection, but could he really defend me?

On his opposite side, Maureen linked arms with him and hummed softly to herself as she walked. I had a spirit guide, a white king, and an empath traveling with me to Key West. I knew it wouldn't last forever, but for now, I relished their companionship as we strolled down the street.

Reaching the B and B, we caught the proprietor just as she was about to lock the doors for the night. As we quietly climbed the stairs, the witches were nowhere to be seen. Once in our room, Solomon sat down in a wing-backed chair close to the balcony. Maureen kicked off her heels and flopped across her bed.

"So, tell us about this uncanny ability you have," Solomon said. "Do you think it's why this biker wants you?" He stretched out his long legs, crossing his ankles and linking his fingers over his stomach.

I looked over at Maureen, who lay on her side, her arm propped against the mattress. She stared back at me, resting her chin in one hand.

"Judas Priest and cherry Popsicles! Do we have to get into this now?" I tossed my purse onto the dresser then thought better of it and stashed it under a pillow. Turning, I looked at Solomon. His gaze brimmed with interest.

"He wants you for some reason," Solomon stated. "He has powers too. I saw what he did to the door at the

Brunswick motel." He studied me for a moment. "What or who is he?"

"I don't know. Whenever he comes to me in my dreams or comes close to me, I...well, I..."

"What?" asked Maureen.

With my face flaming with heat, I whispered, "I have an orgasm."

Solomon muttered a really foul string of profanities under his breath. He met my gaze, and the jealousy and protectiveness in his eyes stunned me.

"We're all tied together somehow," said Maureen. "You, me, Solomon, the bikers and even those witches who have been watching out for you."

"You seem to have an ability all your own too," I pointed out. Unfastening my sandals, I straightened and kicked them off. "You sense things about me and talk about things that haven't happened yet."

She shrugged. "There's nothing to tell, really. I just pick up on thoughts and I get flashes of things that are about to happen and stuff that has already happened but has occurred somewhere else."

"Are you psychic?" Solomon questioned. "Can you look at someone and read their thoughts or know their futures?"

Maureen shook her head. "No, it's not like that." She rolled over onto her belly, her feet in the air. "I hear thoughts at odd moments. It's like listening to a radio station and another station filters in overriding it. And the pictures of things I see just come to me whenever and wherever. It's a handy ability since I travel alone most of the time. It's kept me out of several sticky situations."

Skeptical, I stared at Maureen. It sounded too simplistic for my taste, especially since she'd mentioned Anthony's name. My son was known by no one except for my parents and his adoptive parents.

"What's really weird," Maureen continued, "is that I feel like I know you both, but I've never met either of you before. That's why I approached you on the Interstate, Ruby. The pull was so strong, and when I saw you, I knew you." She shrugged. "I just didn't know "how" I knew you."

"Same here," said Solomon.

Quiet fell over the room. We all stared at one another. The weirdness of the situation was too much for me to bear.

Solomon said, "What about you, Ruby?"

"Yeah, me too," I replied. "It's like I've known you both from somewhere before."

"What do you think it means?" Maureen questioned.

Unease pelted me as I looked back and forth between them. "How the hell should I know?"

"Well," Solomon said, "I don't think its coincidence that we all feel the same way. And I also think this is why the bikers are after you—us."

I sighed and sat on my bed.

"Tell us about your power, Ruby," he prompted. "Maybe it's a part of this too."

"Oh, all right," I muttered, feeling as if I had no choice. "When I was a teenager, the white fire started materializing from my hands or fingertips whenever I became upset or frightened. I glow, my hair and nails change colors, and sometimes the power acts as an invisible force—"

"Like what you did to that biker chick at the museum!" Maureen stated.

"Yeah, but I couldn't control it and still can't—at least not very well. It's one of the reasons I prefer being a loner. It has caused me a lot of problems while growing up, especially in school then later in the workforce."

"Did you ever ask your folks about it?" Solomon questioned.

"It frightened my mother, so she ignored it, but Dad would act as though I were a monster whenever it happened. I worked hard to hide it from him, but finally a day arrived," I gulped and pushed the memory of my mother's death to the back of my mind, "when my father was forced to acknowledge my abilities. However, I know he has answers about why I'm like this, but he won't talk to me about it."

"Ruby's dad doesn't like to talk about the Nutters," Maureen interjected.

I shot her an irritated look.

Solomon straightened in his chair. "What's he got against his family?"

As Solomon's interest in my perverted talent grew, so did my discomfort. Mom's death was something I still couldn't deal with and even tap dancing around the issue made me feel sick and lightheaded.

"I have no idea." I scooted back to lean against the headboard. "But Maureen's right. Dad always says 'the past is in the past' and refuses to say anything more about his family. I don't want to talk about it anymore," I said forcefully. "I'm tired, and we have to hit the road early."

"You're right." Solomon stood, stretching.

Relief washed through me.

"I'll sleep in here with you two," Solomon murmured as he stood. "Both Azazel and Wayne know you're here now, so I think it's wise if I stay in your room tonight. Put one of your wards over the inn too."

I glanced at Maureen, who nodded her agreement.

"Yeah," I said, "You're probably right."

"I'll go change and be right back." Solomon shut the door behind him.

As I turned around, Maureen stood stark naked in the center of the room and kicked her dress and undies over to a pile of our dirty laundry. Bending over at the foot of her bed, she presented me with a view that would give me nightmares for weeks to come.

Maureen retrieved her oversized t-shirt and pulled it over her head. She drew the covers back on the bed and hit the button on the little bedside light.

Bathed in darkness, I stomped toward the bathroom and stood in the crack of illumination spilling through the door as I studied her shape beneath the sheet. What must it be like not to worry about anything? Was it possible to be as carefree as Maureen? Or was it all an act?

I stepped into the bathroom and closed the door. Being carefree was impossible—at least for me. My past and powers haunted my every waking moment.

Finished in the bathroom, I discovered Solomon waiting for me in the room.

"Shall I sleep on the floor?" he asked.

At first I was going to tell him he should, but why fight it? I shook my head and stepped out on the balcony, focusing my strength into my power. A soft glow surrounded me and lit up the balcony. The feeling of electricity bled through my torso and into my arms, down into my hands. This time the invisible force poured forth, and I imagined it over the B and B and even put a ward around the Excursion and Shunka's pen for good measure. Tired, I closed the French doors.

Solomon stood just inside the threshold waiting for me. "Floor or bed?"

"Bed, but we're not doing anything."

"Remember what I said to you earlier tonight?"

Like an unexpected slap, his words penetrated my brain. I sighed grumpily.

He swept the backside of his fingers over my cheek. "Besides, don't you think it would be a bit difficult with Maureen in the room?"

A soft giggle reached me from the other side of the suite.

Fuming, I marched past him and hurriedly donned my Cleveland Browns shirt. Without another word, I climbed into bed.

Long, desirous moments passed as I listened to Solomon undress. The soft whisper of his slacks sliding down his long, muscled legs, the clink of the metal belt buckle and the soft swish of his beater landing on the carpet all sounded erotic in the darkness.

Heaven help me, how I want the man!

Solomon pulled the covers aside and slipped into bed. He rolled with his back to me, and within minutes, his breath grew steady and low as he slept. His body heat warmed the sheets, radiated through them to stoke the flames of my desire.

I lay there quietly a long time battling the need raging through me.

Damn him!

Chapter Twenty-Two

The following morning, I awoke to find Maureen and Solomon gone. Maureen's backpack waited by the door. Figuring they'd both gone downstairs for breakfast, I showered, dressed and finished gathering my things. Later, dressed and ready to go, I stepped into the hall and turned toward the sound of a door opening. Maureen emerged with Mr. Jebbstart. He hugged her and placed a not-so-chaste kiss on her mouth.

"I'll always remember you, my pet," he said with emotion in his voice. He patted something glistening on her arm, kissed her again and closed the door.

She saw me and blushed hot pink.

She didn't! No way!

"Are you all packed?" she asked shakily, her gaze on everything except me.

"Uh, yeah."

"I'll just get my gear before you shut the door." Without meeting my eyes, Maureen leaned through the threshold and retrieved her stuff. "I'll grab your cosmetic case for you since your hands are full."

"Thanks."

As she straightened, my attention landed on her right wrist. A beautiful silver bracelet inlaid with puau pieces encircled her wrist.

"That bracelet is lovely," I said.

"Mr. Jebbstart gave it to me. He makes jewelry and peddles it around Florida and Georgia." She still couldn't look at me, and as she spoke, her cheeks flamed redder. As elderly guys go, Mr. Jebbstart was a debonair man and didn't look his seventy-odd years at all, but to sleep with him? For what? A nice piece of jewelry? Hell, I wasn't sure about anything anymore, and I was the last person to judge someone for their actions when I could barely control my own.

"Hey, it's none of my business." I pulled the door shut.

"Thanks."

"For what?" With my duffle bag slung over one shoulder and a suitcase in each hand, I paused.

"For not asking any questions."

"Remember that the next time you start pelting me with yours." I grinned.

Flushing pink again, she smiled back. "You're a good friend."

Not expecting such a response, I turned away with my cheeks burning and started down the hall.

"Solomon's getting Shunka from the kennel," she stated.

"Then we'll meet him at the SUV."

Downstairs, quiet permeated the inn. The three witches were absent from their usual places in the den. Once we checked out, we headed for the door.

My biggest worry was the bikers and Wayne. Were they nearby, watching and waiting?

Outside under the carport, Solomon loaded the Malamute and our bags. The sunshine gleamed on the Excursion's shiny paint, the wind brought the aroma of fresh coconut, and I was glad to be on our way again.

Solomon rearranged my purchases from the day before so there was room for everything in the luggage area. I pulled a box from the top of a shopping bag.

Maureen climbed into the backseat with the dog.

"Who's driving?" Solomon asked.

"I will."

He tossed me the keys, and I hopped in behind the steering wheel.

"What's in the box?" he asked once he'd settled in the passenger seat.

"I bought something for you and Maureen yesterday."

I slipped the key into the ignition before taking the lid off the white box. Inside it, a pewter sand dollar dusted with fine white sand laid in three pieces, each one with a rawhide strap to go around our necks. I handed one to Maureen, one to Solomon then took mine out and quickly put it on.

"Aw, Ruby, these are so cool!" Maureen said tearfully.

"Oh, no you don't!" I said, looking hard at her. "Don't get sappy on me."

"Okay." She smiled and slipped the necklace over her head. The sand dollar nestled between her monstrous breasts and glittered in the sun.

"Very nice." Solomon donned his too. "Thank you, Ruby." He leaned across the console and brushed his lips across mine, startling me.

"You're welcome." I tried to ignore the pleased smile on his handsome face. Emotion washed over me, and I suddenly fought tears and had to bite my lower lip to keep it from trembling.

****

By noon, the clear skies gave way to silver haze and stifling humidity. We stopped at a rest area and bought sodas and cold-cut sandwiches. Solomon took the dog out to the park's pet area while Maureen and I sat at a picnic table and ate. She stared off into space as she chewed a mouthful of her ham-and-cheese sandwich. The unbearable heat affected everyone. Parents lay on blankets beneath shade trees with their babies while older children immersed themselves in hand-held games or reclined against tree trunks listening to iPods and MP3 players.

The elderly remained in their air-conditioned Park Avenues and Coup de Villes, waiting while their spouses or traveling companions braved the elements in pursuit of a fresh pair of Depends. Big rigs, pickups pulling travel trailers, and RVs all idled in the larger parking lot, their A/C units dripping condensation onto the pavement.

Sighing, I took a long swallow of my Pepsi. We'd already passed Daytona Beach, Titusville and Merritt Island. Melbourne and Vero Beach would soon be behind us as well. If we drove until suppertime, we could be in Florida City by nightfall.

Back on the road, we traveled in silence save for the pop tunes blaring from the SUV's stereo system. I stopped once for gasoline, but after that, Solomon drove all the way through to Florida City. The closer we got to the town, the more subdued Maureen became. Around eight that evening, we rolled into the state's toe-like tip. Since none of the hotels Solomon called would allow animals, he found a pet friendly motel instead.

From there we could drive to Key West in two to three hours, so I didn't see much point in fighting tourists at the peak of vacation season for over-priced lodging in The Keys. Solomon readily agreed with me, but Maureen said nothing.

Our room was the last one at the far end by a high privacy fence. As Solomon unloaded the SUV, I fed and watered the Malamute, who panted in the heat. Striding to the heating-and-cooling unit on the wall, I cranked up the A/C full blast. The expression on the dog's face almost looked like gratitude.

Our room possessed a kitchenette. Thinking of cooking something, I asked, "Do you want to go with me to buy a few groceries, Maureen?"

She lay sprawled on the second double bed. "I guess."

"If you don't want to, you can stay here."

"No, I'll go."

She slipped on her sandals as if it were the biggest chore in the world.

I grabbed my purse and rummaged inside for the wad of hidden money. Quickly, I counted out half of it and offered it to Maureen.

"Here, this is your half of the money."

"You keep it for me," she said. "I'd only lose it."

The fact that she wanted me to hang on to her money shocked me. I'd always figured as soon as Maureen had a couple thousand in her hands she would want to go shopping for more high-heeled shoes.

"Well, do you want some of it to keep in your pocket?"

She shrugged. "I suppose."

Passing her two one-hundred-dollar bills, I asked, "What's wrong?"

"Nothing."

"Are you sure? You don't act like your usual—" I sensed my razor-sharp tongue should be held in check. "You act like you're upset about something. You're not as perky as usual."

"It'll pass." She shoved the bills into her pocket and sashayed to the door. "Are we going or not?"

"Okay, let's go."

Her change in behavior unnerved me. Maureen had such an effervescent personality that the switch to quiet and brooding creeped me out. Then there was the money issue. She trusted me to keep her part of the money for her? I wouldn't trust Maureen, so why did she trust me?

No, I was wrong. I did trust Maureen and that freaked me out even more.

When we stepped outside, Solomon walked toward us with the last of our gear. "Where are you off to?" he asked.

"We're going to pick up a few groceries to stock our kitchen," I answered as Maureen got in the SUV.

"Should you go by yourselves?" he asked.

Shit. I hadn't thought of that. My gaze met his, and the worry in his eyes touched my heart.

I crossed my arms over my breasts. "What do you suggest?"

"You stay here with Shunka and put a ward on the room. I'll take Maureen to the store and be back ASAP."

"Does this mean that from now on I'm going to be a prisoner of motel rooms or always chaperoned?"

"We all just need to be careful," he replied. "At least until we figure out what's going on and how to handle it."

"Whenever that will be," I mumbled.

He kissed me, and I found myself leaning into him. "Please don't kiss me," I whispered.

"It's just a kiss, Ruby."

"No, it's not. It's playing dirty."

"Only if you allow it." He offered me a lopsided grin that urged my heart to thrash crazily. "How about a decent bottle of wine?" he suggested.

"Sure." I looked over at my hitchhiker, who sat quietly in the Excursion's passenger seat looking as if she were about to be driven to the guillotine.

Solomon's gaze followed mine. "Did you find out what's bugging Maureen?"

"No."

"Well, don't press her."

"She's starting to wig me out."

Solomon chuckled. "And you didn't think the woman could ever be quiet."

That made me smile.

****

Later, sprawled on one of the beds, I watched a rerun of *All in the Family*.

"We're back, Ruby," Solomon hollered through the door.

They brought in three plastic sacks of groceries and set them on a small kitchen table.

Solomon gathered his dirty clothes and left for the laundry room. Maureen changed into her bikini and wandered to the pool for an evening swim while I made supper.

One thing I could do well was cook. Since moving out of my dad's place, I didn't cook often, but when I did, I'd go all out to make a scrumptious meal. I took out a package of pork chops and created a marinade with some basic herbs and spices. As I worked, I thought about Maureen's odd behavior and wondered if it had any connection with Mr. Jebbstart.

The door opened, and Solomon entered, hefting a basket of folded laundry. Maureen trailed in behind him.

After tripping over the dog, which had crept into the kitchen area, I booted him in the ass, yelling, "Get out and stay out or I'm going to make a fur rug out of you!"

"I think he's trying to say you're a good cook," Solomon said, laughing as he placed the basket on my bed.

I shook my head. "No, he's proving he's a pig in the disguise of a dog."

"Be nice to Shunka." Maureen walked toward the bathroom just off from the kitchenette. "He's the one who saved you from that big biker."

"It still doesn't mean I have to like the overgrown furball." I finished up the chops and placed them on a plate.

Solomon scooped his clothes out of the basket and disappeared into the suite's tiny back bedroom.

I turned, staring first at the suite's door then at the bathroom door. "Isn't anyone going to eat supper?"

"You bet I am," Solomon said as he sat at a dinette on the other side of the counter. "It smells fantastic."

Maureen called, "I'm not hungry!"

I stared at the bathroom. Prickles of irritation raced over my skin. "What?"

"I said I'm not hungry!"

I strode to the bathroom and hit the door with the heel of my hand. "You're going to eat if I have to knock down that door and drag you to the table!"

Someone rapped on the opposite side of the wall, yelling, "Keep it down over there!"

"Ruby, please, I don't feel well," she whined.

I looked at Solomon for help.

He shrugged. "Maybe she really doesn't feel well." He helped himself to a bowl of salad. "She didn't say but a dozen words when we went shopping."

With a sigh, I contemplated ripping the door off the hinges just to vent some frustration. I wasn't sure why her refusal to eat bugged me so much, but it did.

"Fine," I growled. "Eat leftovers!"

"I'm sorry, Ruby," she said, her voice tearful.

"Aw, hell!" Snatching up the pork chops, I strode to the dinette.

"Calm down," Solomon said. "If Maureen is sick, we'll know soon enough. If something is bothering her, she'll either tell us or she won't. Sit and enjoy the nice meal you cooked."

We ate in silence except for Solomon's occasional contented sighs. The reason I was so pissed at Maureen eluded me. Finally, I felt the weight of Solomon's gaze and looked up from my plate.

"What's with you?" he asked.

I shrugged.

"Look, Ruby," he stabbed a slice of cucumber with his fork, "we have several more days of traveling together. I think it's only fair we all open up a little bit. I know you're fond of Maureen."

I bristled. "What makes you think that?"

He fingered the pewter sand dollar on the suede strap.

Wilting, I focused on the ranch dressing left on my plate, noting that it looked like I felt—mixed up with various ingredients floating in it.

"What set you off just now?" he pressed.

My frustration mounted. I picked up my fork and swirled a radish slice in the dressing. Why was I so pissed? Then it hit me with force. How many times had my father done the same thing to me? How many meals had I cooked for Dad only to have him grab a six-pack, a box of Twinkies, a bag of potato chips and sit in the recliner to watch one sports program after another?

A memory washed through my mind. "Dad," I'd said the night I'd cooked the last meal I vowed to ever cook for him again. "I made fried chicken, mashed potatoes and gravy—"

"Shut up, Ruby," he snapped from his ratty recliner. "The ball game's about to start."

"Why don't you come in here and have supper with me?" I prepared him a plate and set a knife and fork on the table next to it. "I fried the chicken with Mom's recipe, just the way you like it."

"I'm happy with my beer and Twinkies," he said.

"But, Dad, you need to eat right and—"

He never looked at me, never got up from his chair. "Fuck off, Ruby!" His words and tone sliced through me faster than lightning. "I don't need you or your help!"

With tears pouring down my face and trying desperately to keep my sobs quiet so I wouldn't set him off again, I left Dad's plate on the table, packed all the food into containers, put them in the fridge, and left.

I pushed the memory aside and looked up at Solomon with tears in my eyes.

"Ruby?" He put his fork down and reached for my hand, squeezing my fingers. "I'm enjoying the meal," he said. "Doesn't that count?"

With a slight wobble to my lower lip, I replied. "Yeah, but Maureen isn't."

"Sweetheart, you can't control other people's actions."

Solomon's comment shocked me. For a long moment I just sat there staring at him with my mouth ajar. He was right. I couldn't control what others said and did. I'd lived my entire life worrying about everyone else—my father, co-workers, acquaintances, my landlady—and how they would react to me and whether or not they'd like, love or hate me. However, it all boiled down to the fact that I had to live my life, not them.

Standing, I stacked dirty dishes and walked around the counter to deposit them in the sink. Although it seemed as though a ray of sunshine had finally penetrated my dark world, I had to mull over the revelation more, define it and examine it for cracks.

"Ruby," he said, "are you okay?"

The concern in his voice touched me. With my back to him, I began washing and rinsing the dishes. "I'm fine."

"If I offended you, I'm sorry."

I shook my head. "No, you didn't offend me. It's just that...well..."

He stood and walked into the kitchenette. Warm, strong hands settled on my waist. Solomon drew me against him, the heat of his body comforting. For a moment I allowed myself to lean into him.

"What is it, Ruby?"

Solomon's breath caressed my ear, and a delicious shiver wiggled through me. His touch, his aroma and the seduction of his voice all wove a treacherous spell around my body and heart. It would be so easy to give in, take him by the hand and lead him into the tiny back bedroom so he could have his way with me.

It didn't matter that I'd suddenly had a revelation that had given me a dose of much-needed emotional strength. It didn't matter that I desired Solomon's touch and his body straining against mine. I knew the truth, and the truth was that my life was cursed and love wasn't an option. I had to avoid the calamity that would strike my heart if I allowed Solomon to woo me any further.

"Never mind. It's not important." Pulling away from Solomon, I forced resolve into my voice and focused on finishing up the last of the dirty dishes.

"Are you sure?"

For an instant I almost changed my mind, almost spilled all the sorrow and agony I felt on his doorstep. "Yeah, I'm fine. Don't worry about it."

A gusty sight escaped him. Instead of walking away, he withdrew a tea towel from a drawer and dried the dishes. I let the wash and rinse water out of the sinks, sprayed them down, and then stowed the dry dishes in various cupboards. We worked together silently, and I realized how much I enjoyed Solomon's companionship, even while we completed a mundane task.

"So tell me more about yourself," he said, hanging the tall on the oven's handle. He turned and sat at the table.

I placed the leftovers in the mini fridge. "You're lucky you know what little you do about me."

"Why?"

"The more you know, the more likely you'll run."

He arched a white brow. "Seems like I should've run when you first displayed your powers, but I didn't. I'm still here."

Heat rose to my cheeks.

He caught my hand as I passed him and pulled me over to his seat. "We're meant to be together, Ruby. We both know it." His pale gaze bored into mine. "When I saw you that first time, I felt a pull that scared me. Then when you stayed at my home and we," he slipped his hand under my shirt and brushed his thumb back and forth along my belly, "we kissed, there was no doubt in my mind. I don't know how I know you from some-place, but I do." He skimmed his hand around my hip and palmed my ass. "And you can deny it all you want, but something bigger than both of us is going on, and we're the characters in this sinister play. Whatever it is, it's why we need to go to Key West."

Shunka woofed softly from his spot in the center of the kitchenette.

"Traitor," I whispered over my shoulder.

Solomon released my hand and cupped my cheek with it. "Deny it, Ruby. I dare you."

His touch on my belly, my rear, my face—oh, how I wanted him. But he was right. Something bigger than both of us was indeed happening. I only prayed it didn't turn into a catastrophe.

Solomon wrapped his arms around me, his mouth claiming mine.

No, no! I can't let him do this to me! I have to fight...

But the more his mouth moved against mine, the more I wanted from him. Whimpering, I returned his kiss. His tongue tickled the seam of my lips, and I parted them, allowing him access.

The bathroom door screeched open.

"Bathroom's free if anyone wants a shower," Maureen announced.

Solomon pulled away, his eyes dark gray with need, and walked to the tiny bedroom off from the kitchen.

"I'll get out of here so you can change. I'm going to relax for a few minutes."

She smiled at him and removed the towel wrapped around her hair. He stepped through the door and shut it.

"There are leftovers in the fridge." I flipped on the television with the remote and climbed onto the end of my bed.

"I'm sorry I didn't eat," Maureen replied softly. "I really don't feel like eating."

"That's fine."

"Don't be mad at me."

"I'm not."

"You sound like you are."

"Really, I'm not, but if you keep pestering me about it, I will be."

"Sorry."

"There you go again."

She tossed me an apologetic look and tucked the bath sheet tighter between her boobs. Sitting, she silently combed out her hair.

The bed's softness called to me, and I considered retiring early. Surfing channels, I watched Maureen out of the corner of my eye. Without any makeup, she looked extremely young. She leaned over, head between her knees, and combed her hair backward. In many ways, she was so innocent. I wondered what it was like to go through life as she had, drifting from one town to another, viewing the world and people through her eyes.

"Are you feeling better?" I asked, pretending to be more interested in television.

The Malamute padded over and flopped down on the floor between our beds.

"Yeah, I guess." She straightened and smoothed her hair with the comb. "I just had a bad case of nerves."

That got my full attention. "Nerves?"

She dropped the comb on the bedspread, turned and looked at me with such pain-filled eyes I was flabbergasted. Tears welled up in them. Not the sort of tears she usually displayed, but ones of such agony that words failed me.

"I wish I could tell you," she said.

"So talk to me about it."

"I can't. You'll think I'm a horrible person."

"Maureen, I'm the last person to judge anyone." Oh, but hadn't I? Hadn't I assumed she was a brainless hussy when I first met her and that Solomon couldn't be trusted?

Hypocrite! Inwardly, I cringed.

With sorrow in my tone, I added, "No one judges you or thinks badly of you."

"Maybe not, but if I tell you what's bugging me, you'll judge me just the same."

"Try me."

Her mouth worked, but no sound came out. Sighing, she shook her head.

"All right, I'll not press about it."

"You're friendship means too much to me, Ruby," she said with conviction. "I don't want to lose it." She sniffled and used the discarded towel to wipe her eyes.

"Don't you think we'll part ways once the business part of our trip is completed?" I said.

"No."

Blinking, I sat quietly. She had said that one little word with such assurance it left me unsettled.

"Look, if you don't want to tell me, that's fine. If you do, that's fine too." I pointed the remote at the TV, surfing from The Game Show Network to QVC to the SyFy Channel.

"I used to be a prostitute," Maureen blurted. "My mother was a prostitute, and Aunt Lula is the Madame of the cathouse I grew up in."

I dropped the remote on the floor. The back popped off of it, and the batteries rolled helter-skelter across the carpet.

Chapter Twenty-Three

At that moment many things about Maureen suddenly made sense. The means in which she got money for her fancy French-tipped nails despite Lula's wired money, her statement about doing a guy a favor and being paid with a meal, and her reaction to my smart-assed comment about the truck stop hookers. To say I was shocked would have been an understatement, but I had enough faults of my own, so I wasn't about to cast the first stone.

Sobs pelted the room. The door to the back bedroom opened, and Solomon hurried out.

Unsure what to do, I just sat there, feeling helpless and stupid.

"I'm so sorry, Ruby!" Maureen balled the towel and shoved her face into it. "I know you hate me now."

Her muffled words stabbed my heart. How could I hate her? It was then I realized I considered her my best friend—the only true friend I'd ever had. I hadn't known her long, but somehow we knew one another from another time. It didn't make any sense, but our friendship was still something we both recognized.

I moved over to the other bed, my foot catching a battery and sending it careening under the dresser. Solomon leaned against the kitchen counter, his haunting gaze on us.

"Maureen," I said, "it's okay. I don't judge you. I don't care about your past."

On the floor, Shunka whined and placed his muzzle between his paws.

How to comfort her? What could I do to make her feel better?

At a loss, I put one arm around her shoulder and drew her to me. The aroma of deodorant soap and perfumed shampoo tickled my nose. She sobbed harder.

"Judas Priest and cherry Popsicles! Calm down, Maureen. Everything is okay." I shot Solomon a look for help, but he only smiled. Scowling at him, I half hugged my hitchhiker and jostled her shoulders to get her attention. "You're my friend and that's all that matters."

"Do you," she sniffled, "really mean that?" She lowered the towel slightly, her big, watery eyes peeping at me over the edge of it.

The stunned and yet delighted expression in her eyes almost made me burst out laughing, but the sensation fizzled the instant I realized I truly did mean what I'd said.

"Yes." I hated the emotion in my voice. "I really mean it."

Maureen sighed and relaxed against me. She sniffled several times, hiccupped and sniffed harder. Solomon crossed the room, picked up a box of tissues from the dresser and slid the box over the bedspread where I could reach them. He strode back to his room and closed the door.

"I'm sorry I've been so mean to you." I handed her a tissue. "I don't intend for things to come out of my mouth the way they often do, and—"

"It's your defense mechanism," Maureen said. "I understand. You have a lot of secrets and too many scars."

There's nothing like stunning me into silence.

Desperate to turn the discussion away from me, I said, "Do you want to talk about what you just told me?"

"Nothing to tell, really."

She sighed and straightened, looking at me with such a relief that I almost envied her. Oh, to be able to cleanse myself like she'd just done, to unload years of heartache and misery by confiding in someone.

"Want to go out by the pool and talk?" I suggested. "We can look at the stars and enjoy the evening."

Her pleased smile gave her an angelic look. "That would be great."

****

After she dressed in shorts and a t-shirt, we poured ourselves glasses of soda and made our way outside. As promised, I left the door open so Solomon could hear us should we have any unwanted visitors. In the enclosed pool area, we sat on chaises in the far corner beneath a shade tree hanging over the poolside.

The motel lights and moonshine danced upon the pool's surface. Despite the day's humidity and the lights of Florida City, the sky boasted a nice view of the stars. The jagged silhouettes of the surrounding palm trees framed the blue velvet expanse scattered with white pinpoints. A tropical breeze stirred the water, and the filtering system mingled with the sounds of traffic on the main strip. Occasionally a parrot screeched, and I caught the distinct odor of chlorine threaded with the subtle aroma of some sort of night-blooming flower.

Closing my eyes, I let my mind go blank. I couldn't sort through the craziness of the past few days, nor the emotions surging through me like ocean tides. None of it made any sense. It all seemed surreal.

"Tell me about your mom," I said, looking over at Maureen.

She turned on her side and drew her legs up. "I was so young at the time I don't remember much about her except her big green eyes, long blonde hair, and she always smelled like lilacs. She was one of Aunt Lula's girls. There were sixteen to twenty prostitutes who lived in the brothel at all times." She sighed, and her gaze moved to the sky. "One of my mother's regulars fell in love with her, and when she wouldn't quit the business and marry him, he beat her. Lula rushed my mother to the hospital, but Mom died from internal injuries. After that, Lula raised me."

"So you worked in the brothel when you were old enough?" I surmised.

"Yes."

"But you left."

"I knew there was more to life than selling my body. I got a call one day from my son. He'd tracked me down, and I realized I couldn't bear it if he knew the truth about me. I left the brothel and I've been wandering the country ever since."

With my soda halfway to my mouth, I stopped and gaped at her. "You have a son?"

She nodded. "I had him when I was fourteen. Prostitutes in places like Madam Lula's practice safe sex, but sometimes condoms break, and I hadn't been on the pill long enough for it to be effective yet. That's how I got pregnant. I had the baby and put him up for adoption. Once Payton turned eighteen, he tracked me down, but he doesn't know I'm a prostitute, and neither did his adoptive parents."

"How old is he now?"

"Twenty-one."

"So that makes you...?"

"Thirty-five," she replied.

"We're the same age."

She smiled.

"You can't run away from your past, Maureen. Trust me, I know this well. And we're both still young, so we have our entire lives ahead of us. I don't want to spend it running from mistakes, do you?"

"No." She sipped her drink and sat quietly for a few seconds. "I thought maybe if I was out in the world, I'd see and do things that would give me something to talk about with my son. Something besides 'oh, by the way, I'm a high-priced whore.'"

"I lost my mother when I was very young." The admission sprang from my mouth before I could stop it. However, it was liberating to say it aloud.

Her startled gaze flew up to meet mine. "Really?"

I drew in a deep breath and let it out slowly. "I was a young teenager when it happened, the time when a girl needs her mother the most." Pain, as it always did, stabbed my soul. "My father blames me for her death, which is one of many reasons he resents me so much."

"Why does he blame you?"

The question surprised me, and I sucked in a startled breath.

"It's okay," said Maureen. "You don't have to tell me."

Taking the risk, I surged on. "I caused a fire with my power and my mother...she..."

Maureen reached over and threaded her fingers with mind, squeezing gently. I bit my lower lip and drew strength from the pain.

"It's okay," she said. "You don't have to tell me any more."

After several minutes, I squeezed her hand back and said, "We're a lot alike."

"Yes, we are, my friend."

Her words rocketed me back in time. I found myself reclining on a cushioned bench with curled ends as back rests with stags and boars carved into the wood. Next to me, Maureen sat dressed in a long, heavy tunic dress. Even in the vision she was green-eyed and blonde.

"He loves you," she said to me.

"I know this," I replied, "but I put his life in danger as well as yours."

"Those who look down upon a harlot are not without sin themselves." She leaned over and placed a kiss upon my cheek. "I am not worried about my safety. You and the White King are my only concern. Flee with him, my friend. The Sons of God won't stop until they possess you and murder him."

"Ruby?" A warm hand shook my arm. "*Ruby!*"

Jolted out of the vision, I found myself poolside again, the wind rustling the surrounding palm and fern fronds. My gaze snapped up to meet Maureen's.

"What just happened?" she asked.

"A vision."

She smiled. "I mean what was it about?"

"How did—?"

"You forget I hear snippets of what goes on in a person's mind."

I shivered and tried to shake the feeling of doom. The Sons of God? Why did that seem so familiar? Hadn't I compared Solomon to them a few nights ago?

"Ruby?" Maureen urged.

Quickly, I relayed the vision to her and told her about some of the others I'd had over the past few weeks and especially the last few days.

"And when Solomon and his sister were assaulted by those hunters, he said they called him 'White King' too," I finished, wishing for once that the intense Florida heat would chase the chill from my body. "Do you know what the Sons of God are?"

"No, I don't. What do you think it all means?"

"I don't know, but I do know that the trip, the bikers—everything's tied together somehow."

"I think you're right," she said. "History repeats itself."

I frowned curiously.

"History has a way of starting all over again." Maureen stretched out on the chaise and set her now-empty glass on the patio tile between us. "Historians say history runs in cycles, that only the people, names, and places change. It's like fashion. Look at all the clothing styles from thirty and forty years ago that are back on the market now. And the world shares a collective consciousness, so it's only natural history would repeat itself."

What an incredible concept. Could Maureen be right? And wouldn't that mean the three of us had been reincarnated?

"Yes," said Maureen, "reincarnation."

I quirked a brow at her for hearing my thoughts. "I don't believe in reincarnation, and even if it's true, it doesn't explain why we're back together again."

"Unless you're an Atheist, every religion believes in a soul or spirit for each person." She gestured toward the night sky. "Christians believe our souls are pieces of God because we're made in His image. Maybe there's only so many pieces of Him to go around, so He has to recycle a few souls every now and then, especially if the jobs those souls were meant to do go unfinished."

Incredulous, I stared hard at Maureen. What had happened to my ditzy Marilyn Monroe lookalike? Was her naivety and childlike charm a façade?

"No," she answered my unspoken question. "I told you Aunt Lula educated me well. Plus, I love to read."

The thunderous sound of motorcycles assaulted the night. I gasped, stiffening in my chair. Maureen's hand sought mine again, and we sat there waiting, our attention riveted on the motel office and its entranceway.

The bikes slowed, their riders gearing them down. To my dismay, the roar of the steel horses turned into the entrance. One bike after another filed into the parking lot, the sound of their motors vibrating my bones. They all shut down by the office. The big man, who the others had called Azazel, motioned at the psycho redhead. Her boyfriend helped her off the Harley, and she walked inside, ducking slightly as she stepped through the door. Even from the poolside, I could still see the stunned expression on the night clerk's face.

"Ruby! He will sense you. Protect yourself!"

Without hesitation, I called upon the power nestled deep within me and let the invisible force flow out of my hands and over Maureen and I where we sat. She glanced over at me, somehow knowing what I'd just done. Next, I reinforced the ward already in place around the suite where Solomon sat watching television.

He must have heard the racket caused by the bikes. He peeped around the edge of the doorway. I motioned for him to go back inside.

If he steps out now, they'll see him.

He offered me a helpless look, and I again motioned that he stay put. Slowly, he drew back and partially shut the door so that a narrow line of light spilled across the sidewalk.

The red-haired chick exited the office and tossed keys to a few of the others. The thirteen motorcycles roared to life again. They passed us to park two-by-two in the middle parking spaces lining the motel. The choppers shifted from machine to half beast, their snarls, growls and shrieks one with the thrum of the engines.

Maureen hissed in surprise. "What are they riding?"

"You see them too?" I asked. "Demonic animal heads in place of the handlebars and gas tanks?"

"Yes, but how is that possible?" she whispered.

The bikers dismounted, tossing the beasts' silver reins over the seats. They grabbed some of their gear from saddlebags and paired off in twos, threes, and fours into the center section of rooms. The doors shut behind them, and my gaze returned to the beast bikes as they transformed into suicide machines once more.

"Ruby, I'm scared," Maureen said softly.

"So am I."

"What about Solomon?"

"I've cast a protection ward over us and reinforced the one around our suite. Solomon will be fine as long as he doesn't come outside." I stood and pulled her to her feet too. "Just in case, we'll skirt the privacy wall around the parking lot, slip behind the dumpster, and then run to our room from there."

We walked to the pool gate where I halted and looked at her. "Not a word or sound."

She nodded.

Holding hands, we stayed close to the pool's chain-link fence and turned right around its corner to hug the high privacy wall surrounding the motel's lot. Thank God we were both barefoot. With less worry of making noise, we traversed the length of the fence, but I still expected one of those demonic things to let out a piercing scream, alerting the others to our presence.

We reached the back corner and began to creep along the shorter wall until we arrive at the dumpster. There, we stooped, peeking around the back of it, the stench of rotting vegetation and other trash almost unbearable.

From our vantage point, I detected movement through the crack in our suite's door, so I knew Solomon watched and waited.

"Use your power. Pop the security light, then cross to the door in the darkness."

"Did you hear that?" Maureen whispered.

"What?"

"That voice."

I looked at her. "That was in my head. You heard it?"

She nodded, her eyes huge.

This just gets weirder and weirder.

Maureen frowned at me.

"Stop listening to what's going on in my head!"

"I can't. It's like a radio station that filters in and out." She pressed closer, trembles passing through her body.

"It seems your ability is growing stronger," I mused.

"No, it's the fact we're friends now," she replied, "so I can tune into your thoughts easier." She glanced at me. "Whose voice is it?"

"I have no clue. It's been with me since the morning I left to go south." Sighing, I gathered strength from deep inside me. "Okay, I'm going to zap the light, so be ready to move."

Kneeling, I faced the wall and stared up at the security lamp bathing the last two motel rooms in false daylight. This time, the power rose without me really calling upon it, as if it had been waiting for me to summon it. Although surprised, I also realized that the glow and odd hair and nail color didn't occur if I was in control of my power. The awful sting coursed down my arms, into my palms and exited out my extended hands. One short, sparkly white burst hit the lamp, and it popped, its innards dying. Darkness shrouded the last two doors and the dumpster.

"Well?" Maureen said.

I waited, my gaze stuck to the choppers lined up in the spaces. They remained inanimate.

"Nothing's happening," I said. "The bikes are just sitting there." I crouched, poised to sprint to the door. "Okay, let's go."

She took my hand, and together, we rushed to our suite. Once there, I shoved the door open, and we stumbled through. Our feet tangled, and Solomon caught us before we landed on top of one another. With my foot, I nudged the door shut.

"What the hell are you two doing?" Solomon asked as he steadied me on my feet. "I heard those choppers and couldn't think of anything except how to reach you." He pulled me against him and kissed me.

Allowing myself a moment to enjoy the security he offered, I absorbed the comfort and attention. Finally, I stepped back and filled Solomon in on what was going on, and then told him and Maureen about seeing the bikers at St. Augustine's campground.

"We should leave," said Maureen. "We'll wait until about two or three in the morning, when most everyone will be asleep, then quietly check out."

He shook his head. "I think we should stay. Wait them out."

Across the room, the dog emitted a big sigh.

"Don't you think they'll recognize the SUV when they see it in the daytime?" I asked.

"Not unless they took down my plate numbers. There are hundreds of black Excursions driving around," he said. "Look, if we sit tight and let them leave first, they'll be ahead of us instead of following us."

"How's that going to help our situation?" Pacing, I gestured as I spoke to vent stress and frustration. "I don't know where I'm being drawn to, but it seems they're traveling to the same destination. I think it would be a big mistake to let them get there first."

"Ruby's right," Maureen stated.

Running one hand through his hair, Solomon closed his eyes and stood quietly for a moment. "Okay, we'll pack up and then check out about three. That will put us in Key West around six a.m., depending on the morning work traffic."

A knock at the door nearly sent me shooting straight through the ceiling. Maureen and I grabbed one another.

"What do we do?" she whispered.

Solomon strode to the door and peeped through the spy hole. "Whoever he is, he doesn't look like one of the bikers." He turned and placed his index finger over his lips. "Who is it?" he called through the door.

"Anthony."

The name shot through me like a spear.

"Does that name mean anything to either of you?" asked Solomon.

"Let him in," I said, both elated and horrified at Anthony's presence. "It's my son."

"Please," Anthony's voice sliced through the door. "Ruby's in danger. All of you are."

Chapter Twenty-Four

"Son?" Solomon said.

If it wasn't for the severity of our situation, I would've cracked up laughing at his comical expression.

"Yes. The person I went to see in St. Augustine."

Realization passed over Solomon's face.

Maureen nudged me and smiled, an understanding expression in her eyes. I smiled back.

Opening the door, Solomon let Anthony inside.

Close up, I realized how much Anthony looked like me. I saw Cole Vandercourt in him, too, but Anthony looked more like me right down to the high forehead, the widow's peak, and dark green hazel eyes.

Questions raced through my head. Should I hug him? Did he want to hug me? How did he know we were in danger? I began with the most obvious.

"What are you doing here, Anthony? Does Katherine—your mom—know you're here?"

"No. Yes. Well, she knows I went looking for you but that's all."

"You need to go back," I said firmly. "You're putting your life in danger coming here."

"I had to warn you, Ruby. I see..." He gulped and looked away. "I see "things" chasing you. I have dreams, see visions. They're people, but not people." When he finally met my gaze again fear shone in my son's eyes. "And they ride motorcycles that aren't really motorcycles—they're demonic beasts. They bikers need you for something, and that's the part I can't see. It scares the hell out of me."

"You don't know anything about me—"

"These dreams and visions have been coming to me for the last several weeks, but they've grown worse the past few days." He paced by the door. "I knew I had to find you, but when I told Mom about what was happening to me, she changed, started treating me differently like I frightened her." Pausing, he stared at the door for a moment as if he might bolt from the room. "Somehow, I knew you were my real mom." Anthony turned. "I remembered you at the Castillos and had felt and unbelievably pull from you. When I asked Mom if you were my real mother, she said yes and admitted I'd been adopted. She told me that my real mom was strange too."

Something shifted inside me, as if someone had suddenly yanked the bottom out of my stomach. Strange? Had she actually called him that? When she'd found out he was having visions, had she been eager to let him go?

Solomon and Maureen moved into the kitchen. Anthony watched them go then focused on me again.

"This has happened so fast, but I knew I had to find you, warn you, and go with you wherever you're going."

An ear-splitting silence descended on the room.

I sat at the table and indicated that he join me. "I asked your mother about you. She said you weren't like me. Why would she lie?"

He shook his head. "I don't know, but what I do know is that you're in danger. You have to go south. I've been hearing this voice in my head all day and it tells me to go south with you."

"A voice?" A sinking sensation plagued my heart.

"Yeah," he tapped his index finger against one temple, "right here inside my brain."

Cupping the sides of my head, I propped my elbows on the tabletop and closed my eyes, willing everything to go away. I didn't want my son placed in harm's way, and if he traveled with us, he would definitely land in trouble. Why would Katherine lie to me, though? Granted, she hadn't learned about his unique talent until a few weeks ago, so maybe she hadn't processed it yet. Maybe she felt if she ignored it then the baby she'd raised would remain normal.

I ignored my powers for a long time, but it never made them go away.

"What do you want to do, Ruby?" Solomon said from the kitchen. "He's obviously in danger too."

Solomon was right. If my son was being urged south by the same voice, then it meant he was facing the same thing I was.

"We," Maureen said. "You're not facing these bikers alone."

Glancing at her, I realized she'd picked up on my thoughts again.

"I think he should go with us," she voiced.

I sighed, the sound soulful, worn. Straightening my shoulders, I sat back and looked my son in the eye. "You're twenty years old, Anthony. An adult. You do what you feel is right. Do what your inner voice whispers to you to do."

He offered me a sober expression. Finally, he nodded, and a thick lock of mahogany hair fell over his forehead. "I'm going with you," he said. "I have to shut this voice up. It's driving me crazy." He shrugged. "Besides, I've always felt I was cut from a different cloth, that there was something out there for me besides a college education, a career, and the proverbial house with the white picket fence."

I glanced at the clock on the table: 10:50 p.m.

"I have to call Loretta Detzer and let her know we'll be in Key West tomorrow morning." I picked up my purse to find the number stashed with the money. "Will you two tell Anthony about the bikers while I make the call?"

"Come on, Solomon," my hitchhiker stated, crossing the room.

He joined Maureen and Anthony at the table. Solomon and handed me his iPhone. "Here."

I punched in the numbers. The line began to ring. At first, I thought Loretta picked up, but an answering machine message began to play. "This is Loretta Detzer's residence. I'm not home right now, so please leave your name…"

I let the message play out and left one, stating where we were and when we thought we'd reach Key West. I hung up.

"No answer?" Solomon asked.

"Nope. No one answered the last time I checked in with her either." At the table, I sat and accepted a plastic flute of Lambrusco from Maureen, who had retrieved the wine from the kitchen. "I wonder why she gave us her number if no one ever answers it?" A bad feeling began eating its way into my belly and it wasn't the pork chops I'd cooked earlier.

"Let's hope the woman is legitimate." Solomon sipped his wine.

"Yeah, like anything about our trip has been normal," I said, meeting Anthony's worried gaze. I just couldn't shake the weird sensation there was more to Loretta's proposition than merely picking up a document and raking in one hundred grand. However, hadn't I already known that? I would be lying to myself if I thought the idea had never entered my mind. I'd allowed myself to be seduced by dollar signs, but what would really be the price?

****

I reinforced the protection ward around our room and extended it to encompass our vehicles. An hour later, we all decided to retire so we could get a few hours of shuteye before we hit the road at three a.m. I shared Maureen's bed, and Anthony slept in mine. Occasionally, I heard Solomon moving in his room. Against my better judgment, I threw the covers back and padded to his bedroom off the kitchen.

The dog raised his head, perked his ears.

Quietly, I opened the door, poking my head inside. The Malamute shoved his fuzzy mug between my leg and the doorframe. Solomon sat in an easy chair, wearing only a pair of shorts, his legs stretched out, ankles crossed. A small lamp glowed on the tiny nightstand to his right.

He grinned and asked, "Can't sleep?"

"No."

He motioned toward the nightstand. "There's wine left if you want some more."

I shook my head, waiting for the dog to back up before I closed the door. As I gazed at Solomon, I realized why I'd come to his room.

"Something on your mind?"

"Everything is on my mind," I replied, feeling as though I bore the weight of the world on my shoulders.

"Are you worried about Anthony?"

"Amongst other things."

"You have to do what you feel is right, babe." Solomon kicked in the recliner's footrest and stood. He motioned me toward him.

"I tend to let my mind have too much free rein," I said.

He held his arms wide. I hesitated.

"It doesn't hurt to let someone comfort you once in a while."

He was right. I nodded and stepped into his arms. As always, I felt like I was home again, and the fact he'd called me 'babe' instead of Ruby warmed me from head to toe.

He tightened his arms around me. "Care to tell me about your son?"

"Not now."

"I thought you said you weren't ever married?"

I nestled my face against his shoulder and breathed in his tantalizing scent. "I wasn't. I was very young when I had Anthony. Can we please change the subject?"

"What else?" he asked.

"What do you mean?"

I didn't want to look into his powder-blue eyes, but I couldn't help it, couldn't fight it. Raising my head, I locked gazes with him. He stood two or three inches taller than me, but he might as well have been ten feet tall. His magnetism and sexual aura had me feeling tiny and vulnerable.

"Am I on your mind?" Solomon questioned.

The way he asked tugged at my heart. He really needed to know how I felt about him, but if I was honest, what we had now would turn to shit. Whenever I let myself care about someone, I'd lose them somehow. It never failed.

"Do you want my kisses? My touch?" He caressed my face, tracing my jaw line with his index finger, creating invisible sparks along my skin. "Why did you really come to my room, Ruby?"

His breath on my neck awakened gooseflesh.

"Do you want me?" he pressed.

"I just wanted…"

Shame filled me. I was embarrassed to need him, to want him. A lot of years had gone into creating an impenetrable heart guarded by a barbwire mouth.

"Just wanted what?" he asked softly, burying his hand in my hair. "Just wanted me to do this?" His head descended toward me, his lips millimeters from mine. I almost whimpered when he didn't make contact. "Or are you playing more games? Are you testing me, trying to find out if I'm using you only to later kick you to the curb?"

"I came here because…"

Could I say it? He'd told me the next time we were together would be because I went to him first. Oh, how I wanted him!

"Because?"

The same war raged between my head and my heart. Did I dare be honest? And if I walked out of his room, would I regret it?

I couldn't breathe. Anxiety leapt through me and squeezed my heart. What if I said the words and Solomon turned into a different person? Every time I let my guard down with someone new, they proved they were untrustworthy, or worse, a monster in disguise.

"Ruby?" he said.

The hope in his voice forced an answer from me. "Because I need you," I whispered.

"Finally. A step in the right direction." He claimed my mouth in a deep, hungry kiss.

The sensations that swirled through me took my breath away. He urged my lips apart, and our tongues dueled, creating a playful sparring session. He felt so good, his body firm, warm, and mine molded against his as if I were composed of putty. Solomon released my lips and peppered my jaw with kisses and moving down my neck. He slid his hands around my waist and over my ass, kneading each muscle, his fingers biting, yet gentle.

A tremor began in my body. It raced up my legs, shivering through my crotch and torso, shooting through my arms. I sighed with pleasure as his mouth traversed my collarbone. He grasped the hem of my nightshirt and pulled it up over my head, tossing it aside. I stood before him in only my white cotton panties.

"You're such a beauty," Solomon said. He caressed one of my shoulders, his fingers leaving trails of fire upon my upper arm then back up to my neck where he grasped a thick lock of unbraided hair, spreading it over my shoulder and one bare breast.

I closed the distance between us, my breasts brushing his chest. "I want you."

He groaned and pushed me against the bedside. Pulling my panties down, Solomon knelt and swirled his tongue along my inner thighs. I shivered in delight, but knew in moments the heat between us would be our undoing. He stood, grabbed a pillow, dropped it on the floor and knelt again.

"Turn around and kneel over the bedside," he said.

I did as instructed and felt him behind me, his cock proud and eager against me. An overwhelming hunger blazed within my core, and I wriggled closer. He moaned, but instead of penetrating me, he slipped his cock between my legs and rubbed it back and forth in my moist folds.

Gasping, I gripped the bedcovers and reeled at the surge of desire washing through me.

"Don't tease," I whimpered. "I want you. Please, now."

He chuckled and plunged his cock into my body. He filled me, touching that deep, special place. I bit down on the bedspread.

Solomon waited as I adjusted to him. Once I relaxed, he began a rhythm that I met with little backward motions. Electricity coursed through my body, everything funneling into my most intimate place. The sensation kept building, his member stretching me so I felt both skewered and euphoric. Each of his thrusts bumped my womb, and the itch inside me built to dangerous proportions. Solomon moved his hands from my hips, gliding them around my body. He grasped a breast in each one, fondling, squeezing.

He moaned loudly, his excited breathing spurring me on toward that peak which seemed just out of reach. Whenever I thought I could grasp a piece of the heavens, he withdrew, leaving me suddenly void and unsated.

I uttered a disappointed sound. Chuckling, Solomon turned me and deposited me on my back upon the bed. He clutched my legs, shoved them upward, pressing my knees to my breasts. His mouth ravished me, his tongue darting in and out until I could stand it no longer, but just as I was about to find that pending release, Solomon stopped.

"You're driving me insane," I gasped.

"Good." He laughed, pinned me and entered my body again.

His mouth claimed mine, his hips thrusting. My pelvis met his every movement. Faster and faster, our bodies slapped against one another until Solomon slipped his hands under my ass holding my hips stationary as his ground into mine.

Finally, I cried out, and he swallowed my screams. He shuddered, stiffening as he thrust harder. His hot essence spurted into me, and I rode waves of ecstasy, reveling in the sensations, marveling that the human form could feel such pleasure.

Spent, we reclined together, our bodies entwined. I had just started to doze off when he stirred.

"Where are you going?" I protested, raising my head to watch him saunter across the room, his bare rear startling white in the glow of the little lamp.

"I'll be right back."

He stepped into his boxers, opened the door and sauntered out into the kitchenette. The bathroom light popped on then darkness filled the doorway as he closed the door. Moments passed, the door opened again, and then I heard the bathroom dispenser rattle. With a seductive smile on his lips, he entered his bedroom and held up a packet of flavored lubricant for me to see.

A thrill spiraled through me and I giggled. "You're going to wear me out."

Already aroused again, Solomon slipped into bed and helped me lay flat on the mattress in the missionary position. "Good, you'll be too tired to think of any barbed remarks tomorrow."

"I'm never too tired to smart off."

He laughed. "We'll see about that."

I sobered and looked into his pale eyes. "Seriously, though, we need to get up in a while so we'll need some rest."

He kissed me, his tongue dueling with mine, his right hand sliding over my belly to lay at the junction of my thighs, the heat from his palm matching the heat building in my loins.

"Say no and mean it," he whispered against my mouth.

"Yes," I said, parting my legs. It might not be the wisest choice, but I'd never desired a man so much before. The need to be one with him was all-consuming.

He released my lips and then licked all my sensitive places from my neck to my breasts, my belly and my inner thighs until I thought I would go mad with need.

I gasped, wiggling under his ministrations. "Please, Solomon!"

"Not yet." He slipped off the bed, and, on his knees, turned toward me, pulling my hips to the edge of the mattress.

He knelt between my thighs, breath tickling my skin, followed by his mouth on my most intimate place, his tongue delving and lapping. I grabbed a handful of blanket and stuffed it between my teeth as I cried out with pleasure. Shock waves crashed through my body pulsating and thrumming so that my legs drew up involuntarily.

Solomon climbed onto the bed again and sat on its edge. "Come here."

He drew me onto his lap, but I trembled so violently from the orgasm that I had trouble moving. He cradled me across his thighs, his member spearing my body, sealing the pact, binding us as one for a few moments of ecstasy.

At my shout of pleasure and awe, a triumphant sound slipped from Solomon.

His hands grazed my back to follow the curve of my waist where he grasped my hips. He aid me in a rocking motion that had us panting and moaning against one another's mouths, necks and shoulders. An orgasm gripped me so strongly I turned lax in his arms, shuddering against him so that he gripped me tightly. His cries grew more frenzied, and finally he tensed. His essence, warm and welcome, spurted into my body.

Solomon turned us on our sides where we collapsed on the mattress in a jumble of limbs. Breathing heavily, we both enjoyed pleasurable aftershocks and slipped into a light sleep. He roused long enough to pull the sheet over our bodies and then snuggle me.

"I love you, Ruby," he said next to my ear.

Shock sliced through me, followed by disbelief and then hope. Could this be real after all? Did I dare believe him? I couldn't find my voice and just lay there in his arms marveling over his admission.

"I know we haven't known one another long," he continued, his tone firm, "but I do love you and I feel I always have."

I'd never felt so happy or so complete. Most of all, I'd never been so terrified in my entire life. I only hoped he'd forgive me when he found out that Anthony and I had arranged to leave later that night without him or Maureen.

It figured that the one time I had a real chance at love I'd be forced to walk away in order to protect it. If Anthony was being drawn south, too, then I had to continue the journey with my son. It was the only method I could think of to keep Solomon and Maureen out of danger.

I only prayed that Solomon would understand.

Chapter Twenty-Five

Leaving the room proved quite a feat. It took me several agonizing slow, careful maneuvers to extricate myself from Solomon's sleeping form. I quietly dressed in black terry-cloth shorts and a white t-shirt I'd purchased in St. Augustine with a black-and-white screen print of the Castillos on it. Slipping my sneakers on, I watched Shunka out the corner of my eye. He stood by the door anxiously wagging his tail. Anthony had already taken my suitcase out to his car, so I picked up my purse, duffle and cosmetics case. I opened the door and tiptoed out.

Determined to go with me, the dog shoved his head through the opening. I struggled to keep him wedged there between the threshold and the door. My bags and case hit the concrete as I tried to push his massive head back into the room.

"What's wrong?" Anthony whispered loudly.

Still holding the door with one hand and my other on the Malamute's head, I stepped aside.

My son laughed softly and hurried over to help. Together, we managed to shove Shunka out of the way, but not before I heard his plaintive whine. That one pitiful noise awakened a gigantic guilt monster in my gut.

Except for the far corner where the SUV was parked, the security lights bathed the parking lot in silvery light. Insects hummed, and the noise of traffic on The Overseas Highway leading out of the state had dropped considerably. A parrot squawked unexpectedly, and I jumped, my gaze zipping to the middle rooms where the bikers slept.

Anthony quietly tossed my things in the backseat of his blue Mustang.

At the car, I paused and glanced back at our suite. I hoped Maureen wouldn't assume the worst and think I was going after the balance of the money. Quite frankly, I wasn't interested in the money anymore. Solving the craziness of late was foremost on my mind, and if at all possible, I'd keep Solomon and Maureen out of harm's way too.

"Ruby?"

"Yeah?" I didn't turn around, but kept my attention on our suite. As each second passed, my guilt grew into a mountain.

"I can't find my keys."

That got my attention. I spun and looked at Anthony over the top of his car. "Didn't you have them when you came into our room?"

"I thought so. I could've sworn I had them in my pants pocket."

"Well, look around on the floor and in the seats," I said. With my luck, Anthony had probably left the keys in the room, and I'd have to knock on the door, blowing our plans of leaving in the night.

I felt under the passenger seat and over the floor-board. Anthony groped in the crack of the driver's seat and patted around on the floor.

"Looking for these?" Solomon asked behind me.

"Shit," I whispered. My guilt strangled me. I straightened to find him dressed and dangling the keys in front of me.

"Want to explain yourselves?" he asked.

Maureen stood in the open doorway. "Ruby, how could you?" Hurt lurked in her voice.

A lump formed in my throat. "I won't be able to live with myself if something happens to either of you," I replied, trying to speak around the knot. "And no, I'm not after the money, Maureen. I don't give a shit about it anymore. I just want my life to be normal and put an end to all this craziness."

"You're not going anywhere without us." Solomon tossed the keys across the roof to Anthony who caught them. "I figured you'd try something like this, so I took Anthony's keys after you dozed off. We're all in this together." He looked over his shoulder. "Right, Maureen?"

"Right," she said. She set her backpack and Solomon's suitcase on the sidewalk and stepped out, allowing Shunka to follow her. "I've left the keycard on the dresser, so we can go now."

The dog trotted to my side and sat on his haunches. He snorted as if to say, "You're not as smart as you think you are."

Solomon grabbed their things and strode over to the SUV parked in the darkness.

"They seem like really good friends," my son stated.

"They are," I replied, feeling both relief and worry. "But I'm scared for them nonetheless."

Solomon returned to my side and pulled me into his arms. "You're not going anywhere without me. And you're not getting rid of me so easily either." He nuzzled my neck. "I meant what I said earlier. I love you, Ruby."

"Solomon, I—"

"Shh." He kissed my earlobe, and a fire shimmied through my body. "I know you're afraid, so I'm content to wait until you're ready to love me back. For now, though, you should ride with Anthony. Talk to your son and get to know him."

That damn lump formed in my throat again, and I blinked away tears. One thing was certain. Solomon was full of surprises and they were all good ones.

The dog whined and circled us.

"I think Shunka wants to ride with you," Solomon said, releasing me. "Is that okay with you, Anthony?"

"Sure," my son replied. "He's a really cool dog."

"Go on, buddy." Solomon flipped the passenger seat forward, and the Malamute jumped in and sat with his nose pressed to the little side window, leaving a wet smear on the glass.

Regardless of my worry for Solomon and Maureen, I was glad they were going with us. And no matter what

Solomon thought, it wasn't his love that frightened me. It was the fact that something would inevitably happen to screw it up.

Looking into his eyes, I realized one thing. It would kill me if I lost him.

****

Solomon and Maureen followed us in the Excursion. Driving across The Seven Mile Bridge gave me the heebie-jeebies, but I wasn't about to let Anthony know that. He was jittery enough as it was.

The deep blue Atlantic stretched out to the left, and the bright green Gulf of Mexico sprawled on the right. The ocean view reminded me of a child's finger painting, a crooked line separating the two colors.

Dawn brought a brilliant sky. The glare on the water and the blinding sun forced me to dig in my purse for my sunglasses.

Poor Solomon will feel the sun's effects down here.

Inwardly, I groaned. I couldn't get the man off my mind. Our last lovemaking session played in my mind with stunning clarity. All I needed was a bow-chicka-wow-wow soundtrack to complete the scene in my head. Heat rushed to my face.

"That bridge," Anthony pointed, "is the Knights Key-Pigeon Key-Moser Channel-Pacet Channel Bridge, which was built as a railway system in the early 1900s."

"What's the matter?" I quipped. "Couldn't they decide on a name?"

Anthony glanced at me with a peculiar expression then burst out laughing. "A hurricane damaged it badly in 1935. After it was repaired, Hurricane Donna of 1960 tore it up again. This bridge we're on now was completed in 1982." He chuckled again. "Thank you for riding Anthony's Guided Tours."

It was my turn to gape at him. It amazed me how much my son's personality mimicked mine.

He briefed me on the histories of Key Largo and Islamorada as well. He possessed an extensive knowledge of local history, and what made it even cooler was that he didn't sound like he was reciting facts and dates. I truly enjoyed listening to him and learned a lot that I hadn't bothered to learn during my other trips to Florida and its keys.

He told me about his childhood and that his adoptive father had passed away a couple of years ago. A college education loomed ahead of him, but although he had a high I.Q., he really didn't know what he was going to focus on since so many things interested him.

I found it incredible that a child born out of Cole Vandercourt's deceit had become such an amazing person.

"Have you ever thought of looking up your father?" I asked.

He threw me a sidelong glance. "By the tone of your voice, I'm guessing you hate the guy."

Startled, I looked out over The Gulf of Mexico. "You could say that."

"Was he someone you were in love with?"

"Once upon a time."

"What happened?"

Boy was that ever a loaded question. How did I explain to him that his father had used me, tricked me, and then when I thought we were about to make love because we really liked one another, he'd arranged for everyone at the party to barge in and watch him fuck the high school witch all to prove he'd mastered her?

"It just didn't end well, that's all." The distaste for Cole turned into sour bile. "We were just kids."

"Did my father know about me?"

"Yes."

"And he didn't care, did he?"

"No."

He fell silent at that. I realized he wanted answers, but I wondered if he'd hoped for a happier version than I'd given him.

"I did what I felt was best for you, Anthony," I said, fighting the wad of emotion climbing up into my throat. "I was only fifteen."

"I know," he said. "And my adoptive parents have been wonderful, warm and loving. I still miss Dad and think about him every day."

"I can't believe your mother didn't try to stop you from finding me."

"All she would say was that I had a destiny to fulfill."

A cold sensation bled through my heart. "A destiny?"

He nodded and braked for a car pulling onto the road from one of the tiny islands.

"Anthony, why would Kath...why would your mom just let you go on what any other parent would consider a wild goose chase?"

He shrugged. "I don't know. I thought it was odd too, but I was so desperate to reach you and get rid of that damn voice in my head, I didn't ask her about it."

"Has the voice gone quiet?

"Yeah, for now."

Over the next hour, we sat lost in our own thoughts as we passed Marathon Island and Big Pine Key, not to mention all the tiny isles boasting nice homes. I had to wonder about those who weathered one hurricane after another only to return and rebuild. Their insurance premiums must have been up there with the moon.

It took Anthony a little over three hours to drive to Key West. Gawking tourists motoring below the fifty-five speed limit had been bad enough, but I'd forgotten about the slow speed limit through Pine Key due to the endangered key deer. It's not that I was in a hurry, but I wanted all the craziness resolved.

"What's the address where you need to pick up that document?" Anthony asked.

"It's just off Duval Street."

I had no idea how long it would take us to find the address or how long we might have to wait on someone to meet us once we did find the place.

Finding a parking space proved nearly impossible, but I finally paid an exorbitant fee so Anthony could park his Mustang in a city lot where we locked it up. Solomon pulled in the empty spot alongside us. With the way the sun beat down on the asphalt, the vehicles would turn into mobile ovens.

"Wow, this place is wild." Maureen walked around the SUV in short-shorts, a tank top and her new foam sandals. The Malamute's leash dangled from her hand. "Are we taking Shunka with us?"

"Well," Solomon said, kissing me quickly, "we can't leave him in the Excursion. It's too hot." He took the leash and clipped it on the dog's collar. "Which way, Ruby?"

I pointed, and we strode across the parking lot to wander two streets down until we found our way to Duval. From the address, we were on the wrong end of the street. Frowning, I noted the nearest building number, confirming my suspicion.

"Damn," I grumbled. "We need to be on the south end."

"That's okay," said Anthony. "It's been a while since Mom and I," his face flamed a deep red, "have visited here. I'm enjoying the sights."

"Anthony, you don't need to be embarrassed when you call Katherine your mother." I rested my hand on his shoulder. "She is your mother. She raised you."

He nodded and glanced away, his cheeks turning an even deeper crimson.

Maureen acted like a little girl who had been placed in a doll shop. She gawked at everything, exclaimed over the silliest stuff and seemed oblivious to the lusty gazes tossed her way by men and women alike.

Solomon threaded his fingers with mine. Secretly pleased, I squeezed his hand. He squeezed back, but I didn't look at him. If I did, the emotion choking me would erupt and I'd start blubbering.

It felt good to be loved.

Chapter Twenty-Six

We passed a pink clapboard home with a monstrous cactus growing in a tiny garden. It stood in the corner where the sidewalk met the dirt, looking like something straight out of a Western movie. People milled about in the streets, up and down the sidewalks, in and out of the numerous pubs and bars and rode by on the trolleys that clamored past us every few minutes. Couples strolled along with their fingers interlocked or their thumbs hooked in the belt loops of one another's jeans. Married people pushed strollers and tried to manage unruly children while simultaneously reading street maps. Decks leaned out above the street from second and third floors. Parties beneath the colorful patio umbrellas on various verandas bled boisterous noise into the street. On other terraces, women sunbathed in Band-Aid-size bikinis.

I had to admit Key West fascinated me. There was so much activity, so many colors, oddities, shops, racks of merchandise littering the sidewalks, and an abundance of food and drink that I experienced sensory overload. The aroma of fresh pineapple prompted my mouth to water one second, followed by the odor of coconut suntan lotion and then I'd catch a whiff of sea brine and some sort of tropical blossom mixed with the stout scent of beer from a pub as we walked by.

Solomon and I crossed Caroline Street, Eaton Street, Fleming, and Southard Street with Anthony and Maureen following in our footsteps. The amount of restaurants amazed me. The aromas of fried food, booze and fruit oozed out of open doors and windows. Many provided *a fresco* dining, and the customers sat beneath enormous umbrellas drinking from coconuts sporting tiny, colored umbrellas. One pub catered to a group of college-age guys who guzzled dark beer from huge steins.

We eventually turned right onto Catherine Street where we had to look for a two-story, lemon-yellow stucco building. A psychic shop took up the ground floor, and the second floor served as the proprietor's home.

A cyclist rode past us with a sleeping toddler strapped in a kiddie seat behind him. I studied the palm trees, enjoying a cool breeze wafting up an alley from the ocean. An old woman crouched on her knees, a rubber mat beneath them, and pulled straggling weeds from a garden brimming with blooms. Her large straw hat shielded her from the sun, and as we passed, I spotted a big Siamese cat sprawled across the hood of a newly waxed Kia Soul.

"Is that the place?" Anthony asked.

I nodded.

We crossed the road and found the shop closed.

"Great," I muttered.

"The sign says the owner is at the court outside the Gay and Lesbian Center for a community sidewalk sale," Anthony read from the paper posted on the door. "I suppose we could either come back later or walk to the center and look for the," he glanced up at the shingle above the awning, "Mystical Winds Psychic Shoppe."

"We're picking up the document from a psychic?" Defeated, I shrugged. "Let's go to the center and see if we can find our contact."

By the time we reached the place, sweat coated my body and my mouth was so dry I couldn't have spat if my life had depended on it.

Shunka panted. Obviously miserable, he whined loudly.

"How about I buy us something to drink while you look for the psychic's booth?" Anthony suggested. "The dog needs something to drink too."

"Sounds good," said Solomon. "I'll go with you, and the girls can hunt for their contact."

The Key West Information Center stood on one side, and a First National Bank with a line of people at the

ATM resided on the other. Farther down, a sign for the Gay and Lesbian Center hung outside the entrance. Despite the numerous same-sex couples populating the court, I tried to see the names on the venders' booths and tables, but there were just too many people. A fountain in the middle of the court burbled, and several toddlers swished their hands and feet in it as their parents looked on. Many of the parents were same-sex partnerships. That's when I noticed the sign over the court: Gay Capital of the World.

"I never could get into the girl-girl thing," Maureen said.

Stunned, I looked at her sharply. "What?"

"I tried it with a girl once, but it's just not for me."

"Why would you do such a thing?"

"Curiosity, I guess."

"Maureen, you never cease to freak me out."

She frowned. "You talk like being gay is a bad thing."

"I never said that," I replied, shouldering through the crowd. "I just don't see how a person could be interested in the same sex."

Maureen moved aside for a paraplegic man pushed in a wheelchair by a young woman "Many lesbians probably wonder why a woman would stay with a man who beats the shit out of her every night when she could be with another woman who knows how she feels and what she really desires in a relationship."

Pausing, I looked at her, marveling at the wisdom masquerading as a dead ringer for Marilyn Monroe. "True, but there's probably just as many abusive same-sex relationships as there are heterosexual ones." I gauged her expression as she considered that tidbit then added, "I thought you said you tried being with another woman only once?"

"I tried it for a week," she said, gazing through the crowd as if she couldn't bear to look me in the eyes. "Amy was a lovely person, but I couldn't live that way."

"What made you change your mind?"

"I like men much, much better."

I laughed.

"The world is full of all kinds of people, Ruby."

"Yeah, I'm learning that."

Anthony nudged my arm, drawing my attention. He smiled and handed me and Maureen our drinks.

Solomon pulled a Styrofoam bowl from a trashcan, knelt and poured water from a bottle into the bowl for Shunka. He nodded at something across the way. "Isn't that the place we're looking for?"

A large tent sprawled in a shaded corner of the court.

"Yeah," I said. "That looks like the place."

Once the dog had his fill, we pushed through the throng, but it was so crowded around the tent, we couldn't get very close.

An odd sensation washed over me, as if I were about to leap off a precipice into a deep, dark chasm. Despite the day's intense heat, a chill spread gooseflesh along my arms. The feeling of a pending revelation assailed me as I stared at the shadow-shrouded tent.

The same voice that had urged me south filled my mind. *"Well, Ruby Nutter, after centuries you're finally here again."*

A verbal reply traveled to the tip of my tongue, but fell off, landing somewhere amongst my teeth.

In my mind's eye, I saw the woman sitting at a loom, but she could've been in a queen's court if not the queen herself. Clothed in a Lady Guinevere dress of the darkest green, complete with bell sleeves, gold embroidery and seed pearls she looked as if she'd stepped from the past into the present.

Maureen and Solomon stared at me oddly.

"What's wrong?" he asked me.

"I hear her too," Anthony stated, tapping his temple with one finger, his expression incredulous.

"I've been waiting a long time for you to get enough nerve to travel to Key West, but now we're down to the final days. You had no choice but to come." Comfort washed over me as the voice continued. *"Return to my shop, Ruby. You'll find a key under the third brick to the right of the door. Let yourself in and*

make yourselves at home in the upstairs apartment. I'll be there as soon as I can."

That was it? I'd traveled through seven states just to be told to wait in this woman's apartment? With a sigh, I turned and struggled through the crowd.

"Ruby?" Solomon said. "Where are you going?"

"Back to the psychic's store."

"What?"

"She was told to return to the store and wait," Anthony said, tapping his temple again.

"That's fine," Maureen stated. "I'm tired and need a nap anyway."

Shunka remained at my side, pulling Solomon along by the leash. I walked silently, my mind a whir of whys and what ifs.

I couldn't explain it, but I knew I had to listen to the woman. After all, she'd guided me this far.

We meandered through the people milling about making purchases or standing around chatting with friends and venders. Even over the shoppers' chatter, I heard Shunka's weary panting and knew we needed to get him out of the hot Florida sun and find him more cool water.

The only time one of us spoke was when Maureen paused to exclaim over something.

Back at the shoppe, I found the key under the third brick to the right, unlocked the door, and then once everyone had filed inside, I returned the key and relocked the door. A staircase in the back led to the woman's apartment. With everyone following me, I climbed the stairs, pushed open a heavy door and stepped into a richly decorated abode.

Now that I'd finally reached my destination, I had to agree with Maureen about needing a nap. Exhaustion and sleepiness descended on me with vengeance.

Solomon gave the Malamute a bowl of water in the beautiful restaurant-style kitchen. A common, tawny-colored tabby cat perched in the window over the sink. It meowed and blinked large amber eyes at me.

"Hello, kitty." I scratched it behind the ears.

The cat rubbed its head against my hand and purred loudly.

We filtered into the depths of the apartment. Maureen pointed at a bedroom that also served as a study. As I headed toward it, Anthony flopped down on an overstuffed sofa. Maureen motioned she was taking a small bedroom to the right of the one I entered. The sound of bed springs squeaking reached me and so did Maureen's contented sigh and a yawn.

I kicked off my sneakers and crawled across a black, silver and lavender comforter toward a stack of fluffy pillows barely aware of the half-feminine, half-library-like décor.

Minutes later, as I faded off into slumber, Solomon climbed onto the bed and spooned me.

****

Soft evening sunshine filtered through the window. Shunka snored on the floor at my side of the bed. I rolled onto my back to find Solomon's arm thrown over me. The stress of the trip, the fact that none of us had gotten any sleep last night and the idea we'd *finally* reached our destination had all taken its toll. For once, I felt refreshed and I yawned behind my hand.

A gentle tap at the door forced me to sit up.

"Ruby?" Maureen's whispered loudly.

"Yeah, come in."

Solomon stirred and opened his eyes. "Mmph. I slept like a rock."

"I hear voices in the kitchen," said Maureen. "I'll wake Anthony."

Solomon stepped into his Nikes and finger-combed his hair.

We left the room, and Shunka padded out behind us. The second-floor apartment looked like something out of "Home and Gardens." Everything had its place, and every item complemented every other item around it. Hardwood floors covered the entire apartment, polished to a high sheen and great for sock ice-skating.

The living room and kitchen took up the entire front half of the upstairs. Overstuffed furniture in black and silver sprawled across the living area upon black and white alpaca rugs. A large rectangular coffee table squatted in the center of the main seating area. Its glass top housed a collage of letters, photos, dried flowers, seashells and various paraphernalia, which I thought was a unique idea, not to mention a great conversation piece. The cat from the kitchen window now lounged across the tabletop. It blinked sleepily, its amber eyes narrow slits.

On the wall above the stone fireplace hung an intricately carved broadsword, its handle wrapped in black leather studded with turquoise. Solomon stopped and eyed it with wonder. I watched him for a several minutes. He continued to stare at it as if in a trance.

Finally, unease poked me in the back. "Solomon?"

He continued to stare at the sword.

"Solomon."

When he didn't respond, I approached him and nudged his shoulder.

He blinked rapidly and shot me a bewildered look. "That weapon is amazing."

"An authentic antique for sure," I replied. "Are you okay? It seemed like you were in another world."

"Does that weapon seem familiar to you?" he asked. "It's like I've seen it somewhere before."

Studying it, I shook my head. "No, not to me. Maybe you saw it in a magazine or on the Internet?"

"Maybe." But he didn't sound convinced.

Anthony had awakened and vacated the couch, so I assumed he was in the dining room, where I heard the voices of both men and women. I motioned for Solomon to follow me. Turning the corner, I stopped short, and Solomon sucked in a sharp breath.

Seated at the table, Maureen and Anthony joked with Wayne Blacktree.

The dog barked abruptly, scaring the hell out of me, and leaped by us like a gazelle. Solomon grabbed at him but missed.

"Shunka! No!" he shouted.

Everyone in the room whirled startled.

The Malamute launched himself into the air and hit Wayne, knocking him and the chair backward onto the hardwood floor. His body and the chair hit with a hollow thud. The dog growled as if he were about to rip the guy's throat out. Wayne lay flat on his back, feet in the air with the chair under him, and Shunka's jaws grasping him by the throat.

Chapter Twenty-Seven

Except for Shunka's growls, quiet settled over the apartment.

Finally, a woman moved across the dining area. "Your familiar doesn't trust Wayne." Her laughter wrapped around me. "You might know Wayne's former soul, Shunka Wakan, but it is no longer black."

This gal is off her rocker. She's talking to the dog like he's a person.

I shot her a perplexed look but dismissed her as I slowly approached Wayne. The Malamute continued to grasp him by the throat, uttering low warning sounds. Wayne stared up at me, his eyes nearly all white with fear, his chest heaving. I could only imagine the amount of adrenaline surging through his body.

"What's he doing here?" Solomon asked and moved to my side. "That jerk has been hounding Ruby since she ran into him in West Virginia."

"Get Ruby's familiar to let him loose," said the woman, "then all will be explained."

"Shunka? My familiar?" I glanced at first her, wondering if the woman had lost her mind, then looked over at Solomon.

Solomon knelt and peered into Wayne's stricken face. The dining room chandelier created an ethereal gleam upon Solomon's hair, his arms and neck stark against his shirt. He reminded me of an apparition about to administer judgment upon a victim.

"Shunka," he said. "Let him go."

The dog growled louder. I interpreted that to mean 'Like hell I will!'

"Come on, boy," I coaxed. "He's not worth it. Let him go, okay?"

Reluctantly, the dog released Wayne's throat and moved back, pressing against my leg. Shunka snorted with what sounded like pure disgust.

Solomon shot me an odd look and hefted the big man and the chair into an upright position. Wayne gasped and wiped the dog drool from his throat with a nice linen napkin. He sat stone still, his breath wheezing, hands shaking as he reached for a water glass.

"Well, Ruby," said the strange woman, "you certainly know how to make an entrance."

Anger visited me. "And you certainly know how to manipulate people," I retorted. If I lose my temper, she'd end up with sunburn worse than Maureen's. Gulping, I tamped the emotion down. "I had a feeling I should've walked away from Loretta's offer."

She smiled, but her dark eyes held an odd brand of smugness. "You had no choice, dear."

"What the hell do you—?"

"Ruby," the woman said with force. "Sit, have a glass of wine and relax." When I didn't move, she added, "Please. I'll tell you everything if you just sit down and compose yourself. You're amongst friends."

"Friends?" I queried with sarcasm, glaring at Wayne as I sat.

A chuckle escaped her. "Yes, even Wayne is a friend. It took him hundreds of years to realize it, though."

"Who the hell are you?" A tremor had begun deep in my gut.

"Ruby, calm down," Maureen whispered across the table.

"I didn't come all this way just to get more cloak-and-dagger bullshit," I snapped at her.

Anthony studied me from his seat next to Maureen, an expression of wonder and something else I couldn't identify on his face. Inwardly, I cringed. He probably thought I was horrible.

I sat between Wayne and Solomon, uncertain whether to sit quietly and see how things unfolded or blow up in a fit of rage. As I was about to choose the latter, the woman walked into the adjoining kitchen only to return with a chilled bottle of wine. She moved around the table filling our glasses.

"My name is Alice," she said, holding out her hand once she reached me and set the wine bottle down. "Alice Nutter." Her smile broadened. "And he," she pointed at Solomon with her free hand, "is the White King. Your son is the new blood."

Another Nutter? And did she just call Solomon the White King? I glanced at my son. *New blood?*

Taking her hand in mine, I stared at the woman dressed in a dark green, gothic-style dress with flowing sleeves. Long mahogany hair cascaded over one shoulder, and her hazel eyes, ones similar to mine, looked through me.

As our hands touched, and a jolt of sensation assailed me nearly knocking me out of my seat. Alice's gaze frightened me to the very depths of my soul.

"You two look a lot alike," Maureen said with awe.

"In this life I'm a cousin," Alice squeezed my hand, "but when we first met one another, I was your aunt."

What the hell is she talking about?

I had no family save for my father, and even if there were a few Nutters left, it was no wonder he didn't want anything to do with his family. They were insane!

"We've always known one another," she began. "History repeats itself and it's doing so again. Across the centuries, everyone here has been reincarnated over and over." She glanced at Anthony. "But now you've finally had a son, Ruby. That's a new development, and we shall see where it leads."

"You're not making any sense," I whispered.

Alice gripped my hand, and something flowed from her body to mine—something powerful. The room spun. The air seemed to have left the apartment, and sounds became distorted.

"Once again," said Alice as if she were a million miles away, "we face the Sons of God to prevent them from taking over our world. Wayne was used over and over by them to do their dirty work, and now he's finally realized this and has turned against them."

The Sons of God?

The dining room vanished. Dimly, Maureen's cries and Solomon's shouts reached me, and then disappeared altogether.

A black expanse of tumultuous water stretched out before me, the waves' caps frothy white. A stone monolith rose into the air to my right. Once again, a cloaked woman stood nearby, head down, her hands hidden beneath her brown garment. Thunder crashed over the water.

The creatures I'd faced at Solomon's cabin raced toward us, their bodies composed of indigo and gray smoke. The semblance of demonic animals appeared here and there in the twirling masses. Huge riders sat astride their backs. As always, I couldn't see their faces, but somehow I sensed their identities. I raised my hands to the sky...

The scene switched again. I stood in the village I'd dreamed of a few days ago. Riders upon massive warhorses galloped into the community along a narrow dirt road. The same inky smoke monsters fled, their forms bleeding into the ether. There, crouched against the well, cowered the prostitute whom I'd been sneaking food to. As she turned her head toward me, I saw her face clearly for the first time.

Maureen!

Next, I stood in a great room. I saw the White King and he kissed me tenderly. He held me close, his embroidered robes soft against my body. I looked up at him and took in the fresh scars across his face, scars I somehow knew had come from battle, and I admired the ethereal luster of his flaxen locks, the way the jewel-encrusted crown caught the firelight. Maureen sat across the room in a red embroidered gown, her soft weeping permeating the chamber as Solomon comforted me...

"Ruby?"

Blinking, I looked around the dining room. Several pairs of concerned eyes stared back at me.

"Ruby?" Alice said again. "Are you all right?"

"I need to be alone," I replied.

"I'll walk her back to her room," Anthony offered and rose to hurry around the table. "Let me help you. You don't look too steady."

With Shunka close on our heels, my son ushered me through the apartment and into the study that also served as a bedroom. I strode to the window and looked out at the ocean where the sun had begun to bleed into the water's surface. Gold, red and swirls of deep pink floated in all directions and also stained the sky.

Alice's pet tiptoed into the room and leapt up on the windowsill. The feline glanced with disinterest at the dog lying at my feet. The cat perched there as if pretending to be a figurine. It began purring and shut its eyes.

"Our lives are about to change forever, aren't they?" said Anthony. His hand fell on my shoulder and remained there.

"Yes."

Except for the cat's soft purring, quiet settled over us.

Eventually, Anthony said, "And if we don't stop what's coming, the entire world will suffer, right?"

"Yes."

"How do we know this?"

Shaking my head, I replied, "I guess because Alice is right. We've lived many times before. My work isn't done yet and it may never be complete. I think we're here to stop whatever it is that keeps coming back."

"The Sons of God."

I nodded. "Whatever the Sons of God are, I sense they're not good."

"But...doesn't that mean they're of God or from Him?"

"No. It means..." I shrugged. "I don't know what it means. At least not yet."

"Do you want me to stay with you?" Anthony asked.

Turning, I looked up at him. Eyes mirroring mine stared back at me. And, for the very first time, I was glad I had Anthony as my son, that I'd finally taken the plunge to go see him. What Cole had done to me was wrong, and the means by which Anthony was conceived were sad and devastating, but it all had worked out in the wash. Anthony was "my" son and I loved him.

"I'm fine, really. I just need some quiet to think and process everything."

He smiled sadly. "You're a good person, Ruby. It's a shame the weight of the world and all these last few centuries are on your shoulders."

Surprise skewered my insides. "How do you know that?"

"I'm your son and I have visions too."

I returned his smile, but pride resided in mine. *Yes, I'm very glad he's my son.*

****

Slowly I awoke. Snoring came from the bed, and as I turned and stretched, I found Solomon flopped facedown across the bed in only his shorts. I remembered sitting in the wingback chair and watching the sun disappear on the horizon, but after that only slumber. I rose and crossed the room, pulling the sheet up over my lover's white, muscled body. For a moment, I stood gazing upon Solomon as bits and pieces of long-forgotten memories flittered through my brain.

I love you.

I may not be able to tell him due to fear, but I could certainly think it.

Wide-awake and energized, I moved from the bed and looked around. A small clock on the desk showed it was nearly midnight. Quiet seemed to weigh on the apartment. Where was everyone?

As I padded out into the hall, Shunka close on my heels, I straightened my wrinkled t-shirt and enjoyed the sensation of the cool hardwood floors against the soles of my feet. Anthony slept on the couch, and Wayne snored on an air mattresses. How could Alice believe

Wayne was now on the up and up? A leopard never changed its spots, so how was Wayne any different? I didn't believe it. Not without proof.

In the kitchen, I got a glass and filled it from a water dispenser standing against a wall. I gulped down the water and set the glass in the sink. A stain on the front of my shirt caught my attention. The thought of a shower and a change of clothes sounded wonderful, but I figured it was best to just put on my jammies and go to bed.

Shit. The Excursion and Mustang are still in that parking lot. We need our suitcases and gear. All our things are in them.

However, waking someone at that time of night to help me fetch everything didn't seem fair, especially since they were so exhausted. I debated on what to do.

Shunka danced around my feet, his hind quarters shimmying to the beat of "I have to pee ASAP."

"Do you need to go out, boy?"

He answered with a soft woof.

"Okay," I patted him on the head, "I have an idea that will help both of us."

Next to Anthony on an end table lay the keys to his Mustang. I picked them up as I passed and headed into the study bedroom where I pulled the Excursion's keys from Solomon's shorts. Shunka waited in the doorway, his turquoise eyes luminous in the dim lighting.

Pocketing the two sets of keys, I picked up the dog's leash and whispered, "Let's go, mutt."

Outside, I locked up the apartment and returned the key behind the brick. The aroma of brine and coconut oil invaded my nostrils, and every now and then I'd also catch the pungent odor of beer from the neighboring pubs. Laughter from a party somewhere down the street rode the stiff breeze, and sometimes the distinct sound of lapping waves sliced through the din.

The atmosphere of Key West, the palm trees, the ocean breeze, and all the aromas and sounds raised my spirits and heightened my refreshed state of mind. Somewhere along the rocky shoreline a seagull cried. The

Malamute trotted at my side, ears perked, nose twitching with all the fragrances assaulting it. At least the dog would deter anyone from stopping or bothering me.

We made our way past all the pubs and tourist shops. Parties spilled out onto the streets, drunks hollered and dribbled booze on themselves, and young college-age women strutted around with their tits straining the fabric of their bikini tops and low-cut shirts. Gay couples drifted from party to party, their arms around one another's waists. Music pounded from within a nearby pub. As I drew closer, I identified the song as "Sexy Bitch" by David Guetta and Akon, the bass of it throbbing through the bodies dancing on the patio and of those wandering nearby.

A group of young kids burst through the pub's doors as I approached with Shunka. Caught amongst them, I paused, holding my ground as the crowd encompased me. The dog pressed his body against the front of my legs almost like he thought he could prevent them from touching or jostling me. I couldn't hear him growling, but the sound of it vibrated through his ribs.

The high-pitched giggles of one blonde girl filled my ears. Her laughter reminded me of a shrieking bird caught in a cat's claws. The crowd pushed me back. The human mass undulated to and fro like a fleshy tide. Something hit the backs of my knees, I collapsed, and the seat of a chair met with my rear. With relief, I grasped the edge of the table next to me and kept a firm grip on Shunka's tether.

The dog's growls finally rose over the din of voices. A the same moment, the crowd began to disperse. Tourists, locals and college kids filed back into the pub. Others walked in groups of two, three or four to the next bar, while more headed down one end or the other of the street.

"Finally," someone said, "I have you all to myself."

Cold settled between my shoulder blades and oozed upward into my neck. The hairs on my nape stood on end, and the follicles on my head tightened painfully.

Desire flared hot in my loins and seeped into my abdomen.

No! Not him! Not now!

"Come now, Ruby. Why are you so upset? We're meant to be together," the voice rumbled from across the table.

The realization of what Azazel had done descended on me with such force that my equilibrium seesawed. The entire deal with the crowd had been set up by him. He'd imposed his will upon them, made them think they were goofing around and having fun, and then used them to move me into position. I couldn't run, couldn't hide.

Shunka sat next to me and bared his teeth. Menacing growls reverberated through his body.

"I just want to talk," the biker leader said. He barely glanced at the Malamute.

Slowly, I turned my head. Blond, blue-eyed, rugged and yet beautiful, Azazel stared back at me with a sexy smile that almost made me come in my seat. He'd swapped his motorcycle attire for a tight black muscle shirt and relaxed-fit jeans. Wide, powerful shoulders begged me to run my hands across them. His deep tan gave him the appearance of a buff beach god, and coupled with his vibrant blue eyes and strong features, he was the epitome of a Hollywood hunk. Dark brown five o'clock shadow graced his firm jaw line, and Heaven help me, intensified his sex appeal all the more. A black-and-gray tattoo of a raging beast composed of many different animals covered his upper arms and shoulders to disappear behind his neck. Golden hair curled around his neck as if caressing it.

I gulped. Azazel was the pure essence of sex. It screamed from his every pore, wafted around the table in a cloud of pheromones and flowed into me on an invisible current of arousal.

And oh how I wanted him! Lust raged through me and heated my panties.

Shunka whined and laid his head on my knees. I looked down at him. The dog rolled his eyes as if to say I wasn't fighting hard enough. Hell, what did he know? He was a dog and probably found every tree and fencepost in Florida sexy.

"Wh-what do you want?" I managed to say and scratched Shunka's ears in an effort to not only calm him but me too.

"You."

"No, I mean—"

"I know what you mean," he stated, his lips turning up in a lazy smile. "And again, the answer is you."

The need for sex intensified. I shifted on the hard seat and pushed Shunka away. I stifled a whimper, crossing my legs in hopes the tingling in my crotch would stop. Adrenaline whizzed through my system, heightening my desire. I gulped and looked away.

The urge to shag Azazel lessened. It wasn't a lot, but it was enough I noticed it.

He seemed to sense or read my thoughts, so I couldn't clue him in on the fact I'd realized eye contact only made the need for sex stronger. At least it gave me some tiny portion of leverage.

"Why do you want me?" I asked. Instead of meeting his gaze, I focused on the tattoo covering his right shoulder. "Why am I so important to you?"

"You're the only one who can change everything." His voice wrapped around me. It tickled me with its deep timbre, seduced me into a world where only the two of us existed. "You're the key, Ruby, the one who can help us. You can return everything to the way it once was."

"And who says I want to help you?" I uncrossed and re-crossed my legs, the urge to screw so primal it even resonated in my bones.

Azazel leaned forward. "You know you want me," he whispered. "Just admit it."

"What I'm feeling isn't natural." A delicious shudder cascaded through my body. "You're making me feel this way."

Panting, I knew if I didn't leave soon one of two things would happen. I'd either let Azazel whisk me away somewhere to fuck me, or I'd do something horribly embarrassing. I'd be a small feature in tomorrow's Key West newspaper: Horny Woman Humps Pub Furniture! Damage Estimate in the Hundreds!

There was no way I could allow myself to do either. The unexpected appearances of my powers always caused me public embarrassment, but I sensed if Azazel seduced me, it would seal my fate and doom others as well.

It took every ounce of concentration I could manage but I pushed the lust aside just enough that I was able to summon my power. A string of words passed through my mind: vanish, disappear, leave, run, depart, flee! Tingling ravaged my muscles, and dimly I detected a few startled gasps around me. Nausea hit my gut, my equilibrium flip-flopped, and the sound of ocean waves followed. Something hard poked and jabbed my backside as I stared up at the stars.

With a start, I sat up. The world dipped and spun. I gasped at the nauseating sensations, but they soon passed. Seconds later, I realized something terrible.

Although I'd escaped Azazel, I'd failed to bring Shunka with me.

Chapter Twenty-Eight

I rose to my feet on a rocky shore. My knees knocked together as I picked my way across the stones. How could I defend myself against Azazel if he could find me so easily? I'd escaped this time, but what if he found me again? Shaking so hard my bones almost rattled, I stepped up on a big rock, the ocean wind buffeting me, and looked around. Poor Shunka. He'd been trying to protect me and I'd accidentally left him behind. The dog was probably frantic to find me.

The waves lapped at the mini boulders, and the moonlight danced upon the water like vaporous, iridescent flames. Except for an occasional cloud, the sky boasted a googolplex of stars. The moon illuminated a sign nearby that stated: The Southernmost Part of the U.S.

My powers were growing. The ability to vanish in one place and appear in another was something foreign to me as well as disconcerting. The sensation of hurtling through space had left me weak, disoriented and scared silly.

What am I? Who am I?

"You are the one who can set everything right."

About to step off the rock, I froze with my foot in midair. How had he found me so easily, so quickly?

"Magic leaves a trail, Ruby," Azazel said somewhere in the darkness to my left. "I can teach you how to wield your magic. You're more powerful than you know. More powerful than you could ever imagine."

Sill trembling, I tried to steady myself on the rock. "Why can't you just leave me alone?" I yelled, but the wind snatched my words and turned them into a pathetic complaint. "I don't want any part of you, and I don't want anything to do with the others who follow you either."

"You have no choice," he replied, his voice strong and closer than the last time.

"I always have a choice."

"No, you don't," he insisted.

Where was he? Although moonshine bathed the shoreline, the dead-end street and the walls surrounding the military base, shadows still cloaked many areas.

"Your soul wears a cloak of destiny, and fate rules your life." His deep voice touched me in such a way my knees nearly buckled.

Footsteps approached, but the wind distorted them. At first I thought he was off to my left, but as he drew closer, I wasn't so certain.

I'd been foolish to believe I could walk to the parking lot unscathed, even with Shunka by my side. The events over the past week should have proven I wasn't safe alone. I'd been so worried about my presence causing harm to Solomon, Maureen and Anthony that I'd forgotten to protect myself.

Now I'd pay the price.

Perhaps I could disappear again, but where would I go? If I appeared in the apartment, Azazel would follow my path of magic, and as a result, the others would be in serious danger. However, without the ability to control this new power, I might also find myself bobbing around in the middle of the Atlantic and end up zapping ocean predators with my finger-fire. Shark steaks, anyone?

What if I thought of home or...?

Lust sliced through my thoughts, scattering my puny escape plans to the wind. Terror joined that lust. Acting on instinct, I leapt from the rock and managed two steps only to find myself scooped up into Azazel's waiting arms. With his broad chest squeezed against mine, I was painfully aware of the hard length of him, my feet dangling in midair. The word "sex" screamed in my head. I wanted it, needed it, pined for it, but what would such a huge man do to me? If he managed to seduce me, would my body be able to accommodate him?

"Now I shall have you."

"No!" I struggled, Heaven help me did I ever struggle, but his power rolled over me in waves as strong and as heavy as the ones coursing toward the shores of the tiny island. "Please...please, just let me go."

The brilliant moon revealed him in an ethereal daylight. He smiled down at me, his azure eyes bright as quicksilver and aglow with feral sexuality. Thunder rumbled from the south.

Thunder? How was that possible on such a clear, starry night?

"Before I consummate our union," he whispered, "I need you to first remember who you are." Azazel tightened his arms around me, fastening mine firmly to my sides. He nuzzled my hair and breathed deeply. "You smell like fear." He sniffed again, drawing in a deep lungful and holding it a moment before adding, "And I smell your delicious body scent too. Your aroma is of warm, delectable woman, and you want me. Oh, yes! I detect your desire. It's musky-sweet and all mine."

Thunder boomed somewhere far out over the water.

I wanted to lie down, spread my legs and give myself to him. Desire crashed through me, and I turned lax in his arms.

"Yes...that's it," he said softly. "Give yourself to me."

A whimper slipped from my lips. This was wrong on so any levels, but I didn't know how to stop it. Somehow I sensed that once Azazel possessed my body, I was trapped forever.

Lightning lit up the cloudless sky, and more thunder echoed in the night.

Still holding me with one arm, Azazel tugged the elastic band from the end of my braid and unwound my hair with his other hand. My wavy locks floated and whipped in the stiff breeze. He smoothed his hand up my left arm and over my shoulder, and then moved it to cup my cheek. He brushed his thumb back and forth across my lower lip.

Please don't kiss me, please don't kiss me...

The need for sex streaked downward from that simple touch to nestle in my loins where it combusted into flames of desire so hot, so demanding I couldn't move, couldn't protest and struggled to even breathe.

He continued to hold me as if I was a rag doll. At his mercy, transfixed with terror and awe, I met his alluring gaze and waited for his lips to touch mine. The instant our mouths made contact, my power leapt to life within me and surged to the surface. A brilliant white spark snapped between us, singing my tongue. Azazel murmured in approval, his lips firm yet soft, demanding yet delicious, and I couldn't move, couldn't protest.

He raised his head and stared deeply into my eyes. "You are very powerful, indeed."

The fear that sang through me ignited my power further. The illumination burst from my skin, surrounding us and brightening the dark shoreline.

Azazel captured my lips again. As he deepened the kiss, his power, dark and startling, meshed with mine. Still holding me tightly, he sat upon one of the small boulders and cradled me on his lap. More magic flowed from him, and dimly, the sound of grating stone and tumbling rocks permeated my sex-induced haze. A moment later, I found myself lying on damp sand, his mouth still ravaging mine.

He slid his hands over my shoulders, down my sides and slipped them under my hips to palm my ass. With his massive body pinning me to the earth, and the evidence of his arousal against my belly, the only thing I wanted was to have his cock inside me, our naked flesh pressed together, bodies joined tightly.

He broke the kiss and studied me again. Stars framed his beautiful face and moon-silvered hair. I turned my head from side to side quickly surveying the area he'd cleared of rocks so he could make love to me upon the soft, cool sand.

"Now I shall you," he said.

The ocean breeze grew stronger, and thunder sounded in the distance, each boom driving more fear into my heart—the nails to the coffin of my fate.

He ground his hips against mine and kissed me again. My power replied with another brighter, stronger spark that leapt between us. The breeze lifted strands of my hair, each tendril a bright orange-red live wire.

Azazel kissed me, his tongue separating my lips. *"Come,"* he said, his mind linking with mine. *"Allow me to show you who we are, and in doing so, you will remember who you are."*

Visions flashed through my mind as if I'd been plunked in front of a movie screen. From a lofty height, I viewed a mountainous terrain splashed with blues, greens, brown and tan. Off to my right, hundreds of extremely tall, beautiful men and women looked down at the scene sprawling below them.

He towered over me, and I saw him in his true form. Not quite human and not exactly the epitome of angelic paintings, he was awe inspiring. Beautiful proved an inadequate word to describe the angel next to me. He didn't emanate a heavenly glow, but instead exuded power, an underlying malevolence and alarming intelligence. Forgotten knowledge stirred in my brain, memories of things I'd learned over the years, trivia I'd filed away to never use should I need to call upon it. Azazel, one of the angels, a leader of the Fallen Angels after Satan had...

My gaze drifted back to the others surveying the scene below us.

The Sons of God.

Realization slapped me hard. My gaze flew up to meet his. "If you are the Sons of God, how can there be women amongst you?"

"Angels are neither male nor female. We can assume any form we want."

That familiar sensation of doom that often settled in my gut rose within me in the form of darkness. It wrapped around my senses, crushed my lungs and forced me to gasp for breath.

"Let me love you, Ruby...let us be one..."

His mouth moved from my lips, and along my jaw to my ear, jarring me back to the present. Azazel sucked and nipped on my earlobe, eliciting a sudden, excited moan from me. He pushed his hips against mine, his cock rock-hard and huge through his jeans. Desire roiled in me. The battle had shifted in his favor. I had to fight him, had to find a way to extricate myself from the danger about to consume me. He claimed my lips again and returned me to the past over four thousand years ago.

Back on the precipice again, Azazel hooked me under the arms and leapt into the ether with me. Terrified, I screamed and squeezed my eyes shut.

"You are safe, Ruby. You're merely seeing the past. Open your eyes and know the truth."

His words made sense. His kiss permitted me the means to remember. And as long as I remembered that my body lay on the beach I was fine.

Slowly, I opened my eyes.

The other angels took various forms—giant hawks, dragons, eagles, griffins—and descended into the valleys and plains. They posed as handsome, beautiful humans and wooed the peasants, the royalty, the peddlers, politicians, farmers and servants. The females seduced the men, and the males went in unto the lovely women. I witnessed scenes of lovemaking that fueled the flames already consuming my fleshly body lying on the sand.

Angels in disguise pushed their cocks into the lithe, comely bodies of beautiful human women. The angelic females lay upon beds covered in furs as two to three men took turns pleasuring them as well as themselves. Orgasmic cries filled tents, every shady oasis dotting the deserts, and within clay houses, stone palaces, forts, tents and animal-skin huts. The Fallen Ones kissed and caressed their human lovers. They rode the females as if it was the first and last time they would ever mate. The human women locked their legs around the driving hips of their angelic lovers, and each ethereal woman offered herself to the next man with the energy to service them.

Azazel withdrew from the scenes and lifted me to watch from an invisible perch. Time spun and flashed by, and then I saw the heavenly and human women giving birth to babies. Newborns arrived in every village, town and city. Hundreds of new lives voiced their lust for life in every tent, hut and palace.

And the children grew. They grew from infancy into adulthood within a short time instead of years like normal children...but they transformed into giants.

"They are called the Nephilim," Azazel spoke in my ear. *"The offspring of the humans and angels. And giants roamed the earth..."*

But I watched in horror as their offspring ate everything in the lands. The Nephilim consumed the food, the crops. They laid waste to the livestock and the wildlife.

And then, once they realized their food sources had been exhausted, they turned on the humans who had raised them, cared for them. I cried out at the blood, the carnage, and I wept as they slaughtered the people as though they were no more than cattle and ate them.

Releasing my mouth, Azazel raised his head and stared into my eyes. Lightning laced the sky, and thunder crashed around us.

"Do you understand your destiny?" he asked.

"I won't give you a child," I croaked.

Behind him, inkiness spread through the stars. Lightning bolts shredded the blackness. Something was coming, and if I didn't act soon, it would be here any time. What or who was coming? It couldn't be—

"Ah, you are beginning to understand," he said and chuckled.

The sound and vibration of his laughter shot spirals of desire into my body. Against my will, I wiggled beneath him, delighting in the sensation.

His eyes rolled back in his head. "That's it, Ruby. Imagine how my cock shall feel inside your body. And you "will" bear me a child. Through you, the Nephilim will roam the earth once more."

I could barely speak for the lust coursing through my veins. "Stop...this is...wrong..."

"Now why would I," he drove his hips hard against mine, "want to do that when we've waited so long to reclaim this world?"

"Why me?" The answer to that question had taunted me for the last few days, but asking it was more to distract him from taking me. If he tantalized me any further, I'd be defeated.

As red, yellow and silver lightning splintered the sky, Azazel kissed me again, his tongue tasting and jousting with mine. He ground his hips harder, his cock rubbing my belly until it became painful, but regardless, I found myself wanting more.

Again, his kiss propelled me back to ancient times. I glimpsed a dirty nomad woman wrapped in skins next to a fire, chanting unintelligible words, and in the flames, something gyrated as white sparks arced toward the heavens. The images blurred. The sensation of flying through space suffocated me. I gasped, and suddenly the scene of a dark-haired, dark-skinned woman rose in my mind. Her face remained obscured, but she stood upon a mountain overlooking the terrain I'd visited earlier. She called to something above, shouted to something below, and flames shot from her hands.

A fissure opened in the sky. Planets, stars and galaxies swirled and sparkled in the black void. Within that hole another fissure appeared. Beyond it, barren and dusty, a world boasted nothing but sand, rocks and the putrid smell of decay. The woman screamed words I didn't understand. More cobalt and white fire erupted from her palms, and, with her face turned toward the sky, orbs of power spewed from her eyes and mouth. Thunder and lightning scarred the earth as the Fallen Ones rushed from the four corners of the Earth. They arrowed through the heavens, beating their wings of feathers or leather, each angel intent on stopping the woman. Teeth and talons bared, they screamed obscenities to the world, their serpent eyes flashing with fury and fire.

The woman threw her hands out in front of her, and a semi-transparent wall protected her from the angels' vengeance. The fissures widened more, and a tornado appeared to snatch each being from the air. The twister passed through the first slice in the firmament and into the next, followed by both dimensional doors slamming shut behind it, imprisoning the angels. The resulting clap of displaced air triggered avalanches. Earth and rock crumbled to the valley floors, and gargantuan clouds of dust rose into the air to disperse on the wind currents.

Silence followed.

Then, in the darkness and quiet, a thunderous voice sounded.

Rain began. It poured so hard I felt as though I was peering through a waterfall to no avail. The rain filled the valleys, washed across the plains and ascended the mountainsides. People climbed to higher ground, but the floodwaters rose to wash away their footprints. Within a couple of days, the Nephilim and all other life had drowned, and the woman waited for the water to claim her too.

Finally, she turned and showed her face.

Horrified, I stared back at myself.

Chapter Twenty-Nine

Azazel continued to kiss me, propelling my consciousness through time and space.

A Mayan pyramid on Jaguar Hill rose before me. A powerful, olive-skinned priestess lay prostrated on a stone altar. She turned her face toward me. Once again, I stared back at myself. The king sliced the woman's throat, believing Quetzalcoatl would be pleased with the gift of her life and magic, therefore blessing the Mayans with a safe and fruitful existence.

Next, I saw myself dancing as a slave girl during the height of the Roman Empire, a strange medallion pendant nestled between my ample breasts, the power of it surrounding me in an invisible cloud. Other images flooded my mind. Pictures of battles and dying men of various lands pelted my mystical eye. The metallic aroma of blood assailed my senses, but gratitude filled me when the images, sounds and odors dissipated.

Once more, I stood in the middle of the dirt road that snaked through a village. The big, black-armored rider sat astride an ebony warhorse as he pounded toward me. I whirled, racing away from the yellow-haired town harlot who cowered against the well. The warrior snatched me up and draped me across the saddle as if I was no more than a slain rabbit. The next vision showed him pushing me back on a bed covered in furs, the power of his love for me so intense I cried out in pain and loss as the image shifted into another.

Breaking the kiss, Azazel growled, "The White King will not have you." He moved one hand up to my hair and gripped a handful of it so tightly tears pricked my eyes. "He's interfered enough. You belong to "me" now."

He rose slightly, and, palm down and fingers splayed, he waved his hand over my form. The top and bra I'd been wearing vanished and re-appeared on the sand next to me.

"NO!" I moved to slap my hands over my exposed breasts, but he caught them and pinned them over my head.

He scooted down my body and latched on to one of my nipples with his mouth. Fire seared my nerve endings. Heat raced through my veins and with such intensity I remained powerless, unable to even moan let alone resist.

"That is but a taste of how it will feel when I consummate our union," he said as he raised his head. "First, I must finish awakening your memories." His mouth connected with mine again.

I hurtled through darkness. Brilliant stars streaked through it. I wanted to see more of my White King, wanted to learn why our love had ended so tragically.

But how did I know that? Was the answer locked somewhere in my subconscious?

Just remember you belong to me now.

Another year slipped into my mind...1066.

Solomon stood next to a roaring hearth. A long, embroidered robe flowed over his back and swept the edges of the floor. His flaxen locks hung around his shoulders, the color ghostly in the firelight. He turned and looked at me.

"I must lead this battle," he said. "Edward insisted that if anything should ever happen to him, I am to defend his lands until the proper king comes to power."

"It is you who is destined to rule England," I replied. "You know that. The king thought highly of you and kept you in his confidence. He even gave you a stronghold of your own to govern within his realm."

"I am no king," he said with a heavy sigh. "I only defend what belonged to my friend and brother."

"You are the rightful heir!" I insisted. "Shirk your guise of being in his service and reveal that you are Edward's half brother."

"I cannot."

"Why?"

"The people will never accept a king who is as white as a spirit howling upon the moors." He strode across the chamber, his robe stirring the reeds upon the stone floor, and pulled me to my feet.

His gaze met mine, and my soul leapt in response at the love I saw within his eyes.

"The people are content with me defending their homes, but they will never accept me as anything other than their warrior." He threaded his fingers into my hair and brushed my lips with the softest and most poignant of kisses. "As long as I have your love and this fortress around us," he said with emotion thick in his voice, "I am happy to defend Edward's lands until a better man than I can sit upon my brother's throne."

"I fear for your life." Tears trickled over my cheeks. "What if you don't return to me?"

"If I die, I will find you, my love. I promise." My White King enfolded me in his arms and hugged me tightly. "Bring your yellow-haired friend here to stay with you while I am gone. She shall keep you company until I return."

"But the Sons of God cometh—"

"I shall fight them for you."

"Now you understand how you and the White King have crossed paths again."

Azazel palmed one of my breasts, reminding me I still laid prone on the beach. Against my will I responded by parting my legs.

"You had your time with the White King, and now it's my turn."

He kissed me harder, his tongue probing my mouth. Desire heated the depths of my muscles and bones. I groaned with ecstasy, and he eagerly swallowed the noise.

Suddenly I stood upon the shore where I always saw the huge monolith. Lightning ripped the sky open, the colors deep crimson, volcanic-yellow and silver. Vaguely, I was aware of the wind roaring across Key West's shoreline as Azazel kissed and caressed me. Hadn't I seen the same type of lightning illuminating the sky behind him earlier?

Laughter rumbled through his body, and his words filled my mind. *"They will be here soon."*

Back on the channel's windswept shore, I watched the smoke monsters and their riders as they bore down upon me from across an expanse of cold, slate-gray water. Next to me, the woman who had always accompanied me in my vision kneeled upon the sand in a heavy, dark cloak. This time she pushed back the cowl, and I saw her face—Alice. Surprise whispered in my mind. So, she had been telling the truth.

"Watch as Hardrada of Norway and Harold Godwinson, King Edward's advisor, battle with the White King. This is how you lost the man you loved."

But I still love him!

"NO!" His kiss overwhelmed my senses, absorbed my will. *"YOU ARE MINE NOW, NOT HIS!"*

A cry to charge the shoreline echoed over the water. Hardrada of Norway and his Viking warriors leapt from their smaller boats and sloshed onto the beach, weapons drawn and shields up. Blood sprayed in the air, leaving the aroma of copper in its wake. It dripped from swords, maces, daggers, and spears, and spilled upon the ground or splattered across shields and the chain-mailed breasts of the warriors' massive equines. Men screamed in agony and shouted battle cries. Warhorses stomped upon wounded men, grinding their guts and bones into the moist dirt, and other steeds bit and kicked, felling those fighting in the infantry.

Behind them, the Sons of God approached on their steeds of smoke and vengeance. They soared closer, their eyes aglow with feral light, their mounts morphing from one beast into another. As the mortals' battle raged, the sound of metal rang out over the terrain, and I raised my hands to the sky. Fire erupted from my palms, eyes and mouth. The woman at my side chanted loudly, and her power flowed into me, aiding me in my quest to send the Sons of God back to their prison in that god-awful realm of death and decay.

Azazel led his minions inland. He tossed a lightning bolt at me, but I absorbed it and used it to channel more power. The rogue angels hit a semi-transparent wall of energy. The smoke creatures shrieked and roared with frustration and pain as the angels hurled insults, threats and profanities at me.

"Join us!" the Azazel of that time called to me. He reined in his charger of swirling smoke, a creature half demonic panther, half freakish falcon. "You are a comely woman and shall pleasure me greatly. Together we can rule Earth."

"Never!" I hissed and summoned all my power.

First one fissure opened in the firmament, followed by the other amongst the twinkling stars and galaxies. The tornado emerged to whisk the angels away, the fissures closing after them with resounding booms that knocked the fighting warriors to their feet.

I fell to the beach where the woman cradled me against her bosom. Together, we watched as the White King cleaved Hardrada open with his sword. The king's adversary fell dead upon the rocky shoreline, his innards spilling forth.

"Know how the White King was defeated," Azazel ground his cock against the apex of my hips, *"and see why you and I will be joined forever."*

I sighed in ecstasy and bucked my hips under him.

"Yes...yes...that's it..."

He slid his tongue along the seam of my lips and transported me down the shore to Hastings, England, where Harold Godwinson II and his forces fought the defensive against the Norman infantry, both sides striving to win King Edward's throne. The Normans launched a barrage of arrows. The English marched forward, their shields up for protection. Once the arrows stopped falling, the White King charged through on an ebony steed with furry, pail-sized feet. He brandished a broadsword with a handle wrapped in black leather and studded with turquoise.

The sword hanging over the fireplace in Alice's living room!

"An individual's belongings can travel through time to find their owners. How sad that Solomon is now a nothing, a nobody."

I ignored his jibe.

Knocked from his horse by another rider, the White King scrambled to his feet a few yards away from Harold. He battled one-on-one with an adversary, but as he pushed his sword through the man's gullet, and then shoved him off his blade, he looked up to see an archer siting on Harold II.

Wayne Blacktree!

"Ah, yes. That human has been a useful tool in doing our bidding, but the ungrateful wretch had a change of heart after St. Augustine and turned on us to join forces with that witch, Alice."

The archer who resembled Wayne let the arrow fly, and my lover leapt into the air to block it.

The pointed missile skipped off the edge of his shield and shot through the air penetrating Harold's eye. The would-be king of England slumped backward to the ground. Racing to his side, the White King scooped him up in his arms, but Wayne saw his chance and planted another arrow in the back of my lover's neck. Gurgling, blood spurting, the White King fell over Harold's body.

No, no, no...! Loss flew through me, reinforcing our love that had transcended the ages.

"Forget him! He is unimportant. We are together now, and you will be mine forever!"

Briefly, I saw a scene where the news of my lover's death was delivered to me on a parchment sealed with his crest in red wax. I pulled a dagger from my boot as tears of anguish streamed down my face and sobs racked my body. The woman who looked like Maureen, my only and dearest friend then or now, entered the chamber and rushed toward me as I skewered my heart. Her pitiful cries of mourning were the last sounds I heard in that lifetime.

Azazel broke the kiss. I sucked in air and blinked up at the vibrantly colored lightning bolts zigzagging across the sky. The wind had kicked up several knots, and grit and sand peppered my skin, the stinging sensation insignificant in comparison to the lust bubbling within me.

"You see," said Azazel, his voice slicing through the roar of thunder, surf and wind, "each time you've exiled the Sons of God to that dry-rotting prison of death, and although we possess the power to pry open those dimensional doors, it takes us a few hundred years to do so. As a result, we return in hopes of converting you. Each time you've returned, your power is stronger. In this life your magic shows itself in unique ways because the vessel it resides in is too small to contain it." Perplexed, he studied me for a moment. "Why He has allowed you to be His tool to deliver man from our rule is beyond me, but now you're mine. Everything is in the past, where it will remain never to return."

"But why show me the past? Why not just take me and have it done with?"

He rose slightly and looked down the length of me. "I already told you I need you to remember who you are."

"But why?"

"If you remember everything," he explained, "then you recover your power from over the ages too. You're powerful, but even more so now that you remember who you are. To rule this world, I need both my magic and yours."

Angry at what he'd done and at myself for being so weak, I tried to move, determined to stand and fight him.

His gaze scanned my naked form, and my shorts and panties vanished to re-appear beside me with the rest of my clothes. Frightened, I met his gaze, and he offered me a victorious smile. Even knowing I was at the threshold of no return, I still craved to have his cock inside me. Unable to control my actions, I wiggled, bucked, and spread my legs wider, offering myself to him. However, at the same time, disgust riddled me.

He threw his head back and laughed. A strange glow slid over his body. Angelic light was supposed to be bright, blinding and holy, but Azazel possessed an aura that exuded something dark yet not dark, something malevolent. His clothes disappeared. Nude, he settled on me again, his cock nestled firmly at my opening. He released my hands, and, against my better judgment, I wrapped my arms and legs around him, nudging my center against his prick. No matter how huge he was, I wanted him inside me, desired him to thrust hard and long.

Wings unfurled from his back. Not white, downy wings like I'd seen when I first witnessed him from his lofty perch thousands of years ago. Oh no, these webbed wings of leather possessed sharp talons on their tips. He fanned them back and forth as he parted my folds with his cock, edging ever closer to consummating our union.

My gaze moved from his wings to his face. His beautiful features morphed into hard lines and angles. His eyes elongated, and serpentine, fire-yellow pupils stared back at me.

The scream that tore from my lips hopped aboard the wind and left town. Azazel smiled, revealing jagged teeth and top and bottom fangs that glistened in the lightning. A forked tongue exited his mouth and licked the side of my face.

I shuddered and turned my head away with a plaintive mewl of revulsion.

"What's the matter, my love?" he slurred through his teeth. "Don't you love me anymore?"

Déjà vu crashed-landed in the backyard of my mind. Mental images of Cole Vandercourt played like a slideshow. I saw Cole lying on top of me, laughing as he entered my body. I heard my hiss of pain as he broke my hymen, heard his groans of pleasure as he began thrusting.

The shrieks of demonic beasts and fowl grew louder than the sounds of the paranormal storm. The laughter of the bikers joined the raucous noise, followed by the heavy thuds of things landing on the pavement a few yards above us. Motorcycles roared to life, and more laughter punctuated the night.

The Sons of God had arrived.

Panic fluttered through me, and I struggled to no avail. Azazel grabbed another handful of my hair and yanked. Tears sprang to my eyes. He adjusted his body more snugly between my legs, nestled his cock tighter between the lips of my opening. I stiffened in response, waited for what had been disguised as pleasure to become torture.

The guffaws and giggles coming from the landing at the dead-end street reminded me of the students who had looked on as Cole had had his way with me. Their jeers echoed in my mind, and the smug, satisfied look of victory on Cole's face replayed over and over in my head.

No. I will not be a victim again!

I called upon my power. My skin began to glow, and my unbound tresses turned from orange-red to whips of neon lava.

"Stop it," Azazel said. "You are under my control."

Magic swirled up out of that quiet region within my soul and spread up into my brain, out along my arms, and threaded through the fibers and cells that composed my body. Azazel pressed his will upon mine, forced his power on me to drive mine back, but the more I thought about Cole and the kids who had looked on as he'd seduced and then raped me, the more pissed off and determined I became.

"Don't," he snapped. His long, forked tongue whipped out to caress my neck and the shell of my ear. He shifted his weight, lifted his hips—and I blasted the hell out of him with a shield of pure white flames. He flew backward off of me.

Jumping to my feet, the cool ocean breeze bombarding my body, my hair writhing like like snakes, I held the rogue angel in midair in a ball of glowing magic.

"No one, especially the lowly likes of you, will use me again. Man was created over the angels," I screamed into the wind as I moved Azazel from the rocky shore to the landing above the motorcycle gang. "You are to serve me!" With that, I slammed his body against the pavement so hard bone crunched. At the sound, my stomach flip-flopped. The unbelievable rush coursing through my system slowed, leaving me nauseous and slightly disoriented.

Stunned, the angels in disguise stared at their leader sprawled in all his naked, despicable glory upon the pebbled asphalt. The wind died, and the thunder subsided.

Quiet settled over the rocky shore save for the gentle lapping of the waves and the sound of claws clicking and scrabbling across pavement.

Frowning, I looked beyond the Sons of God and their demonic steel horses to see Shunka Wakan running full tilt down the street toward the landing. Once the dog was about a dozen feet from Azazel, he leapt into the air as a snarling, snapping whirling dervish of fur. Amazed, I crossed the sandy clearing to climb up to the street, but halted as Shunka transformed in midair. A brilliant flash and little lights that winked out like embers left an arced trail through the air. As Azazel slowly sat up, the bundle of twinkles landed on him. The ball of brilliance solidified and knocked the angel flat again. Instead of a dog, a furious, raven-haired man with silvered temples appeared.

"No one," the man snarled like a beast from Hell, his knees upon the angel's chest, hands around his throat, "pisses with my mistress. Not even you, Azazel!"

Chapter Thirty

The bikers surrounded Azazel. They linked hands, and a black vapor wound back and forth amongst their bodies.

"Be gone, you foul little spirit!" Azazel growled. He rolled to the side, gripped Shunka by the arms, and stood up with him held out in front of his body. He tossed Shunka through the air as if he were no more than a sack of wet cement.

On impulse, I sent my magic skyward and caught my friend in a protective bubble. Once his feet touched the earth, Shunka transformed back into the form of an Alaskan Malamute and padded to my side. Whining, he rubbed his head against my leg.

"Aren't you full of surprises?" I whispered to him.

He whined louder.

"It's okay." I patted his haunch. "I'm sorry I neglected to bring you here with me."

The Sons of God continued to clasp hands. The motorcycles morphed from mechanical machines into their true smoke forms. They swirled into the semblance of monsters and beasts shifting from one nightmare form into another or blending several forms into one. The creatures padded to their owners on vaporous paws tipped with long yellow claws. Their serpentine eyes lit the street with a Halloween glow.

None of the past memories except for the era of the White King had revealed these creatures, but I felt sure that whatever they were, the angels had found them in their prison world and trained them to obey their commands, to do their bidding by preying on the innocent and for tracking me down.

Enormous sets of wings sprouted from the bikers' backs. Their clothes shredded and fell to the pavement in tatters. Their other garments simply vanished.

Quickly, I snatched up my clothes and stepped into my undies and shorts. I left the bra on the sand and jerked my t-shirt over my head.

"*Ruby!*"

The shout frightened me, and I stuffed my arms through the shirt's sleeves and shoved my feet into my sneakers.

"Ruby, you have been a very, very bad little witch," Azazel rumbled, his tone patient but touched with sarcasm. "I think you need to be punished, but I'll do that after I take you as my mate."

The angels tittered and snorted at his statement.

I forced my power along my arms and out my finger-tips, drawing a protection orb around myself and Shunka. "You're not going to win me over to your dark, twisted plans, Azazel. I'm going to banish you again."

"Let me punish her," the redheaded biker bitch whined.

"Patience," Azazel replied. "There will be plenty of time to bend her to our will."

The sound of collective footsteps permeated the haze of fear pounding through me. The dog woofed softly. I scanned the area for the source of the footfalls. A group of people walked down the center of the street toward us. Here and there, another person would emerge from behind a parked car, out of an alley, or step from the shadows to join them. As their numbers grew, one person stood out from the rest.

Solomon!

Azazel whirled and delivered bursts of short lightning bolts at the group. The power jolts hit an invisible barrier that briefly glowed silver and white before turning invisible again.

The Sons of God finished morphing into their de-sired forms. They stood over ten feet tall, including Azazel, each one sporting fangs, horns, forked tongues and serpentine tails. Leathery wings with pointed tips or talons blocked much of the streetlamps' illumination or cast terrifying shadows over the moonlit areas.

The psycho chick transformed into a bright red, pebble-skinned creature that reminded me of a dragon. She met my gaze and bared her teeth.

As the others drew closer, I saw Maureen, my son, Alice, Wayne Blacktree and even Loretta Detzer. The group encircled the Sons of God and their steeds. Recognition flared in me. There, to the left of Loretta, stood the three witches from the St. Augustine B and B.

A coven!

Many races had joined to combine their powers and offer their support. I saw Cubans, African-Americans, Jamaicans, Haitians, Caucasians, and all of them softly muttered strange words in various dialects.

"Ruby, you must send the Sons of God back to their prison." Alice's gaze connected with mine. *"I don't know how you've done it in the past, but somehow you'll figure it out."*

Solomon looked at me, his gaze full of worry mixed with determination. Maureen grinned and offered me a thumbs-up.

My attention returned to Solomon. Something pulled me to him, something strong and overwhelming.

"Come to me," I said to him. "I'll protect you."

Casting my power over him in a net only I could see, Solomon seemed to feel its presence and walked toward me.

"NO!" Azazel flapped his wings in agitation. Dirt, pebbles and grit shot into the air from the motion. "She is mine!"

Alice, Anthony and Maureen separated from the crowd and escorted Solomon to my side.

With the four of them divided from the coven, I sensed the protective wards lessening around my friends. I intensified my spell around them and myself.

Upon reaching me, Solomon drew me into his arms and kissed me with relief but most of all with love.

Once he released me, Maureen asked, "Are you okay, Ruby?"

I smiled at Anthony as he took my hand and squeezed it. "A little rattled," I answered, "but other than that I'm fine."

Deep reverberating laughter encompassed the area. I looked over at Azazel and his rogue angels.

"You think you've won so easily?" Azazel asked, his eyes aflame with fury. "What you don't realize is that in summoning the power to winch open the dimensional doors, we've also learned how to tap power from other sources. The last one thousand years have given us plenty of time to gather magic and plan our return."

Mounting the smoke creatures, the Sons of God leapt into flight. Their wings and the monsters' combined stirred sand and debris to whip it through the air, across the landing and up the street. Their flapping wings snapped and beat so loudly I thought of prehistoric flying dinosaurs. I glanced over at the coven, who had joined hands and formed a huge circle on the landing.

"What are you going to do?" Solomon asked.

"I'm not sure," I said. "I just know you're part of it."

"She belongs to me!" Azazel's words rolled over the ocean in the form of thunder.

A bolt of lightning hit my magical shield. The strength of it nearly pushed me to my knees.

"Damn!" hissed Alice. "That was really stroong."

Shaking my head, I intensified the magic, feeling it flow out of me in a more concentrated form. My hair grew brighter and the illumination I case almost seared the eyes.

The angels circled overhead. They screamed and shouted taunts and insults.

The next jolt of power struck my ward so hard it bore us across the rocks and into the lapping surf.

"*Run!*" I shouted at my friends as our shield disintegrated. I sat up and snorted saltwater from my sinuses.

They scattered, taking Shunka with them, and slogged through the water to hide behind boulders and stony outcroppings.

Azazel roared with laughter, and the rogue hoard echoed his sentiments.

On the landing, the coven began to chant in a soft, determined manner.

"Pitiful mortals," Azazel said. "You can do nothing to protect her."

Something gripped my innards. It began in the center of my stomach, the sensation similar to a hot ember landing on my skin. It spread, growing hotter as it did so. I grimaced at the pain, but suddenly found myself raising my arms, hands up, palms out. The power burbled upward . It slipped into my breasts, over my shoulders and down along my arms. It rose into my neck and into my head, the pain of it stripping me of rational thought.

The power exited my hands, mouth and eyes in the form of white, lavender-tinted fire that felt both exhilarating and terrifying. It hit Azazel square in the chest. I pointed my left arm skyward and shot the same magic into the winged hoard.

Screams followed. The sound continued for several seconds, until finally I realized they stemmed from me. The screaming stopped, and strange gibberish tumbled from my lips.

The sky rent, and blackness full of twinkling planets and galaxies materialized. A howling sound began, and the wind picked up, whooshing inland. I glimpsed the twister as it exited the prison world and moved into ours.

Something hit me so hard I lifted into the air. Pain sliced through my body. Warm liquid surrounded me, tossed me about.

Hands pulled me upward, air caressed my body, and I cough hard several times. I spat seawater and coughed again as I tried to draw a breath. The grip on me tightened. With the tornado gone, the fissures started closing.

"Your power doesn't work on us anymore," Azazel said, his demonic face inches from mine. His long, forked tongue whipped out to slide over one of my cheeks. "The Sons of God will remain on Earth, and you will be my queen." He gestured at my body. My clothes vanished to re-appear on the water and float away on the waves. "Once I consummate our union, you won't be able to fight me any longer."

He gripped me by my arms and lifted me into the air. The wind buffeted my body, and gooseflesh awoke as the moisture coating my skin evaporated in the balmy air. I glanced down at Azazel's eager cock and screamed my refusal. Movement caught my attention, and I looked over to see Alice standing waist deep in the water with the three B and B witches and Loretta. Alice shouted something I didn't understand and a silvery essence drifted upward from the five women and combined into a large, vaporous sword. It sliced through the air and penetrated Azazel's ribs. He roared with pain and dropped me in the water. Momentarily wounded, he struggled to his feet and climbed back onto the rocky shore.

Shaking seawater from his wings, he gazed skyward. "Kill the others," he ordered, "but Ruby is *mine*."

"Ruby." Solomon swam toward me and gripped me around the waist. "Let's get out of here."

Again, I felt a weird pull to Solomon. "I can't. I have to send the Sons of God back to their prison."

"But how?" he whispered.

I looked sharply at him. "By making me remember my past, Azazel also gave me the means to collect my magic from the centuries, but the angels are stronger now too. I need you to help me strengthen my power even more so I can banish them even farther."

"What?"

"Put one hand on my heart and hold my other hand. I'll do the rest."

"I'll help," said Maureen as she dog-paddled to me.

Relieved to have her support, I smiled.

"Me too," Anthony offered.

"Do it, Ruby, and hurry!"

Alice and her four witch comrades fired another silver fog sword at Azazel. The witches on the landing did the same, but shot them up into the angels flying above the shoreline.

Azazel shrieked in maniacal anger as the vaporous swords hit him over and over. The Sons of God echoed his cries.

Solomon stood behind me and threaded his fingers with mine. He wrapped his other arm around my torso and placed his hand over my heart.

"I love you," he said. "Let's get some payback for Gabriella too."

His sister's murder suddenly made sense. The Sons of God had been on Earth for the past couple of years searching for me, but had stumbled across Solomon in the process. They'd recognized him, so Azazel had his minions murdered Gabriella to pay the White King back for winning my love.

I nodded, a sense of satisfaction wafting over me. "Yes, it's time they get their comeuppance for her death."

Maureen stood on one side of me and placed her other hand on my left arm while Anthony mirrored her actions on my right.

"You know I love you, right?" said Maureen.

"Yes," I said. "We've been friends a very long time."

She grinned.

"I believe in you, Mom," said Anthony.

Startled, I blinked away tears and mouthed the words "thank you" before I lost my composure.

Once again, the power awakened in me. Its heat raced through my body and burst from the eyes and mouths of my friends and my lover. They cried out at its intensity. My heart ached for them, and I fretted that I'd caused them pain, almost stopping it.

Alice's voice snapped loudly in my mind. *Do it! Do it NOW!*

The magic crackled from my hands and spewed from my eyes, mouth, and even my nostrils. White flames streaked into the sky and knocked the angels and their steeds from the air. They crashed into the water. As they struck the surface of it, each one screamed with fury.

Azazel howled his distaste and disbelief to the universe.

The water around us bubbled, and as the steam of it rose, the first firmament re-opened, followed by the second, but instead of the dry, dead world, another door split the space-time continuum, where indescribable things writhed and snarled. Beyond that one, a fourth popped open, the colors both bizarre and beautiful, but dread filled me at the sight of them. Finally, a fifth tear in the dimensional walls revealed utter darkness, a darkness heavy like sludge, suffocating everything within it with its weight. The putrid fragrance of brimstone and the tortured cries of souls reached us.

A tiny grain of poetic justice landed in my soul. Through the ages I'd always managed to open two dimensional doors, but now with Solomon, Maureen and Anthony's help, I could push the angels farther, and hopefully they'd never return.

The tornado appeared. It lowered to the ocean's surface and moved across it in the form of a waterspout. Azazel tried to flee, but the coven kept bombarding him with the mist swords. He screeched in pain and anger.

The Sons of God struggled to lift from the water and fly away, but the waterspout sucked them up, twirling them in its vortex, their outraged screams similar to the shrieks of seagulls.

Azazel finally broke free of the landing and sprang into the air, heading north, beating his fibrous wings faster and faster. "I will return, Ruby," he bellowed with assurance. "You will be mine, and I will rule this world."

No chance of that, you arrogant bastard.

The waterspout cut him off as he rose over the palm trees, wings pummeling the turbulent air. It dipped its funnel top and gulped him into a greedy mouth. With a last thunderous shout of rage, Azazel joined his fellow brethren.

My power subsided, and the four of us leaned upon one another as we stood in the tidal waters and watched the tornado ascend into the firmament where it passed through one fissure after another to deposit the Sons of God and their leader in the world of total blackness. The rents in the dimensions slammed shut one after another. Lightning scarred the sky, and thunder boomed.

A sudden, explosive quiet followed.

Chapter Thirty-One

We sloshed out of the water, over the shore, and up onto the landing. Solomon kept his arm around me, and Anthony flanked my other side. Behind us, Maureen called to Shunka, who barked and scrambled around the tidal wall and up to the street. The coven dispersed in singles and groups of two or more. Some disappeared without a trace.

"You just saved the world, Ruby. Once again The Banishment is complete." Alice said as she approached me with Loretta on her left and Wayne on her right. The ocean breeze tousled the hem of the dark red-velvet cloak Alice wore. She lowered its cowl and swept the garment off her shoulders to throw it around my body.

As I drew the long cape over my nakedness, I met her gaze. Although admiration filled her eyes, it astounded me just how much we resembled one another. With her high forehead, widow's peak, dark, penetrating eyes...she was definitely a Nutter.

"No," I said. "We all saved the world."

She smiled. "Indeed." Gesturing down the street, she indicated that we should return with her. "Battling the Sons of God is a thankless job, and although only a few know the truth, it has been your destiny time and time again."

"Lucky me."

"Come, let's fetch your belongings and go back to my apartment."

As a group, we walked to the parking lot, got in the Excursion and Mustang, and drove to Alice's store where we parked the vehicles. Upstairs in her apartment, we took turns showering. Once it was my turn, Solomon followed me into the bathroom with our things and shut the door.

I started the water and shrugged out of Alice's cloak as Solomon took off his wet, salt-encrusted clothes. He stepped in the shower first and offered me his hand, helping me into the square stall behind him. He first removed a bottle of shampoo from a shelf and poured some of the liquid into his hand. Turning me around, he began the arduous task of washing my long hair. I could only imagine the salt residue coating it, but he took his time and massaged my scalp, all the while his cock bumping and brushing against my ass. Although I knew Azazel's seduction was pure magic to make me comply, it had still left my libido in turmoil. Gulping hard, I tried to ignore the persistent touches on my rear.

Solomon rinsed my hair then took a washcloth from the shelf just outside the door, soaked it and lathered it with a healthy squirt of vanilla-scented gel. Without a word, he drew me closer and began washing me down my arms, over my breasts and scrubbed my back and legs too.

"When I awoke to find you gone from the apartment, I knew what had happened," Solomon finally said as I rinsed the thick lather from my tired body. "I don't know how I knew, but I did."

"Our souls are connected," I replied and put my face in the shower spray. Sputtering a bit in the water, I added, "I saw our past lives together."

"Tell me about it, about us," he said.

"Later...after I've had time to process everything."

"I thought I'd lost you." Emotion gripped his voice. "Ruby, you don't have to love me in this life, but just know I will always love you no matter what."

I stared at him, his pale gaze full of love, hope and sincerity. Could I tell him how I felt? Did I dare say the words? Although we'd defeated supernatural beings together, the scars on my heart still controlled parts of me.

Sudden rapping on the door penetrated the sound of the spray.

"Hey," Maureen called, "Don't use up all the hot water."

"Out in a minute," I yelled back.

"This conversation isn't over," Solomon said. "We need to talk."

I smiled. "I know."

****

Once Solomon and I had changed into fresh clothes, we realized we were still too wound up to sleep. Together, we wandered back into the living area. On the couch, Anthony lay with his arms behind his head sound asleep. I walked over and looked down at my son. Earlier, he'd called me mom. Love and pride swelled in my heart. Overcome with emotion, I wiped tears away with the heel of my hand.

"Loretta is in the kitchen and Alice is out on the deck," said Maureen as she wandered out of her bedroom with nightclothes and a couple of toiletries. "I think we're all too hyper to rest."

She motioned to Wayne sitting in the recliner. He rose and entered the bathroom with her. Tossing me a serene smile over her shoulder, Maureen shut the door.

I looked at Solomon. "No way."

He shrugged and laughed, grasping my hand and leading me through the apartment and into the kitchen where a door opened out onto a second-story deck. At the kitchen isle, Loretta sat eating sliced cantaloupe and paged through one of the shop's catalogues. She said nothing to us as we passed.

Outside, Alice sat at a small patio table on the opposite end of the porch. Half a dozen citronella candles glowed brightly on the glass top, which reflected the yellow flames.

"What time is it?" I asked.

"A little after three a.m.," Alice answered. She picked up a bottle of red wine and poured two more glasses. "I figured you'd need to unwind after tonight. It'll be daylight before any of us settle down to sleep."

I sat down and sank into the vinyl-covered cushion. Despite the calming, balmy tropical wind and the comfort of the brilliant stars above, I couldn't turn my mind off. Every time I shut my eyes, I saw the images of all my past lives, but worse, the vision of the White King's death haunted me. I looked up at Solomon, who sensed my gaze. He reached for my hand and threaded his fingers with mine.

Alice handed me a glass of deep purple wine. As our fingers made contact, a familiar yet bizarre tingle race down my arm, but I jerked away too slowly. Sparks shot out of my fingertips, illuminating the glass. The liquid within it glowed purple-black, and the finger-fire leapt from the glass to whiz up Alice's arm. To my amazement, the magic failed to knock her out of her chair. Instead, her hair blew back from her face as if she'd been blasted by a gust of wind.

"Don't worry." She smiled. "You didn't hurt me, and a good witch always protects herself from the magic of others. You'll soon learn to control and wield your power. You've already learned so much on your own. And the Key West Coven is eager to get to know you too. Many of them will offer to teach you."

"I'm guessing the money and document was all a story to force me here?" I said as Solomon pulled out the other chair and sat next to me.

"You figured right," she answered sheepishly. "I'm sorry that—"

"I understand why you did it." I picked up my glass. The wine tasted heady and sweet. "The greater good," I replied in a faux narrator's voice, "and all that jazz."

Alice nodded, smiling. "There's more to the Nutter family and how you and I know one another." She held her hand out across the tabletop. "Would you like to see?"

"Sure," I replied, but after all that Azazel had shown me of the past, I wasn't actually certain if I wanted to see more. Against my better judgment, I put my hand in hers.

She withdrew a small silver dagger from her robe-style dress and cut a short, shallow incision in the palm of her right hand. "Now yours."

She sliced my palm so quickly I didn't even feel it. A small weal of blood appeared on each of our palms, and she clasped my hand so suddenly I gasped. Our blood meshed, and a jolt shot through me.

Buried memories surfaced and swept me away, bearing me toward yet another era. A picture formed, and I witnessed her, this Alice Nutter, as my great aunt times four and a wealthy noblewoman of Pendle, England. The year 1612 floated through my mind. Alice had been accused of witchcraft, and weeks later, she swung from a tree by a noose. Others hung alongside her, including me and a woman who looked remarkably like Maureen. On the lush, green Pendle Hill, the three of us strangled to death.

She released my hand, and I fell back into my chair, breathing hard and trembling from head to toe.

"Ruby?" Solomon leaned over, gazing into my face. He brushed my hair back.

"I'm...I'm okay." I touched my neck, still feeling the coarse rope choking the life from me. Tears trickled down my face. With embarrassment, I used the hem of my nightshirt to wipe them away then pressed it to the thin wound on my hand.

"Now you understand," said Alice. She pulled a tissue from her dress pocket and placed it on her cut.

"Well, it's obvious why my father hates me and refuses to talk about the Nutters."

Alice snorted in disgust. "Those with unique abilities are treated with suspicion and disdain."

"But I'm his daughter!" Anger rippled through me. I sighed and shook my head. "It doesn't matter. It's time for me to think about my life and what makes me happy instead of trying to live according to Dad's rules and expectations. Besides, I inherited my power through him."

Alice stared at me expectantly.

"You know, don't you?" I said.

"Yes. You're father knows where you are and why." She reached across the table and placed her hand on top of mine. "You do remember why the garage burned, don't you?"

The memory impaled my brain, the pain of it whisking my breath out to sea.

"Ruby?" Solomon said. "Are you all right?"

"She must remember and admit the truth." Alice's voice sounded as if it came from the end of a long tunnel. "She cannot bear the blame any longer."

"I saw my father," I gulped hard, "saw him..." Hot tears rolled down my face. "I walked into the garage to ask my dad if he was going to drive me to the movies when I saw him talking to a..." The word sliced through my tongue but I spat it out anyway. "To a demon."

The memory surfaced clearly in my mind as if I was watching it play out on a big screen. I told Alice and Solomon about the nightmare that my father had summoned. The pentagram for evil had been scrawled on the floor in chalk with black candles burning on each point. Dad was bargaining for riches. Through gambling at the racetrack, he had put us in financial jeopardy and we were about to lose our home, and the creditors were threatening to take him to court.

The demon had granted him money before, but my father had even gambled that away. He'd paid the price by allowing the thing to take five years off his life, but my father's sickness, his greed and desperation had driven him to the brink of insanity. He begged to be rich, to pay off his debts and to always have good financial luck.

"I will grant you payment for only your debts," said the demon. It stomped cloven hooves, the sound thunderous in the little garage. "Unless you are willing to give up your soul, you do not possess enough to bargain for such riches."

"No, I can't do that," Dad said.

"Then only your debts will be rectified and nothing more given to you," the thing said, "but the price is still dear."

"Anything but my soul."

"It is done!" The demon clapped its clawed hands together. It turned toward me and pointed. "Little witch, you will serve as a useful tool."

Fear leapt within me. It permeated my brain, pierced my heart and turned my limbs to lead. The new, unusual power I possessed chose that moment to appear. My body glowed and the magic spilled forth in the form of white fire. I covered my face, backing away. The flames shot from my hands and struck a garbage bag full of grease and paint rags Dad had been too negligent to haul to the curb. Startled, my father yelled and rushed to stomp out the flames, but knocked over an opened can of paint thinner. More fire erupted from the chemicals, and, hearing the disruption, my mother had raced into the garage.

Overwhelmed by the fumes and smoke, I fell to my knees. My mother found me, but she, too, collapsed. "Crawl, Ruby," she wheezed. "Get out of here, honey!"

On all fours, I scrabbled to the first doorway I found.

"I lay outside the garage on the damp evening grass, blinking the smoke from my eyes," I said as I finished my story. "I watched Dad stumble from the garage without my mother. Dad promised that demon anything but his soul, but my father blames me."

Solomon leaned over and kissed my cheek. "Ruby, you were used."

"Yes, I know, but it still hurts."

"Now that you've admitted the truth," said Alice, "your heart can mend."

I stared at Shunka, who lay sprawled on his side by the railing. As if he sensed me looking at him, the dog raised his head and returned my gaze.

A familiar, indeed.

Sam's theory about Shunka's appearance and role in our lives wasn't accurate, but it had been close. Somehow I doubted the truth would surprise the old man. Any person who could hold off a dozen smoke monsters with Native American magic couldn't be shocked by much.

I knew I had a lot to learn, but I felt I could now welcome the one thing I'd always deemed a curse and even enjoy learning about it. My life in Columbus was a part of my past now. I wanted to learn about my power, use it for good and make a new home.

My home was with Solomon, but that nagging part of my brain kept telling me it was too risky.

"What are you thinking about?" Solomon asked.

As a cover, I asked one of the many questions that tumbled through my brain. "Wayne asked if I was related to the Nutters of Nutter Fort. Is Loretta a Nutter too?"

"Yes," Alice answered. "Nutter is Loretta's maiden name."

"This just gets better and better," I said. "And she's a...?

"A witch." The older woman appraised me. "And it didn't take much of her cake to enhance your powers either."

"Cake?" An image of Loretta's Million Dollar Fudge Cake rose in my mind's eye. "So, that's why I began wielding the power so much better after that! What was in it?"

"The same ingredients as always," Loretta said behind me.

Twisting in my chair, I regarded her wrapped in a lightweight satin robe.

"The cake is not only a delicious recipe," Loretta explained as she strode toward us, "but it has a few key ingredients that bring out the powers of those who are unaware they have them or even deny them, but it takes one special ingredient to activate the spell."

"Such as—no, don't tell me!" I held up a trembling hand and shook my head. "I don't really want to know. Obviously that's why no one has ever guessed the secret ingredient and received the one-million dollars."

Loretta chuckled throatily. She dragged a smaller chair over and placed it between me and Alice. Once Loretta had filled a glass with wine, she sat back, crossing her legs, and watched the night sky.

The stars resembled brightly lit pinholes in a black-velvet shroud. The full moon had begun its descent in the ebon expanse, a perfect, white pearl suspended above the Earth. A seagull's cry carried above the laughter drifting down the street from a nearby all-night saloon.

I struggled to wrap my brain around the Sons of God and all the news, images and revelations that had been dumped on me that night. Inwardly, I chuckled. As wild and crazy as it all seemed, I couldn't deny any of it.

"What about Wayne?" Solomon asked. "Will he stay on the good side of things?"

"Well," said Alice, "that's entirely up to him, isn't it?"

"What happens now?" I asked.

"I think you need to learn about your powers and how to use them," Solomon suggested and patted my leg.

"As you saw during tonight's battle, there's a large coven here," said Loretta. "We'd love to teach you about witchcraft."

"What do you say?" Alice asked.

"I think it's definitely something to think about." Taking another sip of wine, I enjoyed the warmth and lethargy spreading through my high-strung nervous system. "Right now, though, I need to just assimilate everything, process it. I know it's real, but it's still difficult to accept."

"Wait until you see the coven's records on your lives," said Loretta, her laughter punctuating the night.

I gaped at them. "You're kidding, right?"

The two women glanced at one another and chuckled harder.

"Great, just great. I'm a poster child for Reincarnation's Most Wanted."

Solomon guffawed at that.

Alice and Loretta finished their glasses of wine and pushed back from the table.

"I need to set up a cot for Loretta," Alice stated with a yawn, "then I'm going to bed."

"I'm leaving tomorrow, Ruby," said Loretta, "but I know we'll talk again soon."

"Goodnight, ladies," said Solomon.

Alice placed her hand on my shoulder and squeezed gently. "I'm sure you have a lot to tell Solomon, so I'll see you both in a few hours."

Once they'd left, Solomon pulled me from my chair and into his lap.

Sighing with contentment, I snuggled against his chest, his arms around my waist, and nestled my head under his chin.

"So," he began, "what's this I hear about me being a White King?"

For a moment I just sat there pondering everything and enjoying the warmth of his body. Solomon waited quietly, his fingers stroking my lower back. I thought about the power that I had evoked for our battle, the strength I'd drawn from Solomon, Maureen and my son, but the memory of Azazel's forced seduction tainted me.

I knew what I had to do.

"Come with me back to the landing where we fought tonight," I said, raising my head.

Frowning curiously, Solomon asked, "What for?"

"There's something we need to do. Something important." I looked over at Shunka. "And you have to stay here, okay?"

He dog issued a disgruntled sigh.

Chapter Thirty-Two

Taking Solomon's Excursion, we drove back to the most southern tip of the island. The only sign of the battle was debris that could have been easily left by a storm.

Solomon parked the Ford. I grabbed a picnic blanket from the back. We got out and threaded our fingers together, walking across the landing and down to the area Azazel had cleared to seduce and claim me.

"What's going on, Ruby?" Solomon asked quietly.

In the center of the sandy clearing, I stared out over the Atlantic Ocean's dark rolling waves. The aroma of fresh water reached me, hinting that it had rained somewhere out at sea.

"Ruby?"

I spread the blanket out on the sand and placed a rock on each corner so the breeze wouldn't ruffle it. Turning, I faced Solomon. "I love you."

He blinked, his expression so comical I burst out laughing, the sound echoing oddly over the shore.

"Really?" he asked.

"Yes. It's amazing how battling paranormal beings and monsters to save the world can put your life into perspective."

He chuckled and enveloped me in a tight, comforting hug. "Besides that, what finally gave you the courage to take this leap?"

With my thumb and index finger barely apart, I held them up in front of Solomon's face and stared into his blue-white eyes. "I came this close to losing myself forever. Azazel almost seduced me. I wanted him so badly, but it was pure carnal lust caused by his power of seduction. It wasn't real, Solomon. I defeated him all by myself, so if I can do that then I can have the strength to love you again and to accept what may come."

Solomon favored me a smile of understanding.

"These past few days have taught me a lot," I said. "I've realized I was afraid of allowing myself to love someone, even Maureen. I was often cruel to her and I was so harsh with you. I welcome her friendship now. I also have a son and I'm determined to enjoy being his mother. And," I kissed him quickly, "I want to be with you, Solomon." I pressed my breasts against his chest, and he groaned with desire. "I'll love you for the rest of our lives, no matter how many more lives we may have."

Solomon picked me up, and I wrapped my legs around his waist. "You want to erase what happened here on the sand, don't you?" he said.

"Yes, we need to make it a place of love."

"I need you, Ruby." He nuzzled my neck. "Let me make love to you."

I slid down his body and took off my clothes. The wind caressed my body as I watched Solomon disrobe too. He pulled me into his arms and stepped onto the blanket with me. Dipping his head, Solomon sampled first one nipple then the next. Desire seared my body, blazing into my core. I arched against him, the need to be one so intense I almost cried out in frustration.

"Tell me you're mine because you want to be," Solomon whispered against my breast.

"I'm...I'm yours," I said. "Forever and always."

Solomon pushed me down on the blanket. I lay on my back staring up at him framed by the first faint traces of dawn. He straddled me and leaned forward, his body pressing me into the sand beneath the blanket.

Writhing under him, my body acted of its own accord. Every flick of his hot tongue, every caress of his callused hands or his fingers upon my body nearly sent me over a precipice of ecstasy I'd only dreamed about. I wanted this man to own me body and soul.

My hands wandered the planes and muscles of Solomon's body, each one taught beneath my fingers. I dug my nails into his buttocks, and he rewarded me with an excited intake of breath.

He rained kisses along my abdomen, his tongue flicking the skin here and there, the ocean's breath cool against the damp places he left behind. He reached the dark, trimmed triangle at the junction of my thighs. I tensed, but the moment his tongue delicately sampled the bud of my sex, I lost all rationale, all thought processes, and knew loving Solomon was the only thing important to me,

He parted my folds, his tongue dipping in like a hummingbird samples a flower's nectar. I arched against him, sounds of euphoria falling from my lips. Blood thundered in my ears. My breathing grew more erratic, and I clenched the blanket until my fingers protested in pain. I thought I'd go mad if he didn't make love to me soon.

Solomon rolled on top of me, and I parted my legs, desperate for him to enter me, the head of his cock nestled at my opening. Still I strained against him, needing him to plunge into me, to send me to the heavens where I could dance with the stars.

"Easy, my vixen," he whispered, looking down at me. "What's your rush?"

"I want you," I gasped.

He smiled and pushed into my body. I adjusted to his girth and length, pacing my breathing, relaxing so I could accommodate him.

"Ruby," he settled against me, his warmth melding with mine, "I don't know how or why, but somehow I know you. Somehow we've been together before." He began thrusting, slowly at first then his pace quickened, and my hips met his every stroke. "I know I've been with you once upon a time."

The one thing I'd learned from Azazel was how to show the past to Solomon. I allowed him to ride me, taking me to that pinnacle I coveted. Grasping both sides of his face, I drew his head down to me and kissed him, using my power to open his mind.

The images flowed from me and into him, forcing his past memories to rise to the surface of his consciousness. Solomon stiffened, his psyche protesting at first, but I bucked my hips, our breathing more labored. He relaxed, enjoying the euphoric sensations, and let his past lives wash through us.

Finally, I released his lips, and he stared down at me, his expression stunned.

"We're together now and that's all that matters," I stated.

He began thrusting again, and our pleasured sounds changed in crescendo, each exhalation filled with emotion and desire so intense it overwhelmed me. My hands couldn't touch enough of Solomon. His body, hard, pliant and silky, created an emotional elixir that intoxicated me. He buried his face in my neck, mumbling endearments, his breath hot as his hips pummeled me.

His cock slid in and out, leaving me bereft, then filling me again until I thought I'd burst only to withdraw so that I felt I'd die without it inside me again. Our bodies grew slick with sweat, and the spring tightening deep within me coiled until I thought I'd go mad.

"Let me have you," he gasped.

Those words shoved me over the edge. The rhythmic pulsing of my inner walls began gently at first, but as he pushed into me and withdrew only to spear my body again, the contractions swept through me. I cried out, the sound foreign, startling but so liberating.

Snapping my legs around his, I rode wave after wave of sensation. I clung to Solomon, fearful I'd exploded into a shower of splinters. Still I moaned and shrieked my release. Just when I didn't think I could handle any more, his seed, hot and welcome, bathed my insides. Solomon thrust so fast and hard he scooted me off the blanket and onto the sand, his shouts of release loud and victorious.

He milked the last of his strength into me and collapsed. I lay quietly beneath him, bathing in our aftershocks. At each one, he sucked in startled, pleasured gasps.

Moments later, he withdrew and spooned in behind me.

We lay that way for a long time and watched the sunrise. Finally, we rose, dressed and gathered the blanket to return to Alice's apartment. Once back in our room, we stripped out of our clothes and climbed into bed.

As I dozed off, I snuggled into Solomon's embrace, relishing the home I'd found in his arms.

****

Hours later, sunshine spilled across the carpet and splashed the comforter with warmth. I crawled out of bed and looked at the clock.

"Mmph," Solomon mumbled as he kicked the sheets back. "What time is it?"

"Almost two o'clock."

"Damn." He sat up on the side of the bed.

"Well," I glanced around for some clothes, "we probably would've had more sleep if you hadn't insisted on sex on the beach."

He rolled to my side of the mattress and bit me on the ass. Squealing, I danced away from him and swatted him with a shirt.

"Who insisted on sex on the beach?" He wore an enticing smile.

For a moment I just grinned at him, admiring his strong, handsome features, and how the sunshine lit his platinum hair as if it was spun silver.

"Keep looking at me like that and I'll spread those gorgeous thighs of yours again," he rumbled.

Flustered, I rummaged in my suitcase, dressed in a clean pair of shorts and a top, and stepped into my foam sandals.

"I love your legs," Solomon said. "They go all the way up to your ass."

Laughing, I said, "They'd better. Otherwise I'd look really weird." He reached for me, but I dodged his advances. Giggles assailed me as I rushed to the door.

The feeling of being loved and being able to return that
love had me nearly floating across the floor. "I'm going
to check on Maureen then see if there's any dinner."

"I'll be there in a few." He stood up naked.

Momentarily distracted, I thought better of it and
ducked through the door.

The extra beds had been deflated, folded and put
away as well as the blankets, sheets and extra pillows.
The aroma of something spicy drifted to me, followed by
laughter and muffled conversation. Rumbling erupted in
my stomach, but instead of following my nose, I moved
to Maureen's closed bedroom door.

I opened it and peeked in.

My jaw dropped.

With sunshine crawling across the sheets, Wayne
spooned Maureen, his arm draped over her upturned
hip. He raised his head and offered me a sheepish grin.

"Morning—or should I say afternoon?" he said.

"Uh, hi." I started to back out of the room, but
Maureen stirred.

"Ruby? Is it afternoon?"

"Yeah."

"I'm hungry," she muttered.

"I smell food," I said. "See you in a few." I shut the
door.

Maureen and Wayne? No way.

But hadn't I seen their instant attraction to one another that day at Loretta's café? And she'd taken him
into the shower with her last night too.

Not sure what to think of those two, I headed for the
kitchen.

We enjoyed the late afternoon hours gathered around
the kitchen's isle counter, eating the amazing Mexican
dishes and finger foods Alice had prepared. We polished
off a pitcher of homemade lemonade and topped it all
off with a sugary, fried Mexican treat that melted in my
mouth.

"Hey," said Anthony. "Did Alice show you today's
morning paper?" He retrieved it from a shelf by the

toaster. Snapping it open, he read, "Freak Ocean Storm Pounds Southernmost Tip of the U.S. Friday Night. Shortly after midnight, a freak storm suddenly blew in and pummeled the southern edge of Key West. Residents reported broken palms, devastated shrubbery and gardens, slats ripped from privacy fences, and missing roofing tiles..."

He continued to read, but my mind drifted elsewhere. Had the coven's chants disguised the battle? Had they prevented locals from seeing or hearing the truth?

"You learn fast, Ruby. Why upset everyone and cause mass hysteria?"

My gaze flew up to meet Alice's.

As Anthony switched from the article to reading a new movie release aloud to everyone, my attention drifted to Maureen. She caught my gaze and smiled.

"What's wrong?" she asked.

"Didn't you have someone you wanted to see in Florida City?" I asked her.

Alarmed, Wayne shot her a worried look.

She patted his hand and answered, "I decided last night that life's too short, so I plan to visit my son when we head back up the state."

"Good." I tugged on a lock of Anthony's unruly hair.

My son smiled up at me, a bright pinpoint of light shining in his eyes. He slipped his arm around my waist. Touched, I blinked away tears and kissed the top of his head.

"I think it's one of the best decisions you'll every make," I managed to whisper.

"Give your son a call before we leave," said Solomon. "We can head back to the motel this evening. It's only a three-hour drive. We'll be back in Florida City by eight p.m."

"Well, if that's the case, I should start packing our stuff." With my belly full, and the warm camaraderie boosting my mood, I headed for the bedroom.

Moments later, as I finished gathering my belongings and Solomon's stuff, Maureen stepped into the room.

"What's up?" I asked.

Worry settled in Maureen's eyes. "Are we going to remain friends?" she asked.

Surprised, I straightened, putting the suitcases, makeup kit and duffel on the foot of the bed. "Of course. What brought that on?"

"You're the only true friend I've ever had." She blinked rapidly, and her lower lip wobbled.

Oh, hell. Not more waterworks. I'll lose it for sure.

"I don't want to lose you." A fat tear rolled down her cheek.

"Aw, jeez," I groaned. "Don't start crying. You'll sniff and lose too many brain cells."

She burst out laughing. "Now that's the Ruby I know."

"Sit." I pointed to the bed.

As I sat next to her, I thought of Cindy Sansberg and Jody Kefferstine. They'd taught me friendship wasn't just about having people like you or finding acceptance. It was caring about others, supporting them, being there for them and knowing their faults were just as much a part of them as their good points. Cindy and Jody might have been cruel to me, but what doesn't kill you makes you stronger. I was just thankful that Maureen had weathered the barbs of my defense mechanism. Few people ever experienced a friendship like the one I had with Maureen.

"I'm sorry for the times I was so mean," I said, my voice cracking.

"Hey, I already said I understand, so it's okay."

I gulped down the knot in my throat and nodded. "You do realize we've been friends for ages, right? Every time we've been reborn, we've found one another again."

She reached for a box of tissues on the nightstand. "I just wanted to be sure you hadn't changed your mind about me."

"You're coming to stay with me and Solomon until you decide what you want to do, aren't you?"

She gaped at me. "Are you serious?"

"Hey, anyone who follows me through time is family." I offered her a lopsided grin.

"I've been thinking about..." She blushed and looked away.

"About what?"

"Well, about going to college and getting a degree, maybe in law." She peeked over at me, gauging my reaction. "I'm still young, so eight years of college doesn't sound too bad—and Lula would be so proud of me."

"And you like to learn."

She smiled. "Yeah, that too."

"Sounds like a plan."

Maureen hugged me so hard she forced a burp out of me. She giggled and rose to cross the carpet.

"I better go pack too." Still laughing, she left the room.

After I checked our lodgings for anything I might've missed, I picked up my purse and duffel to take them to the living room.

"Come on, boy," I said to Shunka.

He followed me out into the little hall and to the next room. The moment I set foot in the living area, a feeling of evil nudged my consciousness.

Something's not right.

Next to me, Shunka growled low and menacing.

"Is Maureen in the bedroom packing?" Wayne suddenly asked from across the room.

I gasped and stumbled back a couple steps. "Uh, yeah."

"Sorry, I didn't mean to startle you." He strode through the apartment. "I'll go help her pack everything up." He closed the bedroom door behind him.

"Yeah," I muttered. "I bet you will."

Still unsettled, I glanced around the living area. The broadsword glimmered over the mantle, all the hardwood floors shone in the late afternoon sunshine streaming in through the upstairs windows, and every shiny surface, including the glass-top coffee table, winked in the light.

"What's wrong?" Solomon asked as he exited the kitchen.

I shook my head. "I don't know. Something just doesn't seem right."

"Nerves?"

"Maybe."

"Well, let's get the rest of our stuff." He kissed me softly on the mouth. "If we stay any longer, we might as well bunk with Alice another night and I don't want to feel as if we're imposing."

I followed him into our room. "I know. Especially after last night. Not every person has to call a coven together to help you fight rogue angels gone wild." I laughed. "That sounds like a kinky sex tape."

His laughter rolled through the bedroom. He grabbed our suitcases, and I picked up my cosmetics kit.

As we passed Maureen's door, moans and grunts drifted out.

"Oh, for God's sake," I grumbled. "Not again."

"Hey, I'd be doing the same with you if given the chance," he quipped.

We placed our belongings on the landing by the stairs and returned to the living room.

"Is that everything?" asked Alice. "You're more than welcome to stay another night. I've enjoyed everyone's company so much."

A quick glance at our stuff convinced me we had everything. "Yes, that's it."

We waited for Maureen's door to open. Anthony made small talk with Alice about his visions and discussed learning witchcraft too. Maureen's squeals forced color into Anthony's cheeks. The more she shrieked, the louder he talked.

Frustrated, I stalked to the bedroom door and pounded on it with my fist. "For God's sake, Wayne! Fire in the hole, and let's hit the road!"

Anthony turned as red as a stop sign and made a mad dash for the kitchen where he busied himself pouring a glass of water. Solomon laughed so hard he had to lean against the couch, and Alice bit her lower lip, trying not to smile as she looked everywhere except at me.

One thing that would never change would be my smart-aleck mouth.

Minutes later, the door opened, and a chagrinned Wayne stepped out carrying Maureen's backpack and his duffel. She emerged from the room with her clothes askew and her hair in disarray. I started to shoot off my mouth again but thought better of it.

"Come on, Shunka," I said. "We better get go—"

I stopped dead still in the center of the living room. I glanced around. The coffee table sat behind me, all the furniture as it should be and all the items in the room in their proper places. The others, including Solomon, were halfway into the kitchen.

The dog growled.

Everyone halted at the sound.

"What's wrong with Shunka?" asked Maureen.

"Something's wrong," I stated as a shiver ran through me and the hair on my body stood at attention.

Alice moved back into the living area. She closed her eyes, tipped her head back and stood quietly for a few seconds before saying, "I feel it too. Since you've all been preparing to leave, I didn't notice it before."

Shunka growled louder, his hackles up. He padded forward one, two, three steps and then stopped, ears perked forward, gaze trained on the big multi-paned window at the far end of the living area.

I turned in that direction.

The window imploded. Something huge and red burst through the glass. It hit me square in the chest, propelling me backward. A cold, hard surface connected with my backside, and the sound of shattering glass bombarded my ears. For a moment I saw stars but shook off the sensation, realizing I'd smashed into Alice's coffee table.

Worse, I found myself looking up into the eyes of a dragon.

That redheaded biker bitch!

"Ah, so you do know who I am," she snarled through dagger teeth. Her eyes flashed yellow, and her serpentine pupils widened to let in more light, "How smug of you to think that the Sons of God are defeated so easily."

Her breath smelled of brimstone, and I gagged.

"I managed to reach the shoreline where I hid until things quieted. Now, I will do what Azazel was too weak to do, and I shall rule Earth instead of him."

Claws gripped my shoulders. She tightened her hold on me and grinned as I winced at the pain. Blood trickled into my armpits and over my upper arms.

The babbling and yells of Solomon and the others fell on my half-deaf ears. Blood roared through my system, but still disoriented, my senses seesawing, I had trouble summoning my power. Something warm leaked into my eyes. The aroma of copper pennies penetrated my nostrils, and dizziness swept over me.

"We can be whatever we want to be, whoever we want to be," said the rogue angel.

Still holding me down, her body began to morph. The red, pebbled hide of the dragon creature twisted and shifted into the smooth, dark skin of a raven-haired man with a neatly trimmed beard and mustache.

"I'll claim you," he said, "then you and your power will be mine, and should Azazel ever return, he will bow to me!"

The angel glanced at my body, and my clothes disappeared.

Movement behind him snared my attention. Solomon put his fingers to his lips and took the broadsword down from its brackets above the mantle. As he raised the weapon to his side, I saw him as the warrior king he'd been a thousand years ago, his cloak billowing behind him, and a turquoise-studded, silver circlet around his head holding his snowy hair back. I blinked, and Solomon swung the heavy blade sideways.

The sword cleaved the angel's head from his shoulders. Hot blood spurted over me and bathed the glass shards and hardwood floor. I sputtered and coughed as the body flopped to the side, and the head flipped over the couch, landing on its cushions.

"Quickly!" Alice cried and ran for the kitchen with Wayne and Maureen on her heels. Rattling, thuds and clinking followed.

Solomon dropped the sword to the floor and rushed to my side. Anthony knelt next to me too. Both men peered down at me.

"You're bleeding," said Solomon. "Are you in pain?"

With Anthony's help, he pulled me into a sitting position. Anthony snatched a throw from a chair and wrapped it around my shoulders.

"It's nothing a few stitches won't cure," I said.

Shunka padded over to the body and sniffed it. Snarling, he curled his lips and hiked his leg, pissing on the corpse.

"Why didn't you use your magic on that thing, Mom?" Anthony questioned.

"It knocked me silly. I couldn't focus."

Alice returned and instructed Wayne and Maureen what herbs and liquids to pour over the head and body and in what quantities. Grabbing the head by the hair, Maureen set it by the corpse and sprinkled a yellow powder over them.

"Good thinking, Solomon. An angel can be killed when in human form and only then, so this is great luck," Alice said, working the spell. "But if the body and head aren't destroyed, they can regenerate, so we have to work quickly." She opened a small book and flipped to a page. "How did you know it could be killed?" she asked, glancing up at him.

"I didn't," he answered. Solomon gathered me into his arms and rocked me as he smoothed my bloody hair back from my face. His heartbeat thundered beneath my cheek. "I just knew I was drawn to the sword."

I smiled against his shirt.

"I don't know what I'd do if I ever lost you, Ruby," he whispered.

"Find me again," I said.

He snorted and hugged me. Finally, he rose, helped me to my feet and drew the throw more securely around me. "Let's get you in the shower and rinse off the blood and glass so we can see how bad your injuries are."

Alice spoke a few words in a bizarre language.

Quiet followed.

Finally, Alice whispered, "Oh, no."

Solomon paused, and together, we turned toward the living room. The others stared at the place where the angel's corpse had been, their expressions shocked and dismayed.

Horrified, I asked, "What happened to the body?"

"We didn't work fast enough," Alice answered.

"And that means...?" Dread filled me.

"That it has regenerated and gone somewhere safe." She swayed and plopped down hard on an ottoman.

"Alice," I took a few steps toward her, "you're scaring me."

She sighed wearily. "Just because Azazel didn't have sex with you and impregnate you doesn't mean that the Nephilim won't return."

"What?" Solomon put his arm around my shoulders again. "Are you saying that this angel can go around siring children regardless?"

Sadly, Alice nodded. Stress lines appeared around her mouth. "Azazel was the leader. With Ruby's powers the rogue angels would have been invincible and they could fuel that combined power into their offspring."

"And it also means that my mom is still in danger, doesn't it?" asked Anthony.

Alice nodded again. "The Nephilim are the offspring of angels and humans. They grow quickly, but worse, they have the power to blend with man. They'll infiltrate the world governments, take positions of power and they'll hold the world's wealth and the lives of millions in the palm of their hands..." She leaned forward, bracing her elbows on her knees and clasped the sides of her head as if she had a terrible headache. A tear slid down her cheek. "If that fallen angel regenerates and awakens, The Banishment was for naught."

"Oh, Solomon," I whispered, dreading choking me, "what do we do?"

"For now, we need to regroup and recuperate," Solomon stated. He turned me around and pointed me toward the bathroom.

"What can I do to help?" asked Anthony.

"For now, help Alice clean up," I said, trying to keep the tremor out of my voice. "It looks like we're staying another night after all."

He hurried into the kitchen.

Maureen threw me a worried look as she followed my son. "We'll help, Anthony," she said and motioned for Wayne to join them.

"I hope this is the last time we'll see the Sons of God," said Solomon. He directed me around the recliner.

"So do I, but I doubt it," I replied, suddenly exhausted. My shoulders ached and burned, and my senses still struggled to right themselves. "You're in love with a witch, so don't forget that."

He stopped and looked down at me. "I'll take that witch any way I can get her."

"You mean that?"

"Yes, and I'll always find you, no matter what." His eyes caught the fading sunshine and glowed. "And no matter what century."

Tracing the main scar that ran down the side of his face, I said, "I love you."

He folded me in his arms, and I melted against his body. After a thousand years, I'd finally found my way back to my White King. I just prayed that our battles were over.

The End

F. L. Bicknell

F. L. Bicknell's work has appeared in a wide range of genres such as Would That It Were, Touch Magazine, GC Magazine, Ohio Writer Magazine, Waxing and Waning (Canada), and The Istanbul Literature Review (Turkey) just to name a few. Faith was a regular contributor to Gent under her pseudonym, Molly Diamond. She has also had fiction published in Hustler's Busty Beauties, Penthouse Variations, Twenty 1 Lashes, and was a regular contributor to Ruthie's Club for three years. In addition, Faith has many e-books and some print titles published under various pen names.

For two years, Faith served as the co-editor of The Tenacity Times and she served as the managing editor for two e-book publishers for thirteen years until she resigned in 2009 to focus on her writing career. She is represented by TriadaUS Literary Agency (www.triadaus.com).

Also from F. L. Bicknell and Turquoise Morning Press

The Most Intimate Wish

If you enjoyed F. L. Bicknell's *Ruby, the White King, and Marilyn Monroe*,

you might also enjoy these urban fantasy/paranormal. authors published by Turquoise Morning Press:

Melissa Ecker, author of *Giving Up The Ghost*

Jan Scarbrough, author of *Tangled Memories*

Margaret Ethridge, author of *Paramour*

Thank you!

For purchasing this book from
Turquoise Morning Press.

We invite you to visit our Web site to learn more about
our quality Trade Paperback and eBook selections.

www.turquoisemorningpress.com

Turquoise Morning Press
Because every good beach deserves a book.
www.turquoisemorningpress.com

~~~~~

Sapphire Nights Books
Because sometimes the beach just isn't hot enough.
www.sapphirenightsbooks.com

Made in the USA
Lexington, KY
22 January 2013